THE MAGIC EYE

Ann Maurer

THE MAGIC EYE

A Novel

Ann Mauer

iUniverse, Inc.
New York Lincoln Shanghai

THE MAGIC EYE

iUniverse books may be ordered through booksellers or by contacting:

iUniverse
2021 Pine Lake Road, Suite 100
Lincoln, NE 68512
www.iuniverse.com
1-800-Authors (1-800-288-4677)

Because of the dynamic nature of the Internet, any Web addresses or links contained in this book may have changed since publication and may no longer be valid.

Certain characters in this work are historical figures, and certain events portrayed did take place. However, this is a work of fiction. All of the other characters, names, and events as well as all places, incidents, organizations, and dialogue in this novel are either the products of the author's imagination or are used fictitiously.

ISBN: 978-0-595-47504-9 (pbk)
ISBN: 978-0-595-91775-4 (ebk)

Printed in the United States of America

To families who have lived with secrets

Acknowledgements

Deepest gratitude to those special ones who tirelessly provided information for this story. Special thanks to Dr. June Tait for her input from start to finish. Thank you to the Colorado School of Mines for permission to use the deans' image on the back cover. To Robert Sorgenfrei, Librarian, Russell L. & Lyn Wood Mining History Archive, Colorado School of Mines, special thanks for unparalleled research assistance.

CHAPTER 1

▼

CALIFORNIA 1920

"Is Mr. TR here?"

Joey usually trembled before ascending the narrow concrete steps to the plain wooden door that said "TR Gimble." The whole world, as far as Joey was concerned, lay behind the door to this austere workshop.

Out of the corner of his eye, the boy saw a dark sedan parked across the street on the other side of the railroad tracks. He paid the auto no mind because the foundry company there had almost as many visitors as Mr. TR's experimental plant.

The inventor's assistant looked up. He placed a drill bit carefully on the table.

"Good to see you, Joey. Thanks for not barging through the door. Too many visitors these days burst in demanding to see the great inventor at once."

Joey laughed.

"I'd never do that."

Walking to the workbench, the boy's anticipation grew. Starting with Hiram, this place was one interesting thing after another. Blue eyes twinkling with humor highlighted Hiram's kind, angular face. There was no question that a brain of gold sat beneath the short, thick mop of curly hair that refused to conform to the day's style and lay flat on Hiram's head. His dark curls nodded toward the work yard behind the building.

"Mr. Gimble's in the middle of something right now. Can you wait fifteen minutes?"

"Sure!" exclaimed Joey.

The gray January day suddenly turned brighter for the boy. Mr. TR was in!

Hiram chuckled to himself and winked at Joey.

"You still calling Mr. Gimble Mr. TR?"

"Why sure," said Joey. "He said for me to call him TR, but he's a grownup and I'm not. Men are the only ones who call each other by their first initials. I have to show my respect, you know?"

"Not to worry," said Hiram, "Your friendship with the man is sealed in eternity. Once he told you it was fine to stop in anytime and that you could call him TR, I knew this place would offer you as fine a welcome as any lad could want."

Joey blushed.

"Maybe when I turn twenty-one, I'll call him TR, but not until then. It's Mister for now."

Hiram resumed his work with an understanding grin. Joey climbed onto one of the drafting stools. He gazed in awe at the fine tools that any craftsman would envy. The walls of the office were lined with books on math and science.

"I bet Mr. TR knows every formula in these books!" exclaimed Joey. "That's why news reporters call him a genius, isn't it?"

The inventor's assistant nodded and gave Joey a thumbs up.

"He's the real deal."

The door opened and a tall, young man with dark hair sprung inside.

"Hi there, Joey!" exclaimed Ty. "What did you cook up today?"

The boy looked up shyly.

"Just a small idea I'm working on. I'd like Mr. TR to see my design."

Mr. Gimble's son didn't ask for details. He exchanged a wink with Hiram, slapped Joey on the shoulder and said, "Good for you, son. I'll go tell my dad."

Ty's enormous smile glowed white as he turned to leave. He angled his broad shoulders to round the tall filing cabinets as he headed out the back door. He was tall like his father and just as handsome.

Hadn't Joey heard that the movie studios invited Ty for a screen test? Yep, he remembered right. It was Ty's sister Winnie who told his friend's sister. But TR's mom and dad put a swift end to the movie studio's request. They wanted none of that frivolous movie business for Ty.

The inventor's son once told Joey he could envision the words 'Tyrone Gimble' written in lights above the theaters downtown, but then he winked and said he knew he'd have to enjoy the silver screen from the same side as the rest of the audience.

Joey knew that seeing the latest moving pictures was fine for mom and the kids in the Gimble family, but Ty was destined for business school and nothing less.

"That makes sense," thought Joey, "Ty must be prepared to run the great inventor's company."

Ty remaining right here at the shop was definitely OK by Joey. It warmed him to think that TR's son liked him as much as the great inventor and Hiram. All these men were important to the wondrous learning Joey enjoyed inside this remarkable place.

Behind the shop, two men watched the boy enter.

One looked through the lens of a large camera.

"So who's the kid?"

"Not sure," said his companion, "probably some hanger-on the guy can't get rid of."

"Damn, there's his son. He's coming to this side of the yard!"

The man with the camera stuffed the bulk in his satchel. They put their heads down and walked toward the foundry across the way.

Ty Gimble came around the side of the building in time to see the two men hurrying off. As they crossed the railroad tracks beyond the fence, he muttered under his breath, "That's right, on your way, you goons!"

Joey quietly looked around the office. Hiram studied machine parts on the workbench. Tiny, brilliant flashes caught Joey's eye as Hiram turned an object under a lighted magnifying lens.

"That must be a big diamond in the drill bit," thought Joey.

He wondered if it was a new kind of stone from some faraway place. Hiram sure was studying this piece of equipment intently.

Off to the side, Joey caught sight of a small, white book. He could barely make out the title at the angle it was laid, 'History of the Ancient Knights.' He wondered what the book had to do with drill bits or inventing. A red shield with a cross was printed on the cover.

"Is Hiram studying something new?" wondered the boy.

The able assistant once declared to Joey, "I never stop learning every day."

Joey knew that Hiram and the other men who worked for TR Gimble studied things from other countries. Joey silently pondered this new mystery.

"I've never seen that book in a store or anyone's library. What does the symbol mean? I should try to find out what it is."

A million questions never ceased to fly through Joey's twelve-year-old mind when visiting this place. But then a million and one new things always seemed to catch his eye every time he stepped inside. For now, he tamed his impulse to ask about the drill bit and the book. If he did, he knew what would happen. His brain would spin into high gear, and he wouldn't be able to stop asking questions. He'd jump from point to point trying to figure out how every new thing he saw fit with everything else that was here. He didn't want twenty questions blurting out of his mouth to disturb Hiram so he stayed quiet and glanced around some more.

A jagged, dark rock that was shiny in a deep, fiery way balanced on a thin, brown book that sat on a thick, typewritten report. These were recent additions to the materials in the office. The strange rock and documents were yet more unknowns among many things Joey absorbed but didn't understand. He quietly breathed the wish he'd made every day since meeting TR Gimble.

"Let me be lucky enough to learn everything!"

Such a thought would have seemed silly for a boy with no prospects of attending university, but after meeting TR Gimble, Joey felt sure that such a dream could come true. It felt possible he just might come awfully close to learning everything. Hadn't Mr. TR?

Joey knew he'd found the right place to start fulfilling his dream because there wasn't a single man with a loafing mind at TR Gimble's plant. Everyone was working on new ideas. Joey was keenly aware that for something to be left out in plain view in the office meant that it was especially important to one or more of the men. They studied new things constantly and shared breaking news about big developments every week. Joey knew that anything he saw in here sizzled with the excitement of discovery.

Inside this intriguing place, men focused intently on their work, but they beamed an amiable grin his way whenever Joey walked in.

"A little TR," one of them once said.

Joey remembered what he thought after hearing that.

"It can't be possible. Maybe I just look like him when he was my age."

Joey never glimpsed a picture of the great inventor when he was a boy. His thoughts tumbled toward what the man must have been like growing up. He shook his head. He couldn't picture Mr. TR as anything other than who he was now. He thought to himself, "I don't even know where he comes from. But I've gotten a closer look at him than most people. I don't have to speculate because I know him!"

Knowing TR Gimble made all things seem possible to Joey. He could see how imagination came to life in TR Gimble's workshop. The office of this experimental plant was a treasure for Joey to behold. He composed in his mind what he'd write of it some day.

"A suitably impressive headquarters for the captain of modern inventions!"

Joey smiled surveying the fine headquarters. Rich detail in the large room included curios from foreign countries. An array of drafting equipment from Germany sat on a ledge above a wide table opposite Hiram's workbench. The longest parallel bar Joey ever saw was attached to pulleys on thin wires spanning the length of a six-foot drafting table. Thick rolls of crisp vellum paper from France stood ready for new designs to be sketched. Maps and diagrams hung on the walls. Freshly inked drawings and typewritten reports filled every corner not occupied by books.

Joey never knew this place to appear messy. He concluded it was kept that way by design. At any hour, a man could think and draw and find things where he needed them. Filing cabinets lined one wall where a typewriter and rows of dated journals were arranged in pleasing symmetry.

"That's it," thought Joey. "Someone figured out an order of geometry for this place. I want my workshop to be just like this some day."

Joey peered through a window to the yard in back. The organized office seemed to flow naturally to the space outside. Materials of learning and exploring that were so neatly compacted inside the office seemed to explode into enormous proportions outside.

Large contraptions consumed much of the space in the yard, yet everything was neatly arranged. New forms of various sizes were taking shape in metal, brick and wood. Each new form was designed to fit with devices already in place.

Furnaces and steam equipment commanded the attention of workers performing detailed chores to keep them running. The activity of men and machines gave off an electrical charge that seemed to make the whole place vibrate with endless forward motion.

Tall, blinking machines were clustered in families. Not long ago, Mr. TR explained to Joey that these families of machines had their own special engineering applications. In some of these clusters, monstrous pipes linked one machine to another. The inventor called these pipes transfer zones for different stages of chemical processing.

Perforated and smooth, different pipes reflected deep hues of green and blue. Joey thought they looked like giant works of art. His eyes saw exotic metal tentacles that rose and dipped and wound around shiny cylinders in noiseless symphony. Joey knew these pipes had been forged from materials found in distant places of the world. He learned these special pipes could withstand terrific heat and also regulate fires inside for optimum chemical unification and processing.

Vats of riveted steel and mortared brick towered beside complex gadgets that pumped liquid and heat to their innards. Iron sentinels with mystery fluids towered skyward surrounded by plywood planks at the intervals of a man's height. Hoses, valves and generators fit into various machines with thick, black connecting tubes. Joey learned it was Malaysia where the inventor had found the kind of hard, pure rubber he liked to use.

Pipes plummeted from the bases of some vats, then reversed angles and ran along the ground in parallel perfection before dropping to tanks below. The way Joey saw it, the vast work yard was Mr. TR's external brain. These machines humming, clicking and whirling day and night were like the master inventor's mind.

Joey's thoughts raced toward the way Mr. TR's novelties got people everywhere talking.

"Only a few people in the world have been inside this place, but I can visit whenever I want. Mr. TR said his ideas aren't just born but grown. Right here is where men are building Gimble marvels that are changing the modern world."

Joey knew another secret, too—that there were more inventions here than were reported to men beyond the workshop door. He had seen these with his own eyes and wondered, "What are these other contraptions for? How incredible could they be?"

CHAPTER 2

▼

Ty walked quickly through the yard of his father's plant. Pulsing energy from large generators pierced the air's gray haze. Pockets of heat surged from elaborate contraptions pushing aside the chill. Toward the rear of the yard, the vibrant young man approached a group of workers. They were huddled around a machine whose tarp was partially open. The tallest worker was knee deep in the soggy dirt of a freshly dug hole. He examined pipes and fittings below the large machine. Ty grinned at the sight of his father working on one of his experimental darlings.

"She doesn't like sitting idle, does she?"

"Not really, son, what's up?"

Ty raised a concerned eyebrow.

"Men were skulking around the other side of the yard."

"Reporters or others?"

"Hard to tell. One guy had a bag. Didn't look like they had weapons or wire cutters, though. There were only two of them, slim build, not muscular. They went across the tracks when I came around the office."

TR kept his eyes trained on the base of the machine.

"Maybe time to consider some plants outside the fence, something with long thorns."

Ty looked thoughtfully across the yard.

"How 'bout cactus?"

"Too obvious. Try natal plum."

"What's that?"

TR wiped his brow and looked up.

"Carissa macrocarpa. Comes from South Africa. There's a nursery Hiram knows. He'll help you order it."

Ty reached in his pant pocket and drew out a small notepad and pencil.

"Caressing who?"

The inventor chuckled.

"Good way to remember the name, son. If you say 'Caressing macrocarpa,' the nursery manager will know what you mean. The plants grow to eighteen feet. A hedge looks lush, almost like ivy. But each branch has spines along its length with spikes at the end of each twig. Can be quite a surprise to visitors!"

Ty laughed.

"Sounds perfect. We'll order some big specimens by express. I'll line up men to plant them right away."

TR pointed toward the fence.

"We'll want half-inch irrigation pipe to there. Lots of water so the hedge can grow to its finest quickly." He winked at his son. "Maybe we'll win a city landscape award … caressing macrocarpa."

The men laughed as they continued studying the large machine.

The office remained quiet as Hiram peered through his magnifying lens at the drill parts. Joey opened the back door. He stepped outside into puffs of steam escaping from vents on some of the lidded boilers. This winter day, there were no heavy fumes lingering over the stained vats swirling with oily concoctions. A visit last July to one corner of the yard had introduced Joey to the kind of smell that makes your eyes water and your lungs wheeze. Today, the work yard smelled lightly of oil and not much else.

"I wonder if Mr. TR found a better way to separate the chemicals and eliminate that putrid smell. I bet he did. After all, if he knows anything about a certain thing, Mr. TR has shown the world he knows how to trap and separate chemicals better than anyone."

Joey heard a low, steady ticking from two machines nearby. Unlike the streetcar he rode to get here, nothing in Mr. TR's plant wobbled or clanked. He admired how all things in this place, in whatever experimental stage they were, spun along with so few hitches.

From his other visits here, Joey knew that a sudden, big hiss of steam or the groan of a gasket straining against a flywheel would bring TR's men running at once. He'd seen them shut down machines, check temperature gauges, then climb the catwalks and slide underneath to analyze seals, gears and pulleys so that whatever was out of balance could be fixed. Ty once commented, "Managing these machines is like caring for a brood of children."

The workshop and vast yard housed less than fifty workers, but Joey observed that the men paid constant attention to every detail. He remembered what Hiram told him.

"Order in the mechanical realm is delivered first through the ears and secondly through the hands."

Mr. TR had added, "All human senses need to remain alert so that these beasts of chemistry and machinery stay contained within the yard!"

Joey looked at the giant wheels and pulleys.

"You mean so no parts fly off and no chemicals pour out?"

TR nodded. Hiram looked solemn as he stroked his chin.

"You know, Joey, machines of such size and power might decide to walk off on their own!"

Joey looked immediately at the heavy bolts and concrete that kept the machines anchored to their berths. He glanced up sideways at Hiram.

"Nah."

Gimble's men roared. That was the first time Joey shared a good laugh with them. His mind flashed to the unforgettable way Mr. TR first described his workers.

"These men have worked the toughest mines and oil fields on earth. They know about running dangerous devices. They've seen horrible wreckage to humans imparted by sloppy, uncontrolled contraptions. Experimenters have died working with the kind of fire and chemicals that my men deal with every day. The least the machines might do is mangle an arm if not kept in balance. Consequences of not running machines correctly do not have to be explained to my men."

It was this toughness and care that made Gimble's work yard such a sensible place to Joey. Man was in control here, but materials from the earth were showing them how to gain more control to deliver ever more powerful machines and fuel.

Joey had read that nations eagerly awaited any proven means of new power. He could see the Gimble operation was extraordinary. He understood why Mr. TR's gurgling babies of invention were always tended with care in this fertile nursery of man's imagination.

Joey also learned that nothing in the plant went to waste. The men assured him that everything had potential value because one little thing could make an invention work better. Joey felt sure that if any group of men were going to scour the earth to divine the best that could be made, these were the men who knew how to invent better than any other group of men.

"What a swell place to work," thought Joey. "Inventing isn't some crazy pipe dream in this place. It happens every minute with the best materials on earth. Here, it's a sacred honor to work with the best of men creating the finest, powerful new things on earth!"

On rare occasions, Joey heard one of the men swear or exclaim out loud, but it didn't happen often at Mr. TR's plant. This place wasn't like other labor yards he'd been near. Joey knew that if someone raised his voice in this place, something big must've happened.

The men ordinarily spoke in low tones and said very little, only what was straight to the point and necessary. The only cause for voices to rise was a quest of big proportions that presented a sudden obstacle or a solution they'd just found that worked to their amazement.

Sometimes Joey overheard whispers as several of the men examined dials and adjusted valves on certain machines. He saw that one man always made notes or sketches while another listed readouts in precise columns in a journal. TR and Hiram often bent their heads together scribbling calculations. Joey repeated his fervent wish.

"I'd give anything to know what all of this is about!"

Joey's thoughts turn to Ty. The inventor's son had an engaging way of enthusiastically encouraging all this ticking of machinery and men's minds so that things moved along in a very relaxed way. Ty acted as if everyone's days were ordinarily arranged this way. Joey knew that TR's eldest son was destined to inherit the important work his father pioneered. Joey wondered how Ty handled the pressure of being Mr. TR's chosen successor.

"He always seems intent on helping the workmen remain at ease. He's good at looking things up to find more answers. When he offers suggestions, he can make men laugh. His method is probably a good way to start out. How else could you possibly handle so much information in your head every day?"

Ty once told Joey, "If you can't relax, you can't think."

Joey tried this in school taking his tests and knew it worked.

"When my own day of responsibility comes, I will manage my men just like Ty does."

"Psst, kid!"

Joey turned toward the fence. A man with a hat pulled low over his eyes was straining to see inside the yard.

"What's your name, boy?" growled the man.

Joey scratched his head. He looked toward the office to see if Hiram was looking out. He whirled toward the rear of the yard where he knew Ty and some of the men were. No one was in sight.

"Can't think of it?' came another growl.

Joey knew this wasn't a Gimble worker. The click of a camera shudder captured Joey's frozen surprise.

The man ducked away before Joey could utter a word. Joey wasn't sure if he should tell Ty or Hiram. He knew that people came to the yard and took pictures sometimes. He was there when whole groups of visitors stopped by. Joey thought, "That was probably some reporter left out in the cold."

Joey knew how it was when special visitors were expected. Today wasn't one of those days. When it was, the workers were scrubbed clean wearing their Sunday best. Mr. TR donned a fine suit and the hat he wore only when going downtown. Hiram replaced his long overalls and sweaty kerchief with gorgeous slacks and a silk shirt. Hiram dressed like pictures Joey had seen of aristocrats in Europe. Joey once asked him, "Where did you get such fine clothes?"

Hiram explained.

"I'm the first son in generations not to become a clothier and join my family's design business. I don't mind having to scrub oil from my nails every night with the work I do for Mr. Gimble, but I still enjoy a time or two dressing up during the year."

Joey thought Hiram in his gentleman's attire looked as dandy as a man ever could, but his curly hair would not stay slicked down. It didn't matter what hair oil he used, Hiram always looked like he'd just stuck his finger in a light socket. He said he tried axle grease one time, but it gave him a headache he couldn't tolerate. Hiram's wiry hair was the first thing he joked about when greeting special visitors to the plant.

"Mr. Gimble hired me because my hair is a special electrical conductor!" he'd announce.

Women giggled and men smiled when Hiram joked about himself while explaining the things at Gimble's plant. He'd hold up pages of computations for the guests to see.

"We do a lot of mathematical calculations here. These are my Hiram-glyph-ics."

When explaining the machine with the most complicated pipes, he'd say, "This is Mr. Gimble's pet octopus!"

Joey learned that more than one visitor viewing Gimble's inventions did not have a university degree. Hiram's way of explaining complex workings involved comparing electrical wires to a spaghetti bowl and chemical vats to a whiskey brewery.

Women visitors would twitter at the mention of alcohol, and all the men, except those from the government, would look hopeful that the inventor might have some libation on hand.

"Sorry to disappoint you gentlemen," Hiram would say with a wink. "There's no alcohol on these premises. Some fine, scholarly men from Scotland simply shared their centuries-old brewing secrets with us. Those mechanics, not alcohol, are what we put to work in these machines."

The assistant's humor went over big with just about everyone who came to see the inventions. A few visitors frowned at first, not convinced by Hiram that technical science was at work. Mr. TR would take such guests aside. He'd sketch, point things out and explain until those visitors finally nodded. The great inventor would have them smiling soon enough, especially after sharing a secret tale from one of his overseas adventures. By the end of the visit, the critics would be downright excited about the latest Gimble invention.

Mr. TR explained the whole affair to Joey.

"These are the toughest critics I have to satisfy. They are university-trained men brought in to shoot down many of the ideas that inventors in the country are working on. There are too many inventors, and there aren't enough resources in the country for everyone's inventions to be manufactured. Big companies and the government hire these technical critics to review experiments and new machines. My own special project, more important than inventing machines, is to show the critics that my inventions are sound and do work scientifically."

Joey stayed off to the side and watched in fascination as visitors were shown the Gimble invention of the day with a flourish. He noted that certain devices at the plant were carefully draped under tarps and said to be 'down for special maintenance.' He knew why no one wondered about those machines. There was so much activity happening everywhere else. Guests were allowed to climb on special scaffolds, play with levers and peer inside machinery through glass-covered openings Mr. TR prepared for just such visits.

Joey saw the inventor explain his methods to doubting critics with the same calm, patient manner Ty always used with the workers in the yard. Son had learned from father, and Joey was learning from them. The boy of twelve realized an important fact:

"You can have all the money and materials in the world, but if you don't have loyal workers and people to advance your dreams, you don't have anything at all!"

He thought of Hiram working quietly in the office.

"He's really different from the other workers. How can the man go from being dead serious and head-to-toe oil-stained to a stylish charmer entertaining special visitors from big cities? Where does he get that kind of magic? Maybe he's a comedian who disguises himself as assistant to a genius."

Joey thought a moment.

"Maybe it's the other way around."

He shook his head. He knew one thing for certain. The visitors always left laughing and didn't stop gushing with excitement over what they'd seen at the Gimble plant through the whole train ride back to Washington, D.C., San Francisco or New York. Soon after, the papers would feature glowing accounts of Gimble's latest invention. Testimony from the same people who'd visited the plant a week earlier appeared in the news, right down to the exclamations from the ladies.

Mr. TR would smile when he'd read the words of university-trained experts acclaiming the scientific genius they observed at his plant. The technical men used university words to explain to the world what they saw. Hiram would chuckle.

"Those experts have their own upside-down way of saying what Mr. Gimble can say with fewer words and a lot more clearly."

CHAPTER 3

▼

Joey admired a small, new machine near the fence. He thought about the man trying to talk to him there.

"Maybe he figured I'd blab about something—but I never would."

Joey knew that reporters went wild speculating about the next revolutionary thing to come from TR Gimble. They wrote that this was not some inventor working from a back shed.

"They have no idea how big his projects are," mused the boy. Then he shook his head.

"I probably have no idea either!"

Joey saw articles stating that TR Gimble invested his money on giant projects ever since receiving his first million-dollars six years ago. The articles didn't specify all the projects.

Joey also read that Gimble was an inventor who could command resources from anywhere in the world. Joey once heard a visitor to the plant tell the man beside him, "No nation offers obstacles too big if resources from foreign shores are what Gimble intends to get!

"Maybe that explains the camera," mused Joey. "The man who took the picture could have been spying for some country. With all this mystery, no wonder I keep coming back!"

As Hiram bent over his work, the office door whooshed open banging against the wall.

"Monsieur!" exclaimed the man who burst inside.

The smell of strong cologne filled the workshop. Hiram placed the drill bit down again. This time he slid it into its wooden box and closed the cover while he turned off the lamp.

"Good, day, Mr. Tiemonet."

The tall, lean Frenchman carried black leather gloves in his left hand although the weather hardly required them. He slid these inside his coat. His top hat and cape looked overblown to Hiram. Perhaps the fashion connoisseur fluffed things up before entering. Hiram masked a chuckle.

"What brings you here?"

The Frenchman looked about.

"Just on our way back from the port. Is the great one here?"

Hiram nodded and glanced out the window.

"The great one is here, but the great one has appointments waiting and is up to his knickers in mud with one of his machines at the moment. I'd be happy to schedule time for you to meet on another day."

"Not a concern. I only wished to bring some papers by."

"What shall I tell Mr. Gimble?"

Hiram reached for the pencil and sketchpad on his desk. The character who stood before him was Louis Tiemonet. He typically brought messages in some assumed code. He had to be a double agent, maybe triple or more, depending on the number of countries who'd pay for his dubious intercessions. Hiram waited for the message.

"Before I give you my communiqué, I must note with great pleasure that you are studying the noble knights."

Tiemonet tapped a manicured forefinger twice in the center of the cross on the red shield printed on the small white book near Hiram's elbow.

"Are you preparing to be raised to the next degree?"

Hiram stifled another chuckle. He didn't answer such questions without adequate forethought. He wanted to set the record straight without insulting the Frenchman and whomever Louis might represent today.

"I am not of the Guild or their higher orders, Mr. Tiemonet. I'm as interested as everyone these days about the history of other people. Men who stood for noble ideals and fought for valiant causes are to be studied. We try to locate books to increase our appreciation of their complex past."

Tiemonet rolled his eyes at Hiram's diplomacy. Then he smiled warily.

"Ah, indeed. The noble men are as complicated as their histories. Not only did they die gallantly in centuries past, they take an interest in all that is happening at the moment!"

Hiram folded his arms across his chest and waited. Tiemonet sniffed and tossed his head. Hiram knew this character who simply had to brandish the last word from his blade of a tongue.

The caped man looked casually toward the window beyond Hiram. Then he brought his sharp nose and piercing eyes level with the face of the inventor's right-hand man.

"Any man joining the Guild can pick up this fine publication within the circle of his brethren."

Hiram stared back unblinking. Then he nodded amiably.

"I'll take your word for it. We're willing to study whatever history may be important to today's events. Our continued aim is to learn all we can to support Mr. Gimble's work."

The Frenchman smiled much too widely, revealing teeth a curious hue of yellow-orange.

When Hiram stared, the Frenchman snarled from the side of his mouth.

"We remain pleased that Mr. Gimble maintains his elite position and good standing in the high order of the Ancient Rite."

His dark eyes scanned the room. Deft as a magician, the Frenchman swiftly reached out and wrapped five bony fingers around the dark, fiery rock. He tipped it to its sharpest point resting atop the slender, brown book and thick report. He spun the dense rock as if it were a coin. His eyes glazed over. He spoke past Hiram to the cologne-filled air above him.

"You know, my man, thousands of Mr. Gimble's brethren in the noble order are responsible for promoting his inventions around the world. They've moved capital to foreign shores and carved mountains on remote islands to increase the great one's fortune. Our noble brethren have caused his empire to grow more rapidly than any other manner he could have employed."

The Frenchman brought his fist down on the rock. Hiram watched as the specimen stood still. Louis Tiemonet smirked, "Would this be our earthly friend, the illustrious marlstone?"

Hiram saw that the rock survived intact. He kept his tone level.

"The fashionable term for organic marlstone these days is shale oil."

"Certainly," crooned Louis. "A man with your background in tailoring would know what's fashionable."

Hiram chuckled.

"I only sews 'em as I sees 'em."

Tiemonet glared.

"You understate your skills. A clothier is so much more. He designs with the magic eye."

Hiram understood Tiemonet's reference to his prosperous, talented family.

"I am none of those things."

The Frenchman toyed with the rock.

"Nice specimen. I imagine you cannot tell me where this sample comes from."

"I imagine I'd leave that to Mr. Gimble if he chooses to disclose it."

The Frenchman shrugged.

"Soon enough, the great one will advertise what he's found. We can count on that!"

With one more sweeping glance around the office, the messenger in the ridiculous cape opted to conclude the gallant mission that some country was paying him to perform.

"You must tell the great one that we've summarized the new policies of the French and other governments concerning tariffs and export fees in the territories. These are in the papers I leave you now. We offer this information as a kind service knowing that the master deals in materials from these regions. We know he does not want delays."

The inventor's assistant accepted the papers.

"How kind of you to come all this way."

Hiram knew without looking that higher prices lay on the horizon for overseas materials Gimble needed.

"That's your full message?"

"That is all for today. I must get going. The travelers outside are weary from their journey overseas."

The Frenchman swooped out the door and left it open. As he bolted down the steps, Hiram looked out the window. He saw long fingers on an ivory, satin-gloved hand lazily dangling a cigarette out the window of a blue sedan.

"Yes, the madam is probably weary at best!" thought Hiram. "Better her than me."

Joey soon forgot about the photographer at the fence as he pondered more questions he knew might not get answered for years.

"How does Mr. TR talk to so many people all over the world? How does Mr. TR order anything he wants without waiting months like other industrialists?"

Joey stretched his logic to simulate some answers.

"Probably Mr. TR's money opens every door fast as lightning."

He paused.

"Maybe there's more to it than that. Mr. TR isn't the only millionaire in the world. There must be some special way he gets what he needs on the double. Maybe it has to do with the same way he gets a lot of grumpy people in this country to cooperate with him. He has a magic of some kind. It must tell him how to open any doors."

Joey imagined half-naked natives running a hundred miles through tropical forests to carry messages from TR Gimble to village chiefs. In the distant corners of far-off nations that the rest of the world hardly knew existed, Joey imagined Mr. TR having entire colonies of remote villages waiting to deliver things for him.

Joey once glimpsed on Hiram's desk a picture of completely naked brown men loading bricks on a boat. This seemed to Joey the kind of thing that Mr. TR must know about. The inventor told Joey of great adventures obtaining materials that Joey couldn't believe would happen in his wildest imaginings.

"I'll have to travel the world to find out more."

He could think of no other soul he read about who could do the same things Mr. TR could do all over the world.

The boy smiled at his profound fortune. He'd gotten to know the inventor first to hold a patent in every country of the world. As he waited and looked around, Joey MacDermott dreamed of working for TR Gimble one day.

The tall inventor climbed out of the hole beside the large machine. He hauled his thick legs over the edge, stood up and shook each boot. It wasn't to get the dirt off but to restart the circulation. Thwap, thwap! A hard slap to each thigh helped to get the feeling back. He decided to take a break and go see the boy.

TR Gimble came striding from the far the corner of the yard. The awestruck lad watched wide, airborne steps made by huge feet attached to legs the size of tree trunks. The man's head was wide like a continent east to west. A breeze picked up, scattering the man's usually perfectly combed locks. A tuft of straight, sandy hair pointed toward the North Star while the rest of his hair spread out like a sundial.

From the man's deep, glowing eyes came an emerald wink aimed Joey's way. TR Gimble stood six foot five. Moving with such power, he seemed even larger than that. Mr. TR's trousers, from Joey's short perspective, seemed taller and wider than the fuel tanks in the yard, and his pant legs were just as black with soot and oil this day. Whatever he'd climbed down and stuck his head into had sure covered him with goo!

As the inventor smiled widely, Joey saw teeth that were bigger and whiter than Ty's. The man's enormous hand waved hello. His thick fingers extended to swallow Joey's slim palm in a man-sized handshake. Joey beamed. How could such a giant greeting not overwhelm a kid?

The inventor breathed the crisp air and delighted in Joey's surprise. The boy was a model of patience and persistence. TR remembered the taste of his own hunger for his inventions to someday be recognized in a world that seemed too stark to bring any hope his way. To see Joey's fresh, inventive mind working things out tugged at TR's heart. His thoughts sailed.

"Children need more encouragement than they get about how far and wide they can go using their minds. Many more children need to know with certainty, rather than doubt, that every human mind holds thousands of solutions for solving problems. Joey has the magic eye to perceive possibilities all around him. He has the heart to feel truth before he can put it into words."

TR dusted off his pants, wiped his hands thoroughly and said, "OK now, Joey. What've you got to show me?"

Joey gulped the biggest breath he could before speaking. To have yet another precious audience with this man was just about the most pure heaven on earth a young inventor could dream of. His mind flashed a prayer of gratitude.

"Thank the saints I met Mr. TR on the train ride to Red River last March. How else could such a busy, famous man have gotten to know an ordinary boy like me?"

Joey decided that plain old luck had just as much to do with it.

"Mr. TR," he said, "Thanks for letting me visit again. I was figuring to make the needle of a phonograph play music records clearer. I studied the machine at my friend's house and drafted this design."

He brought from his jacket pocket a tightly folded paper. He moved it toward his mentor on the bench where they both sat.

"Let's take a look," said TR. He gently smoothed the boy's drawing on the wood slats.

Now it was Joey's turn to huddle for a fantastic moment with TR Gimble.

CHAPTER 4

▼

"Let's not poke along. I don't want to miss anything!"

The young lady in the pink hat beckoned to her friends on the fashionable avenue. They stepped up their pace with heels clicking. Overhead, bright green fronds burst from lush palms lining both sides of the street. Textured shadows waved over fragrant lawns gracing every spacious residence. The home the ladies hurried to lay half a sunny suburb away from the industrial hub where TR Gimble's experimental plant hummed with quiet intrigue.

In Amy Watson's parlor, ladies greeted one another brightly. Women already seated leaned into discussions intently. Comments across the room sparked new conversations.

The parlor's French doors opened to the south. A light breeze created billows inside cream-colored sheers that hung from carved rods above the doors. Puffs of feathery fabric danced with the spring wind to kiss the edges of small, round mahogany tables set around the room. Fourteen high back chairs formed a circle. Their carved claw feet gripped the floor as if to anchor the determination of women seated upon them.

Amy looked with satisfaction at her treasured chairs. The fresh chintz in which they were covered had been a treat to order from San Francisco. An older lady stood beside her.

"I was at your husband's pharmacy yesterday. What a thriving business!" Amy looked at her appreciatively.

"Yes, he has more customers than ever. He said your husband's health has improved. I'm delighted for both of you." The woman beamed.

"He says he'll soon be dancing an Irish jig. We are blessed!"

Amy waved hello to the women arriving through her entry. She was grateful they were not the kind to question that no butler answered her door. She knew they didn't mind that her parlor was basically a standard affair awaiting better decoration. The room surely needed more trappings to fit the fine home into which she and her husband had moved only five short years ago. A young woman came to her side.

"The flowers are beautiful, Amy. And your chairs look stunning. You're amazing always finding time for new projects!" The pharmacist's wife smiled.

"Thank you, Susan. If it's something we can squeeze into the budget, I'll do it."

"Are you enjoying your new job?"

"Yes, it's interesting. Being next to Superior Court brings as much traffic through the attorney's office as my husband's pharmacy! I miss the baby when I'm gone, though. I know my mother keeps close watch so I needn't worry."

Amy paused, a look of concern clouding her pretty face.

"The only thing I worry about is my husband extending so much credit to patients who can't afford their medicines. When some misfortune delivers one of his customers into the hands of the Lord, Watson's pharmacy can take months to get paid. Sometimes remittance is never collected from the departed's family."

The understanding look from her friend prompted Amy to admit a secret.

"Recovery for our customers is something I pray for as devoutly as a minister! I even send up extra prayers that men might return to full employment on a company's healthy payroll. Is that terrible of me?"

"I'd do the same practical praying!" declared Susan.

Amy looked at her parlor filled with women of different ages. Their delight and hope warmed her heart. She turned to Susan again.

"I don't mind working. It's good to get out and about in the city. My husband's supply of medicines is getting more expensive to maintain, but we'll do whatever's needed to keep a well-stocked pharmacy."

The ladies within earshot nodded. They knew that Amy wasn't the only realistic wife of a busy professional working to stave off tomorrow's uncertainties. With her job downtown, Amy was able to add such things as a delicate gold-plated clock and two fine silver candlesticks from England to her tidy but simple parlor.

Eva clapped her hands above the ladies' heads.

"Welcome, my dears. Happy spring! As always, we meet to exchange our insights about these changing times. My idea is to stretch our minds to recount the most exciting scientific discovery we've read of in the news. Let's see if we can describe why one innovation is more critical to the country's future than any other."

The women paused in concentration and then exchanged quiet comments.

"I've read of so many inventions, dozens every week!"

"Several outstanding discoveries caught my eye, but there's not enough detail in the papers for me to be able to compare one to another."

"Our magazines tell us how ladies should please our husbands and serve our families. They don't talk about technical subjects."

"Where can we read news with scientific details we can even understand?"

"I can't open my mouth and speak with any knowledge about these things. Can you?

When no one came forward, Harriet declared the winning truth.

"I suppose the only chemistry we know better than men is the kind that visits us once a month!"

Giggles filled the room as chatter broke out unrestrained. No woman could withhold her opinion on that subject. Eva raised her voice above the feminine clamor.

"There's a lady in France we should note, a Polish scientist named Madame Curie. She won a Nobel Prize in physics in 1903 and second one in chemistry in 1911. No woman scientist I've heard of has matched that!"

"There you go!" said Doreen. "Women scientists should indeed have a chance to excel in this country, too. Does anyone know of a Madame Curie on this side of the Atlantic who has any big American company paying to support her work?"

Curls on the ladies' heads tossed back and forth.

"For shame," they murmured.

Doreen expanded her point.

"In particular, there's no lady in the U.S. I know of who's a top chemist researching fuels. A gentleman I know told me that university scientists are known to elbow out, if not crush, any man not of their academic standing who dares to diagram a formula! With this kind of thinking in general acceptance, women don't stand a chance!"

The ladies figured she was right. They knew she read more avidly than any of them. She could discuss things more confidently with men than they could. She asked smart questions, too.

Doreen looked at the women seated around her.

"No one in this room can name a woman working as anything more than a secretary or accountant at one of the hundreds of new fuel companies mentioned in the papers. There's not a solitary female scientist being written of among the men creating the country's new industrial energy."

Slips and petticoats were adjusted with impatience. Matters regarding science seemed distant enough to these ladies. Anything to do with fuel seemed even more remote. Eva gave voice to their thoughts.

"We've heard enough talk from men to know that these matters involve companies who keep their associations vague. Only when news about the next big discovery fills the headlines do limited details emerge, but only enough to get people excited to buy stock!"

Susan put her chin on her hand as she wondered aloud.

"The country's millionaires are engaged in the development of fuel. These men are not among any employers we know. How will women like us learn more?"

Harriet glanced up from the news article on her lap.

"Fuel companies open new offices ten and twenty at a time! These companies can grow from nothing to occupying every state in the Union in only a few years."

Twyla perked up, happy to add a word.

"It's nothing like the railroads!"

"That's right," said Doreen. "There were miles of open land between railroad tracks, but roads crisscross everywhere. Men are working overtime to pave thousands of miles of highway. And thousands of new fuel stations must be built along every one."

Harriet held up her news article.

"Ladies, we have a whole new country emerging virtually overnight! Unless we start aiming to learn more science, women could be doomed to watch on the sidelines while technical progress explodes!"

Eva looked thoughtful.

"I read that fuel distribution concerns are known for airtight secrecy. Men say their armor cannot be pierced. There are elusive foreign nations, too. No one's sure what's going on overseas. Some nations are what the reporters call belligerents. These countries desperately want fuel. I worry about another war for our children!"

Doreen looked at the concerned women.

"Working ladies might be able to learn things that will help us cast our new votes wisely. It's up to us because, from what I understand, the wives and daughters of wealthy men who control the new energy companies are kept well distant from knowing any details."

Susan looked surprised.

"I can't imagine not sharing everything with a man I would marry. How do you know that?"

"Ladies interviewed by society columnists state as much. One writer said it's looking to her as if families of established fuel companies only associate with other families in the same business. I doubt that women would choose to restrict themselves like that. I read it as the women being instructed in secrecy by the men!"

The ladies looked at each other in wonder.

"If those women can't learn from their own men, how will we learn anything?"

Doreen summarized firmly.

"We're pledged to meet each month and work our minds to make up for centuries of women who lived in general ignorance. We won't figure overnight how we'll put an end to our days of being excluded from knowledge owned by men alone."

"But asking good questions," assured Harriet, "is a great beginning!"

The young ladies exchanged quizzical glances. They looked at the stiff-backed, older women who still wore corsets under ruffled shirts with full, dark skirts that brushed the tops of plain, black shoes. None of them had supplied new thoughts. Many of the young ladies wondered the same thing.

"How can they understand the modern world? If the women who came before us can't help us, who will?"

The younger women sported narrow dresses that flowed above shins and ankles hugged by lisle cotton stockings in pleasing pastels. Long legs crossed and dangled nervously. Dainty feet were crowned with shoes of colored leather. Dressy straps with bows and flowers flounced over pointed toes. This day in Amy's parlor, many of the sweet, young foreheads puckered in frustration. Carefully plucked eyebrows rose in questioning arches.

Harriet surveyed the perplexed faces around her. The contrasting feminine costumes of young and old seemed a bit constricting in the warm, lilac-scented room. The pressures behind the ladies' impatience took form in her thoughts.

"They're distracted with worries that they should have started preparations weeks ago for Easter outfits and decorating. Springtime visitors requiring more cooking and cleaning at their houses aren't helping either."

She folded her hands, remembering how overwhelmed she used to feel with ambitious chores. Somewhere along the way, she relaxed and changed her aims to learn more. She turned to address the older women.

"A ray of hope can be found in the progress you ladies started for us. California ratifying the 19th Amendment last November was magnificent. Our new right to vote can really bring changes to how men once ruled our lives. Over forty years ago, ladies began to meet like this. No one gave them a handbook on how to achieve suffrage. You women had to learn to believe you had the brains to figure it out."

The older ladies' eyes filled with tears. Eva beamed at her friend's wisdom.

"Harriet's right. While we're still new at understanding science and inventions, we're gaining elsewhere. Women own more property than ever before!"

Amy contemplated the attorneys, clients and judges she was meeting at her boss's downtown law firm. She tried to make sense of what she was seeing at her new job but couldn't.

"I'm no expert in these matters, but there seem to be cloudy issues when it comes to women and land. Eva's correct that more women own property. It gets complicated with mineral rights. Laws about oil wells and mines seem impossible to understand!"

Harriet thought a moment.

"Good point, Amy. We're in jeopardy of losing rights we gained if we don't learn more. Remember, a year after our country's Declaration of Independence, every state in America passed laws taking away women's right to vote. We have to make sure we keep moving forward, not backward!"

Amy reflected more about what she witnessed at work. She spoke again.

"It seems we're continually being tested. When women try to handle things in court without a husband or brother to advise them, parasites do crawl out of the woodwork. They can spot a woman in trouble because legal postings advertise it."

Doreen leaned forward.

"You bring up excellent points, Amy. We must remain steadfast to cross miles of hostile, unknown territory in the well-equipped field of men! They are fast becoming armed with intricate technology and laws. If we want to keep our achievements intact for our daughters, we must not lag behind in kitchens and beauty salons! Exclusion from entire worlds of knowledge remains our greatest handicap. Growing complacent makes us vulnerable. It's up to no one but us to steadily improve our course."

Amy remembered a civil case she saw and spoke again.

"Doreen is not exaggerating. There are scoundrels who know the law better than any ladies I know. It can be a murky pond in court. Schools of society's worst bottom-feeders lurk among swamps of men! Some make laws designed to handicap others. Others win cases on interpretations never designed into law. The fact is that men alone rule in every court where women might be called to appear!"

Susan looked at Amy in shock.

"Exactly what are you seeing downtown?"

Her friend answered evenly.

"A new point of view."

Doreen took note.

"It's not fair-minded individuals we need to worry about. A variety of villains stand ready to take back whatever money or rights women might acquire. They're learning about oil wells, new inventions and things of science faster than we are. We're like peasants armed with sticks against Napoleon's army!"

"A good way to put it," agreed Eva.

Doreen winked at Eva. Eva noted her grin.

"Is it Porter time?"

Doreen nodded. It was time for her impersonation of the famous, theatrical lady evangelist they all knew, Annabelle Porter. Doreen clutched her heart, raised her eyes to the ceiling and sang out.

"With desperate certainty, ladies, we surely must not become overly infatuated with the dubious antics and fashions that movie barons in Hollywood would have us thinking of night and day!"

The women laughed although they knew it was true. The character Doreen impersonated was a show woman herself. According to news reports, the lady was raking in millions through her church. The women in Amy's parlor recognized the irony of one smart preacher lady pulling in as much money as the movie barons. They shared their heartfelt agreement.

"We must get cracking to learn more!"

CHAPTER 5

▼

Billy lay flat on his stomach in the dirt near the grill below Amy Watson's parlor. He rested his chin on the back of his hand and drew circles in the dirt.

"C'mon," he thought. "It's bad enough when Mom talks about women voting and all that garbage. She hears that lady preacher on the radio, too. Go back to talking about fuel companies."

The sharp-witted boy of ten figured out months ago that many of Amy's guests were the brightest among the city ladies. He first noticed them at the pharmacy and the market. He overheard their hushed exclamations.

"Guess what I heard at work!"

"You won't believe the letter I typed this morning!"

That got Billy's attention.

Every time he tried to move closer to hear, they ended their chatter the same way.

"I'll tell you more at Amy's!"

Billy finally heard the pharmacist proudly mention 'my wife, Amy.' He guessed the ladies probably met there. He learned that the Watson house wasn't too far from his. He watched the buggies and autos that congregated in the driveway each month. He knew which families still used horses and who drove cars in town. He felt certain there was more to the ladies' socializing than sipping afternoon tea so Billy began to think of his next step.

"I gotta a find a place to hide and listen!"

Using his usual methods with his tow-headed good looks, Billy pretended to chase a cat he threw over the fence into Mrs. Watson's yard. Crawling under the house, he discovered an open grill near the furnace on the parlor floor. This prime listening cavity seemed like a good bet. He carefully carved out a hole near the back gate shrubs where he could circumvent any permission to enter the Watsons' yard. He snuck undetected below the shrubs along the driveway to the back porch. He used branches to camouflage the portal to his crawlspace under the porch. Once he slid through, he wriggled his wiry frame to his secret listening post.

Billy was amazed to hear the details described by the ladies who worked downtown. He knew why it drew them together.

"This stuff's not in the newspapers!"

He heard the excitement from women who didn't work. They asked all kinds of questions. He realized the attraction.

"They're dying to hear downtown gossip!"

The boy noticed that the ladies described things differently than how men reported events in the paper. Best of all, his older brother made him feel that this espionage operation was a grand achievement. Billy's heart swelled with pride thinking how he might be able to help his brother and dad.

"Someday I'll hear something important they don't know is happening downtown!"

Scrunched below the parlor floor, Billy brushed off his hands and waited for more. He remembered the ladies yakking and giggling about some calamity that befell women each month.

"Maybe my sister Winnie knows about that."

Mrs. Berkowitz laid her hand on Mrs. Finny's shoulder and whispered in her good ear.

"That Eva sure has sound logic!"

Mrs. Finny chuckled.

"So does Harriet. And Doreen's such a spitfire. She inspires the women mightily."

Mrs. Finny looked at the eldest of their companions, Mrs. Rhodes.

"Aren't these women terrific?"

Mrs. Rhodes nodded. Then she smiled wistfully and took a small sip of tea. Her weathered hands worked to hold steady a delicate teacup painted with tiny, yellow flowers. She knew that the lovely Queen Anne china belonged to Amy's only collection. Upon entering the large Watson home, the ladies stowed their wraps on the shelves of the room typically used as the china closet in most fine residences. No formal china was arrayed on Amy's shelves. Also absent were any large, velvet-lined wooden boxes storing sets of imported silver.

The older women knew that Amy would have kept shelves of such fine household treasures if she could afford them. But they were wise enough to know that such possessions didn't matter most in life. They admired Amy as the kind of lady who would never lack the highest order of things she needed—friends, love and family. They knew that vast collections of formal china and fine silver never restored one's faith or replaced lasting relationships, nor did they become a woman's dearest treasures once she was their age.

Mrs. Rhodes leaned slightly toward Mrs. Finny.

"Isn't Amy such a considerate dear for including us?"

Billy flicked a spider off his sleeve. A puff of dust blew up. He suppressed a sneeze and wiped his nose on his shoulder.

"I can't hear anything when they whisper!"

Harriett spoke firmly.

"Winning the right to vote is only a start, ladies. The blunt fact is, we'll be relegated to lowly support positions one and all if we don't declare new aims. As things get more complicated, we're more at risk of losing ground than ever before!"

Susan agreed.

"I see that happening where I work. A man tells a woman to sign something, and she simply takes the next streetcar and comes downtown to sign it. Few women ever ask questions. And when they do, all they get is talk they don't understand!"

"That's right," said Doreen. "Since not many women in this country have succeeded in business by themselves, we must bear witness every day and discuss what we see and hear. We need more women who can speak and write about problems so we can learn from each other."

Mrs. Berkowitz shook her crown of silver hair.

"Sometimes I wonder if we did the right thing marching in suffragette parades and boycotting desperate husbands!"

Mrs. Rhodes smiled at the memory.

"It felt right at the time." She looked at Mrs. Graham.

"Do you think we acted too boldly?" Mrs. Graham paused thoughtfully before she spoke.

"I have no regrets. I hope it's the same for these ladies. Few of the women are as sure of themselves as Eva and Doreen. Harriett touches others with her insights. They seem to have decoded more of the men's world than the others. Susan and Amy aren't far behind. Doing what they suggest may take them farther than protesting in streets and bedrooms did for us!"

Mrs. Finny looked at her senior companions.

"I don't know where else we could go to learn what we do here!"

Mrs. Graham smoothed the fabric of her long black skirt. She tipped her bonnet toward her friends.

"I don't know about you, but I'm pleased as punch to still be invited to any socials!"

Below the parlor floor, Billy yawned and shifted onto one elbow. He surveyed the cobwebs in his roost.

"Too bad there isn't a quicker way than this!"

He felt certain that news of supreme consequence would fly out of the women's mouths and into his eager ears. He counted on overhearing tidbits that he could run and tell his brother.

The old ladies giggled in pleasure over being invited to Amy's while trying to hold fast to trembling cups and saucers. Their thirst to learn at a late age could not be quenched by light conversation or any amount of clover tea they sipped down parched, wrinkled throats. Their bony fingers were permanently curled from years of gardening in tough soil. These women had been solely driven their entire lives to meet priorities of feeding and caring for hordes of children in large families. Their crooked backs had carried many a sick child and up to twelve pregnancies. For some, no more than six babies ever grew to full term, only to be followed by gruesome deliveries in fields, buggies and barns on the way to distant country doctors. Rarely did they feel the comforts of cozy, floral bedrooms or clean hospitals where city women were able to give birth these days.

Mrs. Graham saw the faraway look in Mrs. Rhodes' eyes. She whispered to her.

"Little of our past matters now to the young, but maybe simply being here shows how we support their struggle."

Mrs. Rhodes patted her friend's hand. She felt fortunate to remember the details of the past that she did. Few of their female friends survived to very old age. Those who did were often in wretched health or demented by the age of fifty. For the senior ladies in Amy's parlor, being here was an achievement only they could comprehend. How to move forward with such a markedly diverse group of women was a question that might not be answered in their lifetimes. Any small steps of progress the old women saw sparked encouragement to be reflected upon for weeks. They longed to witness strong seeds of independence taking hold in more young ladies. It was this that the fragile, old women yearned to smile quietly about and discuss as often as possible before their days were done.

Billy strained to hear if anything was happening above him, but the low giggles and soft, old voices made it frustrating.

"Maybe they're taking a break."

He tried to remember a tune he liked. He sang the notes in his head as he shifted onto his other elbow. His stomach growled. Then it churned with impatience. The latest news in the papers showed Billy that a lot was happening in every direction with the men in his father's life. Surely the women must have overheard things! He knew the working ladies spent hours every week typing letters, filing, answering calls and greeting visitors. But they weren't talking about those things today. Billy contemplated how he might seek out a group of lady telephone operators. Most of the husbands and bosses of the ladies above him didn't know, as Billy had heard, that the astute ears of certain telephone operators could be bought for a nominal tip.

"Operators probably hear tons more things than these women!"

When Billy reported each month what he overheard under Mrs. Watson's parlor, his older brother patiently explained to him what was probably meant in the things the women discussed. Ty had a knack for knowing how to decipher what people said. He could tell Billy which morsels from the ladies' conversations contained real news and which things didn't matter much to their dad's world or their family. The frustrated lad was getting a headache.

"I'll have nothing juicy to tell Ty! Don't tell me this stupid meeting's going to be a waste!"

Mrs. Graham surveyed the young women.

"I remember being at my wits' end many a day with even less to accomplish than they're trying to achieve. They're overwhelmed, but still, all this talk stirs my heart!"

Mrs. Finny's eyes twinkled as she addressed her friends.

"Amy surely is a treasure for inviting us. I can hardly wait to see what comes next!"

CHAPTER 6

▼

Twyla listened to the statements and whispers from the circle of women gathered in Amy's parlor. She looked up with a pretty sparkle.

"I don't know of any women studying science, but I will say there's a man of chemistry we should be aware of in this town."

Several women glanced at the young lady they knew to be typically vivacious. She'd barely spoken today. Susan was intrigued.

"Who is it?"

Twyla lifted her chin.

"Let me describe what he's like before I tell you his name. That way you'll never forget who he is. I know I wouldn't want to overlook anything about this person after learning what I did! You might want to keep watch if news of him comes your way. I can promise you, anything to do with this man will be of special interest!"

All eyes turned toward Tylwa. Thoughts of spring cleaning and Easter parties blew out the French doors and far beyond the portico. The women leaned forward to hear what Twyla had to say. She was known for her knack of finding ways to meet people, and also for listening to what men said through closed office doors and walls without oak panels.

"When this chemist comes to visit our office, he fills the entire doorway with his large frame. He is so tall, his hat skims the door frame as he enters. He takes off his hat and delivers a beaming hello to everyone. As he steps inside, the room becomes alive with some kind of powerful energy. He's that magnanimous a man!"

Twyla delighted in her own telling with words she'd heard that she plucked from thin air now. Even though she wasn't as smart as some of the ladies in the room, this was her turn to sound every bit as interesting. She basked in everyone's full attention and gushed on.

"You can't ignore a word this chemist says. His intelligence covers every subject you can think of! He spins a tale that keeps young men, as well as old codgers, enraptured in his every word. No one makes a sound or interrupts until his full story is told. Then the most important men in the room ask him dozens of questions to which he provides fascinating answers. These are answers that explain things in ways that everyone can understand! He has traveled everywhere gathering information about machines and fuels. I've heard he's been around the world. I listen to what the men say after he leaves our office. They declare with certainty that he's a man of importance to the future of our country!"

Buoyed by her joyous recall, Twyla sailed on.

"By way of more description, ladies, this chemist has deep, green eyes that shoot off lights when he smiles, and that is very often. He has big white teeth and hair impeccably groomed. He can make the room rumble with the heartiest laugh you ever heard! Electric bulbs sometimes flicker when he's talking."

Doubt began to gather in some of the women's eyes. Undaunted, Twyla continued.

"Now, there were a few men in my boss's office who said they thought that the lights dimming and getting brighter were from some kind of wiring problem in the damp weather, but a number of them felt certain it was some kind of electro-magic method the chemist knows how to employ because no lights flickered up or down after he left the room! This man draws pictures to explain his math calculations and does all of this while calmly speaking to every single person around the room."

Twyla lifted her luminous gaze toward the brim of her pink hat. Her cheeks flushed. She fanned her face with a dainty, pink gloved hand and continued in hushed reverence.

"This man of science is utterly handsome as the sun! No one can deny that he captures your heart immediately. I have heard him whistle a tune on the way out. Nona in my office heard him singing down on Sixth Street when she saw him on her way to the streetcar. She says she was overwhelmed with immediate desire to slide inside his pocket and travel with him wherever he went. He seemed like such a dashing, happy man. But you mustn't tell her Richard what she said! The chemist might visit our office again. Nona wants to find a way to be there when he arrives. You should see what I have seen. The ladies' knees tremble beneath their skirts when he walks in!"

Billy lay on his hands clutching his chest to keep from moving. Any sound he made would have gone through the floorboards and pierced the silent pause hanging over the dead-quiet parlor.

Twyla took a breath and looked around. Female faces peered back with anticipation. She gathered her poise as if she'd walked miles to deliver this illumination. She tipped her head slightly for her final pronouncement.

"That is all I know right now except for one more thing. I heard this chemist keeps his offices on the entire seventh floor of the Taylor Building. That building is the most prestigious in all of downtown!"

Billy stifled a gasp as he realized who the chemist was.

"Dad's headquarters are on the whole seventh floor of the Taylor Building!"

Genevieve's heart was pounding. She immediately adjusted the hair clip at the nape of her neck that was holding tight the bun around which her long, auburn hair was wrapped. She tried to appear casual. She risked a major tumble from grace with her husband if she revealed who she thought the chemist was.

Her husband Frank had just started work as an accounting clerk for a man of this description last week. He mentioned that his office was on the seventh floor and that the views from his employer's suite above Sixth and Broadway were the most impressive he'd ever seen. The similarities between who Twyla described and what her husband mentioned about the man he worked for were unmistakable.

Genevieve had been strictly instructed to hold her tongue on any matters that Frank might ever reveal about his work for this man. The ladies in Amy's parlor knew many people downtown. They would find out soon enough that her husband had ties to this man.

Genevieve didn't want to throw cold water on Twyla's exciting news regarding a man of such interest to all the ladies, but she had to bring him down a peg or two. Allowing intrigue to intensify wouldn't be comfortable later when the ladies found out about her husband's employment. Too many sticky questions might be directed her way. She thought a second and cleared her throat before speaking.

"The man Twyla is talking about sounds like the inventor, TR Gimble."

Below the floorboards, Billy thought he would burst. He didn't dare take a breath.

Susan chimed in.

"I've seen news articles about the man. The reporters always call him an inventor, not a chemist or scientist."

"That's right," said Genevieve. "He's somewhat a chemist, but he also works at times as an engineer and geologist. He seems to be many things at once."

Susan furrowed her brow trying to remember what she read. She never saw anything referring to the inventor as an engineer or geologist either. She looked at Genevieve.

"I'm curious. Where did you read that?"

Genevieve laced her fingers together. She squeezed them tight to stop the shaking and laid her hands calmly on her skirt.

"I overheard a conversation from some men who came to visit my husband. I heard that Mr. Gimble never went to any university though. He's a self-taught inventor, one that government men and fuel companies don't seem to want to take very seriously."

Twyla looked glum. She didn't read the newspapers like she knew she ought to. The humble man she worked for had been an assistant to a university-trained chemist at a small fuel company several years ago. Now he was trying to start his own chemical business.

Twyla was certain that her boss had called Mr. Gimble a chemist. So had all the other men at the small office where she typed correspondence and answered the telephone several days a week. She thought she brought the ladies an exclusive story about a world-famous chemist that would impress them, especially given that the man could steal anyone's heart away in an instant. She rekindled her confidence thinking of what she'd seen and heard when Mr. Gimble had visited their office on two occasions. She doubted this man was some tinker that the experts would take lightly. She straightened her shoulders and declared loudly.

"I didn't hear from anyone who met the man that Mr. Gimble wasn't a chemist!"

Harriet's pragmatic mind weighed the few facts at hand.

"The way you talk about him, Twyla, you could just about build an altar under him and a church around him. You might as well post his likeness above the minister's pulpit!"

The older women chuckled. The way Harriet summarized things delighted them. Twyla's eyes clouded.

"I'm not exaggerating. You can ask Nona when you see her. Men and women both are instantly taken by the man!"

Amy looked thoughtful.

"Maybe Harriet has a point. We should keep our eyes and ears open for more actual facts about this person, facts that we can really discuss. Knowing more about his work or his company may lead us to things we want to learn. Learning matters of fuel science and maybe some of the machines involved could surely help our understanding of all the new technology. We have to start somewhere, and starting with an inventor who's willing to explain things in ways that ordinary people can understand might be worth our time to learn about."

Everyone jubilantly agreed. There wasn't a woman in the parlor, young or old, not filling out an index card with TR Gimble's name and curious occupations for inclusion in their files.

CHAPTER 7

▼

Billy raised his head closer to the floorboards. He could tell by the excited voice speaking that it was one of the younger women in the Watson parlor who met his dad. He tried to picture the ladies.

"Which one is it?"

He scratched his head. Dust sprinkled from his hair.

"Are the women downtown going after my dad?"

Susan winked at the fascinated group.

"We could probably stand to learn a thing or two about someone who's managed to stay a millionaire for years."

Twyla's eyes got big.

"Is the chemist a millionaire?"

"He sure is, according to reports in the newspapers. It's not every company that pays to send only one man to every country in the world. Think about it, Twyla. Why would any big company ever entrust only one person with all of their overseas interests? They typically have executives and managers to purchase, sell or start business in other countries."

Amy looked up in sudden recollection.

"I've seen in papers I file at the office that companies check everything men claim about materials, meetings and whatever else goes on overseas. Disputes between different companies that end up in court are based on the claims of many men. Big companies look to protect their interests, and many eyes and ears must supply sufficient testimony to defend those interests. One man alone cannot adequately defend himself competing against the large conglomerates."

Harriet surmised the facts.

"Then it would appear that Mr. Gimble is likely not just a chemist."

Susan added more.

"Reporters write that he pays for all his new developments himself. That likely includes his travel everywhere. We know how expensive that is! They say that Mr. Gimble continues to play at the top of the heap of millionaires buying land and gosh-knows-what-else year after year. Doing all that and remaining a millionaire must require some fantastic organization!"

Twyla glared at Genevieve.

"Well then, I hardly think the government or anyone else would be taking this man lightly at all!"

Harriet mused and spoke wonderingly.

"That is, unless he were a master conniver or charlatan."

Genevieve smoothed her skirt and refolded her hands while her mind jumped. She hadn't wanted conversation to go down this particular fork in the road. She wanted to dampen the group's enthusiasm about Mr. Gimble, yet she couldn't remain silent hearing any sort of speculation that TR Gimble might be a charlatan. Her husband and she, after all, would not do well if anyone thought Frank was working for a conniver! The women would find out about Frank's employment with the man soon enough. She must redirect the ladies' attention. She held her tone even.

"I think his wife may be of some interest. I don't know if she would ever come speak with us. She does not socialize, but I heard she was an accountant at a fuel company when she met this man."

Genevieve took a long breath and thought to herself.

"There, maybe I did alright pushing interest away from my husband's employer. I hope this works, at least for now."

Genevieve knew she'd require a glass of sherry to steady her rattled nerves once she arrived home. She told no one about the liquor her husband kept. Frank's were the only twinkling eyes she cared madly about.

There was the matter of her growing curiosity about this person who employed her dear Frank. But she knew there'd be plenty of time later to meet the inventor and assess for herself if the man was everything people claimed. She reminded herself of her duty.

"I must keep a cool head now that Frank is working for someone who's famous and controversial. Frank worked for years to get this job. I mustn't say anything that might compromise his position!"

Genevieve smiled. She knew she had a far more excellent chance of getting to know Mr. Gimble and his wife than did any of the ladies in the room who, by now, were dying to catch a mere glimpse of him.

Billy thought he might poop his pants. He tried to hold things tight, but a small oodle of flatulence escaped. It was bad. The big breath he exhaled once the ladies' conversation restarted had carried his nuisance wafting toward the grill. The subterranean cavity where he crouched was getting cold and stuffy. He was certain he'd explode with excitement hearing that both his mom and dad were now going to be under scrutiny by the ladies in Mrs. Watson's parlor.

"Holy Mother!" exclaimed Harriet.

She was seated closest to the floor grill in the parlor when the odor reached her first. She wrinkled her nose at the offensive smell that certainly did not resemble lilacs!

The older ladies immediately shot accusing glances toward each other and shifted atop their voluminous crinoline. The one who had propelled the scent would never fluff the folds of her skirt. The elders casually ruffled fabric without conscience or consequence. They looked around to see if the guilty party would identify herself by holding her hands still in her lap. This was an old, accepted ritual but today, in silence, it revealed that none of the elder ladies was the guilty party. They smiled in satisfaction. They would still be invited to future meetings. This parlor talk was simply too interesting for any of them to miss!

Amy shot a worried glance toward the nursery and wondered.

"Did someone knock over the diaper pail?"

Miss Doreen, the princess of practicality, intervened to put a swift end to the paranoia of mortified women holding their delicate noses in the parlor. She, like they, customarily would rather drop dead on the floor than to ever succumb to such a frightful social error.

"Come, come now, ladies," she soothed. "We've all been through diapers and gastric inconvenience. Let's conclude our meeting and get moving to complete all the spring chores we must attend to. We'll save whatever newspaper articles we find about Mr. Gimble and see if any ladies at the church know anything of Mrs. Gimble. We can talk about other prominent chemists and inventors when we meet again next month. We will not give up our vigilance to learn more! Let's wrap up now and go enjoy the air outside!"

The young women in the room gave a quick shout like traders at the stock exchange.

"Done!"

They quickly gathered parasols and handbags and exited the room. As they exchanged good-byes and hugs in the driveway, no one was the wiser about the presence of little Billy Gimble or his upset stomach after hearing their conversation.

Relieved that his mission was complete, Billy prepared to withdraw from his underground chamber. His reconnaissance had yielded fine results. Billy capped this pleasing moment of triumph. He gave himself a silent salute followed by a satisfied burp. He kept his whisper low.

"Bingo, you got 'em, boy!"

There'd been too much going on in the news for the Gimble name to be overlooked this week, but he never dreamed the ladies would want to know things about both his parents. He knew Ty would be impressed to hear the latest.

Billy backed out from below the Watson parlor on his elbows. As he neared his portal below the back porch, he scrunched himself around. Parting the branches covering the opening, he peeked right and left. No one was in sight. He wiggled through the opening and kicked the debris back in place. Scurrying to the driveway shrubs, he ducked low and waited until the last of the cars and buggies departed. He darted to his hole near the shrubs by the back gate. He slid through and straightened on the sidewalk. From behind he heard a lady's sharp voice.

"Your mother will drop into a dead faint when she sees your filthy clothes!"

Billy whirled around trying not to faint himself. An older lady walked quickly toward him.

"Oh, man!" he thought. "Is she one of them?"

He decided it didn't matter. This was survival! He dropped back to his knees. Sweeping the ground with his hands, he faked a sniffle and pleading wail.

"I can't find my favorite coin! I've been looking high and low. It fell through a hole in my pocket!"

The lady put her hands on her hips. Billy noticed her gaze did not waver from his dirty clothes. He pretended to wipe his sniffle with the back of his sleeve and squinted up at the lady's stern countenance.

"I forgot my glasses! I don't see too well. It's just been a terrible day, ma'm!"

The woman's face softened to gentler lines as she counseled.

"Well, you've simply got to stop crawling around in the dirt! If you've looked so hard, maybe somebody else found your coin. Here, take this shiny new penny. Forget about the old coin. Maybe this will change your luck."

Billy got off his knees and accepted the penny with both hands as if it would become his most prized possession.

"Thank you, kind lady!"

"You should go home now. Can you find your way?"

"Oh, sure. My feet know the way better than my eyes!"

She smiled at the pitiful-looking boy before she walked on.

Billy waited and then slapped the dust from his clothes as hard as he could. Front, back and sides exploded with sandy gray particles. Any fleeting thoughts he had about trying to figure out all the things the women yakked and giggled about fell to the sidewalk with the dust. Nothing was as important as hearing them discuss his dad like they did, or knowing they'd be searching for things to discover about his mom.

He had to find Ty. The talk about his dad capturing women's hearts was the first Billy heard. Ty would know if Dad was really that way. Billy doubted he would ever tell his sister Winnie about any of it even if Dad were. That would worry her something silly.

He knew Winnie's biggest girlie concern was about anything bad happening to Mom or Dad. The thought of other women chasing after Dad would probably make her downright ill! Thinking that their parents might split apart would rip Winnie right through the heart.

A million more dolls added to the huge collection she played with every day could never console poor Winnie if something like that threatened her world. She'd go straight to Mom wailing about her nightmares and concerns. And he knew what would happen next. He'd get a strap to his stinky, dusty bottom for crawling around spying below Mrs. Watson's floor!

Even if Ty never told on him, and even if Mom never knew how Billy found such things out, Billy would receive some punishment. Mom would be certain he was up to his usual mischief anyway.

CHAPTER 8

▼

The Great Southland unfolded its beaches and party canopies to revelers in the light of early summer. At a university in downtown Los Angeles, ornate buildings glistened in the sun. Fragrant avenues of cypress, eucalyptus and pine trees wound gracefully into well-worn paths. The campus sat devoid of students grateful to conclude their last grueling final exams. Walkways usually bustling with excitement held only eternal bronze plaques denoting prominent alumni and donors. A Pacific Ocean breeze swept through outer halls of polished marble and stone, which no longer echoed the laughter and shouts of jubilant graduates.

The great institution's buildings were locked with one exception. A guard stood watch at the door outside the science lecture hall. In the vast descending room, chemistry charts lay face down on a large oak table. Laboratory exhibits draped in black were set off to one side.

Five professors lined the front of the auditorium. Gripping their synchronized stopwatches, their sharp eyes scanned the room's upper windows. TR Gimble was the only person seated front and center amid rows of empty desks rising fifteen tiers behind him.

The mid-morning heat pushed the mercury in downtown thermometers skyward, promising a searing day. The window blinds in the hall were down for cleaning, stacked neatly on back tables awaiting pickup during janitorial rounds. The sun pierced through naked panes of the glass. High windows on the east side of the hall accepted the blazing rays at just the right angle. The university maintenance department had not been informed that a group of men in heavy robes would be standing here for hours, targets for the solar rays under which they baked.

The academic professionals standing behind the long desk in the lower front of the hall were wearing their graduation robes as requested. Beads of sweat formed on their foreheads, dripping off chins onto brightly colored satin stoles. They pondered nothing academic but shared one common question in their minds.

"What hair-brain organizer of this affair forgot to put out water cups and a cold pitcher?"

The deep-set eyes of the world-renown inventor pierced the scene before him. The proportions of the one-armed desk in which he sat were much too modest for a man of his frame. His long legs protruded beyond the last step down to the front of the class. TR Gimble hadn't counted on such a physical squeeze. He had not imagined this setting in his thoughts.

"It's been twenty-nine years since I sat in a classroom!"

Any large movements he made could jeopardize the outcome. He couldn't shift without toppling the desktop under which his legs were squeezed. His mind, however, was at ease remembering the circumstances that brought him here. He paused to reflect how he'd explain this unusual day to his grandchildren.

"I was fortunate to have my talent recognized by Jacob Steiner. He is one smart patent attorney, the kind that every inventor wants to have. He arranged for Regis Petroleum to pay for a comprehensive exam that would determine if I were qualified to discuss technical matters with the men of large oil concerns. I had no college credentials. In fact, I hadn't even set foot in high school. I had no doubts regarding my own abilities, but the company's scientists and engineers did not share my confidence. One of the science professors telegrammed the test administrator at Regis Petroleum to recommend attaching wires to my head! He thought the wires might read the rate of activity in my brain. Well, I certainly protested submitting myself to such a preposterous trial, and I'd recommend you do the same if anyone wants to hook up wires to your head!"

TR chuckled thinking how his grandchildren would giggle. He remembered Jacob Steiner clearing his throat to issue his words to the oil company men.

"Remember our objective, gentlemen. We agreed to test Mr. Gimble the same as any other university graduating senior but at five times the intensity in diverse technical subjects. It should be sufficient for Mr. Gimble to demonstrate scholastic ability to the satisfaction of the invited deans of your panel representing the country's finest academies. I doubt that any readings from wires on Mr. Gimble's skull will make Regis Petroleum any more money than he will make for you being tested without such wires!"

TR Gimble recalled the scene. Spectacles of the accountants at the conference table hung halfway down their noses. Their eyes grew wide hearing talk of an oil company discussing brain experiments. Executive bellies around the room jiggled with familiar chuckles born of years listening to men's wild-flying comments that often reached ludicrous stratospheres, only to be brought down by men wiser in the basic matters of business affairs. TR knew the minds of such men and how he'd describe them to his grandchildren. He silently mimicked their egos.

"Of course this man Gimble needs to serve only one purpose, and that purpose is to make bundles of money for us! We're investing a tidy, royal sum in testing him to placate doubting investors. We'll determine if he has the goods upstairs for expanding our refineries to the kind of production capacity we need globally now. Let mad scientists find quirky, new subjects elsewhere to whom they can attach their gizmos and wires. We just want to see if Gimble knows science and engineering like a top university man."

The room in the basement of the university's largest building grew stuffy. Upper windows could not be opened for instructions were explicit. No one was to enter, leave, approach the windows or move about during the exam.

One professor sighed and looked over to another. He inched forward his left hand from beneath the folds of his robe and silently rubbed his forefingers together. His associate smiled and tilted his head. Indeed they were once again enduring the customary discomforts of the formal, scholastic world to earn their pay.

The distinguished group standing in front of the hall was well aware that completing this assignment would allow each man to purchase a shiny new automobile. A representative of Regis Petroleum had contacted them requesting they administer exams to a man who would be tested before them in secrecy and strict isolation on the campus of a private Southland university. They were told to bring copies of exams customarily given to graduating seniors at the technical institutions where they served as deans. Then they were told to intensify the complexity of formulas and make the questions even trickier.

The seasoned professors questioned who the examinee might be. When they were told it was TR Gimble, most nodded, remembering hearing of this promising innovator in the news. They corresponded among themselves wondering why they'd been called to give such tests to an ascending inventor who'd never been a university student and apparently didn't care to become one. The generous offer from the oil conglomerate that followed had prompted each scholar to respond favorably with no further inquiries. They packed their robes and exam portfolios and boarded trains to travel the necessary miles to assemble here today.

The professors met at the fine downtown hotel before the day of the test. They discussed their strategy for completing their assignment perfectly.

"We must test the inventor in written manner only. Oral exams shall not be administered. We want no swaying of our opinions from any powerful words or personal charms the inventor might convey. We've all heard rumors about this man's significant appeal to men and women! All his answers must be written."

Each academic dean proudly carried a dossier of his institution's most stringent exams. They each selected fifty questions and advanced those queries to the highest levels of difficulty. They congratulated each other with full confidence.

"No one on earth could finish this test with a perfect score in the allotted time!"

CHAPTER 9

▼

The special examination arranged for one man in the great science hall was proceeding according to schedule. TR Gimble scribbled calculations and essays in his bold hand on page after page. The stack of used pencils in the box beside his desk grew in rhythmic plunks. The lead bore down to the wood in seven minutes. In one motion, TR passed the used writing instrument to his left hand, dropping the spent pencil while his right hand reached for a new one.

An occasional dry cough muffled by one of the men in robes accompanied the grate of a misaligned minute hand scraping the glass for one heartbeat with every rotation on the grand wall clock. Five stopwatches moist with sweat ticked seconds into the fourth and final hour.

The inventor turned a paper with a quiet rustle, his pencil poised to answer the next question. A burst of color broke his concentration. He took a deep breath.

"I've got time. Writing the last answers can wait."

TR knew this feeling when it enveloped him. He learned it was important to absorb vivid thoughts when they blazed into his mind. A wise man once told him he must not dismiss whatever knowledge the feelings contained. He remembered the old man's words.

"The mind orders itself in the most magnificent ways. Let not your forward thrust and discipline block out gentle reflections that will lead to greater insights. Pressure sometimes prompts mental flashes that help a person know great meaning in an unexpected moment."

TR Gimble refused to push the feeling aside. If he did, he might sacrifice an instance of awareness that might not return for many a year. Time stopped. He felt himself drift into the past.

"Thomas Roy Gimble! You get over here right now!"

TR heard his mother holler. A small boy scurried across the path from the shed to the porch. His face was covered in soot, his trousers torn. He skidded to a stop in front of his mother.

"I'm sorry, Ma. It blew up awfully loud, didn't it?

His mother's eyes looked scared. He stretched out his hands.

"Look, it didn't hurt anything. The rest of the experiment worked! I thought there'd be a pop instead of a boom."

The boy turned his gaze back toward the shed while his mother examined his face and hands for burns. Now that TR looked back, he saw quiet understanding in her eyes. She saw his little mind at work analyzing the unintended percussion. A wisp of smoke faded into the gray sky. No flames followed. She knew the animals hadn't been harmed and the shed would be okay. Still, she had to let him know much he scared her.

"I thought you killed yourself this time! That was the loudest bang yet!"

The boy gently touched her arm.

"Ma, I was really careful. I only put enough manure in the bucket to heat it to the temperature I needed. I stood back when the metal made contact, and the horses were tied up, too. I told them ahead of time that my experiment would make some noise so they weren't startled too much."

His mother shook her head. She'd seen TR whisper and the horses obey.

"Well, you forgot to tell me what was coming! That's enough for today, Mr. Experimenter. Go get yourself cleaned up. Tonight you'll stay inside. You can help me invent dinner!"

A slight smile crept across the inventor's face. One professor nudged another.

"What's he doing?"

The other professor shrugged.

"The exam's almost over. It doesn't matter as long as he stays put."

TR traveled in his mind to the family farm in Michigan. What a delightful place for his beginnings. Every old thing leaning this way and that offered wonders to explore. The barn and shed held planks, gears, pulleys and metal in every stage of decay.

He saw old neighbors pulling up in their wagons. Loaded in back were materials of every sort. He remembered what they told his father.

"Better your boy be given our unneeded tools and whatnot to play with rather than these things gathering rust beside our barns."

TR recalled sorting and arranging things with his little hands. Stacks and piles of different items grew as he studied their properties and potential for mechanical use.

The farm's organic material helped him understand what affected other things. He studied what evolved though long seasons and short, combustive spurts. He buried different things to see what happened to them under mounds of dirt or metal piled on top. He found that horse and pig manure steamed hot with chemical possibilities.

He'd been able to build a small brick oven after he showed his folks he'd be careful with fire. He remembered asking his pa's permission when he felt sure he was ready.

"Can I see how your gun works, too?

TR saw the trust in his father's eyes. It was a brief second back then, but now it lingered in his mind. His father took the gun from the rack and handed it to his son.

Dark, sparkling waters splashed through colors to pull TR deeper into his memories. He saw the old well standing by the shed. Its mystery fascinated him.

"An infinite river down below keeps water coming to our well!"

Like his ideas, it never ran dry.

TR's thoughts flew to the earth and farm equipment giving him endless assortments of problems and connections to study inside and out.

"No wonder the professor's questions don't perplex me."

From TR's earliest days, he never lacked a rich bounty of materials to learn from. Wobbly, worn-out equipment seemed to beckon him to come and find out why. Unafraid to climb in and around things much larger than he stood, he saw himself studying every angle of how things fit and functioned together. If an improvement to some arrangement was in order, he found a way to make it work. He sprang out of bed before sunrise each morning, did his chores and started playing with inventions.

TR pictured kind, weathered faces and heard the voices of neighbors talking.

"He's only ten, but he finds better ways to put together pieces that come off tools than the men who first designed them."

"He attaches levers and weights to objects I wouldn't think of."

"If I show Tommy something broken, he can be counted on to take matters farther than a basic fix! I see how he improves things. It's ingenious what he figures out!"

"We say he has the magic eye. He can make anything work better."

TR glanced briefly at the papers on the tiny desk before him. Two minutes had ticked by, but his daydream wasn't over. He remembered the day of the note. His family swore they'd tell their grandchildren exactly how it happened. It was two years after he created the last memorable bang in his pa's shed. He handed the small, yellow paper to his mother. She read it aloud.

"Dear Mrs. Gimble: It has been my pleasure to serve as your son's teacher for the last four years. He can read and write without error and has mastered everything I can teach him of history, mathematics and science. A boy such as Thomas Roy should attend university. There is no need to return him to this school as he has learned the sum of what I can teach him."

Nancy pointed at the note and looked down at her son.

"Have you been misbehaving in school?"

Tommy looked surprised.

"No, I've been busy reading."

The next day, she walked Tommy to the schoolhouse. TR remembered smiling and chatting, pointing out his usual endless observations along the way. His teacher explained the note.

"Your Tommy can recite every book on all four shelves of this schoolhouse. He can reason the solution to any problem given him with the logic of a man. We can't afford the advanced books he needs."

There was nothing left for his mother to do but let her son continue to invent and fix things on the farm. With the time not spent at school, the growing boy built an elaborate irrigation system for his family's and the neighbors' farms. He improved the plow with pulleys and weights to make the blades cut deeper, wider and smoother. He motorized the wagon for hauling hay.

After months of cobbling together all that he could invent and build around the place where he was born, his thoughts turned to the world beyond. TR remembered his mother tenderly holding their only family picture with tears welling in her eyes.

The picture showed their family standing around the little boy who sat on the fence that ran in front of the farmhouse. The tall, pitched roof of the family home loomed behind them. In his overalls, Tommy clutched the reins of a horse standing behind the split rail fence.

TR remembered the horse nuzzling close to his head as he peered at the camera wondering how he might examine a machine like that someday.

The large log cabin in which the family lived looked rickety against the Michigan sky, yet this farmhouse was their pride and joy and one of the largest cabins on any farm in the area. Their home held many a memory. There'd been hard times filled with sickness and despair, but laughter and music inside the four rooms helped the family recover and endure.

TR tapped his fingers, remembering tunes he picked out on instruments he created with wire and wood. He could hear his mother's laughter as the family sang along. For an instant, he saw himself through his mother's heart and eyes. He could feel her thinking that the love of the unique boy bursting with talent had touched the life of every person who lived in the home or ever visited the Gimble farm. TR knew why she cried when she held the picture. She was certain he would have to leave.

TR thought of all the extra care his mother had taken raising him. He was skinny back then with a constant, slight cough, but that never stopped him from running outside. He raced to and fro like lightning, certain to stop in order to peer into every barrel and under every trough for new details he might discover. His mother accepted all that he was. Exploring would forever be his passion. He saw her watching while he carefully moved things around and put things together testing different arrangements. He spoke so fast at times, she couldn't understand the thoughts spilling out of his head quicker than he could put his words together.

"Slow down, Tommy," she'd say. "It almost sounds as if you're speaking a foreign language." Then she'd smooth his hair.

"You're a special one among boys your age. We love you very much."

TR remembered looking up without a second thought.

"I know, Ma."

Then he'd run out the door again.

TR knew that his mother cared for him perhaps a bit more than his beleaguered father, who remained sickly but enduring in strong faith. His pa seemed to pull himself together each cold morning with a kind of special deliverance and fiber. TR knew this man often shook off chilly thoughts of his first wife who'd run off with her true love after bearing the first three children of the Gimble brood.

Tommy's two older brothers and sister told him what happened. A man with one arm had shown up at the Gimble farm asking for their mother. He had returned from the Civil War, battered but still very much in love with the woman who had given up waiting for him and thought him dead.

His siblings ran crying after the wagon carrying the young veteran and their departing mother, who refused to look back at her sobbing children running as fast as their tiny legs could carry them through the cloud of dirt churned up by the wagon's wheels. They told Tommy their ma must have ended up in Detroit or another big city. Neither of her children, nor the concerned Gimble neighbors, ever found out where she and her flame had settled. She never wrote to inquire about the children or their father. She never came looking for them, not even once.

TR remembered hearing how the woman named Nancy came into the family like an angel. She picked up the emotional wreckage day by day. Not long after, his father filed for divorce from the mother who ran off. Later, his father and Nancy had his older sister and him.

TR's memory brought him images of this family blending as one. His older siblings remained bruised from the memory of their birth mother's blatant exit, but they were a patched up sort of crew and got along together. TR now realized that his sister's innocence and his own had brought a new kind of love and trust back into the lives of their older siblings. It was the kind of restoration that enables a broken family to start anew. Like the rickety-looking fence and farmhouse in his mother's precious photo, the group remained standing with inward strength and care to help them survive. TR realized how much he owed the woman named Nancy for the duties she assumed. He quietly thought, "Thank you, Mom."

Now at a full stall, TR's mind absorbed the immense hopes his family shared concerning the great crossroads at which he had arrived. He was doing well as an inventor, but when he told them of his prospects for arranging business on his inventions with one of the biggest American oil companies, they went wild with jubilation.

"Someone like you must show the oil men what you know! Like your grade school teacher said, you ought to have university credentials. Your being a little older shouldn't matter one wit to the men at college. We've read the news about scientists and engineers. They are all from distinguished schools. You must go as far as possible with no limitations whatsoever!"

Loving family faces filled his mind. He saw hearts brimming with expectations for this bold step he was taking. The cramps in his legs diminished. He was filled with new resolve.

"Everyone I care most about in this world would want me to excel on this exam."

TR glanced at the box of fresh pencils. Only six remained. The old man from Manchuria was right. Had the great inventor not paused to reflect at the moment his insight burst through, TR Gimble would have run out of pencils.

CHAPTER 10

▼

The faces of the university men registered surprise when TR Gimble stopped writing his exam answers. When the inventor relaxed his neck and closed his eyes, the robed men at the front of the science hall shifted on their heels exchanging nervous glances. They started whispering fiercely, ignoring the rule for total silence.

"He's grinning!"

"Oh, stupendous. Now he's tapping his fingers!"

"I actually thought he might finish, but now he's wasting valuable time."

"He's ruining his chances on one bloody expensive exam!"

The test administrator glared. He put a finger to his lips and sternly shook his head.

The reprimanded professors stood quiet, but their fears did not. The test-taker was known for his vigorous, independent ways. Was he going to decide to boycott this exam?

The men knew that if TR walked away at any point before completing their exam, they could be delayed months in receiving, and may not ever receive, the generous stipend promised them by Regis Petroleum. Disappointment spread across their faces. Several professors were simply curious to see the inventor's answers. Now prospects looked dim.

Suddenly a ray of hope emerged, and the men quickly forgot their vow of silence.

"He's writing again!"

"The stallion's back!"

"Not so fast, something's different."

"Look, he's writing at half the size he was writing before!"

It took one observant professor to figure out why. He whispered through clenched teeth.

"He was running out of pencils. That probably threw his sensitive genius off course!"

The men chuckled. They nodded to the glaring test administrator, affirming they would behave themselves from now on.

TR heard the shuffle but didn't look up. He didn't care what the esteemed group thought. He knew he would ace their test. He decided he also didn't care what the investors or scientists at Regis Petroleum thought. He knew the executives would force him into their ranks, if for no other reason than to use his patents. He already knew this test would be meaningless to scientists uninspired at the thought of working on million-dollar refineries with a man not of their academic standing.

TR's family, however, stayed foremost in his mind. Picturing them helped dissolve the scientists' unfriendly faces and the professors' mocking eyes. He felt reconnected tightly to all the people he loved. He sturdily focused on the last math calculation.

The scholars quieted after TR resumed penciling his answers even faster than before. Relieved drops of sweat fell to the floor beneath their robes. The men glanced at the irritating wall clock. Surely they could hang on one half hour without wilting further or fainting from dehydration. Their ordeal was rapidly coming to a close.

The professors saw TR finish the final question and look up at them as he'd been instructed. All five men in black robes clicked their stopwatches simultaneously. They assumed the esoteric inventor had passed over highly structured academic questions whose language he simply could not understand. TR Gimble finished 15 minutes earlier than anyone else had been known to complete any such cumulative test.

The five professors came forward to examine the pages of TR's exam in each of the respective categories for which they'd been called to test him. Once the test administrator was satisfied that each professor had the pages he would score, he called a break.

TR untangled his large legs from under the small desktop. He got up and slapped his thighs. The professors didn't look up from his test pages now glued to their damp hands. TR walked out, stopped at the water fountain, gulped largely for a few seconds, and then took the stairway to the exit two steps at a time. He pushed open one of the large oak doors of the science building and greeted the man standing guard with a broad smile.

"The test is over. I'm all tested now."

The guard stepped aside as TR walked onto the polished brick landing. The smooth orange pavers simmered in the noon sun. Heat radiated through TR's shoes and eased the stiffness in his legs. He inhaled deeply.

"Ah, real air!"

Jacob Steiner waited on the landing.

"How'd it go?"

TR looked across the quiet campus and breathed in the fragrant lawn.

"The whole thing went well. I finished a little early, and that was it."

Jacob rubbed his chin.

"I'm glad you agreed to take this step sooner than later."

TR cocked his head.

"I don't see why it changes much of anything for me. What do you mean?"

Jacob explained.

"Your having or not having university credentials would always have been a matter for me to address during patent negotiations. You know how the conglomerates hire these technical specialists to cut down inventors' dreams and discourage certain new patent designs. There is, however, one fact that helps us more than you can know. Gossip among men travels faster than the speediest locomotive on any rail line through the country. Word of today's exam will get out soon enough. Men of industry looking for the brightest innovators will talk to one another making mention of how you performed on your exam. The step you've completed today will save us many lengthy letters of introduction, gathering businessmen's testimonials and countless meetings convincing men of industry that you indeed know the science of all your inventions. You can branch out into any other area you like beyond petroleum. No one will question whatever scientific interests you pursue."

TR nodded. If there was anything he'd come to appreciate about Jacob, it was his efficiency managing negotiations. TR had seen Mr. Steiner move swiftly to cut to the chase with men who might delay any transaction waiting for a smarter man to compete with TR or a more lucrative offer to appear the next day. Now Jacob would hold a premium advantage representing this inventor. The patent attorney could effectively put uneasy, questioning minds to rest with a supreme validation that no other inventor to date had acquired.

"He doesn't yet know how well I did," thought TR. "He'll be pleasantly surprised."

TR had no doubts about how he performed on the exam. He was actually interested in what he learned. There was a method he saw in how the academic questions were constructed. It was backward from the way his mind usually worked. The questions were designed to trick a person into several avenues of thought so that a student might doubt the queries themselves and which thought process might derive the correct answer. TR had only to look at the perspiring men lined up behind the desk in front of the room to sense how they might have designed the questions. A magic eye was a handy thing to have. He smiled at his recall of the exercise and something else he noticed.

"I saw a photographer at the rear of the lecture hall."

Jacob laughed.

"All the better for us. Once the pictures are printed, the men of Regis Petroleum will be able to see how the test was conducted. The professor's robes were for nothing more than show. The robes were worn to intimidate you while creating the perfect picture to pass from hand to hand between the men at the oil company and their scientists."

TR took off his coat and chuckled.

"The professors were sweating mightily in their academic gear."

Jacob laughed.

"And they were well paid for their minor inconvenience!"

Jacob looked toward his Model T on the tree-lined avenue.

"May I drive you home?"

"No thank you, Mr. Steiner. I appreciate you coming today, really, I do. It's a fine afternoon to walk. It'll clear my mind, and the warmth will do me good. I'll catch the streetcar home."

TR shook Jacob's hand. As the attorney drove away, the long arm of the lanky man who'd just aced the genius exam paid for by Regis Petroleum waved one brief time.

CHAPTER 11

▼

The professors' damp, wrinkled robes lay in a heap on the long table in front of the science hall. The men's sopping suit coats hung over the backs of desks in the auditorium's front row. A tall pitcher of water had been hastily obtained, along with an unmarked silver flask sneaked in by the test administrator's astute male secretary. As the men stood about in vests with their shirts open at the collar, they sipped from cool mugs and examined the handwritten pages collected from TR Gimble.

One professor's bellow broke the quiet murmurs, his thunder echoing in the science hall.

"This isn't possible! Preliminary calculation of Gimble's cumulative total shows his abilities to be off the charts!"

Another professor mopped his brow and muttered.

"This has to be some anomaly. It's clear we haven't tested the entire test itself to see if the answers to some of the questions point to the answers for others."

A short, stout professor named Victor Atkins commented lightly.

"I'm rather impressed with Mr. Gimble's understanding of earth sciences. That's a unique field. A man would be hard pressed to gather the kind of understanding Gimble shows without having done extensive studies in the field. He knows geological principles, such as the formation of gases, the flow of groundwater, types of rocks and fluids far beneath the earth's crust and many other things we customarily make our students toil for five years minimum to learn. Our students spend months hiking mountains, canyons and deserts to learn these principles before they're allowed to test for graduation."

"That doesn't matter," one professor declared. "Gimble may have to take another test! We can't explain to Regis Petroleum or ourselves how someone scored as perfectly as he did. There's one line on his curriculum vitae, gentlemen. The man attended precisely four years of grade school!"

Another professor agreed.

"We should require the better part of a year to research further in order to create a more stringent test. Only then can we be certain that no clues are provided between different answers."

"Absolutely!" cried another. "We shall initiate a committee to review the combined subjects. We must obtain government funding for this high order of business. Imagine the scandal if more men like Gimble can dupe our tests. Why the academic system we've worked years to establish will be ruined! Our country could become the laughingstock of the world!"

The man looked pale and steadied himself.

Dean Atkins chuckled.

"The men at Regis Petroleum are on a much tighter schedule than that, my friends. We were brought in for a sole purpose. We bent our minds to compile the best questions we could garner from the head of every department at the institutions we serve. We may have to let this instance go. I personally don't want to spend more time trying to outsmart a man as genuinely interested in this many subjects and driven to study each in such detail as TR Gimble. In a year's time, we can be certain that Gimble would devote himself to double or triple the time that any of us would be able to spend exploring all the emerging science and technology. We are tenured professors trying to manage difficult affairs at large institutions."

The men remained silent as Victor concluded.

"Regardless of any compensation, I'm not further motivated to develop testing for just one man. I have limited time to take on any more than I am managing. I prefer to allocate my time toward larger goals."

Another professor eyed Dean Atkins.

"Your business endeavors, in addition to your academic responsibilities and writing books, have been notable. I wish I could do the same. I imagine how little sleep you must get!"

Victor shrugged.

"I am a man of science, and I am passionate about it. Exploring as much as I can between all venues in the hours I can manage is what I aspire to. We professors are wholesale merchants of discoveries made by other men. So we're all businessmen, as is Gimble. With another year expanding his companies, I doubt he'd elect to spend his time on a second test either."

One professor haughtily snorted.

"We all saw Gimble daydreaming. That hardly represents a focused mind!"

His associate, Clarence Glander, stopped gulping water to add his thoughts.

"Is it possible Gimble was using some sort of hypnosis on himself or us? He was tapping some sort of code with his fingers. Gimble could be one of those enabling his mind with strange techniques of which the rest of us have no idea. He could have channeled information from the answer manuals!"

Victor Atkins chuckled addressing his colleague by his well-known nickname.

"Cool yourself, Sweat. How can you possibly figure such a thing?"

Dean Glander narrowed his eyes.

"All sorts of mind trickery are currently being studied by higher orders of the Guild, in particular, the Ancient Rite. Men of wealth and prominence are donating worldly sums to such offbeat organizations. Their counterparts in Europe are unearthing old documents from monastery libraries and castle cellars. Even more dusty manuscripts are being imported from the Middle East! And what's their interest in these old scripts? The men study centuries-old alchemy and other esoterica. They test one other with telepathy, hypnosis and other mind games. Those who prove their capabilities are awarded distinctive honors. Their brethren revere them. They receive large, engraved certificates at gilded ceremonies overseen by prelates and potentates who govern these affairs. I have it on soundest authority that TR Gimble was raised to the Ancient Rite's 32nd Degree!"

The academics mused among themselves.

"We have endless committee meetings at our college."

"Overseeing financial affairs alone is exhausting!"

"I've never been to a secret society meeting."

"I haven't either. I've never set foot inside a temple of any benevolent order!"

Professor Harrington looked thoughtful.

"Men in our line of work are consumed with overlapping institutional and social obligations; however, men's fraternal societies do appear to be growing. The country's great leaders of industry, banking and commerce join enthusiastically. People regard these groups as an asset to society, a genuinely healthy form of brotherly philanthropy. The wives of the men also establish associations. Their groups distribute charitable aid. The men and women assist the disadvantaged here and overseas during war and natural trauma. Their customary function is to perform good deeds while building industry in these times. I'd not want to offend friends of mine by uttering a word contrary to popular public opinion about such groups. Our most substantial donors belong to the Guild!"

Victor Atkins tapped the Gimble test answers in his hand as he addressed his associates.

"It doesn't matter to me if Gimble learned anything from ancient documents. And if he pulled this data into his mind using tricks he's studying with some mystic order, I can do nothing about that. We all know he's an experimenter, and we tried a little of our own on him today. In whatever way Gimble uses his mind, that's his business, not ours. The way the mind really works is neither proven nor taught at institutions of science and technology. We're years away from breaching that ground."

"Practically speaking," said Professor Harrington, "mystic practices are merely another thing we must accept as leaders of the country's institutions of higher learning. The popularity of a variety of groups will likely always remain in our population. America has some of the most prolific experimenters of any free country on earth!"

The men nodded. Professor Harrington went on.

"We cannot afford to be too unyielding. We simply have to advance our methods to establish better communications between our institutions. If we do not keep pace with bright, experimental minds, it will only serve to undermine academics across the country. We cannot be so blind as to think that our testing methods are impervious to human evolution. That evolution may come more rapidly than ever! Look at electrical and telephone lines being connected everywhere. That will make it easier for students to exchange information, as it will for us. It's not inconceivable to imagine that the general intelligence of our students will increase faster than any students who came before them. Apparent geniuses like Gimble could start cropping up everywhere. Let's take this experience under our belts, gentlemen. Gimble has shown us a thing or two today!"

The professors agreed to submit TR's test scores to Regis Petroleum as originally graded without further recommendations. Their thoughts were drifting to the first Sunday drive they'd enjoy in their brand new automobiles. They decided to keep word of the day's exercise discreet as they confirmed their consensus.

"It would not be wise to give anyone cause to direct public acclaim toward TR Gimble for receiving such high marks on one test."

"Certainly, all university tests will now have to be modified many times and ways each year."

"We'd not want other young men becoming encouraged to follow TR's path of choosing mystic studies, if he's indeed participating in such things, versus university training."

"Students experiment with enough trickery already!"

"Further testing for Gimble would be a waste of our time. We have thousands of other bright, young minds in the country to attend to!"

The test administrator quietly gathered the papers with TR's handwriting. His assistant took the papers and test scores to the small office next to the lecture hall. He sat down and copied every exam question and TR's answers one by one while the test administrator ate a sandwich and read a novel.

Three hours later, the administrator's assistant finished copying and was dismissed. The poor man's eyes were blurry from transcribing TR's tiny handwriting on the final pages. He nearly missed the top stair near the exit. His fumbling footsteps followed the long reaches of TR Gimble's confident strides earlier that day and the footprints of five professors dragging their robes departing as eagerly as graduates through the oak doors. Silver trains raced home carrying the tired professors who cheerfully discussed the fine reimbursement they'd be receiving very soon from Regis Petroleum.

"We must be sure to recommend some of our finest graduating seniors for employment at this prestigious oil company!"

"We'll invest in some of the company stock ourselves. It will go nowhere but up!"

The test administrator remained alone in the office of the great science hall. He brought from his leather portfolio two large envelopes. The typewritten label of one said 'Regis Petroleum.' The other read 'United States Government.' He wrote a cover letter for each envelope stating that photographs of the testing conditions and exam participants would be arriving within the month.

The weary man now had an hour to sleep before beginning his train ride. He reached in his pocket and patted five fresh twenty-dollar bills folded inside a new gold-plated money clip. A man had given him this incentive to sit beside him on the way to Washington and study the papers. The test administrator met him outside the science hall only that morning. The young man pondered.

"What was the stranger's name?"

The test administrator pulled out his notepad. The name he'd written was Louis Tiemonet. He adjusted his spectacles and smiled. Five professors weren't the only men cheerfully riding home. He, too, would have money for a shiny, new automobile after he rode the train with the Frenchman and delivered both his parcels into the hands of men awaiting TR Gimble's test results.

CHAPTER 12

▼

The downtown streetcar clanged along its tracks amid the chaos of autos and horse-drawn buggies scurrying out of the way. The bustle of LA's Sixth Street on an early September morning accelerated the flow of blood in every man's veins.

TR could smell the fresh-baked goods through the lunch sacks of workers riding alongside him on the way to their jobs. Shouts of men overhead signaled the movements of steel girders being hoisted atop new buildings. Craftsmen soldered, chiseled and cut the forms of grand designs filling the horizon. Amid the concrete, metal, glass and dust, colorful hopes throbbed wildly. Bright promises beckoned, wrapped in everything from silk to burlap.

As the streetcar rumbled along, exciting scenes emerged to the left and right. Every electric moment brought action that spawned new ideas, making the city as vibrant as ever to the handsome inventor. He jumped off the slowing streetcar humming a happy tune. He landed three blocks from the Tally-Ho Garage where his roadster was ready for pickup.

A German mechanic named Gunther slept soundly in a guest room behind the specialty shop for gentlemen's fine motorcars. The kind couple who ran the Tally-Ho Garage housed and fed the mechanic brought in from back east at Gimble's request. Gunther delighted in the chance to see his inventor friend in Los Angeles. The mechanic's task was as complex as he hoped. It took him three weeks to outfit the man's roadster with the improvements TR drafted late one night.

As the streetcar clanged away, TR grew more eager to check his roadster's modified engine. He imagined its performance on the open road. He started striding toward the garage, his large shoes slapping the pavement in time to the city's rhythm. As he wove among the hurrying throngs of people, TR nodded to familiar faces of the men and women who worked in offices on the street. His height made him instantly recognizable in a crowd. He'd learned to greet, acknowledge and move ahead while never losing his pace.

CJ Niles and his assistant hurried toward TR. They merged to block the tall man's stride. TR was forced to break his gait to avoid knocking them over. With the inventor halted, the well-known promoter proffered a friendly greeting.

"A fine morning to you, Brother Thomas! Will you be meeting with the Guild at this morning's prayer breakfast?"

TR looked distractedly past the men.

"I'm on my way to pick up my motorcar at the shop."

"A pity! I was looking forward to your attendance!"

"Why?"

CJ looked at his assistant who beamed back at his boss. Their eyes shining with pride, they looked toward TR, eager as boys bursting to tell of their discovery of the greatest treasure on earth.

"We've just completed prints of the latest certificates for the new offering from CJ Niles Holdings. This offering is for an oil and mining venture in which a great number of men are interested. I'm presenting the information at our meeting this morning."

TR responded flatly, "At a prayer breakfast."

"Why, of course!" exclaimed the promoter. "What better time for men to listen with clear hearts and minds? I want every potential investor to deliberate with the most genuine introspection, as well as any holy intervention the Good Lord might deem fit! That's the least that should be applied for fairness and equity to be delivered to every man contemplating our fine efforts! I intend to answer all the men's questions on the finest technical points. I will fully explain our endeavor to the satisfaction of our brothers. That is why I anticipated your attendance. No one makes better queries regarding matters of scientific earth prospecting and refining than you, my kind sir!"

TR shook his head.

"You know I don't invest in stocks."

"Well, sir, that may be so up to this point in time. The city's most influential movie producers and bankers have already formed investment pools. By coming together to create large investor groups, they've already been paid significant dividends on the first issue with our stock split in just three weeks' time! I can give you the names of some of these men if you'd like. You can hear their testimonials for yourself. Some of these wise and prudent gentlemen, I might add, are even handling your accounts at the Merchant & Maritime Bank!"

"Then I certainly wish all of you the finest profits. I have all the investments I need right now. I must get going and will see you again, I'm sure. Thank you for the news."

TR set his sights forward and quickly stepped around the men. As he regained his stride, a large automobile slowed on the street beside him. A handsome woman sat in back atop the folded canvas of the convertible's roof. She smiled and waved hello to pedestrians who looked up at her and smiled in return. Violin and piano music played from inside her auto. TR looked over in surprise as he wondered.

"Did a parade start early?"

Annabelle Porter's sharp eyes saw the fine hat on the wide head of the tallest man striding purposefully down Sixth Street. She noticed that people on the crowded sidewalk looked up to the man and stepped aside for his swift passage. A number of pedestrians waved and called out greetings seeming to know him.

"Maybe he is someone I ought to know as well."

Annabelle instructed her driver to slow the car to a crawl. She sat tall and raised her voice.

"Blessings and good morning to you, sir!"

TR smiled, nodded his usual way and kept walking. The lady spoke again, boldly and clearly.

"Salvation is coming! The Lord is near! Have you been saved?"

TR turned his head her way. He tried to keep from grinning.

"Oh yes, madam!"

"What's your name?"

"Gimble, Tom Gimble."

"Mine is Annabelle Porter. Come join us at our Pentecostal Revival on this coming beautiful Sunday, won't you? We'll be at Silverton Park at 7 pm!"

TR kept his pace and answered.

"Thank you."

Annabelle had to turn completely around by now as her cream-colored convertible cruised further down the street. Her immense jewel-studded cross sparkled on the heavy gold chain that dangled in front of her white, satin-draped bosom. She clutched the cross and closed her lavender-dusted eyelids as she cried out.

"Oh yes, Tom Gimble, we do give thanks! For every great thing we have and do, we always give our Lord our most devoted thanks!"

TR mused that the woman sure knew how to make an impression but, by now, he had reached the Tally-Ho Garage. Grateful to exit the sidewalk, he stepped inside.

Losing sight of the tall man, Annabelle spoke to her driver.

"What a handsome fellow! I wonder if he's any relation to that inventor named Gimble? I haven't seen any photographs of the inventor alongside reports of him in the newspapers."

The driver looked at Annabelle in his rear view mirror.

"I believe you just met the man."

"Ohh," murmured Annabelle.

Now she knew where she might find him. A lady preacher was well advised to maintain a keen eye toward successful men who might become sufficient penitents offering substantial donations to the Lord's cause. She well knew that many a soul among the ranks of the city's most prominent men suffered guilty burdens that her Pentecostal nurturing might ease.

Drew and Barry Rheiman at the Tally-Ho Garage saw TR Gimble fill their doorway. As TR stepped inside, Barry smiled.

"Your auto is ready. She growls with power and purrs across the pavement. We took her for a test drive this morning before the city traffic was out."

"Excellent!" said TR. "I've scheduled a drive to Larwin Valley today and intend to thoroughly enjoy the road with that beauty."

Drew came over and handed TR an envelope.

"Some men stopped in shortly before you did. They asked me to give you this."

TR took the white linen envelope. Lovely gold scrolls were embossed around every edge. He opened the envelope, shook his head and smiled. It was another elegant, flattering plea from CJ trying to get TR to purchase the new Niles stock.

TR slipped the letter into his vest pocket. Many other matters lay before him today. He paid Drew and Barry for the garage services and left a plain envelope with a bonus incentive for the couple to give the mechanic once he awoke. He knew that Gunther likely labored through the entire night to finish in time for his early morning deadline.

Jacob Steiner opened the morning newspaper at Emile & Bonnie's Diner over on Fifth. While the fresh tea and bagel warmed his stomach, he spotted a brief article. The words from the small headline read, "NEW WAY TO MAKE IRON." This piqued the attorney's seasoned antennae. The text below, which said, "METAL SMELTED FROM VOLCANIC IRON OXIDE SAND; PROCESS VALUABLE," was the kind of thing Jacob needed to see. He clipped the small article and slid it in his folio. He knew what kind of news attracted TR Gimble.

Around the partition in the corner booth sat a group of men. From their conversation, Jacob figured they were technical specialists. One of the men spoke firmly.

"I still have reservations about starting work with that man. I don't care if they tested every part of his brain!"

Another man's voice sounded anxious.

"The test administrator told me his scores were superior. The official news that we'll be working with him won't be announced to stockholders until the pictures from the test arrive. They want everyone to see exactly how he was tested."

Jacob lowered his newspaper and folded it twice. He set it on the diner table, anchoring it with folded hands. This way, the overhead fan wouldn't rustle pages as he listened.

"I heard Dean Atkins was there."

"That's what I was told."

"Atkins is smart. I attended the American Institute of Mining Geology where he's dean. Everyone knows he wouldn't attest to anyone's capabilities without being thoroughly convinced of the man's skills. Atkins does his homework and won't take any guff from students or college administrators, not even from college supporters! That's why businessmen like dealing with him. He's a straight shooter."

The man with the anxious voice sounded frustrated.

"If Atkins gives his seal of approval, then it doesn't look like we'll have much choice."

Another man spoke with a low sneer.

"Sure. And if we don't like working with the inventor, we might cry!"

"You heard about Gimble protesting having wires hooked to his head?"

"Sure, word leaks out about that stuff. What a sissy. I'd do it. I'd want to know how my brain ticks."

"Well, you know what they're starting to say. Tom be Gimble, Tom be quick!"

A chuckle rippled through the group. Another man scoffed.

"And he'll burn his butt on our candlestick!"

The men's laughter reverberated through the small diner.

Jacob quietly gathered his coat and folio as he mused.

"Yes, there'll be much controversy with this inventor."

The humble patent attorney smiled at the thought of the adventurous road ahead.

CHAPTER 13

▼

The downtown clamor was fading fast behind the sleek automobile gliding north out of Los Angeles. TR Gimble nestled his large frame comfortably onto the freshly polished black leather of his roadster's front seat. He stretched his long arm over the back of the plush passenger cushions and breathed deeply. He exhaled his gratitude.

"Bless you, Ford Motor Company. Your men do not skimp on the space for a man of my proportions!"

Seeing constant innovations from the group of dedicated engineers at the auto company was a distinct pleasure for TR. This was a matter of one inventor wholly appreciating the inspiration and perspiration of kindred spirits led by visionary men. TR Gimble tested improvements such as those just completed on his roadster by Gunther at the Tally-Ho Garage, not because TR wanted to man-ufacture automobiles, but just because he could.

He stepped on the accelerator, and the powerful engine with its modified fuel pulled the magnificent auto onto the open road. Smooth, graceful power blended man and machine. A burst of speed on a tantalizing stretch of fresh, flat asphalt opened up all the channels in TR's mind. There were no avenues through which his spirit didn't race faster than that of his convertible hurtling out of the city.

Ascending the mountains that lay between the city and Larwin Valley, the road curved along stunning sandstone and granite cliffs thrust straight up from the power of earthquakes that came centuries before. Acute, vertical road align-ments raised the car's front end bringing panoramas of pure sky into view. TR enjoyed the sense of eternity on these parts of the highway. He relished the weightless power shooting into portals of rich, heavenly blue. Winding turns tested the roadster's thick tires and suspension. Hairpin maneuvers challenged TR's instincts to outperform his car as he avoided whoever might be clopping uphill around the next bend. The road dropped from time to time into oak-studded valleys where beds of stark river sand and sparkling streams glimmered in the autumn sun.

He thought to himself, "Those rays remind me of the jewels on the cross that lady evangelist wore."

He couldn't help but smile, thinking of all the sideshows one encountered simply walking the streets in downtown Los Angeles.

Larwin Valley lay only fifteen miles from the metropolis, but what a refreshingly different place to clear one's mind. TR knew much labor and travel lay ahead for him with Regis Petroleum. Jacob's negotiations had already begun in secret with the company's top executives. The presentation of TR's test results and exam room photos to the stockholders would merely be for show. Jacob informed TR that everyone had agreed that his test results would never be published, only used to create vast curiosity and rumor. TR sighed.

"This road I'm on will involve a lot of secrecy. My wife and family will have to be patient through all of it!"

He vowed to bring them on the thrilling drive to Larwin Valley in his beautiful, improved motorcar at the first moment he could spare.

Entering the narrow pass into Larwin Valley, TR stopped at Clay's Filling Station. Picnic tables beckoned under massive, ancient oak trees. This friendly destination welcomed horseback riders and drivers at the crest of the winding highway. The mouth of the pass featured jagged terrain at the highest elevation, requiring a slow, rugged climb that drained horses, humans and machines. The highway cut through sheer cliffs, creating the eye of a needle one had to pass through before attaining awe-inspiring views of the valley paradise below.

The man who owned 240 acres directly north of the pass had laid out a small park where travelers could recuperate from the climb. Many enjoyed the property's beautiful hilltops offering views that rolled into pristine valleys with stunning lavender mountains beyond. Clay Henry, the landowner, never lacked for interesting visitors among the folks passing between LA and Larwin Valley. His park sat alongside his fuel dispensary and market at the side of the road.

Clay walked out as the inventor's sleek automobile idled to a stop.

"Wow, TR! You really barreled over that hill! I saw you coming from inside the store."

"A bat out of hell!" laughed TR. "I picked up my car this morning. The engine improvements I told you about were finished. In fact, here's a can of the fuel additive you might pour in the tanks when filling them."

Clay winked.

"Will it blow up on me, TR?"

"Not a bit. We thoroughly tested the additive with many types of gasoline. I had a small can of gas in reserve from your filling station that we tested as well. It mixes and runs perfectly."

"Good enough. I'll fill her up!"

While Clay carefully topped off the roadster's tanks, TR glanced at the oncoming travelers. He thought he recognized the man pulling into Clay's station. The man's Model T sputtered to a stop.

"Mr. Gimble?"

TR studied the man's face but couldn't place it.

"Yes?"

"I'm James Wynn. People call me Scoot. I believe I met you some years ago when you were working at the refinery in Brea."

"Nice to meet you again," said TR. "Those days seem like centuries ago."

The man named Scoot turned off his car's engine with a clunk.

"It was only six years."

TR cocked his head.

"How'd you come to get a name like Scoot?"

"I go after promising opportunities, namely oil. I'm known to scoot right out to any dang, far-off place and take a look for myself! I was looking at oil land down in Orange County back when I met you. I was talking to some of the men at the Brea Refinery. I did purchase some property, not in the north canyons where you worked, but down by the beach. My men and I got down to some prosperous sands after much trial and error—and quite an investment, I might add! I sold everything I had to carry on. That property's finally paying me back with the leases I set up. Of course, I also got involved in Signal Hill. Who didn't? That venture didn't work out as well. There was too much drilling already going on near the parcels that I bought. It was a gambler's field with poor odds for my taste so I sold out. Now I've come to Larwin Valley. I heard of the oil companies' growing interest here. I saw some news about gushers so I decided to head out and check things for myself!"

TR listened while he checked under the roadster's hood and watched Clay filling the fuel tanks. When Scoot finished the story of his wildcatting career, TR turned to him and spoke politely.

"You share some of the same interests I have."

Clay looked up and nodded at TR. The roadster's fuel tanks were topped off. The inventor handed Clay the $2 for his fuel and shook his hand, pressing another $5 into Clay's palm for his efforts to mix up the Gimble additive. Although Scoot was looking down at the maps he had laid out, he didn't miss the transaction between TR and Clay. As TR climbed back into his car, he called to Scoot.

"See you around!"

Scoot's gaze passed enviously over the curves of the growling roadster.

"Most likely. Very good to see you again."

Scoot remembered seeing a younger TR Gimble not that long ago. He hadn't actually met him. He stretched the truth a little on that count. The man Scoot remembered seeing was rather skinny but awfully tall. Scoot noticed he wore overalls he'd acquired working for the Southern Pacific Railroad. Although Gimble was a refinery worker at the time, Scoot remembered the railroad company's faded patch on TR's chest.

The aspiring wildcatter knew that many men who arrived out west at the turn of century worked the railroads first. That was the best route to learning the territory. Scoot hadn't worked the railroads, but he always wanted to learn as much as he could. He remembered the oilmen at Brea pointing out Gimble and saying that he was an odd sort, almost a loner, who studied everything. But Scoot's ears perked up at one man's idle comment.

"He's the smartest damn thing on two long legs!"

Scoot paid attention to smart men. He developed a knack for small talk that invited gossip of every kind. He learned details that always came in handy.

"Why do you say that?

The men exchanged glances and decided to spill the beans.

"Gimble can't help making improvements to everything he lays his hands on!"

"That's right. You come around the corner and there are pieces of equipment lying all over the ground. Gimble hardly looks up. He just puts everything back together and makes a machine run better!"

"The supervisors have just about given up trying to supervise him!"

"Funny thing is, this place hasn't run safer or more profitably in the 50 years this old refinery's been around!"

"Every man working here has learned something from Gimble!"

The men laughed. Another manager stated his view.

"Maybe he's doing it for show and maybe not. We think he's aiming to shorten his time as a roughneck and make it to supervisor in record time!"

One man summarized.

"Any way you cut it, he won't be cleaning oil from his fingernails much longer!"

Scoot chuckled, remembering the clean-cut supervisor. The wildcatter mused.

"The supervisor's prediction was dead on."

On another visit to Brea, Scoot recalled seeing a well-dressed, middle-aged gentleman who drove into the facility to talk with TR and his supervisor. Later, he saw TR holding a perforated pipe and pointing to the stills, explaining something to both of the men.

Scoot remembered learning the name of the man in the suit. It was Steiner. Scoot knew he saw the name Jacob Stenier in news articles about the inventor.

"That must have been the fellow I saw. He helped TR register his patents. Those patents sure ended Gimble's roughneck days in short order! He ascended past supervisor, out of the refinery and right into his own business!"

Concluding that fate had once again laid the perfect opportunity in his lap, Scoot Wynn folded his maps and decided to follow TR. It wasn't going to be easy in his auto. His Model T ran with perhaps a fourth the power of the inventor's roaring machine. It would take some cunning and time to stop and chat with the ever-watchful locals to find out in which directions TR might be heading. Climbing the hills into the steep canyons that the oil companies were already hailing as very promising was going to make it a longer day in Larwin Valley than Scoot had planned.

CHAPTER 14

▼

TR stopped his roadster in a cloud of dust high atop Dockman Road. He spotted the way to the ridgeline. A footpath wound to the highest point overlooking one of the many narrow ravines that crisscrossed Larwin Valley.

Trying to access this ridge, TR looked hard to find the right cutoff hidden amid black shadows of oaks that sprawled over the edges of dirt intersections. The grids on the large geological maps TR studied the night before were imprinted in his mind, but locating actual points on the ground was another matter entirely. Benchmarks mapped years ago by human hands played a game of hide-and-seek with Mother Nature. Every month, vegetation grew tall and wide, followed by rushing rainwater and mudslides that gutted landscapes and tossed boulders like tiny pebbles. Finding boundaries on this terrain was anything but easy.

The inventor's surveys had him driving for several hours. Ready to stretch his legs, he slid from his roadster and hiked quickly through knee-high grass as the wind whipped his tie about his shoulders. His penciled notes and arrows covered the blueprint maps he carried. TR spent the better part of this day reviewing hillsides and canyon cuts to study how water rushed through low-lying areas. He checked parcel characteristics methodically, eliminating sites too risky to set up any kind of operation where annual floods would carry things away.

TR looked with satisfaction down the rugged valley nook that oil company geologists had not yet found. The land lay on the side of a canyon whose road paralleled Larwin Gulch. The Gulch properties in the distance were already known for the black gold that lay beneath their escarpments. The hillsides were dotted with tall wooden derricks and shiny new pumps pulling up oil in varied rhythms. Crews of men angled drills boring through patches of granite while others poured concrete to line more oil wells.

The small valley directly below TR lay silent and untouched. Draped in golden shrubs and grasses, no settlers had established homes there. No outlaws from the valley's earlier days wanted hideouts in this location either for it featured no large rocks or caves, no big, shady trees and no topographic trickery where they could hide from lawmen or dart out to surprise travelers.

This barren, simple property featured the perfect kind of unobstructed opportunity TR liked best. Pulling the title records and figuring how to buy the land that no one seemed to want should be an easy task for his men.

Scoot lost sight of TR's roadster many times throughout the day. He finally spotted the inventor's fine auto winding up the narrow, steep road. Scoot breathed gratefully.

"A break at last! What's he on to?"

Scoot saw TR's tall profile as the inventor walked briskly to the edge of a high ridge where he paused. Scoot decided to leave his Model T at the Dockman cutoff. Light steam seeped out of the radiator. Getting water for himself and his thirsty vehicle would have to wait. An inventor known for his well-laid plans finally stood still in thought. Scoot's pulse quickened.

"I've got to get up there right away!"

As TR mapped out the distance in his mind between the narrow valley and the small station by the railroad tracks, he saw Scoot puffing his way on foot up Dockman Road.

"Hey, sailor!" called TR jokingly. He thought he'd spotted the man's Model T behind him a time or two throughout the day. The hiking wildcatter gulped extra oxygen in order to shout back.

"I wondered if you needed any help assessing the land. I've had some experience with these kinds of valleys."

TR pondered the horizon while he watched Scoot struggle to the ridge. The inventor masked his amusement.

"Is that right?

Scoot stopped a second and winced, pulling a large burr from the ankle of his sock before replying.

"Indeed I have! These canyons out here are not that different from others I've explored. I hiked them all in Brea with the men from the County Park Service who keep those frequent wildfires at bay, you know, the ones started by lightening or vandals in the canyons just over the ridge from the refinery."

"Great," said TR jovially. "Now I know who to call for advisement on fire protection."

Scoot huffed to a stop on the ridgeline.

"No really. I'm just as interested as you or any other man scouting these parts. I'm one who puts out a lot of work just keeping my ear to the ground with local goings-on. I'm not a bright inventor like you. I make many times more errors than a lot of men trying to earn my dollars. There's no attorney like Steiner, I assure you, who'd ever spot genius in me!"

TR laughed out loud. Then he grew earnest.

"Jacob became a friend and honest advisor to me before he ever signed on as my patent attorney. He was best man at my wedding."

Scoot responded emphatically.

"Yes, I'm sure that trust and friendship would be among the most important things to you. In your line of work among the men you deal with, it's crucial!"

TR gazed at the distant mountains in silence. Scoot walked to the inventor's side.

"I manage my affairs the same as you, Mr. Gimble. I must be able to trust the men I hire. I've been lucky enough to find a few I'd trust with my life. They will be with me for the rest of my days. If I'd not found such good men, I'd never even be able to afford my damn auto at the bottom of this road that pooped out before it could make the climb!"

TR surveyed the wildcatter.

"Yet here you stand."

The inventor raised to his eyes what looked to Scoot like binoculars. They were not like any he'd ever seen before. TR peered down the ravine to the bottom of the rugged, little valley. Then he offered Scoot a look.

"Here, check this. I've got my eye on this parcel, but it's highly untested territory."

Scoot wiped his brow and eagerly took the fine lenses. The scene below was magnified many times and crystal clear, showing every stone and blade of wild grass. Scoot lowered the lenses and looked at the inventor.

"I see possible grazing land down there and not much more."

Scoot took out a fresh handkerchief and daubed his sweat from the lens rims and nosepiece while the inventor explained his interest.

"Oil resources may be quite modest, but I like the angle and grade of the road that runs from here to the train station."

Scoot looked up questioningly at the tall man.

"Is it an engineering endeavor you're considering?"

TR smiled.

"No, the natural road alignment offers prospects for my being able to build a small refinery by the tracks connected to this valley."

Scoot gasped at the inventor's revelation and couldn't help the words that flew out of his mouth.

"Hearing that was worth the hike!"

TR grinned knowing full well the wildcatter's transparent motives.

"Once I'd get something like that built and tested properly, it could be fairly profitable. It would stand to reason that large oil concerns drilling out here might want to use my refinery after its capacity and method of refining crude are proven."

Scoot nodded.

"I couldn't agree more. Private drillers I know would be very interested, too."

TR planted his feet apart and folded his arms across his chest. His eyes aimed toward the railroad station.

"My refining facility would be nothing like ones the oil companies are using at the present, nor have any plans to design in the future. If I proposed the refinery I envision to any of the conglomerates today, all of them would refuse my plan."

Scoot looked intrigued.

"Why? You're an established petroleum inventor."

TR shook his head.

"Not entirely. The oil executives and their designers are already explicitly set in their ways. It's getting challenging to sway them and their boards of directors from refinery construction methods other than blueprints they've already accepted. My endeavor would not pan out if I were to propose a plant like the one I have in mind for any of the oil companies' giant refinery locations at ocean ports north and south of here. My inland refinery in Larwin Valley would be simple and streamlined, built with high capacity throughput and direct access to the rail lines."

"Why isn't something like that already in the works out here? There are enough producing oil wells to merit a strong refinery."

TR shrugged.

"I'm not that familiar with the politics yet. Locals may want agriculture, not oil refining."

Scoot nodded, and then added what he'd read.

"They sure are filming more movies out here these days. I guess you won't know more until you propose your plan."

TR pointed to the rail station and then to the mountains ringing the valley to the right and left.

"My refinery will be clean, not a source of pollution to this valley. Its operation will be compatible with farming and any other uses men establish here. No one you'd inform of my plan, however, would believe you. They'd call you nuts for saying that you heard of such a thing from me."

Scoot looked toward the mountains remembering what newspapers said about Gimble's next big moves.

"News reports say you're the key man building the largest port refineries to come."

"That's correct. And men would call me a fool for risking my time and money to build an inland refinery, even more so, one with unproven methods and drilling oil on land with modest potential."

Scoot felt his ears turning bright red. He put on his dusty hat. Scoot never expected to hear such grand information.

"Well, Mr. Gimble," he said humbly, "I certainly appreciate your disclosing these ideas to me. I can assure you that I will tell no man. If I am nothing else, I am a man of my word. You can count on me if I promise something because I surely wouldn't mention it if I didn't intend to keep my promise! I do contemplate carefully before I add anything to men's conversations. Remember, I'm simply not that bright among oilmen, especially the large concerns."

TR had opened a blueprint map on which he was drawing arrows and writing notes. He appeared to be listening so Scoot pressed on breathlessly.

"Look, you can let me know if there's anything you need along the way between now and when your refinery's getting started. You and I will be around in this business for a long time to come. Who knows where in the Southland or anyplace else we may end up working? I'm a good one for supplying what a driller needs, especially when resources get scarce. I always keep good labor men on hand. I build tight, local connections wherever I do business. With you being gone to a lot of other places traveling so much, you might want to give me a ring if there's anything I can help you with in Larwin Valley."

TR studied the blushing, forthright man.

"Thank you."

The inventor knew that the wildcatter was a professional scammer, but there was a streak of good visible in the heart of this man who'd followed TR around the valley and up this road. There was more than a little wit inside Scoot's mind, too. TR could see that the red-eared man didn't think his mind as adept as other men's. But TR knew why. It was often the difference in upbringing and family love that made a boy think he was smart or not.

TR decided to take the telephone number that Scoot offered him. He put Scoot's business card in his coat pocket and looked down the hill.

"I can give you a ride to your car if you like. I've got some extra water to fill that radiator of yours. It should be cooler by now."

James Wynn beamed gratefully.

"Thank you, Mr. Gimble!"

The wildcatter pictured this scene from above in his mind, two oilmen hiking down the rugged ridgeline with their ties flapping in the wind. Arriving at TR's car, Scoot felt elated. He smiled unstoppably as he slid onto the freshly polished, black leather of the passenger seat in TR Gimble's roadster.

CHAPTER 15

▼

Scoot Wynn tried to quiet his tumbling thoughts. A better day in Larwin Valley he couldn't have hoped for. As TR filled the radiator in Scoot's Model T, the wildcatter gushed.

"I must thank you again, Mr. Gimble! You saved me a hike back to Clay's market!"

"No problem," said TR.

The inventor set the water can in the trunk of his roadster. He handed Scoot a card.

"I'll be traveling a great deal, but you can leave a message here with my man Hiram. He'll make sure I get it."

Scoot looked at the card.

"When I learn more about what's up with the folks in Larwin Valley, I'll let you know!"

As TR Gimble drove off, his long arm waved his customary one, brief good-bye.

Scoot sat in his car and let his mind take off.

"I'm going to find some parcels close as possible to the property Gimble's buying! Any news about him locating oil could mean a shortcut to my own prosperity! He's got tons of money to hire the finest geologists and engineers that I can't afford. I'll just ride his tailwind while he investigates details on the land."

Scoot sighed as he reflected.

"It takes so much capital these days to drill oil. Even with all the resources a millionaire or conglomerate can command, finding the best pools is not easy. All the trial and error my partners and I go through is expensive, and that's just to determine how deep the oil sands are. Then analysis has to be done to figure out what kind of oil we hit. Then we spend even more money finding which extraction method will bring up consistent oil we can rely on week after week. No wonder so many men quit trying as oil operators! They just buy stock in the big companies!"

Not one to shy that easily from a good challenge, Scoot Wynn stubbornly pressed on. His Model T sputtered down the road. He looked at all the pockets of available land around oil-rich Larwin Gulch. As he toured the area, he thought about the inventor.

"If Gimble's aim is to start his own refinery, he'll need plenty of continuous oil production on and near his land. Who better than Gimble to show me a thing or two about the latest gadgets and machines to get the drilling and extraction done quickest? Who better than me to hang in through all that trial to see what works! The best thing I can do is stay close to Gimble's land while digging to find my own gusher!"

Scoot had garnered many a return favor from men who'd otherwise never deal with him. All oilmen eventually encountered some emergency where they needed extra laborers, motors or tools. Scoot remained well-connected locally and stocked with essentials he knew oilmen needed. This was how he stayed liquid, especially when his own drilling was hitting nothing but dry holes. Since this arrangement worked for Scoot his whole life, he planned no differently in forging his new relationship with TR Gimble.

Scoot slowed his car to a crawl when he reached Main Street. He saw a building bearing the name 'The Derrick.'

"Perfect. That's where oilmen must gather. Good gossip, here we come!"

Walking inside the wooden building with the miniature oil derrick on top, he saw roughnecks marginally cleaned up from their day in the dusty hills. He looked over and saw one fair-haired man talking quietly to a group of clean-shaven men listening intently. Scoot whistled softly and murmured to himself.

"Well isn't this a fine day! Is that the famous cowboy movie actor?"

Stepping closer, Scoot saw that it was indeed Buck Williams. This was someone Scoot definitely wanted to meet. Williams was a man of means who would have scouted this valley for movie-filming locations with great care. Everyone knew that Buck loved to ride wild along canyons and cliffs in his own movies. He kept horses in Larwin Valley and even a herd of buffalo. Scoot felt his ears turning red.

"He's been all over these parts. He must know where all the oilmen are getting set up!"

The wildcatter bought two sodas. He headed to the table where Buck and the men sat. He placed one soda near the table's edge.

"Howdy, sirs. I'm just askin' to interrupt a second to give my highest regards to Mr. Williams."

The men stopped talking. Buck Williams looked up. Scoot leaned over the table and burst forth with unabashed admiration.

"I'm a great fan of your movies, Mr. Williams! I appreciate every moment of hard work you put into representing cowboys and Indians as they really are. I've read about your passion for showing the Old West more accurately than any other theatre actor attempting to do the same. Your wild rides are far better than any other on the silver screen! It's amazing you can speak the Indians' language, too! Growing up playing side by side with them while your father was establishing flour mills in the West must have been quite an adventure!"

Mr. Williams looked taken aback. His blue eyes grew wide. He was used to fans and men from movie companies, not workmen, flattering him in such detail. Thinking the man might be a tourist from the city, Buck prepared to give an autograph. As he reached for his pen, he addressed the excited man.

"You remembered what you've read about me, sir. Thank you for expressing your appreciation. It's all the fans who've ever paid their hard-earned nickels to see my movies that I aim to please for as long as I'm around!"

The wildcatter beamed.

"I'm not asking for your autograph, Mr. Williams. I saw your glass nearly empty. Just have this soda complementary from me. That would be thanks enough!"

Scoot moved the soda across the table toward Buck. Buck regarded the red-eared man.

"Will you join us?"

"Sure!" said Scoot. He already had his hand on the chair behind him that he nimbly turned around and settled into at the edge of Buck's table.

The men resumed their discussion. A large roll of drawings lay on the table. Scoot didn't say anything as he learned of the actor's plans to build a grand mansion on the hill that overlooked Main Street. As conversation continued, Scoot started understanding the actor's ambitions in Larwin Valley. The wildcatter held his tongue as his mind reacted.

"Thank God I didn't tell these guys what I do!"

Mr. Williams' voice resonated in perfect modulation toward his audience at the table.

"A ranch of 237 acres should be adequate to keep my haven safe from the dust and fumes of oil drilling over at Larwin Gulch. The prevailing winds from the gulch blow parallel to the hill we're building on, not directly at it. I don't wholly object to the oilmen's endeavors, but I'm a man of the same perspective as Clay Henry. I believe you can plan things so that there are fine sanctuaries for vegetation to grow wild. There must be open land for domestic animals to roam and exercise. Natural trails and feeding grounds must not be touched where wildcats and deer cross between this valley and the surrounding mountains. It's good what Clay has done on his property to tuck his few oil wells into hidden valleys where they are no eyesore to people. I intend to take the same care with what I construct. I'm a man who cares for this valley the same as Clay!"

Scoot could see Buck's point about the way Clay managed his property at the crest of the highway. He'd heard that Clay filed plans to build a Prohibitionist colony nearby. It was clear that men such as Clay and Buck valued peace and sanctuary.

The actor spread his hands across his architectural blueprints.

"I'm especially pleased that my grand tower, entry, front windows and balconies that face north on both floors look directly toward the train station. I have every intention of hosting wonderful parties with restful retreats for actors, writers and poets who'll come visit my paradise many times a year. I want to be able to see my guests disembarking the train and riding the carriage up the hillside to my front gates!"

Scoot Wynn gulped. Now he was certain he'd never mention being an oilman.

Buck's voice rose theatrically.

"I'll have a grand veranda on the hilltop plateau projecting to the west. I want an elegant sun room on the first floor where my invalid sister can enjoy sewing and reading each day. I want her nurse to be able to easily wheel her chair straight onto the patio veranda to enjoy cool ocean breezes blowing over the mountains on hot summer afternoons. I also want the veranda to serve the needs of my guests during Western barbeques and festivities I'll host."

The astute wildcatter looked down at an engineering drawing one of the men had opened on the table. The men bent over to study the outline of a small patio. One of the men spoke.

"The size of this won't meet your needs."

The engineer sketched a larger footprint on the plan as he explained.

"We'll need more fill dirt along this side and a thick retaining wall here. These additions are required to expand the size of your veranda."

The map was upside down from Scoot. He had no intention of calling the men's attention to his interest by asking anyone to turn the drawing his way. Reading the upside-down plan, Scoot was still able to determine the local terrain. He quickly assessed the topographic benchmarks and then gulped in realization. He dare not utter his thought.

"Buck's grandiose patio looks straight down on the valley where Gimble intends to drill for oil!"

Scoot slid lower in his chair, trying to become invisible while Buck's enthusiasm grew.

"Indeed, this grand platform will offer spectacular views across pristine valleys. The sundeck angles toward hills that shield my view of Larwin Gulch. While the Gulch will grow with oil wells, there's nothing to spoil the natural beauty we'll enjoy from my huge veranda! The actors and movie producers who attend my parties will be able to dance under millions of stars. I'll install one of those new telescopes for stargazing and invite astronomers from the County Observatory to give us tours of constellations! It's perfect! I can hardly wait to begin construction!"

Scoot forced an awkward smile. He summoned his moxie before commenting.

"These are fine plans indeed! I can see, Mr. Williams, that you're a man of great artistry. I'm coming to realize that your talent and vision extend far beyond the stage and movie production lots. I commend you for caring for your sister, too. She's a lucky lady to have such a considerate brother!"

Buck smiled.

"Thank you, my good man."

The actor turned to his designers.

"It's full steam ahead from here on out! The County's on standby to approve my plans. My money's in the bank to pay the workmen. We won't lack the craftsmen we need. Good men have traveled here from many other locales seeking work. They stop here before entering the big city. Those who can find employment often stay. I want them and their families to build wonderful lives in Larwin Valley, as I intend to do myself!"

Scoot projected all the sincerity he could muster.

"I'm sure the workers will have fine lives, and so will you and your sister!"

The wildcatter rose quickly, shook the actor's hand and bid the men farewell.

Walking to his car Scoot reflected on his day.

"Dang! Those two big plans are each going to cost their owners over two hundred thousand dollars to build! I bet no one else knows that Gimble's plan is in the way of what Buck Williams wants to build. I better stay clear. I wouldn't want to make enemies with either millionaire! I'll stay friendly with the actor, but I'll never disclose that I knew of Gimble's nearby oil drilling and refinery he intends to build at the train station. The review on building permits for the refinery will have to come before the County Board of Supervisors. Whatever comments or opinions people have about Gimble's proposal will surely be in the news. This ought to be quite a tête-à-tête. Maybe I can profit somehow!"

Scoot cheerfully strolled down Main Street as dusk settled over Larwin Valley. He tipped his hat to folks he encountered, treating the locals as if he'd known these people all his life. The wily wildcatter charmed whoever would stop and chat with him.

By the time the town was rolling up its streets, Scoot had a good feel for the people trying to build lives here. He looked for a hotel. Tomorrow he'd unfold his maps once more. He'd set out early to find the jagged property boundaries traversing the hills and valleys near Gimble's land. He pondered his strategy.

"It'll be useful to know the boundaries of Buck Williams' ranch, too. I'll get that at County Records. God knows, I do not want to be messing with noisy drilling equipment adjacent to that man's sanctuary! And I'll make sure my own acquisition is tucked safely behind some big hill. It must be out of sight from Buck's party veranda!"

Scoot thought of all the complicated work ahead.

"It'll be more than three weeks for me to comb through County title records. Then it could take five months for my land acquisition out here. I swear, I'll hire a landman the first chance I can afford one. For now, my money's on Gimble to get what he wants built, and he'll do it fast. Williams will end up like other hilltop dreamers in the city, planting thick trees in front of his balconies and windows. Industry always wins in the end."

CHAPTER 16

Mrs. Berkowitz hummed a tune while she organized folders in the study of her home. She thought about the lively ladies she was going to see next week at Amy Watson's parlor.

"It's wonderful the ladies can show what they're thinking without someone hushing them up! The younger ones especially can bounce complicated subjects around to see what things mean. We all learn. Things we never thought twice about before, we sure pay attention to now!"

She giggled thinking about Twyla, one of her favorites of the younger women. She'd have to let Twyla know once more that she personally did not think the subjects Twyla mentioned made her sound like Twyla the Twit. That was a nickname the girl overheard one time at her office. She nearly stopped attending Amy's meetings. Mrs. Berkowitz remembered what she told the devastated girl.

"I understand your frustration at how your words and emotions are seen by others. But it's not so bad as you think. You and I will talk about how you can use your dramatic flair to make the best of the keen senses you have!"

She and Twyla met a few times. The older woman consoled her.

"Few women can be like Madame Curie. You have great skills of observation and a colorful personality. You can do a lot with those! I know what it's like to try and mingle among the educated. There's no gentleman in my family who hasn't attended university. That was their goal after emigrating from Poland. They learned this country's language so they could speak without an accent. They worked without pay sometimes to make the right connections. All were eventually accepted at universities, and every one of them graduated."

Twyla stared at her hands.

"No one in my family's ever been near a university."

Mrs. Berkowtiz explained more.

"More intimidating than the minds of the men in my family were those of their sharp women! They were able to absorb the men's talk while keeping up with all the newspapers. My mind didn't seem to work as fast as theirs."

Twyla looked surprised. Mrs. Berkowitz continued.

"How I felt back then didn't matter. Through the years, I've come to see how life parlays the odds between brighter and dimmer stars. It's irrelevant if you keep company with professors or millionaires. True, they can influence the way a person might reason, but wisdom acquired over the years comes from plain old living. Love prevails over accomplishments. Wisdom is richer than any sums accrued in a person's bank account. That is the true gold in life."

Twyla still seemed confused so Mrs. Berkowitz drew a clearer picture.

"My dear, at the end of everyone's youth, it's still the same. There are old folks all around you showing faces that read of similar pain and failing health while simply trying to make it through each day. The most blessed elders are those who attain peace. Seek love from a few rather than acceptance by many. How you think and express things is just fine, starting with me and your other friends who love you very dearly."

Twyla understood. She hugged Mrs. Berkowitz. The old woman added.

"The ladies at Amy's can see where your brightness lies. No one there is expected to be the same as the others."

Twyla rejoined the ladies in Amy's parlor with renewed enthusiasm.

Mrs. Berkowitz continued her organizing as she thought of the people who'd accepted her. There were quite a few. Her hand passed over a folio where newspaper clippings hung out over the edges. Every birth and marriage, party and death among the hundreds of people she and her husband knew was noted in the papers.

Newspapers were eagerly read each day for they bore news of friends and relatives. Articles were clipped, shared and saved in her family as in every other. Younger ladies further down the axis of time would surely burn these old things, frustrated at all the space they consumed in drawers and closets, but Mrs. Berkowitz was one who still valued the news of each life and its events, as if a living part of every passing relative or joyous couple could still be felt through the faded ink on the yellowing paper.

Something caught Mrs. Berkowitz's eye. It was a small headline on the edge of one clipping that read, 'Who is Thomas R. Gimble?'

She carefully extracted the paper her husband must have saved.

"How fascinating! We talked about him at Amy's."

There were two reports on the half page describing the inventor and his work. She read the text in the small box on the paper's edge.

"Thomas R. Gimble is a practical inventor, not a wild, theoretical dreamer or a 'blueprint' inventor, meaning a fellow who gets his plan down on paper and never goes further. Gimble is a millionaire due to his inventions. A crude oil refining process, which he conceived, brought him a million dollars. Besides this, he has many other patents operating which bring him large royalties."

"Hmm," thought Mrs. Berkowitz. "The ladies at Amy's might be interested in discussing royalties. Some writers and inventors make a lot of money with those."

Mrs. Berkowitz studied the page. She saw the large photo of a tall man in a jumpsuit. It was Gimble. He looked as big and handsome as Twyla described. The ladies at Amy's meetings discussed the inventor several times since first learning of him last spring, but she and the other women hadn't seen a photo of him yet.

"Maybe this was taken before he stopped allowing his photo to appear in newspapers."

The paper's date was 1916. Standing beside the inventor in the picture was a shorter man. The text below the photo named him as Skip Vanderhooten, a man 'who risked his life to operate the first Gimble submersible under water.' The inventor's large hand rested on the right shoulder of the good-looking, young man in the way that a friend might hold close his finest buddy. She saw in the article that Skip was the son of a Federal judge. She was intrigued at how the article described Gimble's friend.

"Skip, however, is no way interested in law or courts. He is interested, instead, in sprockets and gears and things with wheels."

Mrs. Berkowitz smiled.

"Twyla's imagination will come to life. Harriet, Doreen and some of the other girls might also be interested. Maybe they haven't have seen this."

Mrs. Berkowitz read more.

"A submarine so small it could be tucked in the vest pocket of Uncle Sam, and which, according to its inventor, will be a leading factor in ending the European war, is being perfected by Thomas R. Gimble. Tests made with this queer little craft indicate that it will revolutionize warfare on the water, just as the aeroplane has turned the technique of land fighting topsy-turvy."

"Goodness," thought Mrs. Berkowitz, "This describes a lot!"

She read that the small craft Gimble was testing would run at twice the speed of any of the heavier dreadnaughts. It was light enough to be transported at twenty miles an hour by rail or truck, and one vessel could be built in mere days. She read in amazement.

"Enough of these vessels could be made in 60 days to protect an entire nation. They could furnish an impregnable defense to small countries not equipped with fleets of dreadnaughts. Every battleship in the American Navy could carry a whole family of these little boats. They could be launched from davits as readily as are cutters and skiffs at present."

Mrs. Berkowitz thought of one of the shy women from Amy's parlor. The young lady had blushed deeply admitting her desire to become an engineer.

"Julie would surely appreciate such details!"

The old lady continued reading.

"The secret of the high speed is said to lie in the design and in the gasoline motor, which exhausts into a special trap under water. The principle of this underwater exhaust is considered so valuable that Mr. Gimble says he has not patented it, and will not. Instead of the usual method of submerging by opening intake valves and flooding the submerging chambers, Mr. Gimble's submarine submerges by means of a vertical propeller located under the boat at mid ship. Horizontal planes on each side, fore and aft, are used as stabilizers and also assist in submerging."

Mrs. Berkowitz adjusted her spectacles.

"Oh, this next part will have the women giggling!"

The article reported one of the first launches of Gimble's submarine.

"When Gimble and Vanderhooten finished their first under-sea boat, government submarine experts came to look at it and promptly condemned it. 'The idea of a dreamer!' they said. 'It is impracticable and never will work; a waste of time and money.' When the government men learned that Skip Vanderhooten was actually going to lock himself in 'that crazy contraption' and attempt to sink himself to the bottom of the bay, they took him aside and filled his ear with such cheerful encouragement as this: 'Why, my boy, you might just as well take a six-shooter and blow out your brains. It's suicide. You're going to your doom. Don't be a fool. That ridiculous contrivance will never work. Don't throw your life away in it.' If you think this talk didn't scare Skip Vanderhooten, you are wrong. It did. Why shouldn't it? The speakers were government men—Uncle Sam's submarine experts. But when the time came, Vanderhooten lowered himself into the diver, determined to give the vessel a trial, even if it became his coffin. 'Tell the undertaker my favorite flowers are daisies,' he laughed as they locked the top of the conning tower over his head."

Mrs. Berkwotiz chuckled.

"How thrilling! There's more Julie might appreciate."

The article summarized the test.

"The engine in the little vessel ticked like a watch. It was tuned to perfection. When Skip Vanderhooten jerked the throttle open, the Gimble submarine shot out of its berth into the bay like a fish. 'She did everything the government experts said she wouldn't,' said Gimble. Since that memorable voyage, Gimble and Vanderhooten have completed more craft, which they are now testing. They are guarding the movements of their wonder boat with utmost secrecy.'"

Mrs. Berkowitz gleefully folded the paper.

"This has something for every woman at Amy's!"

She slipped the article into her handbag and finished her organizing with a happy heart.

CHAPTER 17

▼

A week after Mrs. Berkowitz found the article about Gimble's submarine, the women gathered in Amy's parlor. Billy Gimble nestled quietly below the grill near the furnace.

Billy had scrambled out the front door of his house just as his family sat down for lunch. His mother was angry.

"You get back here, William Gimble! You haven't eaten but a mouthful!"

Billy pretended not to hear his mom as he ran off. His stomach was quiet now, and he intended to keep it that way.

As the ladies settled into Amy's treasured chairs, Mrs. Berkowitz opened her news article and read aloud. The information about TR's submersible vessel made the ladies mouths drop open in surprise. So did Billy Gimble's down below.

"No one in my family ever told me Dad had any arrangement with government men!"

The boy was confused. He knew for certain that his mother despised the men in long, black coats who showed up asking for his father. These were official-looking gentlemen in dark sedans who came to the door showing her documents with big, gold seals and circular emblems printed in color ink at the top of long pages.

From what Billy overheard, the strangers seemed to ask a lot of questions about who his dad worked for and corresponded with. He also heard them ask how much money his dad was paid for his inventions. His mother never answered their questions. Billy saw her upset and quiet each time the men left.

Then his dad and Ty would only talk in low tones later in the evening. Now some of it made sense.

"Dad invented something the government men thought was crazy, but he made it work! Hooray for Dad!"

When the ladies grew quiet, Mrs. Rhodes spoke.

"Some of my family's men were in the Royal Navy for generations. Although I married a laborer, whom I still dearly love, I keep in contact with my relatives overseas. I'll write and ask if any of them have heard of such a thing as a Gimble water vessel. I know that all things naval in every country are kept secret, but Navy men sometimes talk. I doubt I'll learn anything new, but I'll refer to Mrs. Berkowitz's article to see if any of them read about this in Britain."

Genevieve McDonnell listened intently. She was as surprised by the news as everyone else. She folded her hands and pondered.

"How odd! Frank never mentioned a word about any maritime devices the inventor's working on. Mr. Gimble probably tried the vessel but found it more lucrative to work for oil companies."

Mrs. Graham adjusted the strings on her bonnet. She leaned toward Mrs. Finny.

"I have all the time in the world to read the papers. I have for years since my children married and moved away. I subscribe to several editions and read them front to back. I never heard of this Gimble vessel."

Mrs. Finny mused.

"I don't remember seeing the article either. How strange no word of it has been written about since."

She turned to Harriet.

"Dear, have you seen or heard a thing about Gimble's submarine before today?"

Harriet scanned the article that Mrs. Berkowitz passed to her.

"No, but I agree with Doreen. We should keep information of something like this on hand. Who knows what part of the watercraft's technology will appear somewhere else?"

Julie spoke softly.

"It would be nice to see if the lightweight metal, engine or fuel that Gimble used in his submarine appears in other inventions."

Amy looked at Julie in surprise. Then her eyes sparked with hope.

"Who knows? We might someday want to invest in stock that uses Gimble technology we heard about today. I'm being optimistic, I know, but I keep thinking that we should be tuning our minds to promising innovations that may one day end up in machines that thousands of people will buy. Investing and learning go hand in hand. Watching technology, even if one invention doesn't pan out, could be fruitful overall!"

Julie twisted her hands nervously, almost too shy to speak again. Then she breathed in more confidence.

"I'd really like a copy of the article. Maybe women will invent things like this someday. I'd like to learn how companies and the government choose which ideas they want to use. I'd like to study the details. How will any of us learn what inventing really is and how to talk about these things if we don't study them?"

Amy looked startled. She never heard Julie utter five sentences altogether in front of the women in her parlor. Amy smiled brightly at her no-longer-timid friend.

"You are so right, Miss Jules! Here's what we can do. I'll ask my husband to bring home the pharmacy's typewriter for one evening. I'll type a copy of the words in the article. I'll pass that copy onto Susan, who can make another copy for someone else, and so on. Mrs. Berkowitz, I'll return your article safely to you next week. Is that OK?"

Mrs. Berkowitz assured her that would be fine.

Then Eva brightened, animated by a new idea.

"Amy, have you seen papers dealing with patents and royalties?"

Amy rolled her eyes.

"Heavens, yes! To the tune of hundreds of pages! Those are complex matters indeed, just like property. Handling infringements on patents and published material has become substantial work at our office."

Susan glanced up from the submarine article Harriet handed her.

"It's unusual that Mr. Gimble felt his vessel's engine design was so unique that he didn't want to patent it. He makes his money with his patents. But I can see where publication of the patent itself would be hard to protect on an underwater craft that can slide in and out of hiding. Maybe what he did to keep his secret was smart. He can keep his design under wraps forever."

Eva agreed.

"He probably found some other way to make money with it. I'd sure like to know more about patents and royalties myself."

"So would I," added Harriet.

Amy grinned.

"Everyone can. I'll bring a copy of a royalty agreement being drafted now, but not with any real names. What I'll bring you is an outline of an oil and gas lease that has stipulations for paying royalties to the signators and their heirs for perpetuity."

Twyla looked perplexed.

"What does all that mean?"

Mrs. Berkowitz smiled at Twyla before exclaiming to the group.

"I'm eager to know about it as well!"

Amy surveyed the women around her parlor.

"I hope I introduce this adequately. One of the most frequent types of royalties being paid these days, other than to writers and inventors, are royalties paid to people who've allowed oil drillers to take oil from the ground under their property. This is complicated business, but the nice thing is that the people who own the property and mineral rights get paid a royalty when drillers bring up oil. Different kinds of lease agreements address things such as minerals, water, oil or natural gas that men can extract from a property and sell."

Mrs. Berkowitz was impressed.

"Talk about learning on the job, Amy! Do you realize how smart you just sounded?"

Amy blushed.

"I just read what I'm given to type."

Eva grew excited.

"No one in my family has ever had such a lease. I can't wait to see a document as complicated as that! I know I'll have a million questions, but answering those questions can be a start to our own business endeavors. Thank you, Amy."

Susan looked thoughtful.

"It could take many of us to answer all the questions we'll have, but I can't wait to start unraveling the mysteries of leases and royalties."

Julie raised her thin hand.

"I'd like to see a patent royalty agreement. It can be later sometime as I know how busy you must be, Amy."

Amy laughed.

"Sure Jules. It sounds like I may need a secretary of my own to keep up with all your interests!"

The ladies chuckled knowingly. It might be years before smart, young Amy was ever recognized as a true legal assistant rather than just a typist.

Amy looked at Julie.

"Seriously, Jules, what I was thinking is that, if you take a look at the toughest kind of royalty agreement I can think of, an oil and gas lease, then understanding a patent royalty will be a piece of cake!"

Julie nodded.

Doreen tapped her pencil firmly on the papers sitting on the table beside her.

"Ladies, we're dragging sorely behind the men in learning the very first things we ought to about all sorts of legal matters. I'm fully in favor of jumping in to take on some of toughest challenges to try and understand first. We have nothing to lose! There's no harm in simply putting the big words and concepts in our minds, especially when we're lucky enough to have someone in our midst working for the kind of downtown attorney that Amy does."

Amy chuckled.

"Those men try to outwit each other every hour of the day and night, but we do have a gold mine to tap for learning more of what they know."

Mrs. Berkowitz winked at Twyla. She knew Twyla wouldn't be studying anything as complicated as royalty agreements any time soon. There were other aspects of business the old woman had learned in the years she overheard the men in her family talking. These were things she listened to while serving meals, such as how to conduct negotiations and close strategic sales. She intended to inform Twyla about some of the secrets behind men's dynamic business exchanges soon enough.

Billy Gimble didn't squirm as he hid beneath the parlor floor.

"Maybe all those whispers between Mom and Dad and Ty have to do with Dad's submarine. Geez, I know less than these ladies and I <u>live</u> with Thomas Gimble!"

CHAPTER 18

▼

The ladies in Amy's parlor stood in small groups. Taking a break from their talk of more challenging ideas, they happily discussed the direction of Amy's new decor. Mrs. Finny saw something she liked.

"That vase is so striking and the colors so brilliant! It looks like wildflowers in spring yet with an Irish mist swirling all around."

Amy looked at her new treasure proudly.

"I was so drawn to this style. It's part of an idea decorators call Craftsman. It's just getting started. It will take us years to renovate just this parlor alone with what I have in mind."

Harriet joined the group.

"I've heard of this style, too. It's actually hailed as a movement. The idea is that lines and colors flow together in organic forms. Prints and textures are supposed to represent things in nature. Critics say the movement promises to revolutionize how we decorate."

Eva studied the vase.

"Is this what could replace our Victorian furnishings?"

Amy smiled.

"Only if you like. It's simply a new choice, but I rather think it goes with our times, and certainly our generation of women who want to make changes."

"How fascinating!" exclaimed Mrs. Berkowitz. "I'm always curious to see what the young ladies like."

Mrs. Rhodes shook her head.

"I'm still such a traditional Brit. I'll probably always adore Victorian style."

Amy laughed.

"Well, Mrs. Rhodes, I'll never stop loving those traditional, beautiful things myself. I discussed my new decorating aims with my husband, and he said to go right ahead and try out what I think might make me happy. I love him for letting me fly toward new horizons with some of my ideas. We haven't invested a great deal in any decorating yet, as you can tell, but we hope to find some things that will add warm, modern touches to this home."

Harriet looked fascinated.

"Have you seen the desks, bureaus and tables that the Craftsmen artisans are creating?"

Amy pointed to a stack of papers on one table.

"Oh, yes. I'm collecting clippings galore with many pictures. It's fun to see what other people are finding, too. Sometimes you have to travel to small towns and villages where the artists have gathered to create and build these things. You can't go downtown and simply shop for this style in one place, certainly not yet. Only certain companies feature these designs. If any of you are interested in bringing pictures of Craftsman style furnishings to share at our meetings, it might be fun to explore. That could be a relaxing break to balance our other discussions. The technical and business matters we're trying to understand can be arduous at times."

Twyla agreed.

"That sounds perfect. I'd like to know more about Craftsman artists."

Doreen joined the ladies.

"As most of you know, my home is no decorator's dream. My rooms will probably never be a delight to the eye, but I think it's a capital idea to include in our meetings discussion of Craftsman artisans and their creations. I can see this movement emerging with as much influence as industry. Whatever can help women change things, consider me in!"

The ladies laughed, always entertained by Doreen's forthright manner.

Twyla noticed her friend Nona staring intently at the news article Mrs. Berkowitz brought. Twyla went to stand beside her.

"How come you haven't said anything today?"

Nona looked up.

"I still haven't met Gimble at our office, and now I'm really curious. This picture does look like the man I saw whistling as he walked down the street. He's as tall and handsome as I remember. You sure were lucky to be working both times he came to meet with the chemists."

Twyla nodded.

"It made those days interesting, that's for sure!"

Nona reflected.

"The idea that Gimble joined with other men to build an experimental submarine seems to fit with the kind of men my Richard's becoming involved with."

Twyla looked intrigued.

"What do you mean?"

"This fellow beside Gimble in the picture, Skip Vanderhooten, reminds me of Richard's friends. The men are intelligent, jovial types whose company Richard enjoys immensely. They share many ideas and love to experiment. Sometimes they laugh for hours. Gimble's friend Skip seems that way, too. Skip joked about facing death while testing Gimble's watercraft."

Twyla looked at the picture.

"You're thinking about Richard just from seeing this picture?"

Nona shook her head.

"There's more. Richard is growing a lot closer to his new friends. I'm getting to know some of their wives and girlfriends, too. We're forming associations around the men's involvement with the fraternal society known as the Guild. Most of Richard's new friends are tradesmen. They work as electricians, carpenters, brick masons and mechanics. Some of the men are business professionals, too, but all of them enjoy practicing many crafts. The ladies talking about craftsmen reminded me of this. Richard's friends also mentioned starting a new movement, one that's like the foundations of this country when people built lives experimenting with crafts and trades. The men Richard knows all have promising careers. They're serious about defining how they will contribute to America."

Twyla saw her friend's puzzled brow.

"Everything with Richard and his friends sounds good. Is something not?"

Nona took a deep breath.

"I am wondering if the man Richard and his friends speak of as Brother Thomas might be TR Gimble."

Twyla swallowed.

"Really?"

"Yes, really. I never thought to ask Richard this, but when his friends joke around speculating wild, new theories, one of them will ask, 'I wonder what Brother Thomas thinks?' Then the men laugh and exchange some symbol with their hands. Afterwards, they become serious and discuss technical matters. They don't do this often in front of the women, but other women have asked me who this Brother Thomas is. The men usually discuss technical things at their workshops or in their own meetings at a downtown lodge. Brother Thomas is someone we can't figure out because we've never seen him. And the men won't tell us anything about what goes on at the lodge."

Twyla began evaluating Nona's mystery.

"What made you think Gimble might be Brother Thomas?"

Nona pointed to the headline on the small box at the edge of the news article.

"This headline, 'Who is Thomas R. Gimble?' I never knew Gimble's first name was Thomas. The men at our office called him TR. As soon as I saw this headline, my mind flashed to Richard and his friends, and then my nagging question, who is Brother Thomas?"

Twyla understood.

"If it's on your mind, why don't you ask the ladies? Some of the older women know about the Guild. They might know if Gimble's involved. They might know if he has a nickname like Brother Thomas."

Nona looked around and wondered if she should. Twyla patted her arm.

"I'll get this going. Don't worry. Now you have me curious."

The ladies returned to their seats after an enjoyable break. Twyla raised her hand.

"I've been trying to bring Nona up to speed after the past few months when she was caring for her mother and couldn't attend our meetings."

Nona smiled shyly as she spoke.

"Mom's doing better now. Thank you for the cards you sent."

Twyla nudged her friend impatiently while the ladies extended good wishes for Nona's mother's complete recovery. Nona went on.

"The doctors expect her to be on her feet again in another two weeks. Twyla's let me know that you've been discussing this inventor with the submarine for several months already, along with other news having to do with science and technology. I've been able to do more reading in the past months. I've been talking about these same ideas with my boyfriend, Richard. All of it is fascinating, and I want to learn more. I was wondering if anyone knows if Mr. Gimble is a member of the Guild."

Mrs. Graham looked interested.

"Why do you ask that?"

Nona clasped the necklace Richard had given her. It was a tiny silver shield with a lily etched the middle.

"Well, Gimble seems to be like the kind of man who'd be involved in that group, you know, craftsmen, experimenters, men exploring new ideas."

She took a breath and added one more thing.

"Perhaps he's been raised to one of their higher orders."

Nona looked around quickly to see if anyone caught her drift. Twyla's bright eyes were scanning the room as well. Twyla saw Mrs. Graham reflecting carefully. Then the older woman made her decision to speak.

"Ah, she knows," thought Twyla. "Nona will get her question answered, and I'll learn some things as well!"

Mrs. Graham spoke gently.

"Dear, there are men of the Guild, and there are also the Men of Great Works."

Nona knew to approach this subject with care.

"I only saw the inventor from a distance, but he seemed like someone prominent. If Gimble is the kind of man that Mrs. Berkowitz's news article declares, and the kind of man that Twyla describes having met him, it would stand to reason in my mind that he would hardly be a doer of good on the most common level of any men's social organization. He'd have to be someone higher up."

Mrs. Graham looked thoughtful.

"You're right, dear. My husband is a member of the Guild, and he is also a member of the Ancient Rite as well. That is an old order. You might know we are descendants of some of Britain's most independent, rugged people. That old men's order is one of the traditional comforts we enjoy with other couples descended of the same. It gives us good cheer during the holidays and extra support in times of need. Many people in Britain know of this old order. It simply made its way across the Atlantic when the Guild decided to start chapters of their society here. You must know that the men who are raised to high degrees in the Ancient Rite rarely talk of what they learn or do in that stricter society of men. I know little, but I can tell you that Mr. Gimble is one of the most highly regarded among the men of the Ancient Rite."

Twyla feared she would collapse into a dead faint. She gripped Nona's arm beneath the folds of Nona's shawl. Twyla had no idea what the Ancient Rite was, but this was something secret and delicious in the manner that the starry-eyed, young lady especially liked.

Nona quietly shook loose the skin of her forearm from beneath Twyla's nails. She straightened the shawl around her delicate shoulders and looked toward Mrs. Graham.

"Mr. Gimble isn't Scottish, is he?"

"No, I don't think so," said Mrs. Graham. "He may be of some British descent, perhaps from some of the early settlers in America. There was a man named Gimble who was an advisor to our first president. George Washington fondly called him Brother Thomas. It seems to me that Gimble's family tree may go back to that person seeing as the inventor is originally from back east in the U.S. I'm simply not certain of any of this for I've seen no documents myself to tell you this is the absolute truth."

Twyla's eyes look misty. She relaxed in her chair. This time it was Nona who discreetly grabbed her friend's arm and nudged her in the ribs.

CHAPTER 19

▼

Twyla glanced at Nona, who peered back at her sharply. Twyla regained her composure and sat silently. The women in Amy's parlor shuffled in their chairs seeing this talk not moving toward science, inventions or even Craftsman furnishings. Each sensed something new unfolding. Quiet Nona, who'd not even been at their recent meetings, was leading the way.

Nona looked appreciatively at Mrs. Graham.

"No wonder Mr. Gimble seems intriguing. The Ancient Rite men and their wives sound like nice people, so he must be too."

The older woman saw Nona's intent look.

"What have you heard about the group?"

Nona blushed.

"Bare little, I think. It's merely been a fun tease for me with my Richard ever since I first heard there was such a fraternity. Richard is not a member. He's too young. He told me a man must be at least thirty-two before being considered for any higher order such as that. As far as anything I've heard, I figured it was some grand fairy tale. It sounded like that to me, but that's what makes my teasing with Richard so fun!"

Harriet wanted to know more.

"What do you mean?"

Nona explained.

"When Richard has spent a lot of time with his men friends, I tease him by acting reluctant to go on another date."

The ladies chuckled. Nona went on.

"It's just our little courting game in good humor. We always end up closer afterwards. When I'm perturbed from being a little overlooked by Richard, I tell him I won't see him again until he discloses one more little thing about the Ancient Rite."

Twyla cast an admiring look at her friend.

"Brilliant!" she thought, "I didn't think this sweet gal had it in her!"

"So what have you heard?" asked Mrs. Graham.

Nona explained.

"First of all, I never would have known the Ancient Rite existed except that Richard had a little book called 'History of the Ancient Knights.' When I first saw it, I was curious and asked what it was. He told me that one of his brothers in the Guild encouraged him to read it. Richard was able to purchase a used copy advertised in the magazine that the Guild publishes. Richard contacted the brother selling the book. He was thrilled to learn it was still available. He told me he paid $3 for it. I knew that paying so much for a book meant it was important to him. Richard explained he was just beginning to read it, but that it was about knights of a holy military order in the eleventh century who went to guard the roads to the Holy Land so that pilgrims from Europe might be able to travel safely through dangerous territory. I got interested in what he was learning. That's when I started to tease him to tell me more. I already knew that you cannot press members of the Guild to disclose things about their organization, but the book wasn't about the group, only men from ancient times. Richard figured he wasn't breaking his oath of secrecy. He said that other brothers were reading the book and probably had to explain when other people saw it, too."

The ladies looked at one another. No one had seen the book that Nona described.

"What else did you learn?" asked Mrs. Graham.

Nona furrowed her brow trying to remember the story. Then she organized her thoughts and recounted.

"The knights were recognized for their brave deeds throughout Europe, and notably by the Pope, but once they got to fighting against certain large, vicious armies in the Middle East, they couldn't always win every battle. Their heroism was legendary, and they amassed a great fortune from grateful European lords and kings. The knights put the money to beneficent use among needy people, but mainly they used the funds to help support their defense of roads to the Holy Land and sacred Christian shrines. Later on, when some of the wars the knights were fighting went poorly, a greedy king turned against them. He wanted their money. The Pope didn't back up the knights with the kind of endorsement they originally received from Rome a century earlier. The king ordered a mass execution of the knights. Nearly all were slaughtered. Some survived with the help of people who protected them. The ones who hid in the British Isles became the Ancient Knights. Apparently, their legend and the knowledge they collected along the way survived in secret for centuries. The legend of the Holy Knights is being studied now by the Guild. This book was written when some of the Holy Knights' grand fortresses and temples in Europe were being restored. For the men involved, it was like discovering something great from the past that was lost. It became very real when the knights' tombs and other artifacts were uncovered. Richard thought it was a fine story. I enjoyed hearing how he spoke of the castles and kings, as well as the devoted monks and valiant knights!"

"You just told me more than I ever knew!" exclaimed Mrs. Graham, "And you're right, it does sound like a sad yet marvelous fairy tale. I can see how intriguing it would be. In my opinion, it has value in its telling for the redemption of men. I, too have heard just a little of this story, but I've not personally read a word of it. I've seen many fortresses and castles still standing in Europe, but there are only a few that people say are part of what the Holy Knights built. I feel that, whatever old tales or new resolves make our men strive to be better, I am all for those ideas. I know that the wives of the men of these orders feel the same as I do. It's likely you'll feel the same someday, too. It sounds like you and Richard are happily moving forward. That's the greatest blessing that matters most."

Twyla's eyes were saucers. This talk was reason for deeper discussions with Nona outside Amy's parlor and far beyond their office. There were no oak-paneled walls where they both worked suitable enough to hold secrets with such scrumptious details. That Nona had mentioned none of this courting game with Richard to Twyla was a surprise. Twyla looked at her friend with silent, begging eyes. Nona glanced back at Twyla, who, by now, was bending her head to put her face in front of her shy friend's. Nona moved back a little and shrugged her shoulders. She glared at Twyla and murmured quietly.

"Well, you never asked!"

Since Mrs. Graham was being so kind, Nona decided to mention one more thing.

"Richard also said that there are certain groups among the men who go farther into ancient studies. They learn of alchemy and other practices that are said to be handed down from the Ancient Knights. The men who study this old knowledge are ones most likely to be recognized in the higher ranks of the Ancient Rite. I know no more than this. I'm certain Richard mentioned the higher order and the word alchemy."

Mrs. Graham raised her eyebrows. Then a veil seemed to come over her face.

"My dear, I have no answers regarding any of that. I'm sure that these men discuss many subjects. Since they do reflect upon the knights of old, they could be aware of some old practices. As I told you before, I have no personal knowledge about any of the things they study. I'm simply content that I can fully trust the men with whom my husband associates. I love their families as dearly as my own."

Twyla noticed the shift in Mrs. Graham's gaze. Where had she seen that before? Oh yes, it was just like Genevieve McDonnell's face when Twyla first mentioned the handsome chemist who turned out to be the inventor, TR Gimble.

"Now wait a minute," thought Twyla, "Here Gimble comes to our office to meet with our chemists, and now we're learning that he's a member of some secret group that studies old alchemy!"

Twyla looked at Mrs. Graham, who had turned abruptly to talk with Amy. The two were discussing the Scottish architect, C.R. Mackintosh.

Mrs. Graham gushed eagerly.

"You should see what he's innovating at the Glasgow School of Art! It's the most beautiful example of Craftsman architecture anyone's seen. Have you heard of the Arts and Crafts Exhibition Society affiliated with Mackintosh's school?"

The other ladies leaned forward, all ears to learn what was happening on the other side of the Atlantic that might influence their exciting, new design choices.

Not to be outdone, Mrs. Finny chimed in.

"The White House was designed by the Irish architect, James Hoban!"

The women giggled, always in need of a breeze of laughter to break up any topic that got too serious.

But Twyla was not done mulling things over. She nudged Nona.

"Did you see how fast Mrs. Graham changed the subject?"

Her friend nodded. Her voice sounded perplexed.

"Now what?"

Twyla kept her eyes and tone low as she muttered.

"It's probably not a good idea to be sharing either of our fascinations with unscientific subjects. I think I learned my lesson months ago. You better keep 'ol Richard's fairy tales to yourself. Otherwise, the ladies will think you're a twit, too!"

Nona smiled.

"You're hardly any twit. I already figured Gimble was some kind of alchemist-magician-experimenter just by your description. Mrs. Berkowitz's news article confirmed it further. Once I thought about what Richard said about the Ancient Knights, I put two and two together. I'm not exactly sure how all this fits. I don't know if there's a shred of any real science behind it. Why do you think I kept all this to myself? You told me what happened when you first talked about Gimble."

Twyla's eyes clouded at the thought of that day. Then she brightened remembering Mrs. Berkowitz's advice. She turned to Nona.

"You and I will go to lunch soon someplace where no one can hear us. Maybe a picnic in the park would be good. We need to air our silliest notions in private. At least now I know I'm not alone in some of the things I've been wondering about."

Nona looked at the other women animatedly discussing architects and buildings.

"I have a feeling I could use an ally separate from women whose men are tied to fraternal societies."

Twyla looked at Genevieve McDonnell and Mrs. Graham chatting amiably.

"You know, we could be complete fools thinking that every woman in this room is willing to be as open and helpful as Amy Watson."

"I agree," said Nona.

Twyla winked.

"We'll talk soon."

Billy Gimble lay on his back in the dirt. He stared blankly toward the parlor's floorboards. In the darkness, his mind whirled in frustration.

"My whole family's keeping secrets! What do Mom and Ty know about all this stuff Dad is doing? Why does everyone seem to know things about my dad that I don't? And why does Mom clip apart so many newspapers? Is she trying to hide things so the kids won't see it?"

The boy resolved to start buying newspapers on his own.

"I'll read the facts for myself. I can't rely on Ty. Winnie and my folks won't tell me the truth either!"

He brushed a sad tear from his cheek with a dusty finger.

CHAPTER 20

▼

"Ouch!"

The photographer dropped his camera in the lush vegetation.

Hiram glanced to the fence beyond the machines that hummed and whirred in TR's work yard. He saw two men shuffling on the other side. Hiram didn't walk over. New shoots on the plants from South Africa sprang skyward, encouraged by the spring rains and extra dousing from constant irrigation. Hiram had no concerns. The shrubs growing around the fence were doing their job keeping uninvited inquirers away from new construction in the yard.

"What is this damn stuff?!" cried the wounded man.

His companion spotted the many long thorns.

"Nothing we can crawl through! Use this crowbar to grab the camera and let's go!"

TR watched the foiled intruders from inside the office. Ty came to his side and looked out the window toward the fence.

"Nice work, Dad."

TR shook his head as the men hurried off. One man was limping with his trousers torn.

"It's going to require more than Carissa macrocarpa on that fence over time. We just may have to bring in cactus!"

Hiram came inside the office.

"Did you see the men?"

Ty and TR nodded.

Hiram grinned.

"They're just a nuisance. As long as Tiemonet doesn't bang through the door, I consider it a good day!"

TR turned to the large map of the world on the office wall. He traced his finger from California to the Midwest and tapped Washington, D.C. Then he moved his finger across the Atlantic past the Middle East to China.

"Where is that scoundrel Frenchman lurking anyway? I've reached the point where I can almost predict which country he'll go interfering with next."

Hiram laughed.

"He follows your endeavors like a game. Too bad men get excited and talk. They keep giving him clues where to go!"

TR tapped the outline of France.

"We'll just have to start dropping misinformation like they do. Pity, it's almost a waste of good men's efforts, but like the fence in the yard, you have to keep constructing new barriers to offset intruders. The men who are covert have far too much idle time on their hands!"

TR pointed to the Western U.S. and looked at Ty.

"As far as traveling, son, the opportunity for you to work with the Regis geologists this summer is a good one."

Ty looked at the travel schedule in his hands. A new opportunity had arrived. His father explained.

"These geologists Regis hired are men fresh out of service from the US Geological Survey. They've acquired the most current knowledge there is. The men you'll travel with recently finished their government business mapping the country. Now they're eager to delineate mineral regions, especially in the West. Regis Petroleum is paying for everything, including your wage as assistant to the geologists. Locating mineral deposits on remote sites is something you ought to learn. This will benefit you greatly in years to come."

The inventor winked knowingly at his son.

"Business school will start soon enough, and then you'll be in the city, closer to all the girls."

Ty laughed.

"Dad, you know I'm willing to learn all parts of this business. You don't have to convince me that working with geologists is something I must learn. I like the kind of men who study rocks and dirt anyway. They're some of the rowdiest yet nicest fellows I've met. They watch out for one another. They have to. The mines and mountainsides where they complete their surveys are some of the most dangerous. One of the chaps from the American School of Mining Geology told me how the dean of the school allows the students to physically drag him through the mud each spring. They have a grand old celebration and basically tear up the town for a week, but that's because they study so intently the rest of the year. They work hard in classrooms and laboratories, then trek all over mountains and deserts in their field studies. They're constantly exhausted and wound up from the effort. They feel they have the toughest studies and exams of any college students they know. I have to admire the grit it takes for them to graduate!"

TR took the travel schedule and checked off his son's survey destinations on his wall map.

"You're right about that, son. I can vouch for the intricate nature of their exams. You couldn't answer many of those questions if your boots hadn't hiked the field. You'll learn a great deal this summer."

Ty grinned.

"I'll be packed and ready to go, Dad."

As Ty left, Hiram glanced at TR.

"You're not holding anything against those sweaty professors are you?"

TR laughed.

"Hardly. Look at all the work we'll be doing for Regis. I have a stack of contracts from every other major oil company as well. Taking the exam was worth my while. I thought about my kids and how they'll have to go through the same thing someday, minus the five sweaty professors. Each of my children will have to be tested at whatever school they attend. It wasn't that way for working people in this country before now. A man could prove his skills on the job and often do better than the academics. Academics were the personal wizards of royalty and the elite. All that has changed. The professors in this country have made a full-fledged business out of educating thousands of minds. They've made their educating business vital to the economy."

Hiram gazed at the wall map thoughtfully.

"And therein lies the controversy. Just as men and companies can debate your test results for years to come, the academics can make a mighty business out of controversy between the government and industry concerning what to teach!"

TR chuckled.

"Consider me a pioneer."

He reached in his coat pocket and placed a badge on Hiram's desk.

"Here, I had these printed. They're more for visitors than anything else."

As TR left to inspect the work yard, Hiram studied the badge. It bore a drafted triangle. Around its three sides were the words, 'Gimble Refining Company.' The inventor's assistant clipped the lacquered card to the strap of his overalls as he reflected.

"Who'd have thought a clothing merchant's son would become assistant to the head of a refining company? Thank goodness exams aren't required here, although I'd probably do fine if they were. These are probably the last years where such a thing is possible. Other refining companies will absolutely require university degrees of men who'll be designing machines and mixing chemicals for oil companies!"

Hiram looked out the window as the inventor mingled with his workers. TR gave them their badges and whistled as he moved on. The men outside walked briskly whistling, too. Just as quickly, they'd stop and gather, studying details on equipment and construction underway. Hiram saw bricklayers and carpenters consulting with electricians and pipe fitters outfitting new machines. TR jumped in to assist a group of men lifting a large plank. TR then stopped to consult with other men checking dials and gauges. He peered into a large engine where workers oiled and fine-tuned the machine's parts. Hiram observed how every man remained comfortable discussing ideas with the boss. The lifeblood of Gimble's plant was not the fuel that jettisoned through fine pipes, but the men whose minds ran free and clear.

Dusk was gathering amid clouds in the crisp, spring sky. Hiram put on his cap and decided to leave. He'd be back well before dawn tomorrow morning.

A half hour later, TR returned to the office where all was quiet. He gathered the contract documents he needed to read on the train. He thought about the chemist he'd be meeting with early the following week. Reginald Hamilton of Regis Petroleum had made an early impression on the team who'd be building the company's newest and largest refinery. TR had learned that the chemist was educated at fine European universities. He also noticed that the man constantly cleaned his spectacles and adjusted his vest so that the notch hung precisely above his belt buckle. Hamilton appeared highly perturbed when TR was around. One of the oil company men told TR what the chemist had stated when asked his opinion about the inventor.

"He's perfectly honest—but you can't believe a word he says!"

Some of the engineers on the Regis team had rushed to explain.

"Hamilton is prone to making such comments of any man possessed of an idea!"

TR quietly listened as the engineers explained.

"Hamilton is known to secretly install thermometers and gauges that take readings from any part of an inventor's machine so as to disprove explanations from the inventor as to how substances proceed through the chambers. He presents findings about isolated pressure and temperature readings using elaborate chemical calculations and algebraic algorithms to assert that a method absolutely will not work. No one can understand him, but company executives act like they do."

Properly warned, TR said nothing when the chemist fiddled with test machines TR set up at Regis' headquarters. TR then noted that a lot of what the chemist scribbled in his reports depicted unproven mathematical theories. TR chuckled and uttered his own deathless comment.

"Hamilton is a convincing sort, driven beyond any chemist I've ever met."

TR had spoken with Hiram about the immense headaches the chemist must endure.

"The man's spent years galloping around America and Europe trying to keep up with every emerging refining method. He cannot, however, crawl inside every experimenter's mind. He tries diligently enough, but there are thousands of inventors doing the same kind of work that we do here."

Hiram had responded.

"If Hamilton's so bright, why isn't he drawing up new patents himself for machines that will do more or better refining than those he attempts to disprove?"

TR had mused.

"It's another brilliant mind attached to idle or perhaps timid hands. Nothing proves a process better to oil executives than one that meets their bottom line. They want speed and highest capacity at lowest cost per barrel. They want crude transformed into oil, kerosene, engine distillate and gasoline in the largest number of barrels and fastest refining times ever known. That's all these oilmen want proven to them in cold, hard reality."

Hiram looked at his desk covered with his own calculations derived from studying refining methods with TR Gimble.

"It seems that this chemist is simply learning on the job the same way I am. His post-graduate studies involve merely learning from practical men. No wonder his confidence needs boosting from lashing out at inventors rather than trying to work with them. He realizes he wasted a lot of time in school while men were hard at work in back sheds working out the real problems and complex chemistry on machines that will handle what the oil executives want."

TR grinned.

"The new port refinery's going to be a great adventure despite the scientists. The men I'll be working with don't believe a word about the exam Regis Petroleum sponsored to demonstrate my technical skills and aptitude. The scientists, led by Hamilton, scoffed at the pictures of the professors in their robes. The oilmen didn't count on what happens once these scientists leave their universities. The graduates feel themselves more practical and skilled than the men who instructed them. It was engineers who informed me that the executives at Regis finally issued an ultimatum to the resistant scientists."

"What was that?" asked Hiram.

"You better get on board working with Gimble or hit the road to other employment!"

Hiram laughed.

"You've always done better working with engineers and geologists than with chemists. Perhaps you and this company will always be more closely aligned with the men who know the earth and how to form things with iron and steel. Chemists aren't so attracted to such raw, limited physical dimensions. Men like us have to be OK with plenty of grime under the fingernails!"

TR laughed recalling Hiram's sense of humor. Then the farmboy-turned-inventor picked up the new identification card he would carry. This badge would be required for him to enter the highly secure port property to start work on the newest Regis Petroleum facility. The company's name was printed at the top of the wallet-size card. Under the company name were the words 'Employee's Temporary Identification Card.' On the line that said 'Name,' TR had written his signature with its usual large flourish. TR smiled at the line on the card that said 'Occupation.' Beside it, a clerk had been instructed to type the word 'Engineer.' The inventor with no university degree was leaving Sunday night to direct engineering on the country's largest new port refinery in the West.

CHAPTER 21

▼

Gertrude Gimble heard the front door open. She paused with the iron in mid-air. She heard the sound of her husband's firm footsteps. She counted the seconds he took to hang his coat and hat in the hall. She resumed ironing as she heard him call out.

"Hi, Mama!"

Gertie pressed the iron firmly on the large white shirt and called back.

"Oh, you can call me the old mama alright! I feel like it after darning and washing all the socks and shirts you and Ty keep tearing up!"

TR entered the large downstairs room. He surveyed the piles of fresh laundry. His eyes conveyed a twinkle, and then a solemn look.

"I'm sure a maid would be highly useful, my dear, but you know I don't like curious eyes inside this house."

Gertie set down the iron while her husband bent to hug her. He smelled lightly of oil and not much else.

"I know we can't have a maid, and I'm not complaining—well, not too much. There are still so many letters I haven't gone through. The day's ended, but my mountain of work stands tall."

TR picked up the stack of mail. He glanced quickly at the return addresses and set the papers down. He looked at his dutiful wife.

"I'm afraid it's not going to get any slower around here. My travel is going to have me gone an awful lot in the coming months."

Gertie sighed.

"More welcome news. I'll have my stationery ready to write you, as I always do."

TR beckoned toward the kitchen.

"Come sit. The rest of the ironing can wait. There'll be plenty of time to catch up on laundry when Ty and I aren't contributing to the piles of it. Nothing looks urgent in the letters that came today."

TR and Gertie sat at the large kitchen table. It was dark outside, and the spring bulbs were closed for the day.

Gertie couldn't help saying the words her husband wouldn't like to hear.

"This house is such an empty place when you're gone!"

"I know," soothed TR. "The hotel rooms I sleep in are nowhere near as comfortable as here. I miss you and the children very much."

Gertie glanced around the spacious kitchen.

"Why did we buy such a sprawling place?"

TR gazed toward the vast dining room where they rarely entertained.

"It's the right investment for our family, something entirely apart from my patents or businesses. You know how men's fortunes can change overnight given any set of wrong circumstances. This home and its land are something we can always sell if needed. Consider it our children's safety net. They need that, and so do you."

Gertie made an effort to smile.

"I know you're right."

TR studied his wife's tired face. Her hair curled in damp ringlets around her flushed cheeks. She had been working hard. He took her hand.

"I want to thank you many times over for all the work you do to keep me and the children in fine, healthy order. Our home accounts are running smoothly. I know all that's a lot of work."

Gertie smiled.

"My work at the oil company has come in handy for managing our accounts. That part of my job proceeds with ease."

TR glanced at the old picnic invitation Gertie kept in a small, brass frame.

"That picnic on July Fourth where I first met you was already 13 years ago."

Gertie remembered well.

"I couldn't have dreamed where it would lead. All I knew was you smiling, singing and roping my heart for all time."

TR laughed.

"I was some cowboy back then, wasn't I? I had no idea how to capture the attention of a woman as smart as you. The men at the refinery called you a pistol. I had no idea what you were like, other than what they said. I was working in the remote north canyon. You were always at the office downtown. The men said you were a city girl born and raised in Los Angeles. And there I was, a farm boy from the East, no more than a railroad worker and roughneck with so much grime on my hands, I thought it would never wash off."

Gertie looked at TR's large hand covering hers.

"Well, you cleaned up rather nicely, TR Gimble. I had no doubts where your future lay. I just didn't see ahead to all the complications that marrying a genius might bring!"

"We'll work through those things, Gertie," said TR gently. "That farmland we have in Riverside will be our ultimate sanctuary after all this running around is through."

Gertie smiled.

"I hope so. This city girl could be a contented farmer's wife one day—as long as you come in from the fields before midnight!"

TR laughed.

"With these old legs getting more stiff over the years, you'll be having to feed my tired bones by four p.m. and tuck me in by eight!"

Gertie looked pensive thinking how fast the years were passing. She looked up at the vibrant man and couldn't ever see him as old and frail. He was always brimming with ideas, even when he was tired. He looked tired now, even as he prepared to speak with what she knew was another grand scheme. She knew that look of contemplation as his mind rapidly calculated details. She knew that look only too well and simply waited.

"I was thinking, Gertie. There are some things I'd like to put in this house that would make your time staying here a world more entertaining for you."

Gertie stared in surprise as TR pulled two folded papers from his shirt pocket and laid his sketches before her.

"I was studying the plans for the floors of this house the other day. Ty and I can easily install for you a grand sewing room here, on the second floor, where you can keep watch over Winnie playing in the front yard. That big tree casts its shadow over that corner of the house so it would keep you warmer in the winter and cooler in the summer."

Gertie stammered.

"I'm amazed, speechless really. You and Ty would do that? Then there'd be enough room for my sister and I to sew together. We could teach Winnie, too."

TR turned over one of the sketches and drew a circle.

"Ty also showed interest in my idea to build you a darkroom here for process-ing your photos in the basement. I know how much you like taking pictures.

Then you'd never have to send out your film and wait those weeks to get your prints. You could process film as artistically as a fine photographer. Ty will take some photos in the deserts and mountains he'll visit this summer with the geologists. He says he can bring you some film that will be a thrill for you to develop. Each picture will be a surprise containing different natural landscapes."

Gertie clasped her hands.

"Oh, that would be wonderful! I very much enjoy working with photochemistry. I know I could get better at it if you'd supply me a little direction on how to best mix the chemicals!"

TR laughed.

"Consider that done, and one more thing. I know how carefully you maintain our correspondence and want to organize the articles you save from newspapers. We'll be getting even more mail at this house over time. I've depended on you as the most reliable secretary a man might ever hope to have, but I've not given you the kind of incentive you surely deserve. I have, therefore, ordered for you a petite walnut desk and matching file cabinet that we can put in the study. We will both have our own desks. It will be a fulfillment of the modern vision for how men and women will work together running businesses and organizing family affairs."

Gertie clapped her hands in delight.

"I can't wait! I never expected my own desk and filing cabinet. It will be so fine for Winnie to see her parents working together in the study. Then she'll want the same for herself. She is such a bright, little lady. I feel she'll make a splendid partner for a man of business someday. Thank you, Thomas. I hardly know what to say. You've really given this some thought. It eases the pain of knowing you'll be gone."

"Ty and I will get right on these things. Now where's my Winnie. Is she already in bed or did I hear her tiny feet tiptoeing by the stairs?"

CHAPTER 22

▼

Winifred crouched on the upper landing of the large staircase in the Gimble home. She looked sideways, startled by her brother Billy who crept up beside her. She brought her finger to her lips and whispered hoarsely.

"Get back in your room! You don't need to get in trouble again!"

Billy hesitated stubbornly. Winnie hissed at him once more. He reluctantly started to shuffle down the long hallway to his bedroom. Winnie cupped her hand and whispered.

"Tiptoe, you fool!"

Then Winnie heard her dad declare that he heard tiny feet by the stairs. She decided to redeem the moment with exuberant love. This didn't always work with Mom but never failed with Dad.

Winnie ran down the stairs clutching her favorite doll. She jumped in front of her dad with one arm reaching high. He bent down and scooped her up in his long arms. She squealed in delight.

"Papa! I missed you so!"

She planted a kiss on his cheek and threw her arms around his neck. TR laughed.

"I was only gone to the office. What are you going to do when I'm gone for weeks?"

Winnie clasped her doll to her heart.

"I will keep Mama good company! I always do. I have more doll friends than ever to help me. Billy and Mama and I are never alone. I hear you with us all the time anyway. I hear you every moment in the music!"

TR laughed and started whistling. The little girl lightened his heart.

TR knew that she and Billy were very inquisitive, always trying to listen to adult conversations. They were bursting with questions, not unlike the boy who visited his work yard from time to time.

TR started to sing with an even lighter heart, thinking of how he'd helped Joey complete his drawings. Jacob Steiner was now setting up the patent agreement and trust fund that would reward the diligent lad with some royalties. It didn't matter that it would be a brief time before other inventors patented a whole new record player whose sound exceeded the MacDermott phonograph needle. One child had received tangible proof seeing how far and wide he could go using his own mind. TR gazed at his equally intelligent daughter.

"Where's that little brother of yours?"

Winnie hugged her dad.

"He's up in his bedroom."

Billy had crept back to the top of the landing. Now he sailed down the stairs. He was standing in front of them quicker than the time it would take to fly through the wall.

TR laughed.

"You must be learning to read minds as well as books up there, Billy! You knew we wanted to see you. How are you doing son?"

Billy studied his father's face. As TR gently set Winnie on her feet, the boy answered cautiously.

"I'm doing fine, Pa."

TR's green eyes pierced Billy's. Billy decided to mumble more.

"Always good to see you, sir."

TR bowed low and shook Billy's hand.

"Always good to see you too, son."

Then TR swiftly reached out and tickled Billy's stomach. He clamped Billy in a bear hug tickling him more as the boy collapsed into giggles. TR ruffled his hair every which way. Billy then returned his hug.

The inventor realized that his own children saw and heard a lot more mystery in their home than young Joey ever witnessed at the Gimble plant. He knew their questions probably contained a lot of fear of the unknown, especially when both he and Ty were gone traveling.

As TR kissed Billy's tousled head, he wondered what answers this boy was able to extract from Gertie, Winnie and Ty, and if those answers satisfied his curiosities in the right way. TR knew that when Billy spoke, his words burst through fears he tried to conceal. TR realized that it was falling more to Gertie and Ty than to himself to give the boy daily guidance.

Trying to explain what the newspapers said about him was the most difficult thing for TR to handle with his children. It was back when Ty learned to read that he started asking his first questions about Papa's work. Luckily, TR found a way to instruct, explain and caution at the same time. The oldest Gimble boy grasped the importance of concepts TR tried to put into little boy words. Ty had adapted to all of it. He'd grown wise and knowing while, at the same time, realizing that the women at home needed a special kind of comfort.

Winnie had Gertie's full attention to answer her inquiries while learning all the things a young girl needed to absorb from her mother. TR smiled at Gertie, thankful that her skills would be transferred to the sharp mind of the little girl clutching her favorite doll. TR kissed his daughter.

"On my coming trip, I'll see if there's another companion for your dolls. I don't know who the lucky little doll will be or what she will look like. Maybe she'll be like your Dottie winking with a magic eye to tell me that she wants to come home and join the family."

"Deliciously delightful!" exclaimed Winnie. "I can't wait to meet her!"

Winnie reached in her nightgown pocket and produced a small diary.

"I have a daily journal like Mama now. I've started writing in it, see?"

TR looked down at the child's careful scrawls.

"Indeed. Your writing is going to be as fine as Mama's."

Gertie looked at TR. He saw the question in her eyes and nodded. It was time to tell Winnie and Billy something he first told Gertie years ago. TR took Winnie's hand as they walked to the couch.

"Let's talk about journals. Come on, Billy. I want you to hear this, too."

Billy looked startled. He knew he wasn't any kind of writer and was pretty sure his dad knew it, too. TR saw the boy's questioning look and smiled with understanding.

"A man's journal can be mighty important for remembering his travels. A journal can remind you of things you saw, or names and dates you don't want to forget. You might also get ideas you'll want to write down."

Billy sat on the couch and put his chin in his hands while Winnie nestled closely on the other side of her dad. TR explained.

"Your journal is a valuable record for your children to know about your life. You will also enjoy reading what you wrote many years later. Your children might ask you things such as, how did you celebrate birthdays and holidays? Did relatives stop in? Did you go to a wedding? Did you visit people or attend parties? You may want to record what you were doing when a great storm arrived or which days were the hottest of the year."

Winnie nodded vigorously.

"I've already started writing all those things about my days, Papa."

TR went on.

"There are other things that shouldn't go in your journals. It's unwise to record your fears in something as precious as this. Keep those feelings tucked somewhere out of reach in your heart, but do not tuck them inside your journal. Put anything you're worried about to bed each night, and pull the covers tightly around such things for those ideas need to go to sleep. Remember that those who love you will always come at once to assist you."

TR looked at Gertie. It was her turn to explain these things in her way. Gertie spoke gently.

"You children know I like to keep a journal. I leave it open so anyone can see it. You can read that I went to Aunt Helen's and how I took the streetcar and if Papa worked on Sunday. A few sentences describing each day will do. I don't write pages about Papa's work. All that is science and subjects you'll learn in school anyway. In your journals, just talk about your day. Papa is good to advise you not to write of fear. You do not want to give credence to worrisome thoughts. Papa, Ty and I handle all the things our family needs. You can come and tell us if something is bothering you."

Winnie looked brightly at her parents.

"I understand. I'll write of pretty Valentines and our puppies and my dolls. I'll tell about my music classes and the beautiful things we share. I surely won't give voice to fear on a page that I will write. Fears are silly to think about anyway 'cause most of them aren't true!"

Gertie laughed and looked at Billy sitting quietly beside TR.

"Do you also understand?"

Billy gazed into the blackness out the window.

"I won't be writing any journals, Ma. You don't have to worry about me. I know you and Ty and Papa take care of things. I'll try to learn what I can do that might be better than keeping a journal. I just haven't found it yet."

TR hugged his son.

"Good for you, Billy. You keep exploring. Give yourself time to find what you can do. Keeping a journal is not required. Enjoy being a boy first and foremost."

Billy looked up earnestly at his father.

"I'm trying, Dad."

After the children were tucked in with their bedroom lights turned out, TR lifted his large suitcase out of the closet. He placed the heavy trunk on the bed in the large master suite he and Gertie shared. He went downstairs to read.

Gertie flattened the freshly ironed shirts and ties she arranged in TR's suitcase. She reflected how there was no such collection of fine clothes when TR worked at the old refinery in Brea.

"He had his railroad overalls and only one white shirt. It had tiny, ragged holes on the top of the collar. I noticed those the first time he held me close."

Gertie smiled, remembering her small frame being swallowed in that giant hug, just like Billy tonight. Gertie recalled how, over the year of their courtship, the tiny holes in TR's shirt collar grew in size until the shirt was replaced. So, too, had her fears of falling for the tall, hardworking roughneck. Her fears had been replaced by amazing fortune.

Gertie thought back to the big, rugged operation at the facility in Brea. It covered an entire region with derricks and smokestacks that towered along canyons rising above the farmer's orange groves in the valley below. She could almost taste the mix of orange blossoms and oil that overwhelmed one's senses upon arriving there. Reminiscing of those days with TR earlier in the evening, and then speaking to her children about not writing frightening details in their journals, prompted the scenes that now flashed through her mind.

She toured the Brea facility soon after hiring on at the fine offices the oil company kept downtown. Gertie remembered the shabby houses at the refinery. The women who lived there complained that they could never keep oil from sticking to everything. They told her it made their children ill. They said it was an awful place to bear a child. No hospitals existed for miles in any direction. Sometimes women fainted trying to help a woman give birth in the unbearable canyon heat. Then one of the men would try and help, their grimy hands never clean enough. The mother or child or both would die not long after. Gertie shuddered. No such things were written in her journals, but that didn't mean the memories of what the refinery wives told her hadn't been etched indelibly in her mind. Gertie wondered.

"What if Jacob Steiner hadn't helped TR? Would some other man have come along to help him? Might I have ended up like one of those women married to a roughneck living in those houses?"

Gertie saw vividly in her mind the photograph of TR at Brea standing with dozens of other workers. He wore overalls, posing on the roof of a refinery building surrounded by other men. He held the perforated pipe that became his first patented invention. The promise of his brilliance was always present, but it took a man as wise as Mr. Steiner to catapult TR out of that place and past many hardships that he and Gertie might otherwise have endured.

She cringed at the thought of how easily life could have dealt her cruel circumstances. Yet here she lived at a young age in a lovely mansion where soon she would have a grand sewing room, her own photo-developing darkroom and a new desk in the large study downstairs. She smiled thinking of the hundreds of books in the vast family library that she loved reading to her children. There were music lessons for Winnie and a baby grand piano for her to practice at in the parlor. There was every opportunity that smart boys like Billy and Ty needed to set them on the path to successful lives. Nothing about her existence could be considered anything less than abundant. TR Gimble was a caring provider. And so it was fitting to teach her children that no fears or woes were ever worth setting down on paper.

As she finished arranging TR's travel clothes, Gertie recollected finding the small note that one of the roughnecks passed to TR some 13 years ago. It was given to him after TR had proposed to her and shared the news with his fellow workers. She found the note in one of TR's shirts while unpacking after their honeymoon.

The pencil sketch showed Gertie standing behind a low wall with a frown on her face and her arms fiercely drawn to her sides. TR was standing in front of the wall with his long arms draped sideways around Gertie's neck. TR had on a hat and suit and was smiling widely. Below the sketch, the cartoonist wrote, "I pity you, my poor man, when Gertie gets a hold on you!"

TR told her he laughed when he saw the note, realizing that people at the company knew Gertie had to be tough working as an accountant among oilmen. Gertie frowned remembering how the men tried every trick they could to thwart her efforts organizing meticulous books. Gertie knew she was no picnic to stand beside at times, but TR married her anyway. She felt hurt the day she found the note, but now she smiled at the memory. She knew TR had seen the toughness that would be required in the woman he would marry. She closed the lid of the large trunk and thought of her plans for spending the coming weeks without TR.

CHAPTER 23

▼

The hills and mountains around Goldenvale, Colorado lay still. They no longer reverberated with the sound of young men whooping and hollering through the town and nearby canyons. Students at the American School of Mining Geology had dragged their college president though the sticky mud in the middle of campus once more. The academic year was officially over.

Victor Atkins exhaled in relief, grateful to be wearing a fresh shirt and clean trousers. The college president gazed past the stack of papers on his desk. Outside, lush growth on aspen and sycamore trees cast shadows over college pathways. One long, thin shadow cut across the campus lawn. It was the tall smokestack from the low building housing the chemistry lab. Victor looked beyond that to the new building under construction. It was the fulfillment of his dream, an experimental fuel plant. Victor smiled. The shadow from the modern six-story building would eclipse the old chemistry lab and its smokestack.

"The future is now," thought Victor. "The work with experimental fuels is coming along great. Only one more step is needed to really make it take off. What can I do to speed up that private venture?"

He searched his mind for answers as he looked out to a Rocky Mountain blue sky filling with puffy clouds. Scrubby, windswept mountainsides rose vertically behind the campus, topped with dense clusters of pines around each apex. High atop a nearby peak, a large, white letter 'M' glared in the sun. The college symbol shone fresh with paint and the dusting of chalk administered after a rowdy climb up the mountain by a team of devoted students. Dean Atkins pondered the man-made symbol and the tower of shale rock that rose behind it.

"Our new professors have no idea how much every college symbol and ritual means to those who live, learn and teach here. And to those men developing new science, this place is downright sacred!"

The dean grinned, remembering the shocked faces of stiff-looking men in suits as he picked himself up from the students' channel of mud. He bellowed heartily as the young men slapped him on the back spraying everyone around them. The formal men had jumped back in horror. Dean Atkins chased the offenders through campus and wrestled several to the ground, pouring mud from his shoes all over their heads. The hilarity went on for several hours. Later, he explained to the new professors.

"This event is simply to blow off steam that otherwise might end up in fist fights or worse in this small town. The boys have to yell. That's all there is to it. Rest up for the summer, gentlemen. Your first year teaching here could be challenging. If you haven't yet figured out how rough a place this school can be, you'll find out soon enough!"

The polite, young professors seemed confused by the dean's admonition. The man had already resigned once, only to have school administrators and alumni ask him to return. The college supporters asserted that only he knew how to manage the kind of school this was. Victor remembered explaining to a new professor the same thing he regularly told his students.

"One has to appreciate what it takes to survive in the various countries to which our graduates are sent. Our men must conduct intricate scientific work amid the shenanigans of corrupt governments. They must endure whatever illogical rules the fuel and mining companies impose on them. And let's not forget the government officials in the U.S. that everyone from this school ultimately ends up serving in one way or another!"

The confused young professor shook his head the same as the college freshmen.

"Ah well," thought Victor, "Let them learn."

This brought to mind the faces of the men from Regis Petroleum. Victor breathed deeply.

"What an affair that Gimble test was!"

Shortly after returning to Goldenvale from the pompous event, Dean Atkins learned of the reaction from the company chemists the test was designed to placate. They scoffed at the entire exam.

Dean Atkins was eager to put to use his stipend from serving on the exam panel. He used the money as additional funding for the new experimental fuel plant at his college. Being excited to move ahead on that, he didn't engage in gossip with other the collegiate men who were upset about Gimble's high scores on the exam.

Victor was fairly certain from the start that the Regis chemists would reject Gimble's exam results. The college president, who understood students and men, knew that once graduates became competitors outside university walls, they showed little mercy toward others who had not been through the same rites of passage they had.

He remembered the professors' discussion when Dean Glander brought up the possibility of Gimble using mind tricks during the exam. Victor shook his head.

"That's just the kind of thing that makes being a professor humorous at times. People use any excuse they can dream up when things go awry!"

Professor Harrington had walked with Dean Atkins as they left the scene of Gimble's exam. Professor Harrington asked Victor his opinion.

"What do you think of Gimble channeling some kind of mystic knowledge?"

Dean Atkins had looked across the California campus and waved his hand as if it held a magician's wand.

"Mysticism can seem a plausible explanation for things we don't understand. It easily replaces logic when men are frustrated. Men have experimented with mental powers for centuries, and yet no one seems to have determined where our limits are."

Harrington commented with a wink.

"Women sure seem to take to mystical matters quite easily."

Atkins smiled.

"Those lovely creatures are perhaps closer to the truth of it all than men will ever be!"

Victor glanced down at the news article that lay atop his stack of papers. There was no mystery about what this news conveyed to him. He thought the article told everything about why Gimble had been tested by the oil company in the first place. Victor murmured.

"It's funny that the professors couldn't see this coming!"

The article's headline read, 'Regis Makes Great Refining Move.' The subtitle below the headline said, 'Chief Chemist Arrives to Work Out New Process Purchased for $1,000,000 Cash.'

The article named the Gimble refining process that Regis purchased from the inventor. The purchase was reported to be a significant step leading to the conglomerate's acquisition of oil pipelines, refineries and topping plants, as well as lands and leased oil lands owned or controlled by other oil companies. The company's president was quoted.

"Reginald Hamilton is the head chemist of Regis Petroleum and is here to look into the Gimble system."

The company president claimed that the arrival of the chemist and several big oilmen at the Hotel Clark was "quite an accident," but that "oil men are waiting with their ears to the ground for the next development."

Victor laughed.

"The Gimble deal was already bought and sealed by the time the man said that. Their head chemist was hardly there to 'look into the Gimble system' or to give his vote of approval for its purchase. It was Regis Petroleum who leaked their rumor to the press. The billions to be made from buying Gimble's process were already being counted as the rumor got leaked. That this chemist arrived amid a fray of eager businessmen simply indicates one more hurdle for Gimble beyond his staged exam. He'll have to spend much of his energy wrangling with the chemist and probably other scientists as well. He'll have his hands full trying to do that in addition to getting his process constructed and installed at major refineries. He's going to be one exhausted man!"

Atkins considered the entire matter between Regis Petroleum and TR Gimble. He turned the situation over in his mind.

"Even though Gimble will be busy, he'll be looking for his next scientific conquest. Driven men like him get bored meeting the same challenges over and over. His wrangling with the chemist will get tiresome. Regis will start patenting improvements to Gimble's process immediately. That Hamilton chemist will get himself and other scientists all riled up about gunning for their own million-dollar deals. They'll change Gimble's refining process to meet their own aims, even if it means lower quality petroleum products. Soon enough, it will be futile for other men to ever sew up a deal as rich as Gimble's attorney was able to negotiate for him. Regis attorneys will draw up all sorts of contracts making any intellectual strides their employees develop the sole property of the conglomerate. Gimble won't be motivated anymore when that happens. Nor will he waste his time trying to placate men's egos just to stay in their fold. I saw that streak in him at the exam. He'll be seeking new horizons, and so will his smart attorney. Steiner is not the kind of man who'll want to gamble the inventor's talent on a losing proposition with a powerful conglomerate. He'll be seeking new avenues for Gimble's talent, and Gimble will be searching the world for the same thing."

Victor knew that the private fuel venture he envisioned would take several years to set up. Only someone like Gimble could reduce its development time. He contemplated his strategy.

"A man like Gimble needs to lead the way for other thinkers. He'll be thoroughly convinced, after this charade with Regis, that he must work with practical men not driven to undermine his efforts."

The president of the American School of Mining Geology realized what he must do. He smoothed on his desk a fresh sheet of linen paper bearing the university seal. He dipped his fine quill pen in black ink and began to compose his letter.

"Dear Mr. Gimble, I met you at the exam and was quite impressed with what you know. I would like to come and meet with you. I have a proposal that may be of interest. I have this fascinating dark rock from Red River that burns brightly amid men of vision. I would like to share with you what we plan. No chemists will be on hand since the rock's properties are well known. Now is the time to see what it can bring in this country. There is no question of its promise among friendly men. Please allow me to schedule a time to visit with you at your earliest convenience."

Victor sealed the letter and placed the envelope under the jagged, dark rock that was shiny in a deep fiery way. The letter would not be mailed with his other university correspondence. He'd post it to the inventor's home himself.

CHAPTER 24

▼

Dean Atkins eagerly inspected his experimental fuel plant under construction at the college in Colorado. He cast a satisfied eye toward the rock crusher and tall brick retort standing inside the six-story building. Conveyor belts, grinders and large steel cogs were stored against one wall. Wood planks and thick pipes were stacked in neat rows beside a large generator. The equipment stood like soldiers awaiting the command to march forward. Victor glowed excitedly beside his assistant.

"The building looks impressive. The Simplex motor will arrive next week. There'll be plenty of heat generated in this place come winter! Soon I hope to hear from the man who'll give us specifics on the best way to configure these machines."

Two weeks later in California, Gertie sifted through a stack of mail delivered to the Gimble mansion. As she shuffled the envelopes and postcards, her disappointment grew. Nothing had come from her husband. She looked more carefully at each piece and saw a letter from the American School of Mining Geology. She noticed the seal of the president's office. She murmured to herself.

"How odd that this was sent to the house. Ty's been picking up Papa's mail at the downtown office and plant. Why wasn't this letter sent to either of those places? Is this college trying to solicit Ty's attendance? If so, why is the letter addressed to Thomas and not Tyrone? Maybe the college secretary mixed up the names."

Gertie clucked in annoyance.

"Such mistakes are becoming commonplace. How inattentive young workers are getting! The envelope is wrinkled, and the secretary didn't even seal it properly. It looks unprofessional. Such sloppiness would never have occurred under my watch at the office I managed. I truly doubt Papa knows a soul at any university. I can't imagine a college president writing to him. But I'll have to remember to tell him about this when he calls. Hopefully that will be this evening."

Two days later, TR Gimble called his wife. This was the first night in weeks he was not working until two a.m. Gertie ran to the phone.

"Hello?"

"Hello, Gertie. I haven't a lot of time to chat, but I knew you were worried not hearing from me. I'm ready to drop with exhaustion. How are you and the kids?"

"We're doing alright. Everyone's healthy. The kids miss you so. Ty is getting restless to leave for his summer assignment. He's nearly finished building the shelves in the sewing room. My new desk arrived with a big scratch across the front, but after my stringent objections, the delivery company called the furniture company, and both have promised me a new desk to replace the scratched one. The matching filing cabinet, for some reason, did not arrive with the desk. I wrote a letter inquiring about that but haven't heard anything back. I must go downtown tomorrow and rattle some cages at the furniture store until someone finds our order and makes it right!"

TR listened quietly. Gertie paused. TR heard paper rustling. Gertie continued.

"You received a letter from the American School of Mining Geology. The seal says it's from the president's office."

"Are you sure that's where it's from?"

"Why Papa, I'm hardly senile yet. I can still read a return address just fine."

"Can you read me what the letter says?"

Gertie opened the envelope and quickly scanned the letter.

"It hardly makes any sense to me. It's just as cryptic as all the other letters I've seen soliciting your involvement in unknown dreams. This is some idle, handwritten note, probably from some mad science professor. He mentions a rock but doesn't even identify it with a proper mineral name! The letter's written in the same vague manner as the things uttered by all those strange people who come to our door asking for money!"

TR summoned his last ounce of patience for the day.

"Gertie, can you please just read me what the letter says?"

Gertie read him the words written by Victor Atkins.

TR was silent. Gertie grew impatient.

"For any reason, would you want me to set up a meeting for you with this rock professor?"

"No, Gertie. His correspondence was all I needed to know. Give the letter to Ty and ask him to carry it to Hiram at the plant. Hiram will take care of arranging what I need. I'm not quite sure when I'll be back."

"Fine then, we'll just keep managing until you return."

TR paused. Then he spoke gently.

"I love you, Gertie."

The inventor's wife held back tears and buried her frustrations.

"I'm sure I feel the same," she replied tartly.

After she hung up the phone, Gertie sat at the table with the letter in front of her and her head hung down. She put her hands over her face.

"Why can I only provide prattle and chatter when he calls? We can't truly discuss anything. Everything he's doing is such a secret. We barely write a word of essence on any postcards or letters. He's too busy at the plant and office to even come home for lunch anymore. I can't even write a thing of this turmoil in my daily journals."

She rubbed her temples a while and then sat up straighter. She was getting so used to this loneliness, she didn't even think her tear ducts worked anymore. She reprimanded herself.

"Head straight, chin up and carry on. Papa sounds like he'll be meeting this professor, and then he'll be off on some new adventure. It will leave me alone again, and who knows for how long. The dean's school is in Colorado so Papa will probably head to the Midwest."

Ty sprang through the front door.

"Hi, Ma!"

Gertie looked up. Ty took one glance at his mother's face and halted.

"What's the matter?"

"Oh nothing. There's a letter here that your dad wants you to take to Hiram."

Ty picked up the Atkins letter and looked with concern at his mother.

"Did you talk to Dad tonight?"

"Just now. He's fine, but he's working very hard and feeling quite tired. He says he misses you and your sister and brother. He sends his love."

Ty hugged his mother.

"I know he misses you a lot, too, Ma."

Gertie showed no reaction. She looked up at her son.

"I thought you were out on a date. Why are you home before the end of the movie?"

Ty sat down and leaned back in the chair with his hands behind his handsome head.

"Well, Ma, some girls just don't value the gray matter between their ears very much."

Gertie looked confused.

"What does that mean?"

Ty laughed.

"You know, the human brain. I took about as much as I could take of the young lady's prattle about movie stars and fashions and gossip about her friends. I kept trying to get her to talk about anything else. She doesn't like to read a thing but assures me she listens very well. I couldn't tell because she never stopped talking!"

Gertie smiled.

"What did you do?"

"I told her I had a bad headache and that I really needed to get home."

"Ouch!" exclaimed Gertie.

Then Ty got serious. He took his mother's hand.

"Really, Ma, how am I ever supposed to find a girl as smart as you, or even as smart as Winnie? I don't know where they gather. I'm always so busy running errands or helping Hiram at the plant. To me, it's a treat just to go and see a movie where I can get things off my mind. All I want is a girl who understands that a young man can work just as hard as an older man. I want a female companion who picks up a newspaper once a week and maybe reads a book in a month's time. Is that so hard to find? Are all the smart ones at home reading at night where I won't meet a single one of them?"

Gertie looked at the boy who was so much like his father.

"Son, there are many places that smart, young women like to gather, but some of those places are in private parlors with other women or at book clubs and socials you wouldn't attend. Too many of them try to climb in social status when choosing the men they'll date. You are like your father in your independence and wouldn't like that kind of girl. I know that our not belonging to any church or social club limits your chances of meeting a lady you'd like. That's to your disadvantage more than other young men. I'm sure, however, that once you're in business school, women only to glad to meet a man like you will swarm all over you.

You'll see I'm right. I'm not saying you'll find a girl trekking around in the mountains or desert this summer, but hang on. Your patience and discretion for selecting someone intelligent and sweet will be rewarded."

Ty got up and put his arms around his mother.

"Well, you and Winnie are just going to have to put up with being my only sweethearts for now. I'm going to bed. I'll take the letter for Dad over to Hiram in the morning."

Gertie watched her son disappear up the stairs. She whispered softly.

"Thank you, Ty."

She thought again how lucky she was for all the good things in her life. Her dear children remained her greatest treasure.

CHAPTER 25

▼

Tucked deep in one of the fingers of harbors nestled inside the vast San Francisco Bay, the town of Martinez hummed busily. The new port refinery for Regis Petroleum was taking form as hundreds of eager workers tackled assignments.

TR Gimble was about as worn out as he could ever remember. Wrapping up the first phase of construction had taken all the effort he could muster. The inventor was looking forward to a much-needed break. The first months of summer promised to be brutally hot. Few men would remain to expend needless energy in the sweltering heat. As soon as late August arrived, there'd be cool fog rolling across the bay with onshore breezes to make the worksite bearable once again.

As the project's supervising engineer, TR always wore a suit. His tie, white shirt and hat were required as he worked in and around facilities under construction. Being called into meetings at every hour of the day, it was not possible for him to don overalls that would have been infinitely more comfortable. Important men arrived fresh from the city expecting the inventor to present himself the same way. As TR thought of his trip home, he recalled a conclusion he'd made early in this assignment.

"A suit is the least suitable clothing a man might wear at a construction site!"

The inventor remained faithful to his contract and spent a great deal of time in meetings, diligently outlining every step of the refinery's assembly with materials and changes needed as the weeks progressed. Working beside the outdoor crews with his engineers was where TR felt most comfortable. Seeing the rigors that workers contended with every hour showed TR the fine details on equipment and systems that had to be adapted to conditions that no one anticipated on such sandy soil.

This was rapid, large-scale construction going on at a dizzying frenzy. Worrying about torn sleeves or trousers was not something TR could be bothered with. He knew Gertie was going to faint over all the mending she would have to do when she saw all the suits and shirts he had ripped during work and then stuffed in his travel trunk at the end of each week. As TR prepared to head home, he mused about his hardworking wife.

"Maybe it's time to simply visit the local tailor, buy new clothes and save Gertie the frustration. She'll be shocked but pleased at receiving no piles of laundry from me."

When TR was finally able to secure his month-long break, he slid inside his beautiful roadster. It felt so alive, as if the machine had been waiting patiently for his big shoe to finally press down hard on the accelerator. Once again, man and roadster roared down the highway.

The open road where he was traveling home was a good place for TR to contemplate. His mind jumped at once to the professor from Colorado who had written to him about the shale. TR mused to himself.

"The rock to which the man refers in his letter can be no other. That part of the country he's from is loaded with the greatest known deposits of shale on earth."

TR tried to remember what little he knew about Victor Atkins.

"He appeared more logical than the other four deans at the Regis exam. His test questions presented the fairest delivery of any on the entire test. It was obvious he didn't just slap together questions and answers handed to him by department heads. He arranged the queries in logical groups and made sure there were no duplications in the types of questions asked."

That was about all TR knew about the man personally, other than one of the executives at Regis who had referred to 'a short, crazy professor who's always talking about shale.' The executive had tossed TR a slim, dusty book written by the dean.

"Here, no one at Regis is ever going to need this."

Most of the other Regis men had laughed in agreement. They boasted heartily.

"As long as we're around, the only fuel that will ever be used on American highways will be petroleum."

TR read the professor's book and found that the man had researched back to the sixteenth century recapping where and how shale had been used for heating and fuel to run machines in many countries. He had carefully mapped out the reasons shale must be developed as a source of American fuel. The dean had written of his visit to see Scottish shale fields and processing plants. TR had gone there also. The inventor chuckled at the ironic outcome of his own visit.

Some of the men in the Ancient Rite had urged him to follow a trail of meetings with different men who promised him copies of old documents containing alchemical secrets for doing even more with the shale rock than anyone else in the world had done. He'd been intrigued at the time, thinking that his invention possibilities would be endless for the shale rock that was known to contain an almost endless supply of minerals and oils trapped inside its hardened form.

No secret alchemical documents ever made it into TR's hands. He gave up inquiring about such things several years after his fraternal brothers had excitedly mentioned that such documents were hidden in monasteries and castles of the British Isles. TR concluded that the ancient documents likely didn't exist in any readable form, or else someone would have made the effort to copy them for a brother inventor going after them, especially one such as he who had the money to explore modern uses for the rock.

After that trip was when TR began to doubt the lore of the Ancient Rite. TR had spent a significant sum of money on their behalf. He didn't say anything about his change of attitude directly to those men, though. They were mostly a good lot and received much-needed encouragement from one another in all their endeavors. They also helped many a family in need.

TR remained friendly with the brothers but decided that he wasn't going to encourage Ty or Billy to be inducted, not even so far as into the Guild. TR came to feel that the Ancient Rite took up even more time than the Guild. The Rite was basically more complex ceremonies, grand conventions and socializing than the time men already spent at the Guild lodge downtown. All this involved activities that TR felt neither of his boys would benefit from. The men in both groups insisted that sons and nephews would be privileged and thankful to join their ranks alongside their fathers and uncles, but TR didn't feel that those men could teach his boys any more than he could.

TR didn't dwell too long on the good-intending brothers or the ancient documents that never brought him any alchemical secrets for using shale. Rather, he thought more about Dean Atkins.

"I know he has a serious interest in shale, and it sounds as if he's got commercial intentions as well. There is, however, the matter of his affiliation with a big university. I doubt this man can deliver on any business promises alongside his responsibilities managing a growing college. Just the same, some conversation and sharing of ideas will be a refreshing break from my focus on petroleum right now. A visit with the dean to see what he intends to explore will probably do my inventor's soul some good!"

After rounding a curve in the highway, he pressed the accelerator further toward the roadster's floorboards.

"I can't wait to see what Gertie and Winnie have cooked up for dinner. I'm starving!"

CHAPTER 26

▼

Bees circled the tall, green, thorny shoots growing over the work yard fence as the Gimble experimental plant buzzed with activity. Inside the office, Hiram read the letter Ty handed him. Hiram looked up quickly, his eyes excited. His curly mass of hair that usually toppled over his brow seemed to stand on end. Moving quickly to the office window, Hiram peered across the busy work yard toward a distant machine not surrounded by workers. He started humming and tapping the stationery.

Ty caught on.

"It's about that rock and the report you had sitting on your desk, isn't it?"

Hiram nodded. He turned to Ty decisively.

"I know your dad will want to set up a meeting with the professor who wrote this letter. We'll schedule a day as soon as he's back and rested from his trip."

Ty looked disappointed.

"That may be weeks out. I'll already be gone for the summer. I like being here when something big and new is happening."

Hiram folded the letter and grinned.

"Oh, I'm sure you'll get the lowdown if anything comes of this."

Hiram hurriedly stepped outside, hailing a group of men in the yard.

Late in the afternoon, Ty saw Hiram still hard at work in the yard. The inventor's assistant was covered from head to toe with oil and grime. He and the men were intently discussing additions they wanted to make to the processing machine at the rear of the plant

The machine on which they focused their attention processed the rock known as shale. Golden yellow at times, there were also samples of the dark, fiery kind in the batches the machine crushed and heated. Rail shipments of the rock arrived from Red River in the Midwest every two months. The rock was dense and heavy, and the men at the rail yard didn't like unloading it. The rock shattered easily and left dust that was different from the coal they were used to working with. The shale dust could not be swept off the ramps and boxcars as easily as coal dust.

Hiram had designed a covered chute suited to the way the rock might unload best from the rail car. Men from the Gimble plant went down to the rail yard to help when the boxcar arrived. Hiram always came back covered in dust, as he was this afternoon. He and the men kept making small improvements to deal with the rock's sticky particles and the small, broken fragments that Hiram called tailings.

The machine at the plant that processed this rock had a pile of tailings beside it that accumulated each month. A tarp was used to cover the pile until it could be trucked away. The machine that processed the shale had not been a high priority project. It was one of the experiments that kept some of the men busy several hours a week. Ty thought of the professor's letter and Hiram's excitement. He observed correctly, "It might be getting time for those men's lighter duties to expand to full-time endeavors." Ty Gimble could sense change coming.

The hugs and kisses and home cooking TR received upon his return brought the color back to his cheeks and some meat back onto his tall frame. Gertie was complimentary about his fine, new business clothes.

"What fine apparel! Where did the clothes you left home with disappear to?"

TR laughed.

"My dear, attorneys could well use my filthy, torn clothes for exhibits in divorce court. I wasn't about to let you see them. It won't be necessary for you to be burdened with that much laundry or mending. My damaged clothes will become no cause of conflict between us!"

TR's good humor returned in rare form. The entire household brightened with TR whistling and singing along with Winnie's piano music in the evenings. TR took his family for a thrilling drive on the winding highway to Larwin Valley and down to the beach for strolls on the pier and picnics on the sand.

Despite the exuberance in the house over his father's return, Billy had never felt so isolated in his life. He tried to grin and act happy with the others, but something gnawed at his gut. He couldn't figure out what it was. He didn't feel he had a place that fit just right for him in this family, not the same as Ty or Winnie or his mom. His impatient mind groaned.

"No one seems to want to share special secrets with me. Everyone goes off in pairs to giggle and share serious talk. Maybe I'll have a separate place in this family forever. Maybe I can fight in a war someplace where I can be a hero."

The boy had seen the clipping his mother had placed on her new desk. It was an advertisement for a military academy in San Diego.

"That must be for me. Ty sure isn't headed there! I wonder if Dad knows about this. I don't want to go away, but maybe they don't want me here. Dang, I try to remember my chores. I try to finish all my homework. But Mom gets really mad at me every day. She nags me to eat. She worries like crazy when I'm gone. I don't think she's told Dad about everything I do that makes her mad. Maybe she's the only one who wants to get rid of me. Ty doesn't say anything when she complains about all the dirt on my clothes. She thinks I've been fighting. She checks my face and chest to see if I've been hit, but I can hardly get hit under Mrs. Watson's parlor! If I have to put up with Mom's unhappiness every day, maybe that's just my job right now."

Ty was getting excited about his summer trip. TR warned him how hot it would be in the California and Nevada deserts where Ty would be traveling.

"Son, you'll be hiking and working mostly in the early morning hours, but you'll need more than one canteen hiking back to camp at midday when the desert heat shows no mercy."

TR drove Ty downtown to visit the Army surplus store. The handsome young man was outfitted with the most rugged desert gear available in the place. TR advised him that the desert portions of the geological survey would be much worse than the work planned in the cool mountains.

"After you see how much you sweat out there, you will not even consider bringing your stinking clothes into Mom's house when you return."

Gertie and Winnie collapsed in giggles when Ty strutted in the house outfitted like a safari hunter. Ty bowed to them as he declared, "This'll be the first and only time you'll see these fine threads. I'm taking my cue from Dad and will not bring you back these clothes to launder and mend!"

Ty looked at his mother.

"But I will want my city shirts and trousers fresh and clean when I return. I'll be a madman in need of a movie date!"

Gertie giggled.

"All the clothes you'll need for your date will be ready and waiting upon your return."

The night before he left with the geologists, Ty decided to take his two family sweethearts and little brother to the movies. His dad was working late with Hiram on the machine at the rear of the plant. They had made the improvements that now required more shipments of the dusty shale. But Ty wasn't going to be in on that machine's experiments anytime soon.

He looked at the downtown movie listings and decided that one of the films starring Buck Williams would be a better movie to see than a romance story where the girls might start crying. Ty knew that his sensitive little brother Billy would hate it if the girls started crying. He knew he would, too. Ty was more in the mood for cowboys and sassy heroes, not any females weeping before he departed.

CHAPTER 27

▼

Ty, Gertie, Winnie and Billy stood in line at the downtown movie theater. The evening was balmy, the city lights sparkling, and people in line to buy tickets were cheerful and chatty. As Gertie and Winnie exchanged remarks about new fashions and shoes the young ladies were wearing, Ty stood quietly with his hand on Billy's shoulder. They listened to Gertie's and Winnie's comments and looked at the people in line.

Ty spotted a group of girls standing several yards away. They were talking to one another and waiting for one more of their party to arrive.

Twyla, Julie, Nona and Susan were engaged in a discussion that spilled over from Amy Watson's parlor. Julie spoke softly.

"I'm becoming more and more interested in seeing if I can study to become a petroleum engineer."

Susan glanced at her friend.

"What a noble goal. I'd like to see you try. I wouldn't ever want to dash any of your hopes, Jules, but I do think you ought to take note of something I heard recently."

"What's that?"

"One of the ladies I work with told me about a female physicist. She escaped from Hungary and received asylum in the U.S. The lady physicist was fortunate enough to land a job at Regis Petroleum."

Julie's eyes widened.

"Really?"

Susan went on authoritatively.

"Yes, that's the good part of the story. In the five years that the lady has been in the States, she's worked there. The scientists know she's a very smart woman, but yet her job to this day is as secretary to a group of them."

Julie remained hopeful.

"So what does she do? Does she get to assist their research experiments?"

Susan shook her head.

"Hardly. I heard that she is frustrated and yet very thankful to have escaped from her homeland with her life. She was too outspoken for government officials in her country to tolerate. She heard that certain officials were going to have her arrested. A friend told her that the officials intended to transport her to a labor camp far away from the city for the rest of her life. The lady physicist came here with only the clothes on her back and one small suitcase. She couldn't even take her documents of family identity because she didn't want to endanger those left behind. She had to change her name. She certainly could not bring her university diploma or any of the letters from her professors attesting to her research studies with them. Unfortunately, even with her talent and past accomplishments, she is not likely to ever become a Madame Curie in the U.S. Her most notable achievement at the company has been to organize the mess created by the scientists' frantic efforts to keep up with all the research that the oil company demands be done so rapidly. Her innovation has been to put color labels on all the folders that identify which categories of science and chemistry the men are working on. Apparently, these color-labeled folders tripled the productivity of all the scientists and managers at the company. The company gave her a certificate of commendation for her accomplishment, but not one cent of any raise in pay."

Julie took a deep breath.

"Thank you for letting me know. Really, Susan, I need to learn about such things. How can I ever overcome these kinds of obstacles if I don't know of them ahead of time?"

Susan put her arm around Julie's shoulder.

"You're right, Jules. I know you can attend university, but you will have to keep your eyes and ears open from the moment you start any associations with the men in your field. It may take years to find the right company that will not hold you back from doing scientific studies with the men."

"I know. Finding the right employer will be a larger job than my college studies will ever be!"

Billy thought he recognized the voice of one of the women. He nudged Ty.

"I think those may be some of those ladies I told you about, the ones who meet in Mrs. Watson's parlor."

Ty smiled down at Billy.

"You've got excellent ears, kid. Now you have me interested, too. I thought I overheard one of them mention the name of the company Dad is building the refinery for right now."

Billy grinned.

"Ah, that was nothing."

He was happy to be sharing a personal confidence with his brother, apart from everyone else. He was even happier to know that what the ladies in the group spoke of did not concern the Gimble family. He whispered to Ty.

"They're just talking about some secretary they know. They talk about other ladies and what happens in their jobs all the time."

Ty nodded and patted his contented, informed little brother on the shoulder.

Winnie tugged at Ty's jacket.

"Look at that pretty girl walking up!"

Ty looked over toward the group of girls he and Billy had been whispering about. Across the sidewalk floated a delicious feminine form. She moved toward her friends in graceful, light steps. She seemed to flow amid beams of light that shone as brilliantly as the sun to Ty. All time came to halt.

The young woman gliding toward the ladies wore a pink organdy skirt that danced in harmony with every twinkling light and fragrant flower blooming in the city that night. Her matching knit sweater clung loosely to her upper body with its folds sweeping gently around her hips. The lucky garment, Ty realized, held as close company with her curves as he was fast becoming anxious to cling.

Her matching pink shoes had heels that were not too high, offering perfect symmetry to compliment her dainty feet. Her stockings had tiny roses embroidered at each ankle. Ty couldn't keep from staring as he absorbed every detail about this dazzling, young woman.

One of her delicate hands with sugar-pink painted nails clutched a small, pink handbag. Ty felt that his heart had already hopped into her handbag. He felt his soul anxiously waiting between the compact powder case and barrel of the lipstick, competing for the chance that she might reach in and need him, too!

She wore pink pearls that rested right at the point Ty ached to softly tickle on her neck. Her matching pink pearl earrings were attached to her lobes right at the point Ty wanted to whisper compliments of her loveliness in her ear.

The young lady's makeup was subdued with not too much color around her crystal blue eyes that shone brightly. Her pleasant mouth smiled with perfect pink arches that matched her outfit and highlighted the roses in her cheeks.

Ty stood mesmerized, wishing for the chance that even one of those blushing square inches of soft skin might be turned his way for the chance to deliver only one tender kiss upon its surface.

The stunning sweep of emotion Ty felt reminded him of his father's words.

"There will enter one woman into your life, son, who eclipses all the others."

This was the Big Eclipse his father had warned him about, and it was happening right at a time he was standing in a movie ticket line, looking as paternal as any other father holding close his son. Circumstances couldn't be worse with the sharp eyes of his mother scanning all persons in the line and Winnie already having seen this girl first!

Ty never had to try so hard to wipe sheer worship off his face, but Winnie had seen it in his eyes. She whispered pertly.

"That's OK, Ty. The girl is so pretty. Why don't you go see if she's a nice girl like you and Mama talked about, you know, one who actually reads a book?"

Gertie overheard and muffled a giggle as she tried to admonish her daughter.

"Oh, Winnie, a man's business about who he decides to meet is entirely his own!"

By now, the young girl in pink had met up with her friends.

"Oh, Kate!" exclaimed Twyla. "I love your whole outfit. You know how I adore pink. You must tell me where you got everything!"

The girl named Kate laughed lightly.

"Of course I will share my shopping secrets. I always do, don't I?

Kate in pink warmly said hello and hugged her friends. Then she giggled with a sly wink.

"Katy did as Katy does, you know."

Her friends gathered around. Susan clutched Kate's arm.

"What happened, Kate? Did you get the chance to audition?"

"Not yet. I won't know for a few more weeks. They told me to go home and try to lose ten pounds because that's how much the camera adds to your weight. I can't imagine fasting any more than I have been."

Nona looked at Kate.

"I wouldn't try to lose the weight! We all know that a man's perception of a woman's face and figure is many times stronger than any camera lens! What you have simply blinds men, Kate!"

As the girls laughed, Ty Gimble stumbled blindly toward the ticket counter.

"Ouch!" cried Billy and Winnie in unison.

Somehow Ty had stepped on one foot of each child trying to step forward. His head appeared straight, but his eyes were not. If it were possible for a man's eyes to be swirling in other directions than where they were pointed, Ty's brain had made this happen. Winnie cried out.

"Your feet are getting as big as Dad's!"

Gertie chuckled. Ty blushed.

"Gosh, I'm sorry kiddies. Let's get our tickets and go see Buck Williams shoot up the silver screen."

Ty could have cared less if the cowboy hero drowned in a bucket of pig slop or died with his beloved horse galloping over a cliff. The girls and Billy enjoyed the movie immensely while Ty sat remembering his father's words.

"This woman you will meet will have a blinding effect. You will not be able to put her out of your mind. Until she declares that you are unsuitable to be her husband, you will pursue her endlessly. But for all the blindness that she delivered to your eyes upon first meeting, she will also deliver the means for you to attain the magic eye. Only then will your vision of all things be complete and clear enough for you to see beyond the sun."

At the time, Ty had wondered what his father meant. He'd sat beside many a woman on countless dates trying to see if any of the fragrant creatures blinded him more than the one who came before. All he could hear was their idle conversation, and so he had decided that some lady at least as literate and insightful as his mother was going to be the one to capture his heart as his mother had once captured his dad's.

Ty had seen a photo booth picture of his mother when she was seventeen. She laughed gaily at the camera and had both arms lifted with her hands tucked together behind her head. Although she wore a starched, pleated shirt with a high, ruffled collar, it was obvious that her laughter and wit burst through the constricting shirt.

This is what his father had seen in the woman he courted and married before Ty was born. This was the essence of the woman who now sat dutifully, and often mournfully, awaiting her husband's return from his long trips. But this woman also managed all the Gimble household affairs. She could be counted on to tirelessly attend to every detail, whether his father called needing $10,000 wired to him the next day or Winnie had a toothache that had to be treated quickly before severe infection threatened her young life. Such depths of a female creature were hard to assess on only a movie date. Ty had wondered why any man would rely on the blinding effect of a lady to guide him in the right direction anyway.

His father had mentioned one more thing that came to Ty's mind now.

"When you can see farther into other realms of awareness than you ordinarily see, that is what's called attaining the Magic Eye."

CHAPTER 28

▼

As he sat in the darkened theater, Ty blocked out the movie and reflected. Attaining the magic eye remained an intriguing concept. He still wasn't sure he grasped it. Each time Ty wondered aloud with new questions, his dad explained a little more.

"The leaders of Ancient Rite lodges might have the men focus their attention to see if all within their visual range can be broken into squares. Now that may only matter if you can then draft up what you see and have it make better sense than what anyone else has ever drawn. The leaders might also have the men focus their minds to see all things in view as swirling circles of color and light. Again, that may only matter if you can paint what you see."

Ty tried this with his own eyes while his father described the exercises. He could make things blurry but not into squares or swirls.

"Isn't that altered way of seeing what artists do naturally anyway? I see curious images sometimes if I have a fever or bad headache, but I can't deliberately make it happen."

His father nodded.

"Precisely. Few people are born with the natural ability to look around them and see patterns of form, line, color and light as distinct, separate and vivid. Groups of men, such as the Ancient Rite, were formed centuries ago to assist ordinary men who showed some talent working with numbers, words or crafts to see different aspects of the world around them with more than the eye could ordinarily see."

Ty didn't understand.

"What's the point?"

"The point is to expand a person's awareness. The more that someone can see into and around things, the more they can absorb and learn. They can also communicate in hidden ways with others who can see these things that ordinary men cannot. You have to practice expanding your mind if seeing into other dimensions doesn't come naturally to you. When you start to see farther into other realms, you can grow more than ever before."

Ty contemplated.

"Is there something in particular you're aiming for with these skills?

His father smiled.

"The point you're aiming for is to combine all highest forms of awareness. The Magic Eye opens your mind's portal. Then you can achieve something the men of the Ancient Rite call the Great Work. It's a mental and physical ascension of sorts while still remaining right here on earth."

Ty thought of stories he had heard.

"Would that be like men who smoke opium or chew cocoa leaves?"

TR shook his head.

"Men have used leaves, seeds and flowers for centuries in different ways to make their brains attain different dimensions. It's true such things will help them to see, feel or do what they cannot ordinarily. Sacred shamans in many cultures govern the use of these strong chemicals. These practices in other countries are similar to the medicine men of American Indians who sometimes smoke peyote for their visions. Son, I don't recommend you experiment with those things. You and I were not raised to know of the dangers of those chemicals, and I doubt our bodies are physically equipped to handle such things. I hear that there are many risks where a man's heart might stop beating and kill him swiftly, or he may wind up helpless and addicted to what he once thought would only lift him higher."

Ty wondered at all the things his father must have seen in his travels. He sounded very sure about avoiding such experiments. Ty had to know more.

"If the chemicals for your mind are as powerful as the chemicals we experiment with in your work yard, does the Ancient Rite teach anything else for men to attain the Great Work?"

TR slowly explained.

"The combination is simple and yet as complex as a man might ever know. It involves coming together so mightily with a woman that the pure sense of lifting up to the heavens with the explosion of stars all around happens at precisely the same instant for both man and woman."

Ty couldn't imagine what that might be like.

"Is it a kind of overwhelming of the senses neither of you ever felt before?"

"Yes. You will never be the same vibration of consciousness again. We are, after all, tiny sparks of powerful electricity living within bodies that are made up of bits of stardust matter. We shine here on earth for only a brief instant in our lives. Upon our souls are etched every experience we have ever encountered or made happen. To connect with all the other stars and threads of life while still living on this soil is the greatest thing a man or woman can achieve. That is why the Ancient Rite calls it the Great Work. I agree with their common desire to illuminate what it is to feel that kind of connection to all other life. It may be more difficult to achieve on one's own rather than coming together in song and prayer that lifts an entire group higher in one gathering, such as at a church or lodge or temple. This is why so many people like attending group assemblies. I'd like our family to learn the way of each individual seeking and knowing their own connection to all life in their own way. You may want to learn these things in the same manner that I have, and then again not. Your quest and seeking, whether it be through a church, the Ancient Rite, your marriage, living alone or joining the Guild, will be up to each of you children entirely."

Ty had one more question.

"And you, Dad, have you ever ascended in that way you described?"

TR smiled.

"Sure, son, but don't fool yourself that the quest for this experience with a woman is the only way to ascend. It is very important indeed, but a single-minded quest for one woman to unlock your journey could become your opium or peyote. You could ruin your life with as many dangers that await you in that quest as in any other. The balance to be achieved in life means going after intelligent ascension in science, harmony in family life, and the brightest enthusiasm you can share with thinking men and women with whom you will develop deliberate visions. These things are needed for you to feel entirely whole. The men of the Ancient Rite spend a great deal of time indoctrinating young men into these ideas. I have given you a summary that will save you a great deal of time trying to fit into their ranks. Maybe it will help Billy, too. You can pass this onto him when the time is right should I be gone traveling."

At that moment, Ty could feel Billy wriggling next to him in the theater. With all that lay ahead for TR Gimble, the inventor's eldest son was certain that the challenge of trying to explain their dad's unique philosophy would fall to him.

CHAPTER 29

▼

Ty looked down at Billy. The boy leaned forward gripping the front of the chair's armrests. His face glowed with vicarious delight. Buck Williams' wild ride along the edge of a sheer cliff had swept the lad into the movie. Ty thought the cliff path and mountain range beyond resembled a place in Larwin Valley to which their dad had driven them. Ty couldn't help but think of all the wild experiences his father must have known and could be acquiring even now as his family sat watching the movie. Ty realized that he'd never have the same kind of experiences to share with Billy if he didn't pursue his own heart as avidly as his father.

There were many trials Ty knew he'd have to overcome to be able to help Billy decide a path in life anywhere near the kind of accomplished life their dad was living. In some ways, the pressure on Ty was immense. He knew he had to serve his family, and yet somewhere among his responsibilities, he had to grow wings and carve out the time and opportunity to fly off on adventures of his own choosing.

His most pressing trial right now was trying to find a way to duck out from the theater where he might be able to intercept the young lady in pink. Ty had to know if she was the one who might be his partner in complete ascension. The possibilities sure seemed promising upon first sight of her!

Ty made his excuse to visit the men's room and slipped past the knees of the couple seated at the end of the row. One thing he knew was that women who cared about looking good after a movie often freshened up in the ladies' lounge before the film ended.

This evening was warm, and the crowded theater had gotten stuffy during the film. Ty headed up the dark aisle into the brightly lit theater lounge. If this girl in pink were an aspiring actress, she'd want to reapply powder to her shiny forehead, nose and chin. Someone banking on her good looks would care about how she appeared to people in a theater lobby.

Right on target, Kate exited the ladies' room looking lovely. She was walking with her friend, who paused and looked at Ty.

Twyla noticed Ty's attentive stare. She murmured quietly.

"He looks familiar, but I never met him. He certainly is tall!"

She saw Kate's head pop up from closing her handbag. Then she heard Kate gasp. Kate's eyes were locked with the young man's. Twyla knew the sheer power of attraction when she felt it, and this time, the man's attraction was not directed toward her. She kept her voice discreet.

"Kate, I'll go pick up the movie's conclusion and be sure to note the production manager names in the credits. It's apparent this man wants to meet you."

As Twyla hurried off, Kate stood gazing at Ty. He walked up to her slowly.

"Hi, my name is Ty. I saw you when I was standing in line for tickets."

Kate smiled and recovered smoothly. This was not an uncommon approach she received from married men. Ty's hands were resting casually in his pockets, usually a sign of a married man attempting to hide his wedding ring.

"Oh, yes, I saw you standing with your little son. Was that your mother and daughter with you, too?"

Ty laughed.

"The boy is my little brother. The ladies are my sister and mother. My dad had to work late this evening."

Kate studied his eyes. They did not appear to be those of a man attempting deceit. She smiled with relief.

"My name is Kate. Nice to meet you."

Ty struggled to appear casual. He maintained an even tone.

"I overheard you saying that you were auditioning for something."

"You have good ears. I'm hoping to become an actress."

Remembering his own brief conversations with movie studio men, Ty's memory cinched his next line.

"Have you read any good scripts lately?"

"Not really. I mostly read Shakespeare and the classics. I'm trying to earn the money for some acting lessons. I have my eye on an academy I want to attend, but I must save more money to be able to pay for it."

"What kind of work do you do to earn money while you and your agent are waiting for auditions? Are you a waitress somewhere?"

Kate laughed.

"Oh, no. My mother won't allow any of her daughters to work in any establishment that serves food. That's her rule. I work part-time at a real estate company. I enjoy learning all I can about land and the steps it takes to buy and sell it. I want to use my earnings as an actress to purchase property. Land is the only thing that lasts. Nothing I wear in any color will hide the fact that I will age someday. Then studios will no longer want to put my face on any silver screen. I want to own some real estate by the time I'm approaching middle age. Hopefully, I will own land someplace where men want to put water lines, highways or oil refineries. That way, I'll be assured of selling at a profit no matter what the rest of the economy does!"

Kate took a breath and waited. This approach saved her a lot of time. Her honesty typically sent men hurrying off in search of a woman with less complicated aims. This young man did not budge. He planted his feet apart and grinned the widest, white smile she'd ever seen from a man not starring in movies—and certainly not from any man after recounting such forthright ambitions.

Ty looked at her chin, uplifted high and set firmly after her words.

"That's some pretty smart thinking. It sounds like you've got your aims figured out."

Ty felt lofty as an appreciative look burst uncontrollably across his face. He could not disguise the hope he felt. Kate saw his eyes simmering with interest. It was her turn.

"What do you do?"

"I work for my father and will attend business school next year. My dad's a busy fellow. He works a lot of nights and travels a great deal."

Then Ty looked awkward for a second as he looked straight into Kate's crystal blue eyes. He spoke softly.

"I hope to do great work like him someday."

Kate stared back at Ty, captivated by the young man's confident tone and deep sincerity. Then Ty continued amiably.

"Right now, I'm getting ready to leave for some work in the mountains and deserts in California and Nevada. I leave tomorrow, but I'd really like to have your number so I can call you when I get back."

"When will that be?"

"It looks like sometime two months out. I know you're probably very busy with all the work you're pursuing," and then he added with a grin, "as well as with men pursuing you. But if there's a spare moment you might have and some space left on your dance card, I'd like to call you when I return."

Kate was surprised that her initial impression had been so wrong about the man and his son. She struggled to contain her excitement. This young man was not dashing off to see the world or serve in the military like so many handsome men she'd met before. He would only be gone for two months and then hopefully back in the city to stay. She'd met no man as engaging as this. She smiled up at Ty and stepped closer.

"Do you have a card or two? I will carry yours, and I will write my number on one of the cards for you to carry. I want a dance card with only your name on it."

Ty blushed and suppressed his strong desire to pull Kate into his arms that instant. His long arm instead fumbled its way into his vest pocket where he luckily found two of his father's cards.

"I'll have my own cards printed after I graduate from business school. That's my dad's rule."

While Ty wrote Kate's number on the back of one of the cards, Twyla held back Kate's eager girlfriends in the distance. They had abandoned the movie's conclusion and were now clustered behind Twyla, peeking over each of her shoulders from inside the darkened theater to see the handsome, young man talking with Kate in the lobby.

After writing Kate's number on the first card, Ty handed Kate the second card. As his fingertips touched her palm, they both registered shock at the electricity that passed between them. If it were possible for a woman's eyes to be swirling in other directions than where they were pointed, Kate felt her brain making this happen. She instantly lowered her eyes in embarrassment and lifted them only briefly when Ty said his good-bye with a wide smile.

Something exciting had happened. A charge had ignited. There was no other way to conclude their exchange except by establishing denial nearly the instant after it happened. Ty was leaving town the next morning, and each knew that the passage of time brought many things to interfere with young lives.

Kate's girlfriends noted Ty writing down Kate's number. They excitedly watched the business cards change hands and saw the stunned look that the young woman in pink exchanged with the tall, dark-haired man.

As Ty started striding to return to his seat inside the theater, Kate's girlfriends ducked back inside. They hurriedly bounced into empty chairs in the back row and hid their faces under cover of darkness. After the young man rejoined his family further down the theater aisle, the girls nearly collided into one another clamoring back to where Kate stood in the lobby with a dazed smile.

Susan grabbed Kate's arm.

"Who is he?"

Kate didn't move but spoke quietly.

"I have no idea other than his name is Ty. He's not married and he's not going off to the army."

"His business card," demanded Nona. "You slid it into your handbag without looking. Open your purse and retrieve it. Let's see what it says!"

Kate handed her purse to Twyla.

"Here, you find it. I'm numb. I can't even see straight."

Twyla grabbed the pink purse and dug inside. She pulled out the card.

"Oh no! This can't be right. The man must have given you the wrong card or one he found on the street. Kate, that guy is not TR Gimble!"

Nona took the card.

"Of course he's not, but he looks a little like him and he's tall like him."

Kate looked at her friends.

"He is Ty. He said he works for his father. That's his father's business card."

Julie was beside herself.

"Oh heavens! He's TR Gimble's son!"

Twyla looked at Kate who was swiftly turning pale.

"Get some water, Jules! I think our dear friend is going to swoon with infatuation!"

Ty returned to his seat beside his family.

Winnie tugged at his sleeve.

"You missed the ending!"

Ty kissed his little sister's hair.

"I was actually watching the beginning."

Billy glanced over at Ty.

"Did you see that lady in pink that you liked?"

Ty winked.

"In the men's room, Billy?"

"No, Ty, in the lobby. You look all excited about something."

Ty put his arm around Billy's shoulder.

"My man, you will go through events down the road in your life that will show you some things Dad and I simply can't explain right now."

Billy's eyes narrowed.

"You're going to call her, aren't you?"

Ty leaned to Billy's ear.

"Now what good would that do with me out of town the rest of summer?"

Billy said nothing more. He didn't move. His closest confidant and pal out of anyone in the family would be gone for weeks. When Ty returned, he would likely be caught up courting the lady in pink. Billy felt his stomach turn into a disappointed knot as the movie's credits rolled.

"Oh gee," thought Billy, "what a great time for my stomach to be upset! Unless I knock over people in the aisles, I'm stuck here for ten more minutes!"

As Billy's stomach turned further upside down, he realized he had a critical decision to make. His mom would take him home in a jiffy with no ice cream treat for dessert if he passed one iota of gas in the crowded theater. The boy measured his options.

"Maybe I can burp. That only gets me a whack to the head."

He swallowed hard, covered his mouth and breathed a long, relieving belch. Winnie and Gertie looked over at him and glared. Gertie swiftly delivered the sharp whap to the side of his head that Billy knew was coming.

"Really sorry, Ma," he muttered.

Ty didn't hear a thing. He stood gazing toward the lobby thinking of Kate.

CHAPTER 30

▼

TR Gimble handed his son the last of his travel bags from the roadster's trunk. The silver passenger train stood steaming on the tracks as people exchanged farewells at the Los Angeles train station.

"Stay aware out there, son," advised TR. "If animals are scampering away from someplace in the wild, you follow, too. Don't go in any direction they're running from in droves! I'm sure the geologists will take good care of you. Learn all you can from them."

Ty grinned.

"You know I will, Dad. Thanks for everything."

They shared a quick hug. Ty waved once more as the porter took his bags to the luggage car. Watching his dad speed away from the station, Ty thought how good it felt to be leaving on an adventure of his own. Assisting geologists conducting new surveys for Regis Petroleum sounded like a quality assignment. He'd been proud to tell Kate last night after meeting her that this is what he was doing. Ty settled back and wondered about the smart, attractive young lady as the train sped down the tracks.

When TR pulled up to his experimental plant, Victor Atkins stood chatting and laughing with Hiram. The dean called out above the roadster's growl.

"Beautiful wheels! You modified the engine, didn't you?"

TR nodded. He shook the professor's hand.

"Good trip?"

"Fine as any."

The three men walked inside the office.

Hiram was dressed in his fine gentleman's clothes, but he had no need to play the role of comedian today. He had read the professor's book and report before the man arrived. The inventor's assistant simply had on hand the machine specifications and shale quantities if Dean Atkins wanted to see them.

The academic visitor appeared fully at ease with every workman in the yard. He admired the complex pipes connecting the machines and rapidly took in all aspects of Gimble's operation.

TR was surprised to learn how many successful investment endeavors the professor had been involved with. He also learned about the new laboratory Victor was building at the American School of Mining Geology. The professor explained.

"The lab's research will focus on shale and other fuel-producing substances. We're delving into work involving a vehicle gasoline that can be made from shale."

Victor pointed to the pile of rock tailings beside the Gimble shale processor.

"I assume you normally accumulate a small mountain of that material."

Hiram nodded. The professor continued.

"There are other shale products that researchers are testing as well. They're making use of the tailings and rock with less concentrations of shale. There's a physician from the East who developed medicinal oils from shale. And here's a sample vial from a German chemist who's extracted from the rock certain powders that are isolated to produce unique colors of high-quality fabric dyes."

Hiram grew excited.

"I hadn't heard of that. My family men are all merchants in the clothing business. Let me give you the name of my uncle who's head of the company. His designers are always looking for new dyes."

Victor slapped Hiram on the back.

"Excellent! Write it down now so I don't leave without an important participant in the future of shale!"

Victor grew more enthused as he admired the machine in the rear of the yard.

"This looks like the rock from Red River in your grinders. You have chutes in six diameters. What method are you testing?"

TR explained.

"I tested many samples that I located in my travels. The properties of the Red River shale showed the most promise. The distribution of heat is the trickiest thing to achieve between different types and sizes of shale. You can fire up the retort fast and hot if you carefully mix the rock. A maximum number of particles must trap the heat for oil to be refined as quickly as possible. We're aiming for the cleanest delivery of fuel at the least expense, but if you've tested this material, you know it's easier said than done. We have a ton of Red River shale shipped in every two months. The stuff's messy, but Hiram and the men have developed methods to keep the dust and tailings contained during transport and processing. The chutes pour different size rock into sections for our test mixtures."

Victor gazed at the complex machine.

"Gasoline products distilled from shale are mainly what I came to talk to you about. It was obvious to me in your answers on the Regis exam that you knew more about these methods than any other researchers I've met."

TR grinned.

"You placed those questions on the exam to see what I knew, didn't you?"

"I did," admitted Victor. "I know of several hundred men developing shale oil refining patents. We already know that petroleum will be depleted in about 100 years and that there's more shale in the U.S. than any place on earth. I don't believe we should focus solely on petrol. Even though there seems to be plenty of oil in the ground now, there'll come a day when America's shale resources will have to be tapped. It may be at a time when our country is so dependent on gasoline that we cannot switch immediately to steam and other powered machines. We'll have to transition past dwindling oil resources with some type of shale gasoline similar to petroleum. This is why government scientists have been exploring shale as eagerly as private researchers like you. You've read of some of the early test refineries the government has built for refining shale in Colorado, haven't you?"

TR looked thoughtful.

"I've seen photographs. Their refineries look pretty rickety to me. They erect one rock crusher and a single smokestack. They'll never refine profitably at that scale. My experiments at this plant have shown the need for specially processed, high-durability steel to be used in any such refinery. I acquired a metals company in San Francisco after working for five years with researchers at the finest metals company in LA. Brick retorts are adequate for refining petroleum but do not serve shale processing very well. We need to work with heat held steadily at 800 degrees Fahrenheit or higher for production to make good money. Specialty steel is the key."

Victor looked impressed.

"You know what it takes to build proper shale oil refining. I know you're extremely busy, but I wanted to let you know that there's a group of men getting together to try and build the best shale oil processing plant in the country. It will be located right out there in Red River. One of the men is working with the county people and tribes right now to secure a site loaded with quality shale. This is a long-term vision for a substantial operation. We've spotted a place that provides the best conditions for a refinery. What we need is someone to draw up the plans. Are you interested?"

TR thought a moment before replying.

"This Gimble contraption processing shale here is one eighth the size of what would be needed to give people a return on their investment from a location as remote as Red River. The distance of the place requires significant transport along the rail lines and highways in order for usable product to reach large cities. We've tested the maximum volume of gasoline and distillates that can be refined through this kind of processor in one day. Out in Red River, you'd have to build a multi-stage refinery and have its access located immediately along the highway and rail line. The plant would need to be eight times the size of what you see here. No less than four smokestacks would be required. The condensers, engines, pumps, retorts and stills could be generally contained in a building standing three stories tall."

Victor Atkins winked.

"I thought you'd know a thing or two about the scale required. We're acquiring 10,000 acres behind a prime parcel that sits right between the river and the highway. The processing site will be located downslope of the shale cliffs to the west of town."

TR remembered seeing the place.

"It's that flat stretch at the base of the second tier of cliffs along the river, just before the highway turns into town, isn't it?"

"Correct you are, sir. No doubt there's a lot of work ahead and more than a little wrangling with the landowners and government men over how to assemble the title and mineral rights. Just the same, I wanted you to know about this endeavor and to consider being our man to design the refinery. Our work will require four years. You could work on the plans when you have time. Please consider and let me know over the next few months."

TR's eyes shone.

"I don't have to think about it. I'm already drawing plans and elevations in my mind. Just let me know the progress of your land acquisition, and I'll get the refinery plans drawn."

Victor beamed.

"Excellent! We're not asking that you become an investor, only our inventor. Any process patents you devise will be your own. You have sole control over any engineers or chemists you may want to hire. What I'd like to offer is my personal endorsement to the public regarding you inventing the technology to be used. I have certain resources at the university that may be of some assistance to you, but any technology you develop is your own. Our visionaries want to show the town of Red River and investors across the country that we have the best team assembled to make this refinery happen. My endorsement and your reputable achievements will speak volumes during the issuance of stock."

TR thought of the situation involving stock schemes so prevalent in every major city across the country.

"I can think of a few stock issuers, such as CJ Niles, whose reputation would not bode well for a quality endeavor such as yours. He has not proven that a majority of his claims about his refineries and mines can be brought to fruition. Investors remain dubious about a great number of stock issuers such as Niles. Men like CJ are accumulating negative portfolios of unproven schemes. I'm interested in your venture inasmuch as all claims to potential investors are thoroughly proven ahead of any publication. I'd want to read any technical information regarding the refinery's design and anticipated throughput. I'll work with you regarding anything that may be written before information is published anywhere."

Victor agreed.

"That is essential, Mr. Gimble. We'll work closely on any words to be published regarding the refinery. We will not handle stock issuance as CJ Niles has done. I cannot imagine how that man has not yet been indicted for issuing stock so far in advance of his endeavors even getting started! Our men will not issue one stock certificate until we know that the land and minerals are secured in our name. Your plans will be final and approved for construction. The initial technology will be properly tested at the site. The investing public will have a full year to study the prospectus and observe the progress of the refinery's construction. Right now, it would simply be good if I can tell our team that we can move forward based on your collaboration with me."

TR wrote down notes and checked a small date calendar.

"I'd like to meet your men. I've read your book and compared it to the reports of others studying shale. I'm impressed with your practical ideas about the rock. Other men are developing investment plans with shale oil based on scant scientific knowledge and field information. The government's shale experiments have turned out dismally so far. All this is only fueling the disgust of chemists and engineers at petroleum companies. Private entrepreneurs with half-baked schemes will not do well under watchful government eyes or with any faithful investors. It will take a lot of substance in anyone's efforts to be dealing with this mineral. Men must be wholly committed to support the mining and refining endeavors for years. Both efforts are critical for shale. Either operation could stumble at times due to the many difficulties I already know must be overcome to produce oil and gas from shale. I agree that a strong collaboration by men who do not back down from such challenges is what's needed for any kind of shale oil endeavor to succeed in Red River."

Victor accepted the notepad paper with the dates TR had marked.

"I'll convey to the men all that you have said. I'll check the men's schedules and call you to see when it would be possible for us to meet with you. We understand how busy you are building the new refineries for Regis."

TR nodded.

"I'll have only short breaks of time available on those weeks I noted. I must not leave my family totally abandoned through the efforts I'm pursuing. There are more refineries to be constructed for Regis and for other petroleum companies as well, but I want to make at least one trip to Red River before drawing your refinery plan. I must examine the site closely in order to render it complete."

Victor concurred.

"Call me when your schedule looks clear enough for you to get out to Red River. The men and I will meet you there."

TR shook the professor's hand.

"Sounds good, Victor. I appreciate your traveling here to see my plant and extending your offer for my involvement."

Victor laughed.

"See? The Regis exam wasn't a complete waste, was it?"

TR chuckled.

"Hardly. Opportunities can manifest in the oddest forms."

CHAPTER 31

▼

Hiram drove Victor Atkins to the Los Angles train station from which Ty Gimble had departed early that morning. The inventor stayed behind at the experimental plant drawing preliminary sketches for a large shale oil refinery.

After an hour, his thoughts turned to his eldest son and how enthused he looked riding outbound to his new adventure. He had probably unpacked his gear by now, and TR missed him already. His family would feel the absence of both him and Ty in the coming weeks. TR Gimble was eager for nothing more than a good, home-cooked meal and some welcoming hugs.

The inventor turned out the lights in the workshop. Locking the front door to the office, he heard some rustling beyond the cypress trees in front. He peered into the darkness but saw no one. His car was a few feet away. As TR started his four long strides to reach the car, a crowbar grabbed his right arm.

TR pulled away immediately casting the iron to the ground. As it banged, the man in a cape stepped up from behind.

"Tiemonet!" growled TR. "You could've just knocked. Is it too much to ask anymore that you make a gentleman's appointment?"

The Frenchman's eyes looked wild.

"It's hard to keep up with you these days. You should be glad my man used nothing more than a crowbar. Your wife is already a widow enough without her becoming one in truth."

TR turned to his car ready to kick the Frenchman to the ground if he stepped any closer.

Tiemonet didn't move. His lungs rattled and his voice called out in raspy urgency.

"Wait! There is only one thing tonight. At the same time you draw up your design for Red River you will draw the same for a plant in Fushun."

TR couldn't believe what he was hearing.

"Manchuria."

"Yes, the Japanese are ready to do the same, but they will control the outcome. They've banished the Russians who are no more in that territory. There will be no Regis Petroleum and no American bureaucrats standing in the way of Japan's total success in Fushun."

TR sighed. Then he turned to Tiemonet.

"No."

"Why not? Your payment will be handsome."

"And so would yours. No, I'm not traveling to China again."

"You don't have to. I just got back."

"No doubt. The answer is still no."

"You don't have to see the site. It's a flat ledge near the river between a highway and rail line, just like the place in Red River."

TR opened his car door, slid inside and slammed the metal.

"This meeting is concluded."

Tiemonet crept closer.

"Then you will see that I am not the only messenger of this directive."

TR plunged his key in the ignition and turned it. The roadster fired up and TR turned the wheel. Running the Frenchman to the ground would be a delight.

But a man grabbed Tiemonet who stumbled backward. The crowbar had been retrieved without notice and skillfully put to service twice that night.

Gertie brought her husband's steaming plate to the table.

"How did your meeting with Dean Atkins go?"

TR looked at his food and saw his wife's loving care in its preparation.

"It went very well."

"Will you be traveling to Colorado for a new venture?"

"Not any time soon, but I was impressed with the professor's understanding of shale."

TR winked at his wife and added, "Shale is the correct mineral name of the mystery rock the man referred to in his letter."

"Oh, Papa" said Gertie with exasperation.

TR finished his meal and gave her a hug.

"What's going to happen is that I'll draw up some plans for Victor and his partners. Then I'll sell more patents for new inventions. We'll accumulate a bit more capital. That is all. I might have to make one brief trip to Red River for a couple of days to examine the refinery site. I will not return there for several more years, not until the new refinery opens. Do those sound like travel plans you can endure?"

"Of course," said Gertie. "I simply wondered what the man wanted. I figured money. It was hard to know what to think from his letter."

TR fingered the monogram of his shirt cuff. He saw it remained spotless today. He looked up.

"I was surprised to learn all that I did about Victor, especially after meeting him under such strange circumstances at the Regis exam. It turns out he inserted questions to see what I knew about mining and processing shale. I thought those subjects were simply something new they were teaching at the university, but Victor says no. People now are much more interested in petroleum than shale. With conglomerates like Regis investing millions in refineries and pipelines, petroleum is the only subject people think young adults should be studying. Victor says universities in Texas, Oklahoma, Colorado and California teach more about petroleum law and science than anything to do with shale."

TR touched Gertie's hand.

"Dear, I couldn't have predicted I'd be approached by a professor to design a refinery, but it's happened. Whatever comes of people in the U.S. buying shale fuel in great quantity or not is out of my hands. I will simply make the most streamlined process I can design. It will be up to other men to bring shale oil products to market and sell them at an equitable profit."

Gertie frowned.

"It surely sounds like a lot of work."

"No doubt it will be much work for many men some day. I'm merely the point man on one refinery. I have a well-tested prototype working at the experimental yard. I simply need to increase its volume and fit it onto the site. My engineer will supervise building it in Red River."

Gertie brightened at the news that a man other than her husband would be gone to Red River for weeks at a time. Then she frowned once more.

"Do you think there'll be any conflict with your work for Regis?"

TR chuckled.

"Not a bit. They're convinced that shale oil is already a complete failure. The only reason designing a plant in Red River appeals to me is because of the professor. He sounds as if he's involved with a dedicated group. For our family's benefit, I can see at least eight more patents to register, own and sell the rights to.

Whoever uses those patents will do well in their progress with shale oil, but I will not invest in shale oil stock myself."

Gertie studied her husband's face.

"What if your refinery in Red River is highly successful? What if a few other shale oil operations also succeed and start being seen as a threat to the oil companies? Didn't you tell me that shale gasoline would cost pennies compared to petroleum?"

TR stroked his chin.

"That was years ago, Mama. Since then, the need for specialty metals to refine shale has become clear to me. That will increase refining costs. I'm not certain by how much. I'm establishing Gimble Metals Company for numerous reasons. And you know I've had the fledging business I named Gimble Coal and Shale Oil Company. Coal is more important to process than shale right now, and it requires new metals for innovations. Shale will never be my sole aim, but I will not give up my fascination with it, Gertie. I enjoy the quest the same as other men who appreciate solving its mysteries. I'll continue to invent related machines and processes, but don't worry. We can divest of anything to do with shale if there comes any conflict with oil."

TR bypassed the mention of Tiemonet's rude visit and any foreign governments. Gertie's threshold for worry was not that wide.

Gertie learned long ago that it was impossible to know the inventor's ever-changing tapestry of ideas, so she brought up something simpler.

"How is that boy you met on your train ride to Red River?"

"Joey MacDermott?"

"Yes. He sounds like someone Billy might enjoy as a friend."

"Joey is doing well working on several new inventions. He's becoming a fine, young man. I would not, however, want to force Billy to become friends with anyone. The boy must choose his companions on his own. I can see the independent streak in Billy, and it's best he explore whatever suits him in his own way. I have a lot faith in Billy. He is, after all, a Gimble in the Gimble tradition of hard-working, intelligent men."

Gertie glanced toward the stairwell. TR cupped his hand and directed his voice up the staircase.

"Did you hear that, son?"

Gertie and TR laughed as they heard the boy's feet scamper down the hallway back into his bedroom.

"At least his stomach behaved today," said Gertie with a chuckle.

TR took his wife's hand.

"Don't make that a capital issue, Gertie. You'll only make him more self-conscious than he already is. It's got to be upsetting for a young boy like him trying to find his way when our family is growing so fast. Now that Ty and I are getting involved with work that takes us away from the home fires more often, it will only get tougher on Billy. Be patient with him, Gertie. I know he's trying."

"You're right, Papa. I won't entertain any more thoughts of him attending military academy unless he really earns his way into that school."

"Good. Leave the dishes until morning. Let's put out the lights and get our rest."

As TR picked up his suit coat from the downstairs hall, he turned over the right sleeve and exhaled. There was no rip or mark left by the crowbar.

CHAPTER 32

▼

Skip Vanderhooten stepped halfway out of the train's passenger car. Holding onto the side rail, he leaned out beyond the side of the train, peering right and left. Skip called back to his traveling companion inside the coach.

"I thought this was the right stop. I never heard the porter announce Larwin Valley when we pulled in. You had me too enchanted!"

Skip assisted his young lady down the coach's steps. Ellie daintily stepped onto the station platform. She reached over and straightened the three daisies on Skip's white jacket lapel.

"I think your flowers got a little wilted on the ride."

Skip kissed her forehead.

"But you, my dear, remain the freshest flower of them all."

Ellie squeezed his hand and angled her hat to block the sun's rays.

"It's going to be hot out here today."

"No matter," said Skip, "There are always plenty of fresh daisies to be had at any flower shop. Maybe Clay Henry has a florist by now. I heard he's building a cemetery on a hill near the crest of the highway. An undertaker would surely need daisies to host a proper funeral."

Ellie laughed and kissed his cheek.

"Please don't be morbid, Skip. All I want to do is laugh and sing. I'm not in a serious mood for visiting headstones. If the daisies wilt, we'll toss them. I'll be your bouquet for the day."

Skip grinned. Ellie didn't yet know that his favorite flower sent a message. He liked to show his friendship with the inventor. Some remembered Skip looking death in the face as he climbed into TR Gimble's submarine for its first ride around the bay. The launch of the watercraft seemed long ago, but those who didn't forget how it inspired them never failed to remark. Skip's daisies reminded them what he said to news reporters about notifying the undertaker that those were his favorite flowers. The success of that time was a hallmark for Skip, even though the Navy decided they didn't want one-man submarines. With Gimble now engineering refineries, there were no more vessels for Skip to risk his life aboard. Men received explicit training for the kind of maneuvers Skip once performed for TR. Proving the seaworthiness of experimental subs with Gimble turned out to be not much more than a parenthesis in each of their lives.

Skip patted his wilted daisies as he observed the scene.

"It looks like this dusty old town is growing. No wonder I didn't recognize it. They made the platform and station house bigger and painted everything new colors. I bet 'ol Buck had something to do with these improvements. Let's see if we can find the carriage up to his place he said we'd be able to catch."

Ellie smoothed the collar of her new organdy dress.

"I'm glad I brought my parasol and you wore your straw hat. I feel festive, and the barbecue will be wonderful!"

They looked around the station but didn't see any colorful carriage bearing a Spanish name as Buck had promised.

Then Ellie cried out, "Look!"

Skip saw her gazing up a hill directly behind the station.

"That's it!" exclaimed Skip. "That's Buck Williams' new sanctum sanctorum officially under construction."

Ellie gasped.

"It's large!"

"Ten thousand square feet, my dear. It's costing our beloved cowboy actor a quarter of a million dollars. The round structure on the left that looks like a castle tower must be the entrance he described. I see the windows for his large music room being framed up, and the square, three-story tower in the middle will become his study. Look at all the balconies! He's probably looking out one of them now where he can see us standing here. I bet his buggy will arrive in no time."

Just then, the buggy arrived, festooned with colorful ribbons and balloons. A green, canvas biminy provided shade over the carriage, its gold tassels bouncing in time to the beat of the horse's hooves. As buggy and driver reined to a stop, other guests from the train joined Skip and Ellie for the ride up the hill. The ladies chatted gaily and complimented one another on their beautiful summer outfits. The men looked across the valley, commenting on the new pumps and derricks in the oil gulch. Progress in a thriving town unfolded before them. Buck Williams was leading the way by building his glamorous destination for city visitors to experience the new excitement in these parts.

The buggy reached two exquisitely crafted, white iron gates that were closed. A man with a wide sombrero stood before them. The buggy's passengers glimpsed a grand driveway beyond, winding up to the site of the home. A six-foot high, white masonry wall wove gracefully around the entire hill. The wall began and ended at the gates connected to the round two-story structure resembling a castle tower.

As the buggy clattered to a stop, the male passengers brought from their vest pockets gold engraved invitations. The handsome, Mexican man smiled and nodded as he checked each one. Then he stepped back, took off his wide sombrero, and swept it in a wide arc as he bowed to the guests.

"I am Francisco Alvarez. It is my pleasure to welcome you to the estate of Mr. Buck Williams. He has decided to call this place La Loma de Oro. That means the Hill of Gold. When you see this carriage with that name on it, you know you can ride up the hill and that you are welcome as his guest. The home is called La Casa Blanco de La Loma de Oro, the White House on the Golden Hill. The house is not yet completed, so your barbecue will be held under the big white tent on La Loma!"

The guests applauded and everyone repeated Francisco's Spanish words, trying to make the words they pronounced sound as beautiful as Francisco announced them. Ready for a good time, the cheerful guests rode through the gates Francisco held open.

After the buggy passed through, Francisco closed the gates and returned to his post inside the white tower. His English was getting better every day. He counted his blessings, grateful to have landed at this beautiful ranch, guarding the gates with one of Buck Williams' great danes and a six-shooter the cowboy showed him how to use.

California was proving a very interesting place for Francisco and his family. His hard work digging tunnels in the hills below the lady preacher's mansion had earned him the proper references to be able to work for Mr. Williams. He thought how strange it was that Miss Porter built her mansion similar to Buck Williams but with such different decoration. Being a lady preacher of sorts, Annabelle's hilltop home in El Lago featured gold turrets and Moorish towers, East Indian arches and a large gold cross. Francisco heard people question if a preacher could properly represent Christian folks having built the shapes and forms of religions from all over the world. Francisco didn't care how anyone decorated their mansion, as long as it meant steady work and a good life for his family.

Buck's home was not mysterious like the lady preacher's. His manor was straightforward, just like the actor himself. Buck's home spread across the top of a sprawling hill with commanding views in every direction. Francisco's duties here were much easier than digging tunnels in the hard clay below the Porter mansion. Francisco enjoyed greeting all Buck's visitors and seeing the fine collection of American Indian artifacts being brought to Mr. Williams' new rooms as they were completed. He learned that the actor spoke certain Native American languages. He was especially pleased when his boss asked him to teach him Spanish. Francisco learned that's just how Buck was, always interested in people wherever he lived. Francisco thought of several Spanish expressions to explain to Mr. Williams, along with more of his people's history. He smiled. The fine cowboy movie actor who wanted to learn more would welcome this knowledge from Francisco.

The guests riding in the buggy disembarked at the end of the grand driveway. A cool breeze floated across the top of the golden hill, taming the summer heat. As Buck's mansion came into full view, his guests exclaimed over the scale of the building under construction.

After they viewed the lower grounds, they strolled to the base of a winding outdoor staircase on the north side of the home. The men gazed up at the lush shrubs already filling in to hold firm the wide slope. They admired the intelligent way the large home was set into the hill.

Ellie looked up at the staircase.

"Oh, how gorgeous! Let's go!"

The ladies' petite heels clicked up the twenty-six concrete steps, their delicate fingers tracing the edges of sculpted balustrades on each side of the stairs. The landing on top offered the guests even more scenic delights. The staircase brought them to the apex of the hill at level with the home's second story. Stone walkways lined with fragrant flowers served the home's rear doors and spacious patios. The walkways merged and swung out the opposite direction, leading to a western-style arch that framed the entry to a vast stone sun deck suspended over a valley.

A large, white party cabana provided abundant shade over the sun deck's stone patio. A barbecue was already steaming with large steaks simmering on the grill. Guests bedecked in fine summer apparel and fresh corsages chatted and sang along with the smiling mariachi band. Several men discussed a movie screenplay, studying its pages while sitting on the sun deck's low stone wall. Men and women admired Buck's new telescope near the outer edge of the patio. An astronomer from the county observatory described constellations they would see that night.

Beyond the low stone wall, a rocky slope dropped steeply. Views across a pristine, golden valley gave way to the sight of massive, ancient oak trees clinging to the sides of canyons below. The view swept up to distant oak-studded hills and canyons with purple mountains beyond. Buck stood describing how the hills in the distance were part of Henry Clay's property at the edge of the valley.

An enormous eucalyptus tree towered above Buck's white party canopy. Its leaves swayed over the stone wall that curved around its base. When Buck's guests admired the specimen, he described how it was part of the original hill and how his construction men built the sun deck to fit around the massive trunk.

Ellie clapped her hands delightedly.

"What a perfect setting! Let's dance!"

"Of course, my dear," agreed Skip. "One dance, then we'll get something to drink. And I must compliment Buck on what he's done with the place."

Skip took Ellie's hand. They circled together and clicked their heels with two other couples who couldn't resist the festive music.

As Francisco sat on the bench inside the cool, white tower, he tapped the toe of his boot in time to the distant mariachi music. He remembered the fun on his wedding day many years ago. What a fiesta that was! Francisco looked up sharply as he heard a thundering sound coming up the dirt road. Mr. Williams had clearly instructed his guests to take the buggy up the hill and not to drive their cars. Mr. Williams wanted the flavor of the festivities to start at the base of the hill so guests would leave all city worries behind and be carried away as soon as possible by the valley's beautiful setting.

Two dark sedans roared to a stop in front of Francisco's iron gates. Francisco leapt up from his bench and ran into the cloud of dust. Two men dressed in dark suits, completely out of keeping with a summer barbecue party, got out of each of the cars. Francisco felt weak, never expecting intruders on this sunny afternoon. His heart sank, knowing he didn't even have enough bullets in his gun to handle them. There had been prowlers at night sometimes, but never men or vandals daring to enter the ranch during the day.

"Francisco!" said one of the men.

The gatekeeper froze. How did they know his name?

"Cool it," said the man. "You introduce yourself to everyone who comes up this road. We are here for Mr. Williams' party."

Francisco hesitated then stepped forward.

"May I see your invitations?"

The men smiled wryly at one another.

"Where's that invite?" asked one of men.

A man's hand extended from inside one of the cars holding one of Buck's gold engraved invitations.

"Here."

The man who stood before Francisco shoved the document toward him.

Francisco studied the wrinkled invitation.

"This is only one name. I do not remember Mr. Williams telling me that there were any groups this large who were asked to come with only one invitation."

The man studying Francisco narrowed his eyes.

"Don't test my patience. We are definitely associates of the cowboy. Open the gates and let us through."

Francisco tried stubborn insistence.

"Who are you? I must know."

One of the men said in a low growl, "We are patrons of The Saint. Buck knows who we are. We will discuss nothing further with you."

Francisco quickly looked up and down the driveway to see if the gardener or any of the ranch hands were coming after the sound of big autos on the road. No one was in sight. Buck's great dane was snarling, but Francisco knew the strangers could leap back in their cars if he told the dog to attack. One of the men nearest Francisco wiped his brow and made sure that Francisco could see the large weapon strapped to his chest.

"It's getting very hot out here," said the armed man. "Now are you going to open these gates or are we going to have to give Mr. Williams' puppy and you the gift of a limp you two may be lucky enough to walk around with for the rest of your days?"

Francisco shrugged. The gates were unlocked anyway. All anyone had to do was push them open. The ceremony of opening the gates was simply for the benefit of welcoming guests in a pleasing fashion. These men were not breaking through. They had only stopped at this point to not damage the hood of a car. Certainly no one in Mr. Williams' household had been expecting such an intrusion. Francisco opened the gates, and the two sedans pulled through.

CHAPTER 33

▼

Francisco started to panic after the sedans rolled through the gates. His hands shook closing the wrought iron. Agonized thoughts flooded his mind.

"God help us! Buck's fiesta will be a disaster!"

Francisco pictured men and women gunned down, dangling over the walls of the sun deck with the ladies' high heels and bracelets dropping to the valley below. His mind wailed in sorrow, ready to accept his earthly penance and eternal banishment for allowing harm to come to so many souls.

"This will be the massacre of Larwin Valley! It will be my fault! I have failed all who trusted me!"

He saw through a blur his sombrero lying on the bench of the white tower. The large hat looked as useless as he felt. Francisco decided he must not abandon his post. A second group of terrible men could be coming up the road as he'd seen before in Mexico.

Just when he decided he must die in honor defending the gates against the next intruders, the great dane snarled loudly and pawed at the ground. Francisco heard the dog panting as he bit at the rope attached to its collar. He watched Francisco with wide, expectant eyes. The man realized that the giant dog could run straight up the hill on its powerful legs. As he bent down and quickly untied the rope from the dog's collar, Francisco whispered in the great dane's ear.

"Run, Buster! Go find Master Buck. Get Master Buck right now!"

The dog pounced forward in one great leap out the castle tower's low front door. He ran to the top of the steep slope below Buck's mansion before Francisco could fully exhale. As swiftly as the mountain lions that roamed these beautiful hills, Buster found his quickest shortcut through the thick brush on the hillside and ran at lightning speed to his destination.

The great dane came charging through the veranda entry and onto the stone patio, leaping to slap both paws on Buck's shoulders, nearly knocking him over. Women shrieked at the sight of the charging canine that appeared to them as large as one of Buck's beloved horses.

"Whoaa, Buster!" cried Buck.

The men wondered aloud if this was some stunt the actor had planned as part of the afternoon's festivities.

"It's OK," announced Buck with a breathless laugh as he soothed the dog. "Buster is not acting, and neither am I. He must've gotten loose. You know he's the friendly mutt who greeted you at the front gates with Francisco. I was missing him, and he must've felt the same way!"

Skip Vanderhooten looked quickly at Buck Williams. In the instant their eyes met, they both knew something was up. With rapid steps, Skip joined Buck and the great dane.

"Here, I'll help take him down the hill."

As they started walking, Buck grabbed a rope near the veranda entrance. He quickly tied it around the dog's collar. The two men half-ran across the hilltop's paths and flew down the concrete stairs. Buck knew Skip had come here with a lovely starlet who would soon be starring in feature films. And Buck also knew the history behind the daisies on Skip's coat. Two of the wilted flowers had fallen on the stone veranda. One remained on Skip's lapel.

"Someone's paying you a visit," breathed Skip.

Buck's eyes scanned his property.

"I'm certain of that!"

He pulled the great dane closer as he and Skip walked quickly toward the wide circular drive at the mansion's entrance. As Buck reined in the dog, he looked at Skip.

"Better that we meet and greet out here than on the sun deck."

The men in the dark sedans had pulled up. Two of them were standing beside each car. Skip and Buck and the dog walked up to the four men.

"Gentlemen," said Buck. "What can we do for you?"

One of the men flicked a cigarette ash toward the dog. Buster got ready to leap, but Buck held him back. Lighting the dry brush outside the wall surrounding the hill was a trick these men might pull if provoked.

Ignoring Buck's dog, the man who flicked the ash took another slow drag on his cigarette. As his smoke quickly dispersed toward the mansion, he spoke nonchalantly.

"It's a lovely day indeed, Mr. Williams, a little hot for my preference, but not too unbearable with that breeze. The music sounds inviting. We do have another party to attend today so aren't dressed in quite the right fashion for yours."

Skip quickly surveyed the men. Two of them looked familiar. Skip recalled seeing them near the Gimble backyard when he and TR were building the first submarine. He saw them again outside the experimental plant before the second sub was launched. One of them looked at Skip.

"We'll get to the point. You, daisy boy, might want to hear this, too."

While the great dane growled and tugged at the rope held tightly by Buck, Skip leveled his eyes at the man.

"What might your point be?"

The man turned his steely gaze toward Buck.

"The Saint watches over what's happening in this valley. He wants you and the folks you party with to be clear about the direction things will go. What's in the Gulch is none of your business, and we don't want to hear your point of view about what's going on. We know you have a tendency to chat with 'ol Clay Henry on the neighboring ranch, and that you're getting to know more people here in town. We know you like to sit around with poets and artists talking about how industry is going to ruin things like the beach up in Santa Barbara. Well, this place is different. We know where the oil is down here, and it's not on any beach. Our recommendation is that you stay friendly with one and all, and that includes the oilmen who'll be doing a lot of work in the hills around your place."

Buck replied in a stage actor's voice so that all ears could hear.

"I bought enough land so that won't be a problem. I endorse oil drilling in general and know that it's a dirty job getting to the black gold. Men did what they had to years ago on the other side of the canyon when they first found yellow gold there, but that canyon's still a decent place for man and wildlife. I watched my father establish flour mills in towns across the East and West to refine what they called white gold in those days. I'm quite familiar with what any kind of gold means to men of motive. I planned ahead when I decided to build out here. I have land enough to enjoy adequate peace. I ask for nothing more. You didn't have to come crash my party to deliver this message from The Saint, whoever he is!"

The men looked back at the sedans. A hand waved them back. As they turned to leave, one of the men Skip recognized spoke gruffly.

"Just stay clear on this message so we don't have to remind you. And, daisy boy, you can tell your old pal that we're watching him, too."

Skip returned the man's stare and spoke evenly.

"Some things never change."

Buster broke free from Buck's grip, which he'd loosened on the rope attached to Buster's collar. The last man had to dive inside the sedan to avert having his leg torn apart by the powerful dog. Buck kept barking as the cars skidded around the drive and headed down the hill.

Francisco heard the roar of the engines and hurriedly opened the gates. He stood back as the cars swept past, struggling to keep himself from weeping. Relief flooded to his bones. Whatever happened on the hill was over quickly. Francisco didn't hear yells or gunshots and thanked God a thousand times. He heard Buster barking and saw the great dane charge past, chasing the cars to the base of the hill.

Francisco finally breathed. At least he'd been able to give the dog's master some warning. The gatekeeper was sure that Buster would soon be getting several new canine companions of larger size to join the other animals at the cowboy's ranch. He surveyed the wall of the castle tower. It was just big enough for a rack of guns to be mounted inside.

CHAPTER 34

▼

Buck Williams and Skip Vanderhooten left the great dane at the castle tower with Francisco. They hurried up the winding staircase to rejoin the party. There was no need to discuss between them that the incident with the men who showed up unannounced would go without mention to the guests on the upper veranda.

"That capricious dog!" exclaimed Skip as he stepped beside Ellie.
Ellie looked concerned.
"Is everything alright?"
Skip slipped his arm around Ellie's waist.
"Sure. I think it's time for a cool drink and another dance with my daisy. Once you get famous, I'll regret not having spent every minute possible by your side."
Ellie clasped Skip's hand around her waist. She murmured softly.
"I would never forget you, Skip."

Buck returned to mingle with his guests. Skip overheard the actor talking jovially to the men and women gathered around him.
"And then I ran outside, still in my skivvies, mind you! I saw this dang-blasted airplane circling over this very hill. I darn near killed myself running inside to grab pencil and paper and run back out. But I got the serial number of the plane. It was flying so low I could read the numbers clearly. I thought, 'If that crazy pilot is going to crash on my land, I'll need to notify the authorities pronto! If not, I'm raising one helluva complaint about such risk and disturbance over my home!'"

"What happened next?" asked one of the men.

"Well, as it turned out, ladies and gents, the plane did not crash, and this pilot was a lady of all things! I thought she must've gone nuts in the cockpit. The dives and turns she had that bird doing were making the engine scream!"

"Did you find out who it was, Mr. Williams?" asked a lady with her eyes shining.

"My dear," said Buck, "It was some young woman named Emily Browning. I called the authorities at the airport, and they knew all about her. I told them how she was darting around like a bat so low over my property. They laughed and said she was training for some difficult landings and flights she intends to take cross-country. Then they said she'd drive over and apologize in person for disturbing my sister and me. Miss Browning saw me run out half naked taking down the number of the plane."

"Did you meet her?" asked the same lady.

"Not yet," said Buck, "but I'll keep you posted on what happens. Folks, it was just another adventurous day in Larwin Valley. You never know what can happen out here in the wild, wild west!"

The actor looked over at Skip Vanderhooten and winked.

As Skip and Ellie mingled amid the guests at the barbecue, they heard a great deal of interesting talk.

"It's so decent of Buck to care for his invalid sister. He's built every amenity in this house to ensure she's comfortable and happy."

"He's so talented a man who can act and write screenplays. Have you read his poetry, too?"

"Indeed. He's also working on his third book, an autobiography, in addition to his collections of short stories."

"What a prolific mind!"

"Buck is known in our circle for encouraging the talent of painters and sculptors. He's helped many an artist build their career by giving them proper introductions to celebrities and people of influence."

"Buck definitely is a friend of the arts. We're hoping he'll help sponsor our movement to head off destruction caused by the men of industry. Too many greedy barons are ruining thousands of acres of land, plus the air and water!"

"Isn't it revolting how oilmen destroy everything they touch?"

"Without a doubt! Treacherous deeds by these capitalists destroy safe havens for man, as well as animals! It's enough to make you weep in despair!"

"Not so fast. I've heard that Buck does have a great eye and many ideas for how things can be fixed after businessmen take what they want from the land."

"Well, he can't fix everything. You must have noticed the irreparable damage to the coastline in Santa Barbara. There are hundreds of oil derricks on the sand and rising up from the ocean. The same horror is befalling Huntington Beach. Beachhead refineries ooze contamination onto land and sea, killing everything for miles around! The locals had no power whatsoever to stop the destruction of beaches we all once enjoyed."

"Didn't a lot of the locals sell out to the oilmen and profit handsomely?"

"Some did, but tell me, who was selling the beach sands and the ocean floor?"

"Only men like Buck Williams have enough influence over Wall Street and Congress to stop such horrible crimes."

"It's not only the shoreline. Let's not forget Signal Hill! And what about Santa Fe Springs? Those massive oil fires are noxious beyond compare! Desecration of the land will never end without strong intervention!"

"Mark my words, people. More killing of nature's majesty is yet to come! Those places in California are just the beginning. Buck will get active, I assure you, once he sees how extensive the drilling becomes in Larwin Valley. Dirty workers will overrun the town. Companies will pump oil night and day over every square foot without regard for the valley's delicate natural abundance!"

Skip had to conclude that the things the men in the dark sedans had mentioned about Buck's friends were true. Ellie tugged at his sleeve.

"Do you think Buck will join the artists' movement against industrialists?"

Skip looked across the pristine valley whose view they enjoyed at the edge of the veranda.

"My dear, this is only my opinion, but listen carefully. Buck has built a beautiful place here, but not without cost to the environment which once ran freely across this terrain. Millions of cubic yards of earth were moved aside and rearranged to provide the massive foundation for his mansion. Hundreds of plants, not native to these parts, were brought in to grow on the slopes and along the pathways. The veranda we're standing on would not exist without tons of boulders and rocks dug up from nearby riverbeds. The stones were dragged up the hill to be set in concrete. Making the concrete required dynamite blasting, then scooping sand and gravel out of ugly pits. All the construction just to build this hilltop oasis for Buck Williams and his sister displaced thousands of native creatures living here and in hills adjacent. Those creatures existed without interference before Buck's workmen appeared."

Ellie furrowed her brow.

"Does that mean Mr. Williams is just as awful as the men of industry?"

"Anyone could say so, sweet Ellie, except for looking at it another way. This sanctuary the actor created represents a marriage of man's technology and a certain fixing up of the land. It's a vision for how men can use land then restore it in certain ways. Plants and animals will flourish here for years to come. But as nice a job as Buck has done to build his mansion while preserving acres of natural habitat, his home will stand witness for decades facing the scourge of grading and contamination on the hills across the valley in the oil gulch."

Ellie remembered the derricks on barren hillsides.

"Do you think they'll restore the land in the Gulch after they've taken the oil?"

Skip chuckled.

"Probably not so likely, my dear. Maybe that will happen much later. Maybe it will be when government men can agree on how to make oil companies set the land right. For now, the government itself needs the oil. They need it desperately, even from these nearby hills."

Ellie contemplated.

"So the government is responsible for destruction to land and living things?"

"In a way, yes, Ellie. But if you were trying to lay blame on one department, you could not exclude people like you and me. Do you wonder if the artists uttering such angry words about oilmen stopped to think how long it would have taken them to ride mules or horses rather than trains and cars to get here? I have, and so have other men. It's not as if the artists themselves do not make use of the modern comforts oil brings us."

Ellie looked at the cowboy actor chatting amiably with his friends.

"So what do you think Buck might do?"

"It's hard to say, my dear. Buck's a pretty smart guy. He is, after all, a tradesman and craftsman himself. He belongs to the Guild like a lot of the other men you don't see vocalizing against industrialists. Buck's been raised to a high degree in the Guild. I'd bet on him acting with a lot of discretion before he'd use his influence in any all-out campaign against men of industry. He'll care a great deal about this parcel he's on. He'll watch over it like a hawk. With all the activity to come in Larwin Valley, he might participate in the town's development. He may help work things out before oil drilling goes haywire here like in some of the really damaged places these artists mention."

Ellie looked up at her clever date who spoke with such regard for all men's point of view.

"I really won't forget, you, Skip.

He kissed her cheek.

"I hope not, Ellie. I want you to go ahead and get your lovely face on the silver screen. See how things work out for you and how you feel after making some movies. A lot will happen quickly for you, but I'd like it if your fondness for me is one of the things that never changes. I'd like to remain a part of your life."

Ellie rested her head on Skip's shoulder and sighed.

"I have a feeling I'll always want that, too."

CHAPTER 35

▼

Francisco was furious. The men who intruded on Mr. Williams' property were worthy of death in his mind. He kicked at the dirt and thought about the number of guns he'd need to be able to shoot out the tires of two cars and men like those who might invade the hill in the future.

After the party ended, Buck Williams walked down the hill to the gates by the castle tower. He looked satisfied, not angry. Francisco thanked his Almighty God once more. Buck called out.

"Good thinking!"

Francisco could not hide his exasperation.

"I didn't know what else to do!"

Buck grinned.

"Buster made it up the hill and into the party in seconds flat to warn me. That gave me and a friend just enough time to go out front and approach the men."

Francisco looked at the ground. Buck could see the man's complete shame over his failure to guard the gates he wasn't really assigned to guard with his life. Buck saw Francisco battling sorrowful tears.

"Hey, Francisco, I suppose I could stand here and listen to you say 'lo siento' a hundred times, but I already know that expression. You don't have to teach me the words for 'I'm sorry.' You surely don't have to apologize to me for those men coming through! We simply weren't equipped for daytime intruders. The gates only serve as decoration anyway, especially for events like this party. We'll have to change that and install some heavy locks on the gates. This place isn't some movie set. It's my home, and I must get more cautious. We can't change the fact that certain men we don't want here may feel the need to barge in. I learned from today."

Francisco looked up hopefully.

"Surely we can install barbed wire and gun turrets along the big wall, can't we?"

"Gosh, no, Francisco. This place is not a war zone. I don't have much here except some old Indian artifacts that no one but me thinks have any value. I don't care if men want to sneak up and steal pewter from my kitchen. That'd make the cook mad, but I'm mostly concerned about my sister in her wheelchair. You and I will figure out what kind of measures here at the gate and lower down the hill might create enough delay for any intruders on foot, horseback or car. That way, my foreman or I can have the extra minutes to take the necessary precautions against someone trying to force their way into the house."

Francisco remained worried.

"You know, where I come from, big landowners use cactus along their property boundaries."

"That's a capital idea, Francisco. It wouldn't be necessary to plant them everywhere on these hills. There's a lot of rugged terrain where even the mountain lions don't tread. We could plant large cactus here at the gates and along those ravines and ridges where someone might try to ride or hike in. We can leave some gullies open for the wild animals to traverse under thick scrub, but we can work on spotting the vulnerable places where men might sneak in. You can work with the gardener to get the fastest-growing, meanest cactus species planted in the open spots. That would help us do a better job of securing this property."

Francisco beamed.

"I'd like that very much."

Then he paused.

"Mr. Williams, did the men tell you who they were?"

Buck looked down the driveway.

"None of them mentioned their names, but my friend thought he remembered seeing a couple of them before. We figure they were thugs for hire, you know, the worst kind of cowards who can't find a job doing anything else."

Francisco scratched his head.

"When I asked them who they were, one of the men said, 'We are patrons of the Saint. Buck knows who we are.'"

"Maybe that was the same man who also mentioned the Saint to me. He lied, Francisco. I don't know anyone by that name. He said someone called the Saint watches over this valley. Sounds like some terrible individual, but men sometimes get dramatic when they're trying extra hard to terrorize others. God knows I've seen enough acting in my life to know that. If it weren't for their expensive autos, I'd really discount those fellows. But I paid attention to what they said. They didn't warn me of anything I'm not already aware of. They want people here to let the oilmen have their way, which is fine to wish for because we have government officials who can help keep Larwin Valley a little cleaner than some of the other oil drilling places in this state. I'm not too worried about who this Saint guy might be, nor am I trying to find out."

Francisco looked across the blackness of evening in the dark valley.

"Whoever he is, he is not a Saint. He is El Diablo, the devil!"

Buck nodded.

"Well then, that's who this mystery terrorist will be to you and me. We'll get that cactus installed and remain on the watch for any of his goons who feel the need to visit again."

"That sounds good."

"Go home and be with your family. The party was a smashing success. The guests never knew about the goons anyway. Don't give this day's events a second thought."

Francisco took his sombrero and headed down the path toward home. Buck Williams gathered the leash for his great dane. He and Buster headed toward the cabin to speak with the men who lived there while the mansion was under construction.

Francisco would not forget El Diablo. The evil men could have sent a wire or simply one envoy to deliver their message to Mr. Williams, but they entered the property through those gates, his gates, where he was proudly doing his job. On this visit, the men did not interfere with Mr. Williams' guests, but there were many more parties planned once the house on the golden hill was finished. Francisco vowed he would never forget the faces of the evil men or the shame they caused him on that sunny afternoon.

CHAPTER 36

Skip cradled the telephone on his shoulder while he waited for his call to be answered. A familiar woman's voice came on the line.

"Hello?"

"My dear Gertie!"

"Skip Vanderhooten! It's been ages since you called! How are you?"

"Doin' great, Mrs. G. How are you and the kids?"

"Fine, really fine. Ty is off on a geological survey, and Winnie is studying her music. Billy is … well, just Billy, but he promises to do his homework without my nagging this coming school year."

Skip laughed.

"Is the gentleman of the house in town?"

"Yes, he happens to be, but not for much longer. He'll be returning to Martinez soon to continue work on the port refinery for Regis. He's at the yard right now. Is everything alright?"

"Oh, Gertie, of course. No more experimental subs means no more armed guards around the house. All is well. I'm going to see if I can intercept the 'ol inventor and Hiram. I'd love to see what they're up to."

"They'd love to see you, too. Oh, and Skip, is there a future Mrs. Vanderhooten yet?"

"Not yet, Mrs. G., but the one I'd love to ask is a gal named Ellie. She's really sweet. You'd approve."

"Well, best of luck to both of you. And keep me posted. It's been forever since we attended a wedding. Yours would be very special!"

"I will. Take care, Mrs. G."

Skip pulled into the familiar work yard, amazed at how much the Gimble facility had grown. He burst through the office door.

"Hi, Hiram!"

The curly-haired inventor's assistant look startled, then he wiped his brow and hands. He grinned widely.

"Been quite a long time since you set foot in this old place."

"Those were adventurous days indeed."

They walked out the back door of the office. Some of the workmen hollered hello to Skip. He let out a low whistle.

"Look at all the gadgets and gismos you have working here. I'm impressed."

Hiram laughed.

"I never knew gasoline could be made from so many different things myself. I'd never have dreamed you could mix this stuff up from rocks and corn and whatnot."

"Some of the men from the movie studios who use your Gimble fuel swear by it."

"Yep, they call it a secret mix. They do come eagerly around back, willing to pay whatever we charge for it. Those contraptions they put together to make cinema effects sometimes require a lot of thrust and explosion."

Skip ran his hand over a shiny, clean pipe, waiting to be installed on the machine it rested beside.

"Rockets will be next for you, I'm sure."

TR came striding into view from the back of the yard. He was wearing his old overalls from the railroads.

"Geez, TR!" exclaimed Skip, "Haven't you tossed those old things yet? They must be able to stand up in a corner by themselves."

TR laughed heartily and slapped Skip on the back.

"How are you, you old buzzard?"

"Aside from not doing any more submarine maneuvers, I'm quite the same. I'm dating a nice gal who thinks she wants to become a movie star. I'm going to wait it out again to see if she dumps me or keeps me once she's made her first movie. We went to Larwin Valley last weekend for a barbecue out at Buck Williams' new place. I can't believe how much that valley has grown."

"It sure has. I found a few parcels there that caught my eye, some property not too far from Henry Clay's ranch. What I'm planning is not something that I want in any news reports, but I want to build a small refinery using some of this new machinery that is quite clean and compact. My actual oil drilling will be very limited, but it'll be located on some veins that aren't being tapped in the Gulch. There'll be plenty of small and large oil drillers in that valley soon enough. I want to have my refinery and an oil and gas lease in place by the time I exit the rat race."

"By rat race, do you mean building refineries for Regis and other oil companies?"

"Yes. I see firsthand how they're expanding. Believe it or not, the bigger they grow, the more rigid they're stuck in their ways. Managers afraid of losing high-paid jobs won't make decisions without countless meetings. Makes it hard to find better ways to do things as quickly as we need. That's not an inventor's preference. I'm grateful for the contracts, but I don't see that kind of work in my future. With all the travel those companies require, Gertie would divorce me for abandonment long before I'd retire. I want a couple of businesses and a small refinery. I'll keep generating new patents and licensing them to others as Jacob and I have done. Then I'll work our farmland out in Riverside where the boys and I can plant grapevines and watch the sun set."

"That still sounds like plenty to keep you busy."

"We'll see. My intent was always to burn out before I rust out. I'll never be able to sit around idle. Gertie knows this, and my kids will probably be the same. They're all bright and love to learn. I want to help them find the things that suit them. They already know I'll be inventing until I'm an old codger. There's no doubt about that."

Skip told TR about his travels and conversations with the movie business people. Then he told TR about the intruders at Buck Williams' party. TR frowned.

"That's odd a whole group showed their faces in the light of day. They usually skulk around at night and don't go further than cryptic notes or telegrams. They must have wanted to identify to Buck that there's one ringleader and the fact that this guy has a small militia and enough money to cause some harm. It's clear that whoever it is has their ear to the ground in Larwin Valley. They mentioned the kind of details about Henry Clay and Buck's friends that'd have to come from circles both inside and outside town. I wonder if they would've mentioned your old pal if you hadn't been standing next to Buck."

"Maybe they know about your land purchase in Larwin Valley. It's easy enough to learn that information from one trip to County Records."

"I did tell one wildcatter out there what I was thinking of doing, but as far as I can tell, he's a lone operator who'd undercut his own mother to make a dime. I figured him as crafty enough to set his words and feet carefully wherever he treads. It doesn't sound like he'd want to anger the group run by Buck's party intruders because he's not big enough to match resources against someone like that Saint person. Maybe the wildcatter, Scoot Wynn, did leak the word about my plans. Whoever's plotting big maneuvers out there probably feels threatened by my entering the fray in Larwin Valley. If you want to put the word out in the scuttle, let the men in Larwin Valley and downtown know that I have no plans whatsoever to partner with any of the large conglomerates or small operators intending to drill oil in that valley. Mine will be a sole venture, away from the Gulch properties. Believe me, there's plenty of oil to make a lot of men millionaires over the next 80 years!"

"If I get the chance, I'll do that. The movie people are buying land and entering oil and gas leases in greater numbers each week. Then there are all the attorneys and judges getting involved, plus guys like CJ Niles running around drumming up all sorts of rumors. It's quite a circus."

"That's what I mean about the rat race, Skip. It's all tied together north, south, east and west. It's very hard to exit that network once you've gotten yourself tangled with those men."

TR invited Skip into the office.

"Here, I want to show you something."

TR brought out a large wooden box and opened it. Inside was a gun with an odd barrel.

"I just had this design patented. It can be adapted to most any standard firing weapon. There's only this one and another slightly larger prototype. The other modified gun is with Ty right now. I hope he doesn't have to use this thing in front of the other men in his survey party, but I sent him off with it in case it's needed to save his life."

Skip examined the gun while TR explained.

"My patent creates a miniature plumbing system for a gun's gases. This system doesn't introduce new gases into the gun chamber. It reuses gases that normally escape out the top of a gun when it's fired. The chamber here compresses and directs these gases directly behind the bullet, causing a small, super-explosion in a millisecond when the gun is fired. By trapping and directing gunpowder-released hydrocarbon, this improvement propels a bullet farther, faster and with more accuracy than a normal gun barrel. My little system here gives a bullet more stopping power with more penetration at more foot-pounds than a normal gun would."

Skip whistled between his teeth.

"Wow! This would've been deadly on guns attached to your old submarine!"

TR laughed.

"That might've sold the Navy better on the one-man sub, but their own missile improvements for submerged ordnance have been coming along just fine. Their main objection to my sub was not having any second person backing up the captain."

Skip smiled, remembering how scary it had been thinking that failure of the hatch or any systems on TR's sub could have cost him his life.

"Are you thinking of selling this design to gun manufacturers?"

"Possibly. I don't have any brochures printed or salesmen on the road. I rather like this as a private design for now. It's something Ty, Hiram or I might find handy some time. You let me know if you could use one, too. Presently, I've been too busy supervising refinery construction to register very many new patents. I've also agreed to draw up a design for a new shale oil refinery in Red River."

"Another venture?

"Not exactly. I've been working on methods for refining shale into gasoline and other distillates for a number of years right here in the yard. I got together with a university professor from Colorado recently who's working with a group of businessmen to mine 10,000 acres of shale property in Red River. The refinery will be located along a railroad line and highway out there. If that refinery proves even marginally profitable, my patents for refining shale could be sold elsewhere. I'm not investing in their venture, just enlarging the capacity methods I tested here. I'm drafting a unique refinery design."

"Gosh, TR. I never fail to be impressed reading in the newspapers about what you're doing, but I should always remember that there are at least a hundred other inventions you're cogitating in that big head of yours!"

TR laughed.

"No news there. It's a blessing and hopefully not a curse."

TR and Hiram left to go home to their wives and families. Skip pulled onto the boulevard back to LA. He was glad he met with TR in person. It sounded like the inventor would be in high demand in the coming months and years.

Skip thought about the dejected gatekeeper he'd passed when Buck's carriage took him and the guests down the hill after Buck's party. The humiliated gatekeeper was one man Skip could think of who'd love to have one of those guns improved with TR's patent. Skip chuckled thinking of the man's sombrero flying as he whirled around to fire a warning shot that would penetrate car hoods and knock down trees, sending branches flying down the hill. He mused.

"That's all it would take to intimidate any intruders because TR's gun looks to be that powerful. If there's any more nonsense from that Saint or his goons, I'll ask Hiram for my own prototype. Why not? Things are only getting crazier with that network of men all tied together north, south, east and west. I've seen enough to know that what TR described is accurate. These are men from whom you cannot extricate your life once you're involved in the same affairs that they are. Problem is knowing who's really involved and who's not!"

That brought to Skip's mind the image of one more person he forgot to mention to TR. It was the flamboyant attorney, Harry Ritz, whom Skip and Ellie met briefly at Buck's party. Harry had been stumbling around with a movie starlet on each arm, boasting about his association with a man named Frank McDonnell. People at the party were chuckling over the fact that no one knew who this McDonnell guy was, so exactly how were they supposed to be impressed? One of the starlets had flickered her long lashes and exclaimed that McDonnell worked downtown in the fancy offices of that handsome inventor. Skip couldn't be sure if the inventor the young woman referred to was TR Gimble, but it was something about the way she fluttered her eyes. Gimble did have an intoxicating effect on women. The starlet's dazed opinion probably meant nothing. People's thoughts got mixed up, and they talked a lot of nonsense when swaggering around parties, but Skip made a mental note to remember the attorney's name and the name of the man who apparently worked for the inventor.

CHAPTER 37

▼

Looking out over Larwin Valley, Francisco tried to comfort himself as he picked cactus needles out of his arms. The tiniest needles that a man could not see were indeed the most painful. Only when a red spot indicated that the pierce might be infected did Francisco's wife help him at night by applying poultices to draw out the stinging tips.

The head gardener at Buck Williams' ranch watched in amazement each day all of Francisco's tireless efforts helping him install two hundred cactus plants on the ridges and ravines. Francisco dedicated each plant and stinging cactus needle to his enduring hatred for El Diablo.

After planting cactus one afternoon, Francisco spotted a dark sedan in the valley below Mr. Williams' home. Francisco crouched on the sun deck like a cat and peered over the low, stone wall. He saw a man get out of the car. He watched the man hike down a trail to the bottom of the valley. The man marked stones with dabs of paint.

Francisco watched with wary eyes. The man did not look like other surveyors Francisco had seen. He wore a dark suit, had no partner and carried no surveying instruments. The man hiked quickly, looking frequently up the hill toward Buck's mansion. He carried only a small piece of paper and his can of white paint.

Francisco heard alarm bells in his mind.

"I must warn Mr. Williams!"

He skidded backward, nearly spraining an ankle. He ran breathless to his boss.

"Another of El Diablo's men is invading the property! He's in the ravine below the sundeck!"

Buck quickly saddled a horse and rode down a steep trail running north behind the stone veranda.

Francisco saw Mr. Williams stop on the valley floor as he came upon the hiking man. They spoke. Then Buck tipped his hat and rode back up the ridgeline. Francisco made a silent vow to plant more cactus in that area. The cowboy actor rode up looking unconcerned.

"The man wasn't on my property after all. It only looked like he was. He was marking boundaries for an adjacent parcel he wants to use for horse grazing. I met him before. His name is Scoot Wynn. The man's not unfriendly. He'd have no intention of breaking in."

Francisco gazed down the hill silently as Buck unsaddled his horse. The gatekeeper turned away, unconvinced that a man with the unlikely name of Scoot Wynn would be harmless.

Later that night, Francisco warned his family's people who lived in the valley.

"As far as I may know, any man who loiters beside Mr. Williams' property could be connected with El Diablo. The evil that calls itself 'The Saint' has penetrated this land. Our work keeps us in the hills and ravines each day. It is up to us to watch for suspicious intruders!"

The Alvarez men agreed.

"We believe this evil has come as you say, Francisco. The men in our family have noted forty oil companies getting established in Larwin Valley. The men from these companies drive big, dark sedans. Their workers roam the hills looking at maps and digging holes. It's impossible to tell who may be El Diablo. This makes us nervous. We could end up not knowing we work for the evil one!"

A young Alvarez cousin leaned forward.

"We must have a man we can trust to let us know information about such men we cannot learn for ourselves."

Francisco's nephew offered a suggestion.

"What about Clay Henry? He is settled here a long while and is building the town cemetery. He knows who oilmen are having his own wells and gas station. He sees people at the crest of the highway coming and going from Los Angeles."

Francisco approved.

"Mr. Henry is a good, Christian man. He warns us which drunken workers to avoid on the highway and dark paths that cross our valley under thick oaks. Our women and children are safer because he watches. We can trust his opinion of men."

Clay Henry remained watchful of the comings and goings of Scoot Wynn. He observed a man who was planning something more aggressive on the land than ranching. He saw Scoot truck in drilling equipment on occasion and hire local men for short periods of time. He learned that Scoot's patch of land was tucked away from view near the oil gulch.

Although the wildcatter insisted he wanted nothing more than to keep horses on his property, Clay Henry was not deceived. The man was looking for oil. From what Clay could tell, the wildcatter hadn't yet struck black gold, but he had a feeling that Scoot wouldn't stop trying until he did.

Clay's own land was turning out to be a veritable bonanza of opportunity. He had TR Gimble to thank for his added fortune. TR convinced Clay some years ago that he did not need to purchase oil from a large company to keep his service station replenished with fuel.

While farmers with much larger acreage than Clay scoured their hills and valleys with university-trained geologists, they had no luck locating oil. Clay hiked to a spot with the inventor. TR Gimble quietly pointed out to Clay where to drill, how deep to drill, and at what angle he might strike oil in two of the most hidden ravines on his property that no one else would think to look.

A small refinery across the highway from Clay's land processed the oil he pumped. Clay Henry's productive oil wells, busy gas station and market were a complement to his new cemetery. His endeavors at the crest of the highway were making Clay Henry a wealthy man.

Larwin Valley itself was turning out to be one of the most important crossroads in the Southland. Once enough companies had men fanning out across the hills, oil and natural gas were located in paying quantities. The wealth began to flow. A new aqueduct brought in fresh water from the north. Agriculture and ranching flourished as never before. Adding even more to local abundance was a thriving movie filming business that made use of the valley's beautiful, natural scenery. Buck Williams filmed his cowboy movies and brought to the valley more cinema men to film theirs. Buck's mansion near downtown increased the town's prominence. Clay Henry watched the value of his own property quadruple.

Annabelle Porter decided it was time to drive out to Larwin Valley. She read of the men and families prospering quickly. There seemed to her a goodly number of people she ought to get to know and, without question, bring the Lord's salvation their way.

A week later, Miss Porter's white convertible pulled into Clay's filling station. Clay approached her auto.

"Greetings!" she cried out.

He immediately noticed the jewel-studded cross on her bosom. He remembered seeing her picture in the paper.

"How are you, Miss Porter?"

"Just glorious! Blessings to you!"

"What brings you out this way?"

"Meeting and greeting the wonderful people of Larwin Valley!"

"Well then, I'm Clay Henry."

Annabelle looked around.

"You don't have workers to top off an auto's fuel tanks?"

"I do, but I still like to do a fair amount of meetin' and greetin' myself around these parts."

Annabelle smiled knowingly.

"Oh, I certainly understand! There's nothing as important! I'm very interested in this valley. I'm landscaping my house on a hill in the town of El Lago, something like Buck Williams has here. I wanted to see the features his men are designing. I heard his landscape is divine. I thought there might be plants he's using around his property that I could use on mine."

Clay pointed toward the train station.

"His home is just beyond the depot. He has an excellent gardener. Knows a lot about horticulture."

Annabelle gazed at the hilltop.

"The setting is marvelous! So many oak trees!"

She turned to Clay.

"I'm also hoping to see a former employee of mine who works there now. His name is Francisco Alvarez."

Clay nodded.

"We know the Alvarez family well, Miss Porter. Good men and women. Francisco is working hard on Buck's estate, even helping the gardener these days."

A clanking sound coming up the hill interrupted their conversation. A dark sedan rattled heavily into Clay's filling station.

The driver got out and rushed madly over to Clay. He gasped breathlessly.

"Please, you must help us! There's something wrong with the engine. We're late for an appointment. We fear we won't make it in time!"

Clay looked at Annabelle.

"Excuse me, Miss Porter."

Annabelle glanced with intrigue at the dark sedan and its occupants.

"I can wait."

Clay walked to the auto where the breathless driver struggled clumsily with the hood. Clay reached over.

"Here, I can do that."

As Clay opened the hood and peered into the engine, a passenger got out. He lit a cigarette and leaned against the rear of the car. A voice from inside beckoned him back to a rear passenger window. As the man leaned in talking, Clay glanced around the hood.

The man grimaced in the glaring sun, revealing teeth of yellowish orange. Clay heard only murmuring, but he recognized the language as French.

The driver, who stood beside Clay, anxiously mopped his brow. Clay reached in and located the loose belt in the engine. He looked at the sweating driver.

"I have to see if I have one of these on hand."

As Clay walked to the garage behind the market, Annabelle stepped closer to the visitors' car. She said nothing. The man finished his conversation with the passenger in the rear. He hurried past Annabelle in great distraction. He stopped at the picnic area beside the market, lighting another cigarette.

A woman's hand beckoned out of the rear passenger window. A voice, thick and raspy, called out to Annabelle.

"Come here, healer."

The lady evangelist heeded the call. As she leaned toward the window, she saw a beautiful, middle-aged woman with sad, gray eyes. Before Annabelle could take a breath to offer her greetings and blessings, the woman spoke.

"Here, you help so many."

Annabelle stepped back in surprise. The woman held out two one hundred dollar bills. Annabelle gushed.

"Why thank you, kind lady! This will feed many a hungry child! I'll hold a service at the temple in your name. To whom shall I credit this beneficence, my dear one?"

The woman gazed past Annabelle, almost not seeing her. Then she spoke firmly.

"Credit no one. That is not necessary. You work miracles. You touch people and heal the ailments of thousands. You are a saint. Just take it. That is all."

The lady disappeared behind the window, laying back her head and closing her eyes.

The heat was growing unbearable. Annabelle realized this group was under some kind of pressure and decided they could do without preaching today. She turned and walked toward her car.

The man who finished his cigarette in the shade of Clay Henry's picnic area rushed at Annabelle. He grabbed her arm and snarled.

"I saw that, you hypocrite! Your fraudulence doesn't fool me for a minute!"

Annabelle looked down at her arm. She saw the man's gold ring with its secret society emblem. She responded calmly.

"I have no idea what healing you're in need of, but the spirit moves within me now."

The man tightened his grip.

"Chrissake, lady! You don't get it! Better you leave preaching to the mechanic here or any man than stepping your high-heeled foot inside a pulpit!"

Annabelle quaked. Her entire body shook. She closed her eyes and breathed. The man loosened his grip.

"Go on, pass out! Heat stroke'll do ya some good! At least it'll keep your mouth shut! And stay away from that woman in the car!"

Annabelle's eyes fluttered open. The trembling passed. Peace flooded her body. She spoke calmly, looking squarely into the man's beady eyes.

"Your car will be fixed, sir, and you will go about your business today. But it shall not be fruitful."

The man's eyes widened in fury. He tightened his grip and shook her arm violently. He raised his other hand, poking a bony finger at her face.

"I'll tell ya who's not gonna be fruitful! You and your damn church and your fancy car and big 'ol mansion! The District Attorney's getting all over your ass. Your crooked books in the rectory will soon be front-page news. You'll learn there is only one 'Saint,' and it ain't you, lady!"

Annabelle felt no fear. She spoke calmly once more.

"By your ring, sir, I see you are a man of the Ancient Rite. There must be some good inside you, but it is lost. Now look at the gash on your hand. It is healed."

The man quickly dropped Annabelle's arm. As he stared in disbelief at the healed wound on his palm, Annabelle spun around and walked to her car.

Clay Henry came around the market and saw Annabelle behind the wheel of her white convertible. He called out.

"Thanks, Miss Porter! Stop in again on your way out of town!"

Annabelle waved good-bye and pulled away.

Clay worked quickly replacing the belt in the visitors' auto. A woman's hand in the rear seat reached out with cash for the nervous driver. The man seemed more anxious than ever.

The driver paid Clay and told him to keep the change. As the man rushed to get back in the car, his dark suit coat blew open. Clay noted the holster and gun at his side.

CHAPTER 38

▼

Two young ladies dallied along the sidewalk on their way to a summer meeting at Amy Watson's. Stopping in the shade of a large palm tree, Twyla asked Kate, "Are you sure you don't want to mention that you met the son of TR Gimble?"

Kate sighed.

"That one meeting with Ty will never mean a thing if he doesn't call me. He might forget about me after his surveys in the mountains and deserts. I simply cannot hide how attracted to him I feel right now. I don't want to face inquiries from the ladies. Better no word of this is known."

Twyla agreed.

"I know. Facing a group of women already so interested in anything to do with the Gimbles could be tricky. Sharing this anticipation with four of your closest friends is plenty. Sharing it with thirteen women would make your waiting agony!"

Kate glanced at the simmering, blue sky, wondering if Ty was hiking under a burning sun.

"I think about him every minute, Twyla. The ladies' questioning looks alone would drive me nuts!"

Susan, Julie and Nona waved to Kate and Twyla. Before they caught up with them, the girls speculated about their beautiful friend and the inventor's son.

"Do you think this is simply another fellow who'll abandon his interest in Kate once some heiress comes along with a handsome dowry?

"Mothers of millionaire sons are known for keeping their sons directed only toward proper debutantes. They want to ensure their sons marry a woman who'll keep the family money intact—and growing with future inheritances."

"Kate revealed to him that she was a working girl aiming to become an actress. That could've spoiled her chances of ever impressing the Gimble matriarch. I wonder what his mother is like."

Before entering Amy Watson's house, Kate shared her final thoughts with her dearest friends.

"The Gimble name is simply too high profile in the news for me to feel comfortable discussing Ty with anyone outside this group."

The girls gathered closer. Kate continued in a practical manner.

"If word about me dating someone like Ty Gimble ever got out, any head of a movie studio would instantly think I was trying to land a millionaire's son over a role working in movies. I don't want to throw away my chances to act on screen. I must get my shot. I can't have any known involvement with notable men."

The girls smiled. Every one of them wished for Kate the same thing, a quiet, torrid affair that would leave them breathless for further details. They made a pact to stand by Kate as she waited for Ty to call her, and to not say a word to anyone else.

Mrs. Berkowitz opened the door at Amy's and hugged Twyla.

"How's my girl with the dramatic flair?"

Twyla grinned.

"Just fine, Mrs. B. Thank you for our discussions."

The girl with the dramatic flair was maturing quickly. With kind words from Mrs. Berkowitz, Twyla was coming to realize how a woman's good looks were simply icing on the cake. She now understood such things didn't last forever. She also realized that others' opinions about a woman faded quite rapidly, as quickly as the next distraction appeared.

"I'm not as worried anymore about how I express myself, Mrs. B. I've decided to learn how to sell real estate. My aim is to sell homes to wealthy people in the movie business. I plan to join Kate in buying some real estate as soon as we can make enough money to purchase the smallest parcel of land!"

The girls gathered round the parlor and started their discussions. Amy had piqued their interest in learning about royalties. She did as she promised and brought a copy of an oil and gas lease for the ladies to peruse. Kate looked with interest at the document.

"I see how such resources offer additional value to a property. I intend to learn more about mineral rights."

Kate nudged her studious friend sitting beside her.

"More than ever, Jules, I think you need to get studying to become an engineer. Twyla and I will need to consult with you about oil and natural gas before buying land. We wouldn't even know how to look at the right maps showing these things!"

Julie brought out a folded paper she had tucked under her arm.

"I think I figured out the right kind of newspaper I should be reading. This is one of several different ones where we can find the latest information on what's happening in specific industries. News such as this is not spectacular most of the time. Most people might even find it boring, but it tells us where there are newly discovered resources in our state."

Twyla was intrigued.

"What kind of newspaper is it?"

Julie explained.

"This one's called Oil World. There are other specialty newspapers as well. There are chronicles published by chemical and engineering societies. They discuss men doing research on new projects and companies buying patents. They name who's getting into new manufacturing and oil drilling. I met a young man who was kind enough to show me which special newspapers to look for on these subjects."

"Jules!" exclaimed Twyla. "Are you telling me you're flirting with nice, young men so you can peek at their professional news journals?"

Julie lowered her glasses and looked at Twyla.

"Why, of course, my dear."

The older ladies giggled in excitement.

Harriet looked up from the notes on her lap.

"Listen to this everyone. I was searching through old news articles at my aunt's house. I was trying to find ones that mentioned patents. One article I found talked about royalties paid to TR Gimble. This news is two years older than the article about Gimble's submarine that Mrs. Berkowitz found. This article tells about the inventor being paid a million dollars in royalties for his refining patents. The article says that the Gimble Refining Company 'carries on no business and has merely the clerical expense of collecting and checking royalties.' Then I found another article about Regis Petroleum paying Gimble a million dollars cash to purchase one of his patents."

Harriet whistled.

"What a lot of money for one guy to make!"

Susan looked at Nona and winked.

"You're right. That's a ton of money. Twyla was sure right months ago when she assured us that anything to do with this man would be of special interest. I'd like to see any charlatan pulling in that kind of gold! I remember saying that doing all the inventing Gimble did and staying at the top of the heap of millionaires probably required some fantastic organization. Well, ladies, it looks like if your patent is good enough, the only organization required is to collect and cash your royalty checks!"

The ladies chuckled.

Susan turned to Mrs. McDonnell.

"Genevieve, were you able to find out if Mrs. Gimble belongs to any social clubs or churches?"

Kate leaned forward in her chair. If this woman knew anything about Ty's mom, Kate was eager to know.

Genevieve cleared her throat.

"All I know is what I told you before. The Gimble woman does not socialize. I've never seen a word about her working with charities or appearing at any parties, not even at any of the ladies' picnics for women married to men of the Guild. Am I right, Mrs. Graham, Mrs. Rhodes? Have you ever met someone named Gertrude Gimble at these affairs?"

Both elder women shook their heads. Genevieve went on.

"I'm sure she has a full time job counting and spending all those millions. They must live like royalty. I doubt Mrs. Gimble feels the need to circulate among women like us."

Amy sensed a certain tone in Genevieve's statements. Amy disliked another woman receiving an unfair sentence so she spoke out.

"Just because the woman might be reclusive doesn't mean she's uppity. We ought to reserve judgment. I know that when my husband's customers do not pay at the pharmacy, I get worried and may appear testy to those who don't know the hardship we're enduring."

Doreen looked at Amy.

"Doesn't the Gimble woman have quite the opposite problem?"

"Precisely," said Amy. "With so much money, she probably has many complicated affairs to manage. She must also endure the headaches that go with being married to someone as notable as her husband."

Kate couldn't imagine having problems from too much money. Instead, she imagined all the servants in the Gimble household. She looked up inquisitively.

"But Amy, what kind of headaches would Mrs. Gimble have?"

"First of all, the inventor travels a lot. Secondly, she has to be both mother and father to her children most of the time. I don't know how many children she has, but my husband tells me about women customers at the pharmacy who come in frantic for their children's medicines. That trauma alone, if a man is not around much, is enough to turn a woman's hair gray."

The older women nodded, touching their silver hair. Amy went on.

"Imagine the secrecy she must have to live with. There are likely scammers and scoundrels coming at their household from every angle. She has to deal with them and figure out which visitors are safe. Genevieve told us Mrs. Gimble worked for an oil company as an accountant before she got married. Think of how tough that must have been so early in all women's careers. Think of how smart she must have been to attract someone like the inventor. He would have been looking for a strong, intelligent partner, knowing what his aims were. There this woman was with everything he might need to succeed. And time has proven she must've been one tough cookie to carry on with all the loneliness and worry, as well as Gimble's success. I've not read of Gimble divorcing a wife, have any of you?"

The ladies shook their heads. Doreen looked thoughtful.

"Amy's right. I can see the woman being preoccupied with many concerns that would keep her awake at night, and then with no one to warm her bed for weeks or months on end!"

The women started chattering about that subject.

Eva held up a paper and addressed the group.

"Ladies, I have another article of interest. I thought it would be intriguing for our unmarried women to hear, but now it seems this may also help us understand the Gimble lady. This could apply to any of us one day."

"Read it to us," said Susan.

Eva began, "The title says 'Why Great Men Seldom Make Women Happy.' The article reads, 'It has without a doubt often occurred to one to ask why it is that great men as a rule make their wives or sweethearts so unhappy. And why their marriages usually turn out so miserably! It would seem that great men ought to make women happier than unknown ones in exact proportion to how much more distinguished they are. But this is not really so. It may shock you, but I believe with Bacon that no really great man can feel great love; or that if at some period of his life he does feel it, he never permits himself to indulge in it for very long. And this is the reason they do not make women very happy.'"

Eva looked up.

"Do you want to hear the rest?"

"Yes!" burst Genevieve. Then she realized how loudly she had spoken. She looked down at her hands while Eva continued.

"By a great man, I mean one who achieves vast things, not one who is trying to achieve and succeeds only spasmodically. The former's mind is too continuously occupied for the mental agitation of love to take hold upon it. He can only be under the influence of love in his rare moments of leisure. For if he let any emotion become irresistible, he would cease to be a great man! He might be a genius, because geniuses are frequently the prey of emotions, but a great man who makes history conveys the impression of strength and complete self-domination. Therefore, if a woman wants continuous love and devotion, she must seek a man of mediocre mentality, who may possess every honorable quality as well as charm, but who will not have that supreme brain which impels him to achievement at a large scale. If she finds that she has grown to love a very great man, she must be content, and even grateful, for whatever he can spare of time to give her and not feel aggrieved or neglected because his work must always come first. How many men who could perhaps have risen to a fair amount of greatness have found it impossible to attain it because of the exactingness of their wives or beloved ones!"

The older women had tears in their eyes. Mrs. Graham addressed the young ladies.

"The article reveals painful truths regarding women married to most any man trying to achieve greatness in his endeavors."

She looked at Mrs. McDonnell.

"I, for one, would not judge Mrs. Gimble with any less mercy than I would want to be judged."

Genevieve looked bashful.

"I suppose you're right," she murmured.

The accountant's wife had not yet revealed that her husband worked for Mr. Gimble, and none of the ladies had found out. Things had been going very well for Frank. Genevieve blushed knowing they were accumulating large sums in their bank account. She'd not been able to arrange any meeting with the elusive

Mrs. Gimble, but she decided it was time to see exactly how the royal Gimbles lived.

The ladies chatted some more and bid their good-byes. Billy Gimble did not make his exit under the parlor floor. Home with the flu, the boy missed hearing the ladies discuss the millions his father made. Billy would have disputed the royal household they thought he lived in. He also missed hearing the poignant words in Eva's article that applied completely to his mother's situation.

CHAPTER 39

▼

Downtown Los Angeles sparkled pleasingly to Frank McDonnell. The streetlights and neon of the city flickered in the haze of late summer heat. He passed people rushing off to home-cooked meals as others strolled into fine restaurants.

The short drive home from the Taylor Building at dusk was his favorite respite after hours spent straining over columns of numbers. Frank anticipated his beloved Genevieve waiting with his sustenance. As he cruised down the boulevard, he relished the interesting news he would share with her.

The smell of roast beef greeted his nostrils as Frank dashed up the walkway. He swept past the colorful flowers and neatly trimmed hedges to the rear of the building. Their four-bedroom flat on a fashionable lane just outside the city stood before him. Unable to resist sharing his good news at once, Frank burst through the door.

"Genevieve, darling, I'm home! I'm happy to announce that I'm now working with Harry Ritz."

Genevieve hugged him and touched his flushed cheeks.

"Is this a new job?"

"No, Gen, I'm still with Gimble, but this is really great. Mr. Ritz is a top-notch attorney. He knows all the guys downtown. He's active with the Guild. He attends lodge meetings up in Ventura and Larwin Valley, and then as far east as Riverside and El Lago. Harry has a huge network of associates! It's my chance to finally meet men I ought to know. I can move beyond having my nose stuck in Gimble's ledgers!"

Genevieve smiled. Her husband was rather shy and bookish, but he was a devoted partner to her and diligent in anything he took on.

"I'm proud of all you do, my darling. If someone as excellent as Harry Ritz will be working with you, then your job as an accountant in the Gimble organization will soon become more than that."

Frank blushed deeply and clasped Genevieve's hand.

"No man could be luckier than I."

"I know you work very hard, my dear. I never mind the evenings when you must stay downtown to finish the books and draw up checks. I get a lot of sewing and reading done. I'm pleased that a prominent attorney has seen fit to strengthen his association with you. The man has made a wise choice indeed."

Frank smiled.

"We will do well, my pet. We will do very well indeed. Soon we'll buy our own home."

Genevieve thought a moment.

"Frank, I had no doubt we'd achieve anything less with your fine skills. Speaking of homes, do you think it would be possible to visit the Gimbles sometime? I'd be delighted to meet the woman and her children. I know nothing about her, and yet we do share in common having to remain discrete about our husbands' affairs. I'd think she'd like to meet the wife of one of her husband's accountants. You told me she was once an accountant herself. She must be curious about the quality of people upon whom her husband relies."

"That's a fine idea, Gen. I never thought that the two of you could become friends. If the possibility exists for us to visit with them, we should try to arrange a meeting."

A week later, Frank and Genevieve eagerly drove up the long drive leading to the front of TR Gimble's mansion. The home was a large, two-story, four-sided white stucco building with many grids of square windows. Under a four-sided tile roof, the home featured a long, shady porch with large breezeway openings amid square columns spaced evenly along more than half of the home's front.

Genevieve was surprised that the Gimble residence had no turrets, arches, towers or flourished decoration of any sort. The large home was a simple Italian villa with a tall brick chimney rising squarely above the plain roofline.

An enormous tree stood close to the house, spreading over more than half of the lowest and highest pitches of the roof. Thick masses of leaves on the multi-trunk tree dusted the large home nestled below it.

Frank pointed to the massive tree.

"That old specimen is perhaps ninety feet tall."

Genevieve looked up.

"I've never seen one so vast anywhere else."

Genevieve nestled close to Frank in their auto. She was grateful Frank had only to ask once, and the Gimbles agreed to have them over for a short visit with tea and dessert. With TR preparing to go out of town, Genevieve insisted Frank accept their offer for the brief visit. She didn't need long to look around and absorb what she wanted to know about Gertrude and the Gimble household.

Winnie Gimble came to the door, holding a fine doll and hiding behind her mother's skirts.

"It's OK, girlie," assured Gertrude. "These are visitors Mama and Papa invited."

The little girl stayed clinging as she looked up at her mother with worried eyes.

Gertrude turned to Frank and Genevieve.

"Hello," she said. "This is Winnie, and Winnie is going upstairs right now, aren't you dear?"

Winnie shook her head up and down, held her doll close to her heart, and turned to scurry upstairs. Gertie smoothed her hair.

"Of course, I'm Gertrude Gimble. Did you find the house alright?"

Genevieve took Gertie's hand.

"We located your residence just fine. Thank you for having us. What a lovely tree out front. What kind is it?"

Gertie laughed.

"I'm told it's the largest rubber tree in the Southland."

TR came down and joined his wife and the couple. He left minutes later to answer a phone call. As he stayed talking in the kitchen, Gertie kept up casual conversation. Gertie barely looked up as TR came in and out of the drawing room during dessert. Then she asked if Genevieve would like to see her new desk.

"How wonderful!" exclaimed Genevieve. "I would love to have my own desk to work beside Frank."

Gertie led the way into the study. Genevieve admired the fine walnut desk and matching file cabinet. Gertie pointed out her tidy rows of accounting books.

"Everything's arranged by date and topic with this book serving as a cross index to all the volumes."

Genevieve could see that the woman's accounting books were massive enough to summarize every dime spent in the Gimble household. Genevieve glanced at an open daily journal on Gertie's desk. Neatly written words on a page under the day's printed date said, "Weather was nice today. Papa has to go to Red River."

There was no more detail than that on the page, and Genevieve understood why. This woman was bound to secrecy, even in her personal diary.

Under Gertie's journal lay a number of newspapers clippings, not stacked neatly, but left in hurried array. She saw one article about the lady evangelist, Annabelle Porter, another about raising ostriches, and yet others about child rearing and family nutrition. Then Genevieve's eye caught glimpse of a partial page sticking out beyond the other articles. The portion of title that was visible read, "Why Great Men Seldom ..."

Genevieve knew what the rest of the article said. She was fairly certain that Gertrude's great man seldom made this woman happy.

Gertie saw Genevieve's eyes scanning the items on her desk. She hurriedly invited Genevieve to come and see the library. Genevieve understood the woman's embarrassment and quickly turned away from Gertrude's things.

Surveying the library, Genevieve couldn't help being impressed. Shelves built to the ceiling brimmed with titles of every kind.

"Oh, what marvelous books! I can see how many children's books you have. Your darlings have such a wide variety of stories to learn from!"

Gertie smiled.

"My sweetest, treasured moments are reading to my children each night. They each seem to take something special from these stories. It delights me to see how they learn."

Genevieve glanced at the clock. She had but a few moments left in their visit to ask Gertrude about her social involvements.

"Do you ever attend any events with the women from the Chamber of Commerce or the wives of men of the Guild?"

Gertie's face fell.

"I'm afraid not. My duties here are all I can keep up with."

"Is there no church your family attends?" pressed Genevieve. "Frank and I were thinking about attending a church in this area. It would be nice to see you and your children at least once in a while at Sunday service."

Gertie frowned.

"My mother, sister and I used to attend church. Now that Mr. Gimble is so involved with his inventions, I'm afraid I haven't found it too uplifting to attend church without my husband. I'd rather be here with his meals prepared should he come home. He usually works at the plant on Sundays when his downtown offices are closed, that is, when he's here in town and not away. If I can be here when he comes in for a Sunday meal or needing company for a drive to the country, I'd rather be praising those moments with him than sitting in a church praising the Lord while my husband comes home to an empty house."

Genevieve could clearly see how the inventor's wife was living. She didn't bother to ask if Gertrude belonged to any more ladies' societies. She knew what Gertrude's answer would be. The woman was living in near total isolation, except for the daily comfort of her children.

"Who are your other children besides Winnie?"

Gertie brightened.

"There's Ty, who's the oldest. He works much of the time for his dad and is away right now on geological surveys. And then there's Billy, the youngest. No doubt he'll be a pistol like I once was as an accountant."

"What do you mean by pistol?"

"I mean that I had to have a sly head on my shoulders and a temper at times to deal with the oil men where I worked. There wasn't a day that went by that the men weren't trying to pull the wool over my eyes regarding their field accounts or royalties to be disbursed or readings from the oil wells. It became a game of sorts for me to figure out inconsistencies. I'm not saying that all men attempted to cheat the numbers. It was entertaining for me to find out where honest mistakes were made and which men indulged in certain, um, frequent patterns of reporting errors."

"I bet your work was very valuable to the oil company."

Gertie looked at the accountant's wife with a sharp eye.

"You can be sure they made a few more dollars than other oil concerns who did not have anyone watching the books as closely."

Frank was bored sitting alone in the drawing room. He came to the library door in time to hear Gertie's last comment. He beckoned Genevieve with a frown.

"It's time to leave, my dear. These busy people have much to do."

Genevieve turned to Gertie.

"I so appreciate you letting us stop in. I hope you know that you can call me any time you or the children need anything. You can be assured we share the same discretion. We want to do everything in your best interests."

Gertie forced a smile. She ushered the accountant and his wife to the front door. Winnie ran downstairs clinging to her favorite doll. She held her mother's skirts once more.

"Good-bye," called Gertie with a wave.

After the McDonnells left, TR came downstairs. Gertie sighed.

"She was just curious, Papa, but still, it was nice to have a lady visitor other than my sister."

TR looked out the window into the darkness.

"I know, Gertie. Just watch your back."

Winnie sucked her thumb and didn't utter a word. Gertie stroked the child's hair and glanced at her husband.

"I'll go see if Billy is feeling better."

TR beckoned to Winnie.

"It's time to read a story to my next-to-most-favorite sweetheart. Upstairs we go, Winnie. Let's find that book about the panther and the hunter that you like."

"Swell!" exclaimed Winnie. She brightened and took her thumb from her lips.

CHAPTER 40

▼

As Frank and Genevieve drove away from the Gimble mansion, the accountant's wife could barely contain her excitement.

"They are so entirely different than I imagined!"

Frank kept his eyes on the road.

"What do you mean, Mrs. McDonnell?"

"Why, I would have imagined them living like royalty with a doorman and servants galore. Their home was so simple, not decorated end to end with regal, Victorian furnishings like I would have thought. Surely, with all the man's travels, he has seen the inside of courts and fancy estates. Yet their home was nothing like that."

Frank nodded.

"That's pretty much how Mr. Gimble is. The man prefers overalls and any place outdoors to fancy offices or fine suits. It is a conundrum for Mr. Ritz and I to figure out. Why a man and woman like the Gimbles would want all the money they have is beyond reason to us. Now I see you notice the paradox, too."

"Of course I do. What a mysterious couple. Maybe they enjoy hiding what they have instead of flaunting it. Maybe the two of them are like hunters who simply want to pounce on more millions and eat up their prey. Maybe they enjoy licking their chops and laughing all the way to the bank. It could be that we aren't really seeing what they're like at all."

"Somewhere amid what you just said, my pet, I think you're perceiving what Harry and I have somewhat determined."

"What's that?"

Frank's voice dropped to cautious, measured tones.

"Well, it seems to Harry and me there may be a lot more capital in the Gimble fortune than we can seem to lay eyes on in the Gimble accounts that we know of."

"Really, Frank?"

"Really, Gen. What's needed to run the man's companies always appears on demand. There's never any shortage of funds. There are never imbalances in the books, and there's never an endeavor the inventor wants to pursue or a company he wants to purchase that ever seems out of his reach. In addition to funding all of his own interests, he puts large sums of money into other men's endeavors. And in addition to all that, my sweet, he sends money to French orphans, remote villages and needy people in other parts of the world. Don't be fooled that these people do not appear in the social pages or attend charity balls and the like. Their money seems to be flowing out in many directions. What little I've seen and heard about is staggering."

"So let me understand this correctly, Frank. You have no idea how much money these people really have?"

"That's right, my dear, not a clue."

"Holy heavens! You never mentioned this before, but maybe I can understand why. You're supposed to know these things that most accountants would know about their employers. I can't imagine the kind of wealth you describe, and I can't imagine hiding it from the entire world while spending it everywhere! Aren't you as close as any of the other accountants working with Gimble's funds?"

"I am, I assure you, at least so far as any of the accountants who work in Gimble's downtown office. Harry Ritz is going to be recommending elevating my position to head accountant. So far, Gimble has not determined any accountant to hold a position such as that in any of his companies. I honestly think Gertrude has held the reins until now. It will be interesting to see if I gain any further insights in a more expanded role."

"Well, dear, that determines what we must do."

"What's that?"

"It's clear that we should try to enter into some kind of legal business arrangement with this couple. If there's that much money to spare in their accounts, it would seem perfectly legitimate for us to become business partners on just one deal with the Gimbles. That would help us garner more capital for our own lives. The man does not pay you enough for all the work you do at his office. If you're going to take on even greater responsibilities, maybe think about not requesting a big raise in pay. Ask for a modest pay increase, but tell him that you would like in on one business deal that you know can make us good money we can retire on. I only want to live splendidly in my old age, Frank. One lucrative opportunity with this man who has such a golden touch in business would be enough to set us up for the rest of time."

"That's an interesting notion, Gen. I'll probably need Harry's advice to determine what kind of deal that would be."

"I can think of one."

"Such as?"

"How about an oil and gas lease?"

"Hmm. I'd have to study the ones he has. And there are more he's planning for the future. You know, he has lease partnerships in place on literally thousands of acres of land here in California, all over the West, and even down in Mexico and up in Canada."

"Dear Lord! I was only thinking about maybe one. Our arrangement doesn't need to get too complicated. It should be some location on land here in California where the entire deal would be a nice arrangement they'd enjoy participating in with us. Local property would allow us to keep watch over other parties who might become involved. We'd want it in a legal jurisdiction where we are living, not overseas or out of the country. We'd want to be able to visit our little nest egg. It would be fun to take drives out to see the oil drilling and new facilities that will be making us our royalties. Wouldn't that be wonderful, Frank?"

"Gosh, Gen. It sounds like you've gone to college. Where did you learn these things?"

"I've been listening to other women learning about property and mineral rights."

"Where?"

"At Amy Watson's, you know, those meetings I attend each month when I can."

"Is that the pharmacist's wife?"

"Yes. Do you know her husband?"

"Not personally. Harry mentioned Amy Watson worked for his downtown staff. He mentioned wanting to sponsor her husband into the Guild. He even went so far as to say that the pharmacist has the makings for a brother in the Ancient Rite if he can pass the tests of merit."

"Really, Frank. I had no idea someone like a big city attorney would be interested in sponsoring a neighborhood pharmacist."

Frank glanced out the car window. He accelerated and changed lanes several times. He relaxed back in his seat.

"I have to say, Gen, I admire your spunk in contemplating a plan to engage in an oil and gas lease with the Gimbles. That's very forward thinking. I'll have to see if I can match your bright thoughts. You've given me a grand homework assignment. How I love you for your studious eyes and smart mind."

"Thank you, my dear."

Gertie laid her hand on Frank's thigh. She moved her shoulders toward him as she nestled closer and purred.

"Let's snuggle mightily tonight."

"Sure thing!" exclaimed Frank.

He barely avoided running into the curb.

CHAPTER 41

▼

Ty gasped, his eyesight swimming above the simmering hills. Fiery air rattled inside his lungs. Once-colorful blossoms blew past him dry and shriveled. Life born from spring rains merged with dusty particles in the midday desert hell of summer's end. Ty tried to grab blindly for his canteen, but the metal scalded his fingertips. He felt sure he'd be next to collapse onto the sand.

"Don't you be eyeballin' that mule, son," said Devon, the tall, black geologist leading the troupe. "She's loaded up enough as it is and just as tired as you. No one's allowed to unload anything more on her back. We have just enough water for us and 'ol Bessie to make it to camp. Step it up and don't think about the heat. Think of anything you want, son, but do NOT think about the heat!"

As young men are apt to do, most in the party did not pace themselves. Older, more experienced surveyors like Devon knew how. The young men burst out of their tents each morning, wrestling and pulling pranks before departing on their trek. Devon knew about saving his strength to endure the climbing and hiking back to camp in the sun's heat. He proved even smarter weeks into the surveys knowing that a man would get tired all the more quickly after consecutive days of such arduous work.

Hours earlier, the geology team had hiked six miles into a canyon. The air felt surprisingly cool for the first time in weeks, but that was before dawn broke. The group was jovial as they set up their equipment. Under the first rays of sunrise, the men chipped away rock samples from the cliffs, took survey points and drew maps of mineral veins.

Intent on learning all he could, Ty made sure he helped with each of the tasks. The technical instruments of this trade came easy to the inventor's son. The men noted his adeptness in mathematics, writing and sketching. His skills and easy humor with the men were much appreciated, but Ty was not as desert-hardy as they.

As the sun streaked over the mountains, Ty had run up a steep embankment. The sunrise photos he captured for his mother were stunning. He knew she'd be pleased developing these in her new darkroom in the basement. Now close to noon, the dead weight of the camera felt like a pound of lead on his back. Like everything else he carried, it seemed to weigh three times more than it really did. Every ounce in his pack kept his legs from walking faster back to camp on the other side of the hills.

Ty's eyes rolled back above the horizon, his tongue as dry as cardboard in his mouth. He felt lightheaded and hoped for some kind of deliverance cooler than the water in his canteen.

A vision of an angel swept into his mind. She stood twice as tall as the distant hills with a sheer, pink gown draped around her lovely figure. Ty blocked out the windswept hills and strained to see each gentle curve of the angel's body. The gown blew softly around her form.

As he tried to focus better, Ty saw gentle breezes pick up folds of the sheer fabric, stretching the gown and rearranging it into places where he could see more of her body.

"Oh please let the wind press her gown closer to the front of her," prayed Ty.

He exhaled several deep breaths to help the wind's mission. He kept his legs wobbling forward and his eyes trained on every detail of the lovely angel's breasts, waist and thighs outlined by the gown's caresses kissing those wonderful things.

The hot wind touched the back of his neck as he felt her sweet, warm breath. She sighed, leaning forward and kissing him on the forehead. Her warm, full lips lingered along his brow before softly touching his nose, his lips and chin. As beads of sweat trickled down his face and into his beard, Ty felt the angel's kisses touch lightly upon his face.

Her soft hands rested upon his chest. No matter that the straps of his backpack were actually pressing here, it was her fingertips caressing the curves of his chest and circling smoothly upward to lie upon his shoulders. Each tug he felt on his neck and shoulders was the angel pulling him closer to her heart. Eager to join her vibrant energy, his heart increased its beats. The angel and Ty were flowing in rhythms together, swirling and circling into the blazing heat toward the sun.

Ty felt suddenly virile in his loins. Glowing strength seemed to carry his legs and lift his feet adeptly over rocks and sand. The angel was breathing upon him and calling his name intently. His head leaned forward to rest on the pink bosom that leaned toward him. Her golden hair swirled and paused upon his face. Ty reached out his hands to encircle her waist, his palms coming to rest at the perfect small of her back. Her hips moved forward under the sheer gown, lifting upward toward Ty with the beautiful curve of her arching back.

The hills were coming closer. They burst forth into full view with the angel's fiery warmth. Heat radiated from the hollow of her golden hips. Ty's lips felt the soft smoothness of her skin as he explored the curves and valleys up to her neck. His fingers traveled in concentric circles, tracing blazing trails that ignited passion deep in the angel's body.

The angel's fingertips met his, and their eyes locked. Deep blue sparks flew from Ty's trembling hand. The angel clasped and steadied his hand. Ruby explosions from her fingertips pierced the endless cyan desert sky. The circle became complete. There loomed no distance between his vision and reality in these hills. The heavenly angel and Ty were now ascending as one in a beam of pure light, merging with all things earth and sky and flesh.

A huge blast suddenly shattered the sound waves inside the glow where Ty traveled upward with his vision. He stumbled, laying face down in the sand. Men came running from their scattered line along the trail. Devon stood with the handgun, but it wasn't smoking.

"Dang, kid!" he declared, "I've never seen a rattler blown apart like that. Hell, the blast left a crater in the desert!"

As Ty got up and dusted himself off, he quickly adjusted his belt and made sure that everything was dangling loosely where it needed to be. Devon had spotted a snake on the path, coiled and ready to take down the mule. The wise surveyor had grabbed the gun he remembered seeing Ty stash high up in the mule's saddle pack. It was the modified gun TR had given Ty. The other men ran up and examined the sizeable crater left by the gun's blast. They were fascinated with the obvious power this gun delivered.

"I swear I barely aimed the thing!" exclaimed Devon.

Ty grinned. His mind was still wafting upward toward his memories of the pink angel.

"It's a gun my dad wanted me to bring along in case we needed it."

The inventor's son spoke quietly as he put the weapon into his pack.

"A regular gun would do just fine for a snake. Keep this one in mind if something's far away. We'd want the bullets for that."

Within minutes, the men arrived at camp. They gulped water and ate seeds to replenish the salts they sweated. The relaxation felt good as they talked about the closing days of their work. They sat under a large tarp attached to the water wagon. Stretched tight with stakes dug deeply into the hill's sandy soil, the tarp held firm against the gusty winds. On this hill, the breezes blew cooler than on the deathly desert floor. The men packed their equipment and organized survey information. They talked about future assignments and new teams each would be joining after completing this job.

"I've got Larwin Valley coming up next," said one of the men. "There's some guy named Scoot Wynn who's been poking around for oil on his land for months. He says he needs a pro to point out where he can drill. He said he can only afford to hire me for a few days, but I've been wanting to head to that valley. This Scoot is just a small-time operator, but I want to get to know some of the men from the large oil concerns out there. I think it'd be steady work. Who knows? I might meet a gal and settle down out there."

"That's a choice location," said another man. "I'm heading farther north to that new refinery for Regis. I hear it's ungodly busy up there. I'd prefer some work in a clean lab after all this crawling around."

Devon hadn't said anything. Ty studied the experienced surveyor.

"Where are you headed next?"

"I've got some things to do for this guy whose name I don't know. Some of his men contacted me when I was at a Regis meeting downtown. When I asked who was running the survey, they laughed and said to call him the Saint. That's OK by me. I'll call him whatever he wants. You stick around this business long enough, you know you don't always need to meet the boss. You just tell 'em to make sure the ink's dry on the money."

"Hmm," said Ty. "I hope they aren't mean sons of bitches, just elusive. It's not so unusual in oil and mining for men to keep their affiliations secret. Things get pretty crazy in competition trying to find the right veins to tap. But you can handle a gun. I'd keep one near if I was working for someone I didn't know."

Devon looked thoughtful.

"Lady Wilderness is the only entity that none of us can ever completely know. She has more tricks up her sleeve than man can ever dream up. She gives you a lot of clues, but I'd say she's the toughest boss of all!"

The men chuckled. Devon continued.

"Men are cowards, a lot of them. The ones who aren't flashing big guns are braver in my book than those who do. But men who hide in the shadows and never allow you any fight at all are the worst cowards of all. I've worked with every sort of coward and brave heart probably out there. I'm sure I'll see a lot more in my time. I hope to work with you again someday, Ty. For a millionaire's son, you really do have your feet on the ground."

"Thanks," said Ty, "I'd like that, too. And thanks for everything you showed me. I won't forget."

That night, cool breezes returned. Ty lay on his cot and wondered if the angel in pink would come and visit him in his dreams. When their eyes had locked in his desert vision that day, Ty knew in a blinding flash that the angel was Kate. His brief memory of her had ascended above any other young lady he could recall. His vision of her had not grown dim or fuzzy in the desert. It amplified to some unknown quantum power that brought him safely across the toughest stretch he'd hiked.

He ached to call her but was nowhere near a telephone. He wouldn't be near any town for another week. He hoped she hadn't met some dashing young fellow who stole her heart. He hoped that by now she wasn't some concubine for one of the movie studio men.

Somehow, Ty could deal with men seeing her pretty face and lovely body on the silver screen, but he knew she wouldn't be the same woman if one of the movie men did things she would regret. He thought of the powerful gun and the kind of men it should be used on. They were rattlers indeed, striking at prey with no sort of conscience. Ty was not prone to violence, but the only person he could think of ever bringing that kind of force to bear upon would be someone who left their rubbish upon his angel.

The thought of Kate's peaches and cream loveliness helped Ty to slumber deeply. Once again, she appeared in the sheer gown. This time she took his hand. They walked together through a forest thick with fragrant shrubs and flowers, where giant trees loomed overhead.

A storm was approaching, and they cuddled in the nook of the largest tree, its branches splattering fresh raindrops upon her delicate cheeks and lovely breasts. He took her face in his hands and pressed his lips to hers. She responded lovingly and completely, holding firmly his back and shoulders just as she had done earlier that day. He felt her strength. It added something undefined and magnificent to his essence, which seemed humble by comparison now to hers.

They slid down deeper onto the ground. Their legs tangled, thighs melting together, approaching the heat of fire. Once again, her hips were gold and powerful, begging for him to connect with her. Somehow he had no clothes to untangle or toss beside the tree. He was bare and strong and ready to find her inner beauty with all he had become. Sheer deliverance met his essence in a powerful explosion. This time, no gun blast shattered the air around them. The blast was all of them, both of them, clean and pure, with no one and nothing else to matter. Kate and Ty ascended as one form in a beam of light, merging with all things earth and sky and flesh. Heavenly peace descended upon Kate and Ty lying under the vast tree inside his dream.

A white streak of light glared across the sky. They could see the light shatter the clouds through the dense, heavy branches above. Kate grabbed Ty with all her might. It should have been the other way around, but he stumbled and fell helplessly. Kate caught him in her arms and pushed him from under the tree. She leapt out of the way just as heavy, sopping trees branches crashed to the ground where they'd been curled in passion seconds before.

Ty awoke, breathless and exhausted.

"Oh, geez," he thought. "Maybe I can sneak out and wash these things quickly, but it's too damn quiet."

He folded the blanket out of sight planning to spill some water on his cot and rub that clean. The men joked about washing one sock in the mornings when the desert heat could dry it quickly. Ty showed no less restraint than the other fellows, but now he realized with a smile that his clothes would soon be tossed. This pair of shorts needn't go home to his mother's laundering. The only thing he cared about was calling Kate the moment he returned.

CHAPTER 42

▼

"Kate!" exclaimed Ty when she picked up the phone. "It's Ty, Ty Gimble, but you wouldn't recognize me with the lumberjack beard I've grown."

Kate laughed.

"You sound out of breath."

"I just got in. I'm still at the train station. Luckily you're still at your mom's house!"

Kate pinched herself and tried to keep her voice even.

"Well, I think my mom's is a pretty fine place to live for now."

They talked briefly and arranged a date the coming weekend. Kate sounded gleeful.

"I actually have an audition to attend on Friday. My girlfriends and I are engaged in deliberations about exactly the right outfit and jewelry I should wear. Of course, we're discussing these things amid our talk about buying a piece of property in Larwin Valley."

Ty remained breathless.

"Save the details. I'll want to hear about everything when I see you."

"That'll be fun," giggled Kate.

"I'll call you later"

Ty elatedly hung up the phone, hitting his elbow as he dashed from the phone booth.

Gertie laughed and kissed the news article. The words couldn't have made her happier. The report described how completion was anticipated within the week for the new Regis port refinery. Her husband would be home soon.

She picked up another newspaper, a small, out-of-state publication. Like the special science and engineering chronicles received at their house, it came addressed to Thomas Gimble. Billy was gone to the newsstand to pick up a local newspaper. Gertie decided she had time to browse through this other paper she ordinarily wouldn't read.

The banner on the fourth page announced, "Shale Plant Now Assured." Gertie felt her heart descend. This first breaking story about the Red River venture meant that her husband now had intense hours of work ahead. His sole focus would be on the design of the new refinery. Gertie frowned. A quick scan of the article showed no date for the refinery's opening. She wondered how long the work for her husband would last. She read the text.

"Producing gasoline from oil shale bids fair to be one of Red River's most important industries and threatens, also, to revolutionize the entire oil industry, according to JE Hempton, president of the Red River Oil Products Company."

Something about that line made Gertie shudder. She read on.

"The company has already expended about $50,000 for labor, equipment, machinery and supplies on their Red River holdings, and have an ambitious program for the coming year which contemplates the erection of one or more units to their elaborate manufacturing plant. The Gimble process for extracting oil from shale is no longer an experiment. It is, according to Mr. Hempton, and many other authorities on oil shale, an assured success. Gimble, the inventor of the process which promises to solve the problem raised by the constantly diminishing supply of crude oil in the United States, has already erected a plant in California, and this plant is now being successfully operated."

The article explained the plan for the new refinery to be designed by her husband. It told how stockholders would be allowed the unique opportunity to participate in the profits of the company by purchasing gasoline at the cost of manufacture at the plant near Red River.

Gertie shook her head.

"So all this is coming to pass."

She wondered about the words 'threaten' and 'revolutionize' from the news article. She'd seen those words years ago when news reporters wrote with great excitement of her husband's submarine. She wondered if the same words describing her husband's inventions for refining shale meant more guards posted around their home every night. This new adventure would mean another thing she couldn't talk about with anyone, not even with that curious wife of TR's accountant.

Gertie looked at her desk with the folio of freshly printed checks her husband handed her weeks earlier. The checks were for a new account she was to solely manage. She didn't think anything would become active with this account for years. Apparently she was wrong.

The checks were imprinted with 'Gimble Coal & Shale Oil Company.' She chuckled silently. Coal could be crushed and sold for pennies compared to the amount of money TR was investing in a steel company designing metals to process shale. The word 'coal' on the Gimble company name was likely registered to ensure that shale oil didn't seem like such a threat to oil companies. They would care if shale oil succeeded in a big way and threatened their skyrocketing petroleum profits.

Gertie knew there were other details of which she wasn't aware. Each venture her husband embarked upon brought surprising, new information that TR often forgot to tell her up front. She looked around for Billy. He should have arrived home by now.

Billy whistled a tune and enjoyed his stroll. It was cold out today, but the brisk air felt fine. He appreciated this walk to complete an errand requested by his mother. He'd been cooped up in the house a long time with the flu. All the chicken soup and castor oil his mother forced down his throat had helped to calm his stomach. Winnie, too, had been extra nice to him, bringing her dolls outside his door and chatting during little tea parties she hosted to help keep him from feeling bored. Billy's thoughts wandered as autumn leaved crackled under his shoes.

"Maybe things will go okay with our family this winter. Maybe Dad will get some time off to spend with us in front of a fire. Maybe Ty will even have time to spend with me over Christmas. Seeing another movie with Ty would be fun! Maybe Ty will get all wobbly again seeing another girl. He must've forgotten about the other one by now."

Billy had missed his daily walks to the newsstand when he was sick. He looked forward to previewing Gimble news articles on his own. He could see that reporters didn't tell the same story about his dad from one article to the next, that is, unless they were completely copying someone else's story. Sometimes two different newspapers ran the exact same article about his dad, wrong facts and all. Some newspapers didn't even spell his dad's name correctly.

Billy decided there was a lot to be discounted concerning claims that different reporters made about what his dad was doing. Some reporters' stories sounded to

Billy as if they should be scenes in a Buck Williams movie. Those reporters made everything they wrote sound like a grand adventure, or some horrible scandal or mysterious evil that people ought to panic over. Billy felt assured, realizing that he was learning to see things a little more practically, just as his dad and Ty urged him to do.

As he walked up to the newsstand, Billy saw a boy a little older than he. Billy was feeling friendly.

"Is that a brand new bike?

"It is," affirmed the boy.

"Neat."

The older boy had a newspaper in his hands. He was straddling his bike reading the inside pages. Billy saw the boy's paper open to a page that had the Gimble name printed in large letters at the top of a column. Billy peered over the top of the paper.

"Is that a story about the inventor?"

"Sure is. I follow everything that Mr. TR, I mean Mr. Gimble, does. I actually know him."

"Me, too," said Billy. "How did you meet him?"

The boy smiled brightly.

"I was riding the train one summer out to Red River. I sat next to this man, and we started talking. He asked me all kinds of interesting questions, questions that made me think about some of the small inventions I was working on. I told him I was from California. He asked what part, and I told him Los Angeles. Then he told me that his name was TR Gimble. He said that I could come by his plant where he does his experimental work. I stop by there once in a while. I've gotten to know his assistant, a guy with crazy, curly hair named Hiram. I also got to know his son, Ty. I get along real good with Mr. Gimble, Hiram and Ty. I try not to bother them too much, and I sure try not to ask too many questions."

Billy's curiosity grew.

"So do you and the Gimble father and son do anything?"

"Not too much anymore," said the older boy. "They both travel a lot now, but I did have something terrific happen. The inventor helped me patent something!"

The boy's eyes were shining as he recounted the story of how he came up with the idea for a phonograph needle that played records a little clearer than other needles.

"Mr. Gimble helped me draw up my design and write a proper description. I had to explain how the record needle I put together was different from any other.

He helped me make the sentences correct. Then his attorney drew up an application, and we submitted it to the U.S. Patent Office!"

The boy laughed.

"My parents about fainted when my first royalty check came. A small company made a certain number of my needles, and some of them sold. Then a record company asked to buy the patent so we sold that, too. I didn't mind a bit when other companies came along and invented new record-playing machines that didn't need my phonograph needle. Mr. TR told me ahead of time that would happen, and it happened just like he said. I learned that my idea was a design improvement patent. Those don't usually last too long before another inventor comes along and makes a better improvement on the last improvement that the previous inventor invented."

Billy could barely keep up.

"Gosh, you sure talk fast."

"Oh sorry. My brain just gets going, and sometimes I don't think to turn it off so someone else can talk. By the way, my name is Joey MacDermott. What's yours?"

Billy had a funny look on his face, almost as if he was thinking of throwing up.

"Er, my name is Billy Gimble."

"Really? You're his son? I'm really glad to meet you! I never saw you at the plant."

"Well, my sister and I don't go there. We're mostly at the house. In fact, I need to get back now. My mom wanted something, and I was supposed to get right back."

Joey grinned.

"Well, heck, Billy, it was super to meet another one of Mr. TR's, I mean, Mr. Gimble's sons. I'm sure you're every bit as smart as Ty. I won't keep you any longer. Bye!"

As Joey rode off on his new bike, Billy could feel the familiar twist in his stomach. The boy obviously adored his dad and Ty. Billy remembered hearing his mother mention Joey MacDermott's name. Billy had been listening over the balcony that night. It was the night his dad actually said nice things about Billy. Nevertheless, this was a kid that his dad and his dad's attorney had actually registered a patent for!

Billy felt angry that the boy had been so nice to him. Billy wanted to hate him outright. But it sounded like his mom knew Joey was nice, too, and it sure seemed like this kid was close with both his brother and dad and even Hiram! Billy was completely frustrated that he couldn't even hate someone he was jealous of!

Everything Billy might have loved about his family felt like it had finally slipped away. He kicked the newspaper stand with all his might. The cover on top of the newspapers popped open. Billy didn't even look right or left as he spat on the ground. His mother could go to hell. She knew all about this favorite boy! She probably loved Joey more than she loved Billy, just like Pa and Ty!

Billy grabbed a newspaper from the open stand without inserting his money. He didn't care who saw him. It was the first time Billy Gimble ever stole anything in his life. He didn't run down the sidewalk. He didn't sob. He just didn't care. He was going to take his own sweet time doing whatever he wanted from now on, and consequences be damned!

CHAPTER 43

▼

Friday morning arrived. Kate had every strand of hair curled and secured around her face, each eyebrow carefully penciled to a pleasing arch. She'd reapplied her rose lipstick three times to outline her mouth as voluptuously as possible. Her aqua blue outfit was spotless and ironed, her shoes shined to creamy perfection. There was nothing further she could do to compete with any other woman vying for stardom on the silver screen.

Kate's natural endowments were dolled up with the best downtown cosmetics and jewelry she could afford. There was nothing left to do but wait in the lobby until her name was called.

Auditions were running late. It was looking as if Kate might have to spend the entire day here. She told her boss at the real estate company she'd be back in the office by one, but now it looked like she might have to work on Saturday to catch up on the papers piling up on her desk through the afternoon. It appeared that movie studios didn't run on quite the same efficient schedule as her office.

Three hours passed before her name was called. Kate boarded the elevator to the fifth floor, only to find more rows of hopeful young ladies waiting on black metal chairs in another room upstairs. Some of the girls were reading scripts for other auditions. Novices who didn't know they ought to appear as if they were reading scripts were reading romance novels. Kate brought nothing to read. She wanted to catch the eye of every secretary and assistant scurrying about. Now she wished she'd brought her copy of Amy's oil and gas lease to study. This was a perfect time to bone up on technical matters in case this audition didn't work out.

Kate chuckled over how pragmatic she was becoming. She was not the youngest flower in the bouquet of blossoming womanhood here today. Some of the girls looked to be as young as fourteen. Kate could see their innocence and naiveté shining on their faces under heavy makeup. Kate knew she was smarter for waiting to take this step. She'd listened carefully to the warnings of women who'd been through auditions at too early an age. They were mostly girls who arrived in the big city from small towns in the Midwest. Without their mothers alongside them, some had sordid experiences. Kate felt she could handle herself with the confidence she had now.

Her sharp skills at the real estate office increased her knowledge about how to deal with brazen men. The talks with the women in Amy's parlor helped Kate form stronger views. She knew today was just a stepping stone, but still, she wanted to cut the mustard with these men. They controlled the portals onto movie studio lots and the kind of income she hoped to make.

A stocky man in a white straw hat came striding in. He tipped his hat to the girls and planted himself in front of the secretary's desk.

"Tell him CJ Niles is here."

He added with a chuckle.

"And no, you pretty thing, I am not here for an audition."

The door to the inner office stood slightly ajar, following no response after the secretary's light tap. Mr. Niles pushed past the secretary into the office. Everyone heard Niles roar.

"Barry! How the hell are you?"

The wide-eyed girls saw Mr. Niles skillfully kick the door shut behind him. The girls shifted in their chairs. This was going to mean more delay than the agonizing waits they already endured between auditions. The telephone never stopped ringing with calls for the man in the office. The secretary informed him of half of the callers, and the director asked for half of those to be patched through to his office.

The young woman seated beside Kate sighed heavily.

"You know we could be asked back next week if they don't get to all of us today."

Kate smoothed her hair.

"That won't go well with my schedule."

The hopeful candidate studied the older girl.

"That's why, if you want to be in movies, you have to waitress at night."

Kate gazed intently at the director's closed door.

"I'm here on the chance I'll be called in today."

Moments later, CJ Niles opened burst through the director's door. As he walked out, he bellowed over his shoulder.

"You're gonna be sorry you didn't pick up more shares! This one's on fire. Everyone else is buying 20,000 minimum!"

Kate leaned forward a bit and looked at the inner office. She saw the back of a hand waving Mr. Niles out the door. The secretary quickly got up and closed it. The phone rang again. Kate heard the secretary answer politely.

"Why yes, Miss Porter, how are you today? Oh, and blessings to you, too. I do think the man is available for just a moment. You want me to write down what? Oh, I see, $500 for a ticket to the celebrity revival at Silverton Park. And what else? You think he might be needing twelve tickets? No problem. I wrote down exactly what you said. Let me see if he can take your call."

Kate swallowed hard thinking about the value of these casual transactions expected by solicitors interrupting the director without a care for the man's appointments that day. What money and what a business! She wondered if solicitors were just as frequent at the Gimble offices and residence. They must be. The inventor appeared to be as wealthy as any of these movie studio heads, maybe even more!

Kate decided not to think about the inventor or Ty. It could be that she might not even be able to make her date. It was possible she would have to work long hours on Saturday. It was much harder to get her paperwork done when she couldn't call the parties she needed to talk to and get the right information she needed to fill in the real estate forms. Her schedule wasn't looking too promising at the moment.

The girls in the hard, black metal chairs shifted uncomfortably. Each wondered how many more interruptions there'd be before their names were called. Kate felt stuck, but decided she might as well wait.

Two more girls were called.

"Oh, great," thought Kate. "Now they're doubling up candidates to make up for lost time."

The two girls lasted exactly one and a half minutes with the director. Their dejected faces told their story to the other girls. Those remaining looked down at their laps, and then exchanged more worried glances with one another. Amazingly, Kate was called next. And amazingly, she was called in alone.

She entered the director's office.

"A little bit older of a sweetie pie," said the smiling, older man. "Please have a seat."

Kate saw two plump chairs in front of the director. Heavy oak-paneled walls lined the entire room except for one window that provided a sweeping view to the movie lot outside. A massive armoire stood on the wall that separated this man's office from the outer office. Next to that was a tall bookcase filled to bursting with thick manuscripts and binders.

"Soundproofing," Kate instantly thought. "Well, no matter. Here I am. I've waited all this time, and I know where the exit is!"

The door wasn't locked so she gave it her best shot.

"Is my age the reason you called me in by myself?"

"I'll ask the questions," barked the man.

He frowned and studied her written profile. He tapped on her black and white photo.

"I don't think this picture does you any good. No one can see your gams. You can barely see anything below your face. Directors want to see all the way to the gams, and clearly. Tits, ass, face, gams, in that order. Don't forget it. You'll need more than one picture with your resume."

Kate took a deep breath.

"Welcome to the industry," she thought.

She didn't have anything to say which would capitalize on much theater experience since she'd only had time to act in some plays during high school. She didn't want to sit there making lame excuses, so she used her most articulate voice.

"Sir, I can memorize scripts rapidly. I can swoon, act coy or angry and give the biggest yell you ever heard."

"Got talent, you think, huh?" chuckled the director. "Go over to that couch. Lie on it like you want to seduce me."

Kate hadn't figured her interview would come to the fabled casting couch so soon. No wonder the girls scooted out so fast. This man didn't mess around with formalities, plus he was running far behind the audition schedules at this point. Not that he cared about inconveniencing the countless candidates, Kate knew he was probably missing his early cocktail hour. Kate got up. Just then, the phone rang. Kate sat back down. She knew his calls weren't patched through unless it was someone he'd already cleared with his secretary to allow.

As she guessed, he picked up the phone.

"Yyello," he said. "Uh-hum. Yeah. Larwin Valley? Nah. The Saint? Who in Christ's name is the Saint? Can't say? Why not? Oh."

The director looked at Kate. She looked right back, staring him down with her wide blue eyes. He turned back to his phone.

"What about any entitlements? You don't say. Who's got the homestead on the minerals, Nash? Not a problem. What? That'd be the guys over at the bank. Well, yes, of course their money's liquid, you nut. They got more stinkin' liquidity than you got sperm!"

He looked up at Kate. She crossed her legs and smoothed her skirt. He rose to peer at her knees over his desk. He plopped back down in his chair.

"I got a hot babe in here for an audition right now. What? Oh no. She's a challenge. Look, send me a map with boundaries. I'll have my guys take a look at it. If you want me to be talking this up to the other fellows, we gotta have some answers, and I mean all the details. Yeah, right. ALL the information. Actually, stop by with it. I might have some questions. Yeah, right, next Thursday. See ya then. Bye."

Kate felt she had nothing to lose at this point.

"Real estate?" she ventured.

"Maybe," said the director eyeing her blouse.

Kate smoothed her hair and spoke evenly.

"Just about anything in Larwin Valley, short of the aqueduct right-of-way, is a solid investment right now."

The director named Barry looked like he was going to fall out of his chair.

"Now what in Christ's name would you know about any of that?"

"I work for a realty company, and I pay attention. I told you I was good at memorizing. I'm pretty good at taking directions and following through as well. You know, dotting the i's and crossing the t's. How long will it take your guy to get you the land information?"

The director relaxed in his chair and crossed his hands behind his head.

"Aw, those pinheads. They couldn't put together a proper prospectus if their lives depended on it. I usually have to go in talking to everyone else with some half-baked proposal and then hire all my own landmen to make any sense of it."

He looked like he couldn't believe what had just come out of his mouth, but he realized he was comfortable talking to this young woman.

"Well," said Kate, "What if you give me the chance to prove that my associate and I can put together more accurate information than the pinhead who just called you?"

The director shook his head.

"This stuff has to be done by licensed realtors, not secretaries. Someone known to my guys has to sign off on everything. There are all these two-bit realty outfits running around town. Those bonebrains don't know their ass from a hole in the ground. Got anyone you work with of any standing in the real estate business?"

Kate stood up and put one cream-colored pump on the chair, making sure her skirt parted so her right knee was visible. She leaned forward and put her elbow on her knee.

"Albert Sherman is his name, and real estate is his game. Your representatives would be Twyla and Kate, that's me. Here's the business card for Sherman's downtown office. As we say, they ain't makin' any more land, so our outfit goes for the best and helps you get it. We'll list in detail for you any liens, leases or other encumbrances on the land so you can buy them out or clear them up as swiftly as clerks will move. Our aim is to help you secure all right, title and interest, including the mineral and water rights and, of course, oil and natural gas if those can be had."

"Well, ain't you a gas yourself!" cried Barry. "Sit your ass back down."

Kate took her foot off the chair, smoothed her skirt, but remained standing.

"Look, I have to get going. I've got a pile of work to do. If you want our assistance putting together the title search and boundary maps, I can have it in your hands next Thursday morning. You can compare what we prepare to what you get from the pinhead. I'd dearly love to act in movies. You can imagine how I've already figured out the kind of income I need to be able to purchase land. Think about supporting roles for me, an older sister, a secretary, something that could provide a gal like me some steady income. That's all I ask for you to consider casting me in. I can act as well as I can research titles. I won't let you down."

"Fair enough," said the director. "Let my secretary know that you'll be stopping by with the info. I'm sure she has some notes on where the parcel is so you gals can pull the right maps at County records. Meanwhile, get yourself some better photos. Supporting characters still need to appear luscious. You've got what it takes."

"Fine," said Kate. "Nice to meet you."

"You, too, darlin'," said the director with a wink.

Kate walked confidently out of Barry's office and closed the door quietly behind her. Every girl in the outer waiting room looked at Kate expectantly. She fluffed her hair and addressed them.

"Don't settle for anything less than what you want ladies. He wanted me to be screen siren, but I wanted to be in comedy!"

Puzzled eyes stared at Kate in disbelief. Then a few of the girls started laughing. Kate laughed with them, told them to be strong and then went on her way. She was beginning to think she might like her second job as a supporting actress. She couldn't wait to tell Twyla what happened. They had a ton of work ahead of them!

CHAPTER 44

▼

"How'd you get that black eye?" asked Ty with exasperation. "You've only been here a week!"

Billy looked at the floor and didn't reply.

"You know, Billy, Nelson Naval Academy has an isolation area. Do you want to be put in a restricted dorm only to be more alone than you already are?"

A tear slid down Billy's face. Ty sat down on the bed opposite the one on which his little brother sat. Ty leaned over and put his hand on Billy's shoulder. The boy seemed very small, and he was shaking.

Ty could see the boy didn't like it at the school. Ty didn't want to be here either. He was disappointed Kate cancelled their date two weekends ago and seemed too busy to schedule another. He only made the drive to San Diego when his mother fainted after receiving the call about Billy's fight.

Gertie noticed Billy acting terribly the day Billy returned from the newsstand three hours overdue. The boy threw the paper in front of his mother with a curse and ran out the front door.

Stunned, Gertie watched Billy's behavior deteriorate. It was the start of the academic year, and Billy took to skipping school. Gertie went to the school thinking that Billy was having some kind of problem with his teacher. The teacher was kind and told Gertie she tried to give the boy extra attention and small rewards, but that only seemed to make him act worse. The teacher could no longer control the child.

With TR gone traveling again, Gertie wrung her hands. Billy showed up several times at the Gimble plant when Hiram didn't know he was coming. Hiram called Gertie later to report that Billy came in and appeared nonchalant, but that several pieces of drafting equipment appeared deliberately bent and broken after Billy left.

Ty had been at the plant one time when Billy showed up. Ty thought Billy was curious about the activity there or simply wanted to say hello to some of the workers who'd been nice to him. Billy nearly burned himself trying to climb the scaffold surrounding one of the heating units. A worker pulled him away in the nick of time.

Ty thought Billy might be seeking companionship, so Ty allowed Billy back into the yard again. On the next two visits, Billy broke machine gauges and got his shoe caught under a grill that he was trying to kick in. Ty had to ban Billy from entering his father's plant.

"If you're seeking attention, kid, you sure aren't doing it very smartly."

Billy responded frantically.

"I won't tell you what I hear under Mrs. Watson's parlor anymore!"

"Frankly, Billy, that won't change a thing. Nothing the ladies discuss makes a difference to our family. Life will go on as it has. You better shape up."

Billy continued to refuse to eat meals at home. He all but ceased doing his homework and chores. He cut the heads off of several of Winnie's dolls and made her cry by telling her she would hide behind her mama's skirts forever.

Gertie decided she had enough. She could not allow the boy to become more of a terror than he already was. She called the Nelson Naval Academy. Within days, Billy was on his way to the school in the white and blue bus the academy sent to the house to pick up the youngest son of the famous millionaire.

The school was eager to add the Gimble name to the roster of children reformed and educated to the delight of their wealthy families.

Almost immediately, Gertie got the call from the school's director informing her that Billy started a fight with the son of a prominent judge. Heartbroken, Gertie asked Ty to please drive to the school and see what happened.

Billy stopped trembling under Ty's comforting hand. The boy tearfully looked up at his older brother.

"Vincent said that Dad was a traitor to the United States."

Ty's eyes grew wide.

"What?"

Billy sniffled.

"Vince is one of the older boys. He said that his dad is friends with men high up in the military. He said our dad was under suspicion by the government for selling his inventions to bad guys."

"Did Vince say which invention the men were worried about Dad selling to bad guys?"

Billy blew his nose.

"One of them is the submarine."

"What did he say about it?"

"Vincent said the article he saw in the newspaper had our family name in big letters at the top. He even quoted it from memory. The article that talked about our dad said, 'While reluctant to discuss the disposal of his one-man submarine, he intimates that he has marketed it with a big steel company back east, which in turn will sell it to one of the European belligerents now so arduously engaged in the butcher business across the ocean.'"

Billy looked wide-eyed at his brother.

"Vincent said that our family was rich only because we were as bad as butchers!"

Ty shook his head.

"Billy, that was years ago. As far as I know, Dad built only two experimental subs. Hundreds of other subs have been built since then. Two tiny, old vessels wouldn't make a hill of beans difference in any sort of war."

"I know," said Billy tearfully. "I tried to explain that Dad wasn't building any more subs. I tried to tell him that Dad tested things but never got into building lots of machines like cars or boats. I told him all sorts of things are assumed about Dad's work but that the papers are often wrong."

"That was the right thing to do, Billy. You're learning that news reports can sound hysterical, if not hilarious. So how did you end up in a fight?"

Billy touched his swollen eye.

"Once I explained that newspapers aren't all they're cracked up to be as far as printing true stories, Vincent got even madder. He said that the men his father knows are also worried about our dad building that new refinery in Red River."

Ty frowned.

"That will only HELP the military's supply of crude oil. Did he say why the men wouldn't want more fuel?"

Billy shook his head.

"Vincent said that our dad was going to sell his patents to bad guys again, and that if we lost a war, American blood would be on our hands. He said he'd let everyone know that this curse included my whole family and me! He said we'd be hated in history and maybe even run out of the country. That's when I punched him in the gut. Other boys came over. They were standing around listening to all the junk Vincent said. Once I hit him, he punched me in the eye. I didn't duck fast enough 'cause I'm just learning how to fight. What was I supposed to do, Ty? Stand there and let him call our dad a traitor and smear our name? You know some reporter would be only to glad to print giant headlines and a story full of those lies!"

Ty spoke slowly.

"You realize a lot of things, Billy, but no reporter has printed such a story. Dad would intervene right away if someone started that kind of trouble in the news. The first thing that anyone would do is launch some kind of investigation in the government. Nothing like that has come to pass. I doubt it ever will. No one wants to shut down new ideas being patented. If that happened, then it'd shut down innovation in the whole country. And then the U.S. wouldn't be much better than countries ruled by dictators. Dad's businesses are legitimate. It's his right to sell his patents to the highest bidder. What any country does with his ideas or inventions after they buy those things is their business. It's the same with any patents Americans buy. Men in our country do what they want with patents from overseas. It's called trade, Billy. It's gone on for centuries between countries. Just like you, I don't like the fact that news reporters start rumors, but you have to learn to walk away when anyone starts talking hysterical nonsense. There were no facts to bear out anything Vincent said. That's all you had to tell him. Then walk away, don't punch."

Billy slouched, looking weak and tired.

"I don't seem able to do that anymore."

Ty's voice was gentle.

"That's because you're angry inside. Mom wanted me to come down here and explain we understand. It is a mystery to us all the things that keep you so upset all the time, but we understand, even Winnie. It scares us to think that some nut could think we are bad people. They could kidnap Winnie or cause harm to us somehow, but that's why you have to stay strong with us. We need your strength in our family along with ours. That's the only thing that keeps us together."

Billy looked glum as Ty continued.

"You have to trust that Mom, Dad, I and even Winnie would come to your side if anything threatened our family."

Billy looked away.

"Well, I don't feel like there's anything I can do for anyone else. Everyone seems to hide things from everyone else in this family. I can't trust people who don't know our family either. Why do you wonder I feel alone? I AM alone."

"Not so," said Ty, "You simply are not. There's only one thing that'll ensure you're alone in life, and that's your own behavior. You're smart, and you're going to learn about things even faster from here on out. You'll learn lots of technical things like Dad and I learn, and you'll also come to understand why people say certain things and act as they do. A lot of it has to do with people feeling small and scared. You're not helpless with all the smart people who love you and can help you. You don't have to turn into a Billy the Bully to survive. That's not the loyal, quiet way a Gimble should act. We know plenty to outsmart any people who would throw stones at our family. And if, for some reason, we couldn't outsmart an enemy, we sure know a lot of methods and places to get safely out of harm's way. Dad and I can help you with any sticky situations you encounter. Dad has more resources than you know among all his inventions and the men he knows. You're strong, Billy, a pistol like Ma. There's that strong temperament that both of you have, but then there are ways to temper that steel in your constitution, just like Dad and the men at the plant temper steel into shapes that help things run better. You can take that cold, useless metal inside of you and reshape it constructively."

Billy looked up.

"I get the part about shaping steel."

Ty kept trying.

"Just hold your tongue, then, on all the family matters outside our home. The Gimbles won't abandon you as long as you keep that rule. It's the same honor, decency and discretion that the teachers here are going to try and drill into the heads of the boys at this school. But I think you're smart enough to already understand this."

The thought of years at the academy made Billy tearful again.

"I just don't want to be here!"

Ty grinned.

"Ya know, kid, everyone in our family is someplace they don't want to be a lot of the time. Dad doesn't have fun sleeping in hotels so many nights. Imagine how he can't sleep at all with his skull bumping the headboard and his big 'ol feet hanging off the bed!"

Billy laughed at the thought of his dad's large frame draped across some tiny hotel bed. Ty went on.

"Your ma doesn't like having to be alone so much of the time either. You know that for a fact!"

Billy nodded his head vigorously.

"And Winnie sure could use more real live girlfriends than all those dolls she has."

Billy looked up and exclaimed, "She still sucks her thumb for Chrissake!"

Then he looked contrite.

"Sorry. Sometimes I wonder, though, is she just going to stay home the rest of her life?"

Ty shrugged.

"I don't know, Billy. Ma is scared because the daughters of other people with money are kidnapped and held for ransom. That's having a big impact on how much Winnie can get out and play freely with other girls her own age. Sometimes the other girls' moms don't even want Winnie over because they think that their child playing with a Gimble daughter might mean that their own child could be kidnapped, too. Do you see how complicated it gets?"

Billy reflected.

"I never thought about that."

"Well, it's time you did start thinking even more practically about these things than you've been trying to. I know you've been trying, Billy, but you simply haven't understood everything yet."

Billy studied his older brother.

"Hey, what about that girl you flipped over at the theater before you left this summer?"

Ty grinned. Then he frowned.

"Not so good, my man. She doesn't seem to want to go on a date with me."

"Gosh, Ty. You can get a date with any girl. I wonder what the scary reason is for her not wanting to go out with you."

CHAPTER 45

▼

Ty didn't want to think about Kate. His trip to San Diego was a welcome distraction, and he was here to help Billy. He looked at his little brother.

"Let's take a walk. It's stuffy in here."

Billy and Ty passed the empty rooms of boys gone home for the weekend. They stepped outside the dormitory into the crisp autumn twilight.

"I'll show you the baseball field," said Billy.

Ty put his hand on the boy's shoulder as they walked.

"I don't have all the answers, Billy, such as why the girl we saw at the theater won't go on a date with me. Did you ever think that maybe I would've liked to be in movies?"

Billy looked up in surprise at his handsome brother.

"No. I thought you liked working for Dad. I thought you didn't want to do anything else."

"I do like working for Dad, but there was a time when men from the movie studios asked Mom and Dad if I could come in for a screen test. That's what movie people do to see if you can act. They photograph you and take moving pictures to see how you appear on camera. Well, Billy, I never got to try that. I was told I must go to business school. Sometimes I wonder how fun it might've been to be in movies. I'd be dating pretty ladies all the time. I'd be attending parties and cruising on big yachts with movie directors instead of hiking in the desert doing geological surveys."

Billy's eyes grew wide.

"Wow! Being in movies would be fun. You could ride horses like Buck Williams. I bet that girl in pink would jump at the chance for a date if you were a movie star!"

"That's my point, Billy. Family is more important to me than being in the movies. No matter how much fun that might've been, I'd still rather be fulfilling my duty to family as best I can. Dad doesn't drink, gamble or buy stocks, or even like movies all that much, so right now, that's how I live, too. Our parents know what's best for this family. I'm trying my hardest to make things work so I can carry on Dad's business."

Billy looked thoughtful.

"Why doesn't Dad like movie people? What's wrong with them?"

"Well, a lot of them live risky lives. You have to realize, Billy, that Dad already takes big risks every day. Every time he starts a new invention or business, Mom worries. It costs them a lot of money to start up things, more money than most men put into stocks, drinking or gambling. Dad doesn't wholly dislike movie people. In fact, he and Hiram sell special fuel to movie studios. It's the part about movie starlets and the way men treat them that Dad doesn't like at all."

Billy looked perplexed so Ty tried to explain it better.

"Dad told me when he was young, he went places with his friend Skip. One time, Skip took Dad to a party at the castle of a big newspaper publisher. There were lots of movie and political people there. Dad told me he could see how all these people mingled together trying to impress one another, but a lot of movie people spoke against men of industry."

"Why?"

"Lots of reasons, Billy. What Dad observed was that movie men figured out that entertainment sells everything, including newspapers. Why do you think some newspaper stories sound so dramatic like movies? Politicians figured out that newspapers peddle influence. Newspapers and politicians can make or break a businessman. If certain businessmen get more successful, then those guys can give more money to support the politicians. If someone gets mad at a businessman, the papers can print a damaging story about the guy. Everyone supporting everyone else is how things work in general."

Billy studied his smart brother. Ty continued.

"The people at the party had strong opinions about men like Dad trying to get new ideas off the ground. Dad saw that the people at the party exerted influence to decide whose ideas should be brought to the American public and whose ideas should be 'canned,' as Dad put it. That means squelched, Billy. Dad also said he saw women being treated poorly at this party. He said the women he saw mostly acted confused, maybe drunk or something. A girl got raped when people were in the big pool. Dad saw her crying and being comforted by other girls. All this came together in Dad's mind to form his opinion that he then shared with Mom. That's why I'm not going to be in movies, Billy. They don't see that helping our family."

Billy thought a moment.

"Gosh, Dad doesn't feel that way about baseball, does he?"

Ty laughed.

"Not at all. Sure, some men place bets and act crazy. Some of the players even go to parties with movie stars and people drinking, but Dad feels the sport itself prevails over any other scuttle. He likes sports heroes as much as anyone else. It's the spirit of competing he likes because he competes himself."

They arrived at the edge of the academy's baseball diamond.

"I like this field," said Billy. "I'm glad Dad likes the game because I want to join the team. I know I have to wait 'til after I get through serving my punishment for punching Vince, though."

Ty laughed.

"Good. While you watch your p's and q's down here, I'll see which weekends Mom and I can schedule when Dad's in town. We'll get some tickets so we can all go see some college baseball."

Billy looked happy for the first time.

"That'd be swell!"

Ty sniffed the air.

"Who's smoking out here?"

Billy smelled it, too.

"Aw, it's probably kids under the bleachers."

Ty peered toward the bleachers but didn't see any movement.

"No, it's closer than that."

A man rushed up behind them. Ty whirled around, pulling Billy close and shielding him. The man chuckled.

"Well, if it's not Gimble the elder and Gimble the younger!"

The man's cigarette smoldered between his forefingers. Ty watched as he stamped it on the ground. Billy wriggled under Ty's firm grip.

"You boys thinkin' 'bout baseball, are ya?"

Ty studied the brutish man, trying to remain calm as he spoke.

"Nothing unusual there."

"I'll tell ya what's unusual," said the man slowly, "that your pa ain't interested in building someplace else what he's gonna build in Red River. Your old man's always lookin' for money on his ideas. Tell him he'll get paid well."

Ty pulled Billy and started to walk away. The man roughly grabbed Ty's arm.

"Listen here, Ty. Tell your old man to pay attention when he gets a good offer. Just tell him that his services will be rendered for Red River as well as the other place."

Ty shook loose his arm and glared at the man.

"Tell him yourself."

Billy broke free and swung hard at the center of the man's britches, but the man saw it coming and merely stepped back. Then Ty saw the man's face turn red with fury. As the man grabbed for Billy, Ty landed a punch to the man's ribs. The man swung back, catching Ty's cheekbone below the eye with his fist.

Ty reeled backward. Billy put all his might into a kick to the man's shin. The man stumbled. The boy yelled.

"Come on, Ty!"

Billy pulled hard on Ty's arm bringing his brother upright. The Gimble brothers ran.

Reaching the front parking lot, Ty pulled Billy inside their dad's sedan and locked the door.

"You're bleeding!" exclaimed Billy.

"It's nothing," said Ty, "nothing a hankie can't handle while I drive back. Look, Billy, I want you to stay in your room and report this to the officer in your dorm. They'll take care of you. Just don't wander around anywhere by yourself. Keep your nose down, go to classes, and stay out of fights, OK? I have to figure out what all this means."

Billy fought back his tears.

"I want to go with you!"

"No, Billy. I actually think you're safer down here than out on the highway with me. That coward won't come inside your dorm. He was just delivering a message. He's limping back to whatever hole he crawled out of. Plus, I felt his rib pop when I hit him."

Billy hugged his older brother. Ty hugged him back hard, still holding his hankie over his cheek and swelling eye.

"Go on now. Get back in there and report this, and don't leave your room. I'll call the school when I get home to be sure you're OK."

Billy curled up on his bed after Ty left. The dorm officer stood outside his door. What happened tonight was the business of secrets he knew would haunt his family forever. His talk with his brother had been the best he'd ever had. His thoughts spun.

"Ty tried to walk away from that guy, but he had to punch him just like I had to punch Vincent. Ty got his own black eye. Now Ma's really gonna faint!"

He hoped Ty's face would heal and that the girl in pink would let his brother take her on a date. Billy knew that Ty would treat her nicely, but he was also proud seeing how hard Ty could hit when he needed to.

"My family's gonna figure out what the man's message was, but I'm sure they won't tell me. I wonder if they think I'm a scaredy cat?"

He thought about his sister Winnie and wondered if she'd ever go on a date in her whole life. He decided probably not. The tears began to fall. His whole body shook with sobs. He realized he'd been just as scared as Winnie many times, even tonight, only he never sucked his thumb. All he did was get stomach aches.

Somehow crying helped untangle the knots inside his belly, even though he had questions and worries and missed his family terribly. Since trouble seemed to be creeping toward the family anyway, Billy vowed he'd never go sneaking under Mrs. Watson's parlor looking for more. He swore he wouldn't let his family down, not ever again.

CHAPTER 46

▼

"What a grand vision this is!" exclaimed Victor Atkins. "I love this place. The air is pure and bright, and the ground utterly screams with mineral resources of every kind!"

TR looked around and could only agree. Giant cliffs of brilliant red and gold stood above them on one side. A wide river moseyed past them on the other. The railroad tracks beyond the river blazed a straight trail through a plateau of low, sandy-colored cliffs in the distance. A highway cut through a tier of cliffs behind them, coming in across the Midwest plains exactly as the railroad did on the other side of the river.

The place called Red River was just as the inventor remembered it. TR and Victor stood at the refinery site with their fellow men launching a bold plan.

The fall air was electric for the group gathered here. It breathed the kind of opportunity and leadership that all men loved. Everyone had plenty of tasks to do. The goal was as high and clear as the sky above them. The challenges they must overcome were as daunting as those faced by other entrepreneurs building two hundred shale oil refineries across America.

As far as these men knew, Gimble's plant was the only one to be constructed in the unique way he designed it. The thrill of conquest made every man's heart swell with anticipation, and it tasted good on every man's tongue.

All looked ready to go on the ground. The men studied TR's sketches and discussed the site. It would be an ambitious scheme to build a tramway across the highway. TR pointed to where the tram would go.

"That's the shortest route between the raw shale on the cliffs and the tall crushers into which tons of rock must be dumped. Natural gravity is our best ally.

Gravity and pulleys will bring the heaviest shale across the highway in a straight line as the crow flies. It'd take men hours to haul the rock down the cliffs and across the highway. This way, it will take only minutes."

One man queried.

"We're with you on that concept, Mr. Gimble. What about local suppliers? Should we start rounding up companies to build machine parts while you finish your working drawings?"

TR shook his head.

"I have special steel I want to use to maximize production and minimize wear and tear. This refinery needs high speed and super temperatures. Volumes of distillates must process fast enough to make your venture profitable. As soon as these plans are approved, you can help me negotiate rates with the rail lines in this area. I want to transport the major working parts from California out to this site for construction. See if you can get some strong work crews locally. We need men with proven ability to work well together. I want the kind of men who'll awaken clear-headed and ready to follow complex instructions. They're the only kind to get this refinery built as fast as you'd like to open."

The men agreed that they'd find the best local work crews and inform them that they'd be working under the supervision of TR's head engineer.

Several men appeared toward the edge of the refinery site. Victor spotted one man with a camera. Victor tapped TR's arm.

"The reporters are here."

The inventor turned toward the approaching men.

"I supposed it's so calm in these parts that six men inspecting a piece of dirt is cause for a ruckus."

Victor chuckled.

"No doubt. You want to talk to them?"

"We should. They'll report on our visit whether we talk to them or not. Might as well make a statement rather than leaving everything to speculation."

Victor, TR and the men started walking toward the reporters. The man with the camera was busy, shooting pictures as fast as he could. Victor called out.

"How are you?"

"Curious," replied one of the reporters. "Can we ask Mr. Gimble some questions?"

"Sure," said Victor, "fire away."

The reporters had dug into the latest filings at County Records. They knew of the thousands of acres being acquired. They sensed an enormous undertaking. They wanted to know how it would affect the town and region

TR gave them estimates for initial production and told them that future expansion would depend on many factors, most importantly, the public liking the new gasoline.

"If all this is so speculative," asked one reporter, "why do it? I hear the investment of your group has already surpassed $50,000."

TR turned to the reporter.

"I'd like to think that Americans will always welcome new inventions. This country's people are the most eager experimenters on earth. They have the most free hands and minds to try new things of any people living united under one God and flag. Such a people will only come to anger and frustration being limited regarding things that impact their lives greatly. Economic ruin would follow such despair if people felt funneled like lemmings running over a cliff to accept only one choice, such as only petroleum fuel."

The man scratched his head.

"What exactly do you mean, Mr. Gimble?"

"Petroleum running out with nothing to replace it would be a serious problem, don't you think? One monopoly in energy linked to yet another in housing linked to still others that would force singular choices upon Americans eventually wouldn't fly. That would be cause, I would think, for unrest. People are already used to varied choices in transportation, education, houses, the clothes they wear and utterly every aspect of their lives. Whenever men and women feel limited, I'd bet on things to change dramatically."

"Do I gather from your words, Mr. Gimble, that you identify what you're building in Red River as a source of revolution in the fuel industry?"

"Not entirely. Other reporters have used that word when referring to experiments with shale and new shale oil refineries being tested in this country. I prefer to use the word choice. This refinery is about offering people a choice for fuel made from a source other than oil in the ground. Rock fuel, gentlemen, you can refer to this endeavor as bringing a choice for rock fuel to Americans, in addition to good petroleum."

The reporters looked at one another and repeated the term 'rock fuel' as if to test how it might appear in the papers. TR Gimble's large ears overheard the reporters' comments.

"Too general," said one man.

"Won't sell papers," said another.

"Let's keep digging on the revolutionary angle."

"This whole deal could go bust up like a lot of other schemes in this town."

"That's it! This is a boom-and-bust town. We'll interview the locals and get their opinions on how prosperous they think they'll become from rock fuel."

The reporters laughed and bid farewell. TR and Victor remained standing on their refinery site with their fellow men of vision.

TR winked at Victor.

"'If it ain't bleedin', it ain't good readin.' Isn't that what editors say?"

Victor laughed.

"They'll screw it all up. Let's go have lunch at the diner. The sandwiches there are good. I also want you to read what I wrote for publication. It doesn't resemble any other prospectus you've seen in print. It'd be hard to stir up any controversy from the facts I've outlined. You said you wanted to go over details about the refinery we're printing, so we brought a draft of the words and pictures."

The sandwiches at the Red River diner were just as good as Victor declared. The men who met to review the plans sat in adjoining booths. They examined the details of the full-page spread being readied for publication. The headline announced, "An Unparalleled Opportunity for Investment in the World's Most Essential and Profitable Industry."

"That's pretty strong," said TR. "When is this going to be published?"

The men assured him that the information would not be printed until the plant was approved and the venture cleared for stock issuance. Shares would be offered at ten dollars. The generous price was people's unparalleled opportunity. The direct benefit to the town of Red River and surrounding region was that folks could buy their gasoline at cost by pulling into a filling station at the shale refinery. This was proving a popular concept by word of mouth already. TR joined their enthusiasm.

"This entire news page will create quite a stir. I'm moved just seeing it. I can see lines of cars and trucks ready for fill-ups on opening day. We'll need production going at full steam. The people's needs must be met to start momentum that'll make headlines around the world."

TR admired the five large pictures arranged below the headline.

"Victor, you were right. This is a unique layout for a new stock offering. Looks solid."

Each of the pictures showed views of the refinery site and mining areas. Visitors would have only to look at the pictures and drive a mile west outside town to see where the photos were taken. A vision of vast supplies of shale and the refinery site along the river would meet their expectations. The vision looked almost as good on the page as it appeared in reality.

Paragraphs noted that the company owned shale deposits worth at least two hundred million dollars potentially. They said the company and its offering were directed by a group of executives thoroughly acquainted with every phase of the business. The Gimble process for refining shale oil was noted throughout the page. The capacities and fuel quality of the Gimble process were compared and rated better than other refining processes at plants owned by other concerns.

The data TR and Victor had discussed about the refinery was outlined clearly, as well as paragraphs describing the purpose of the company, the purpose of the stock issue and the tremendous importance of oil shale. TR was impressed.

"Compliments to you all for including the fact about 5,814 dry holes drilled for regular oil in only two years, which represents a wasted $58 million dollars of oil investors' money. Such waste of investor capital will not occur in Red River where the rock is ready to be scooped off the ground."

A separate paragraph noted the seven men comprising the managing personnel of the Red River Oil Products Company. Their credentials were impressive. A box in the lower right corner contained a form people could cut out and send to the new company for shares of capital stock to be purchased outright or reserved by monthly payments. Again, the offer was generous. Purchasers paying over time could determine any amount suitable for their own budgets. TR noted this.

"You've made stock obtainable to everyone. I like that you're making the refinery friendly to citizens here as well. Mining impact within the town will be minimal, but benefits will be enormous. Shale mining occurs only outside the town limits. Mining can be phased to balance extraction between cliffs in view and those out of sight behind the highway. Restoration of disturbed sites where people would see cuts in the cliffs could occur in several ways."

The men sat taking notes on the ideas the inventor brought forth.

TR had no doubt about Victor Atkins' regard for him when he read what the man wrote. The highly accredited professor wrote the finest description of TR Gimble an inventor might hope to see printed.

"As a young man, he went to work in the oil fields and gained health and experience in well drilling, pipe line construction and refining, and so became a master of the details of the entire oil industry. Through his own efforts, aided by natural talents, he has made himself the inventive genius of the oil business. He is the inventor of three highly important advances in the industry, the Gimble Refining Process, the Gimble Cracking Process and the Gimble Gas Trap. His inventions are used all over the world wherever oil is produced. Six years ago, he began attacking the oil shale problem. His experience in oil stood him in good stead in the solution of this new problem. Retort after retort to process shale has been erected and found useless. Gimble's present plant in California unites the retorting and refining process in one continuous operation. It is the apex of his work. Inasmuch as Mr. Gimble is a man of means, he asks no financial aid but meets all expenses from his own resources. As Mr. Gimble has made an enviable record in the well oil industry, it is quite likely that he will be known as the oil shale genius of this decade."

As they were leaving the diner, TR thanked Victor for his fine endorsement.

"The apex of my work, eh, Victor?"

The professor laughed.

"Doubtful."

TR gazed toward the promising shale cliffs towering above the town. With insuppressible good humor, Victor absorbed the sight of the inventor standing before their giant dream. Victor had to reach to slap TR on the back. They laughed and headed downtown.

They made an odd couple, the tall, larger-than-life inventor and the stocky, studious professor. People watching them walk down Main Street in Red River noted the pair. Something about these strangers to the small town made folks wonder if these two characters were carving a place in history.

CHAPTER 47

▼

Night fell over the cliffs of Red River. While the small town slept, TR surveyed his short hotel bed. Before laying down for a night of restless tossing with his feet hanging over the edge, he decided to call home. His son answered.

"Ty, how's that cut on your cheek? Has your eye healed?"

"Sure, Dad. That tape Hiram stretched across the cut worked better than stitches. By the time I got home, Mom hardly noticed. She was upset anyway so I suppose I can thank God for that. I told her I got bruised wrestling with Billy. So far, no lingering questions. Maybe she was glad she didn't go down to the school to try and talk with Billy herself. She doesn't want to talk about him now. She's at her sister's tonight. How's Red River treating you?"

"So far so good."

"Are you going to heed the guy's warning?"

"If he was referring to my designing another shale oil refinery, maybe. Now that I see what the deal is out here, I might be able to work up something for overseas. The problem will be the metal I'm using in the design at Red River. There's that and a thousand other details that may not work out on a foreign site. I'm certain the man who assaulted you was referring to plans they want. Any more trouble at the plant or Billy's school?"

"No, Dad, not since then."

"What was Billy's problem down there when he first got into a fight?"

"This kid was talking some nonsense about the subs you built. Seems he saw the old news reports. The kid was saying that men are concerned about which countries you sell your patents to. It was the usual hysterical garbage, except that it upset Billy a lot, and he punched the kid."

"Oh, Ty, those old reports were one of the reasons I stopped talking to reporters for so long. I hope you set Billy straight on those things."

"I'm pretty sure I did, Dad. Would it be possible for us to get tickets to some baseball games and head out to a few with Billy?"

"Sure. Just figure out which teams you want to see and let me know the dates. I'll do everything I can to join you."

"Thanks, Dad.

"For someone who got assaulted, Ty, you sound awfully jovial.

"I am, Dad. That girl I told you about that I met before I left this summer finally decided to give me a chance to see her. We went on our first date. Simply stated, I'm in love with an angel."

"Good for you, son. Remember what I told you about coming to me first if you get into any situations with her."

"Oh, Dad. I'm careful. You know that. This one's my ticket to heaven."

"You mean the Great Work?"

"Absolutely. No doubt in my mind."

"Well, enjoy the best flight of your life, son. I'm pleased that Lady Fortune has come your way. Let Mom know I'll be gone for a few more days. Victor and I are heading out to see a shale oil plant that's opening a hundred miles north of here."

"I will. She'll moan, but I'll tell her. Oh, there's a letter you should know about. An entourage of government officials wants to come to the plant and see your shale oil processor. Should Hiram schedule the tour?"

"Yes, tell him to do that. He'll be happy to get all dressed up again. Give Mom and Winnie a hug and a kiss for me. I'm finally sleepy enough to crawl into this miniature bed."

Ty laughed.

"Sleep tight, Dad."

Victor and TR rose early to catch the train the next morning. The autumn air pushed icy drafts into the heat of the locomotive that pulled its passenger cars to the high elevations. The scent of Rocky Mountain pines greeted another promising day for the men who rode with Victor and TR.

The latest shale oil refinery to begin operations was built on the side of a mountain. The grade was so steep that the visionaries had to build the processing unit sideways instead of vertically. This refinery was too exceptional for any of the men on the train to miss viewing.

Investors and government men arrived in town, along with reporters carrying big cameras to record the event. All had to ride up the side of the mountain in open trucks. TR made everyone laugh when he remarked that the tour vans with colorful flags must all be in use over at Signal Hill. The men in the open truck were familiar with how investors were lured out to California oil fields where hundreds of busy oil derricks dotted the horizon. Vans with colorful flags were packed with the curious and novices trying to figure out how to make money in oil. Visitors drank stale lemonade and ate dry corndogs, listening to sales pitches by men with big voices and red faces. Visitors were beckoned to come and play the oil game by men in pastel suits with white straw hats. The people bought their stock with bags of dimes and nickels.

Out here on the side of this cold, rugged mountain, the new shale oil refinery attracted a different breed. Men in black top hats and long, dark coats talked in low voices while they milled around the operating equipment. An articulate head worker in clean corduroy pants, heavy plaid shirt and a new cap pointed out parts of the machines. Bright-eyed men answered technical questions while serious visitors scribbled notes. Hot steaks were grilling on an open barbecue pit. None of the food was stale, and the men did not go away hungry or dissatisfied with the new technology they'd seen.

The visiting men commented that this was the future of cheap gasoline, and it was going to blow the balls straight off the petroleum industry. This taste of the future was just as good as the thick, juicy steaks they enjoyed.

Victor eyed the scene and leaned toward TR.

"You've heard about some of the scammers that are entering the shale oil game, haven't you? Men on the streets of Boston are selling capital stock certificates for plants whose drawings are nowhere near complete, and the land has only been looked at but not purchased."

TR grinned.

"I wonder which of those men will end up sitting in the same pokey as CJ Niles. It's only a matter of time after the first claims of fraud are filed and the indictments handed down."

As they came off the mountain from leaving the refinery site, TR noticed two dark sedans. Most of the men visiting the new refinery had traveled in on the train, but the two sedans, it appeared, were tailing TR and Victor as they walked back to the station. The windows of both sedans were tinted dark. There were no license plates on the front grills.

TR picked up his step and told Victor to hurry. The sedans kept pace, crawling slowly behind them. The professor looked up and saw TR's head directed straight ahead, but his eyes were darting right and left, checking every doorway and window. Victor didn't ask but picked up his gait to a near gallop to match the strides from TR's long legs. The sedans accelerated. Victor saw a rear window rolling down slowly on the front sedan nearest them. A gun barrel poked through.

"Split!" urged TR hoarsely.

Victor immediately dove left while TR jumped right. Each man ducked into a doorway on the opposite sides of the street. Two shots rang out in either direction.

Victor thought his heart would break in two. It was not because he'd been hit. It was the mere thought of the brilliant inventor being struck down.

The two sedans screeched down the main street of town and onto the open highway heading west. Victor flew across the street toward TR. The inventor clutched his stomach. Victor gasped.

"Are you alright?"

TR scowled as he fingered his shirt ripped across his belly, noting the nail sticking out of the doorway frame. He dusted off his coat sleeve.

"Coward bastards!" he growled. "I'm fine. You're OK, right?"

Victor patted his chest and arms.

"I'm still upright with no blood on my clothes so the answer is yes."

TR watched the dust settle behind the cars now gone from town. He turned to Victor.

"That was just a warning shot. I hate idiots like that."

TR saw a large paper in the middle of the street. It was left there with a chunk of shale rock thrown on top. He walked over and picked up the dark rock and heavy paper. He shook off the bits of broken shale. The paper had Japanese letters scrawled roughly across the top. The words in English below declared, "You will deliver the plans to my hands. Gentleman's appointment at your plant on 15 October."

TR folded the paper in half and slid it inside his coat pocket. This could only be from goons sent by Louis Tiemonet, the emissary of all things irritating. TR remembered telling Louis to make a gentleman's appointment the last time the Frenchman confronted him after lurking in the dark outside his plant. This was how the terrorist decided to make his appointment.

Victor set his hat on his head and walked to the middle of the street to join TR.

"I take it you've been in touch with these fellows?"

"Yeah," muttered TR. "This time they're being explicit."

"Was that their calling card in the street?"

TR nodded.

"The last time these characters popped up, it took me two years to figure out which invention they were angry about. Then it took me another year and a half to get rid of it so they'd stop prowling around."

Victor looked at the inventor inquiringly. TR shook his head.

"When it comes to men like these, things can get murky. I have a lot of different inventions in the works at all times. I keep a tight lid on details at the plant. But I have more attorneys and accountants than ever working for me now. I'm not in my downtown offices often enough to always see what they see. I've kept our shale oil refinery plans locked up at the plant, but still, I think men can figure out what I'm doing. Too many eyes and ears can be bought these days."

Victor surveyed the street. Everything appeared normal. TR clasped Victor's shoulder.

"It's OK. They fired their warning shots. Now they're gone. They won't be back since they've delivered their message. And don't worry. They won't hurt us because they need something from me. The next move is mine to figure out how to get them off my back."

The professor and the inventor resumed their walk to the train station. Then TR started to laugh.

"You know, it's the darnedest thing, Victor. You can do something you think is going one direction, but it starts a whole chain reaction in another direction, usually among men you don't even know. It can become a domino effect. Men get crazy thinking that you invaded on some whole other deal that involves kings and barons and other nations. I've reached the point where I don't even try to guess who's involved. So don't give this a second thought yourself. It's not worth it. The Red River plant is going to get built. That's not what this warning was about. I'll put my men on watch and have them help me figure out how to win the peace."

Victor looked perplexed.

"Peace with whom over what?"

TR shrugged.

"With these men, you rarely get to find out who's involved. I have a clue how to settle the matter though."

CHAPTER 48

▼

TR came home to another rousing welcome at his front door. He brought a doll in country western clothes for Winnie and new phonograph records for Gertie. He thought Gertie might like the ladies yodeling country western melodies on the records, and she did.

TR was pleased to be needed less by Regis Petroleum for a while. Gertie was more than pleased. The household brightened once more

Ty seemed to be floating on air with all the attention he was receiving from his new girlfriend. Billy was doing amazingly well at Nelson Naval Academy and looking forward to baseball season. Winnie was learning more complicated music on the piano. She giggled and sang her way through every day, thoroughly enjoying her dolls and school and music, but not half as much as all the hugs and tickles she received from Ty and her dad.

TR's refining and cracking processes were working excellently at the new port refinery, making the conglomerate all the millions they hoped to acquire and then some. The Gimble Gas Trap was installed at more refineries throughout the world. The Gimble receivables clerks remained busy, cashing the royalty checks each week.

Hiram was dressed up in his finery the day the government men came to see TR's shale processor at the experimental plant. The entourage inspected the operation to their satisfaction and laughed at Hiram's comical explanations. The shop was quiet and dark as TR loosened his tie.

"That was a fine tour, Hiram. I think we answered most of their questions about how to make shale oil profitable. I'm finished with the plans for the overseas shale refinery. I'm going to lock these drawings in the safe in back. You know where the extra key is. If I'm out for some reason when Tiemonet comes, just give him this roll of drawings. Who knows if he'll arrive when he said he would. Receiving my plans should at least ferry him off these shores for a while."

The inventor's assistant grinned. Then his eyes grew serious.

"You're spending more time downtown these days. Are you making any headway getting the accountants and attorneys squared away?"

"Can't say that I am, Hiram. I understand how they're setting things up, but I don't agree with their interpretations of the new laws. I either have to haul all that stuff back home and dump it in Gertie's lap or try to make do with how they're arranging things. Taking entire sets of company books home to Gertie is simply not an option anymore. She hates those guys downtown. It'd never work out."

"No one is more loyal to your interests than your wife—or more skilled at balancing numbers."

"You're right, Hiram. But for now I have to let things proceed as they are in the downtown office. The Red River plant and this other drawing have taken all the energy I have. I need to rest."

"I'll keep watch here, boss. You don't have to worry. I'm in touch with Jacob and Skip. We've got the guys out at Brea and other refineries keeping their ear to the ground for any scuttle with the oil men. No one's heard a word about any character named the Saint, and Tiemont's not skulking around their facilities."

"Yes," said TR, "that makes me feel special indeed."

"Go on home, boss. Get your rest."

The Frenchman arrived at TR's plant three weeks earlier than his planned appointment. He burst through the door looking haggard. Hiram noticed the absence of the scent of French cologne wafting about his head. Tiemonet spoke hoarsely.

"Are the plans finished?"

Hiram nodded.

"I'll have one of the workers go get the boss."

Tiemonet waited quietly without picking up the shale sample or tossing snide remarks Hiram's way. The haggard visitor sat on a chair picking at his knuckles.

As soon as he came in from the work yard, TR noticed the fresh gash on Tiemonet's cheek.

"Looks like you ran into a pretty sharp blade," said the inventor.

Tiemonet growled.

"The men who want your plans are not pleasant types."

TR handed Tiemonet the roll of drawings.

"There's much more for men to figure out in the field beyond what I've drawn and specified in these plans. It's all site-intensive work that building supervisors with experience should handle."

Tiemonet grasped the roll.

"Don't worry about their men. They can figure it out."

TR's gaze remained steady, peering into Tiemonet's tired, beady eyes.

"Perhaps the Russians were more equitable to deal with than the Japanese. Their swords aren't drawn quite as readily during negotiations. This must be why you had to compel me to draw these plans by firing shots, and out of state no less."

Tiemonet threw his cape over his shoulder and winced.

"There is no better way to stress the urgency of a situation than with bullets."

TR thought of his modified gun.

"I'll certainly remember that."

After the Frenchman shoved past the furniture and dashed out the door, TR turned to Hiram.

"This ought to satisfy whoever's so intent on getting shale oil started on a big scale in Asia."

Hiram handed TR a letter.

"This came this afternoon. I saw the government seal. It looks like they're sending their comments on the tour."

TR opened the letter. He read it, and then he put his head in his hands.

"What?" asked Hiram.

"This letter thanks us for the providing the tour of our plant and urges us not to engage in any sale of shale oil patents to any government other than the U.S. They put it as a recommendation, not a directive, but they mention, in particular, the land of the rising sun."

Hiram sat quietly. He folded his hands on his desk.

"All areas of China aren't under control of Japan. Do you think U.S. officials will learn about such a distant shale oil plant? How would they even know that one is being built with your design?"

TR looked up, gazing at the large map of the world on his office wall.

"U.S. men are in just about every country, Hiram. They'll find out, especially if a government actually starts erecting a large plant. It's only a matter of time for men to figure out the similarities between the foreign plant and the one at Red River. How long this would take, I don't know."

"Is there any way out of this tangle?"

TR pondered. Then he stood decisively.

"Here's what I'll do. Since I've conveyed some new technology for the Asian plant, I'll have Jacob draft up new patents containing the design improvements I improvised for processing shale there. Much of it has to do with building more complicated retort systems that wouldn't require the special steel I'm using in Red River. There'll be five new patents in all that Jacob will register under my name. I'll donate all five to the U.S. government and tell them to do with them what they want. This way, no domestic or foreign emissaries can claim that I'm trying to draw allegiance toward one country or another. No one can claim I'm trying to profit from secret designs sold to foreign belligerents. Regarding those five patents, I'll simply forfeit my gain."

Hiram grinned.

"Since we don't know which side men are on these days, that seems like the only solution."

TR tapped the government letter.

"Any government attempting to build one of my sketched designs will have a hard time making it work without cooperation between visionary entrepreneurs and government men. Either set of men working alone is likely doomed because legal rights regarding the shale rock on the land are proving tricky for private entrepreneurs here. On foreign soil, government scientists and men trying to construct shale oil refineries become frustrated over politics that force them to use metals and other building materials unfit for the heavy tasks of mining, crushing, heating and refining the shale. A shale oil refinery under full government control overseas will take years to construct and prove operable. Even if U.S. men tell the government that a refinery of my design is being constructed overseas, I know it'll take much experimenting there to make the endeavor profitable enough to make any dent in U.S. shale oil profits. Basically, men won't care once they see how slow shale oil is proceeding overseas. In the meantime, I will have divulged my inventions to the global public. Then I'll invent different designs and register other patents unrelated to any I've devised so far."

Hiram grinned.

"I see no better way to wash your hands of Tiemonet and that whole mess. Now go on home, boss, and get your rest."

CHAPTER 49

▼

TR spoke quietly to Ty in the work yard.

"I've supplied the oil shale refinery design to the Asians. Jacob is getting my five patents prepared for registration. I'll give the patents to our government by sending them with a letter to one of the government men who visited here. There should be no more trouble with that whole affair."

"That's good," said Ty. "I'd have a devil of a time explaining all this to a new wife, if she'd ever agree to marry me after catching wind of danger to this family."

"I understand, son. That's why I'm doing everything I can to steer as far afield of such trouble as I can. Look, we took care of settling the trouble with the submarines. We can handle this, too."

Hiram came running into the work yard.

"You're not going to believe this. Tiemonet is back!"

Ty looked at his father.

"Do you want me to step inside?"

"No, Ty. Stay out here. Don't even let the man see your face. I'll handle whatever it is."

TR walked with Hiram into the office.

The Frenchman was standing with his hands in his pockets.

"I must barge in again. Our business is not quite finished."

TR eyed Louis suspiciously.

"I gave you the plans. At some point, you must leave us alone."

"The plans were agreeable. This next matter barely concerns you at all. There's a certain, uh, request regarding some men in your downtown office."

TR stared at the Frenchman. Then he noticed the man's eyes were not as hard. He realized Tiemonet was battling excruciating pain. He noticed how oddly the Frenchman's hands were dug into his pockets. The man never stood that way. He was always tossing his head, flapping his cape and fiddling with things near Hiram's desk. TR moved toward the terrorist.

"What do you think you're going to try and extract from me now?"

Tiemonet stepped back.

"Why, nothing at all. You're simply going to quit interfering with the men running your downtown office. They've tried to politely inform you of the laws and regulations by which all companies are conforming, that is, companies preferring not to be troubled by tax officials. You seem to be resisting the winds of change that are sweeping across this country. Therefore, you must relinquish your grip on those affairs."

TR's eyes widened in disbelief. He could not contain his anger. He barreled forward and grabbed Tiemonet by the neck of his cape.

"Over my dead body, you scum!"

Stunned and surprised, Tiemonet's hands flew out of his pockets. TR dropped the neck of his cape as Hiram gasped.

"He's missing a finger!"

Tiemonet's eyes glazed over with pain as he shoved his oozing, bandaged hand back into his pocket.

"It's not your concern. I still have nine good ones and, mind you, I can still pull a trigger if needed. Don't make me. Elevate that accountant and turn over your downtown affairs to him and Ritz. No one cares about this old yard or office. And don't lay a hand on me again or I'll send men that'll make me look like the Prince of Kindness!"

Hiram and TR both started toward Tiemonet at once.

Hiram grabbed a long, metal t-square, ready to gash the Frenchman's unscarred cheek or take his ankle out from under him. He stopped abruptly.

Tiemonet had a gun at Hiram's chest.

"Calmly, gentlemen," soothed the Frenchman. "Just make the change calmly."

As he backed out the door, he kept talking.

"Alert no one. It won't do you any good. We're watching every soul in your family and well beyond."

He whirled and stepped out of the office. He jumped in a waiting sedan, and the driver took off.

Ty heard the screeching tires. He ran into the office.
"What happened?"
Hiram looked pale. TR cast a look of concern at his son.
"They only want money now."
Ty got water for Hiram.
"And how's that gonna happen?"
"We don't know," said TR slowly. "I guess we'll find out. If I knew what amount, I'd give them the cash, but no amount was specified."
Hiram gulped his water.
"I say, let them cut off his whole hand. We've put up with his threats long enough! Armed guards have to be posted here."
TR nodded.
"And at the house again, unfortunately."
Ty whistled softly.
"Ma's gonna shit."

Each day at the experimental plant thereafter, Hiram found a different newspaper in a brown envelope that arrived in the mail. Each paper had bold headlines and custom-printed articles inserted amid the day's regular news.
"American Inventor Sacked: Famous Petroleum Inventor Performs Great Work with Lady Evangelist."
"Inventor Destroys Regis Conglomerate: New Gimble Shale Oil Patent Promises to Annihilate American Petroleum Industry."
American Inventor Indicted: Famous Stock Swindler, CJ Niles, Joined in LA Pokey by TR Gimble."

TR did not tell Gertie about Tiemonet's visit or the false newspapers. Ty agreed to stay silent as he watched Winnie and his mother closely. Gertie surprisingly did not object to the night watchmen at the house.
"Winnie's maturing a little," she said, "I actually feel better knowing a man's on guard as we sleep."

TR did not institute any changes at his downtown office. He spoke with Hiram.

"Someone's getting experience creating these fake newspaper layouts. This is purely intimidation."

A week later, another brown envelope arrived. The false newspaper headline read, "Boy Killed in Inventor's Work Yard." Joey MacDermott's frozen look was captured in the front-page photo.

Still, TR negated the threat.

"Look at the barren tree, Hiram. That picture was taken last winter. That was when photographers were lurking around the yard. They must have been gathering ammunition back then."

Hiram agreed.

"Joey never mentioned seeing anyone with a camera, but you're right. Joey's face looks a little older now."

Within another week, TR was run off the road on his way home. The dark sedan that rammed his auto's running board knew in just which pocket of darkness to stop the inventor's car. As TR reached under the seat for his modified gun, a familiar, hoarse voice called out.

"Move faster with those changes. Don't force me to involve your family!"

TR called into the blackness.

"Go to hell!"

As he readied his aim to fire a shot, a hand flew out the sedan window. The white of the bandage showed clearly. It was smaller. Another of Tiemonet's fingers was missing.

No one got out of the sedan. TR lowered his gun. The sedan roared off.

TR decided to start making certain changes downtown before things got worse. His first move was to tell Gertie he was going to change banks for the account on his coal and shale oil company. The account had been with a local bank where Gertie knew the president and all the managers on a first-name basis. The bank people were so appreciative of the Gimble account that they sent Gertie Pig 'n Whistle chocolates on every holiday.

TR informed Gertie that the account was being transferred to a big bank downtown where his new head accountant, Frank McDonnell could more easily manage the account's growing activity. Gertie frowned but didn't say anything. She had read plenty in the newspapers about the executives at the Merchant & Maritime Bank where TR's account was being transferred. The bank executives and their wives were socially prominent. Most of the executives belonged to the Guild. Despite the high social standing of the bank executives and their families, scandals involving these people rippled through the headlines or social pages at least once every couple of months.

Gertie also remembered seeing the names of some of the bank executives in the little roster book listing TR's fellow brethren from the Ancient Rite lodge downtown. Some of the men raised to the highest leadership positions in that order would be in charge of TR's new bank account for his shale oil company.

Although TR no longer attended meetings for the Ancient Rite, he remained on gentlemen's terms with the members. Gertie felt that the men must have convinced TR that he needed a larger bank to handle interstate financial transactions for his new shale oil company.

Gertie began to see the attorney named Harry Ritz advancing to a stronger advisory and management role in TR's downtown office. She didn't know how to tell her husband that she didn't feel she could trust this man any farther than she could throw him. So far, she hadn't said anything to her husband. She snarled like a junkyard dog whenever he called TR at the house, giving her orders for where and when the inventor was to call him back or execute documents he prepared.

Mrs. Gimble did not like Harry Ritz at all, but she was unaware of all the circumstances. She fretted over why her husband was allowing that man to increase his prominence in TR's organization, as TR quietly extricated himself from the organization Ritz and McDonnell thought was becoming their new empire.

CHAPTER 50

▼

The calm afternoon unfolded with relaxing ambiance in the sunny, fashionable suburb surrounding the Gimble home. The clock in the entry hall ticked steadily, the only sound in the quiet house. While Ty, TR and Billy Gimble withheld secrets about dangerous men, Gertie remained secluded from grave concerns. The Gimble mother stayed watchful over her daughter, giving her more attention than the men in her family. This was no different than in other families, where men banded together separately in their own opinions of serious matters.

A man rang the bell at Gertie's front door. She peeked out the curtains in the living room and saw a van stopped on the street bearing the name of a local tree trimming company. She'd not called any workmen. She figured the man must be lost, trying to find another address. Winnie was gone to her music lesson. The girl would not be frightened seeing her mother talk to the man. Gertie opened the door.

"May I help you?"

The man in the crisp, white shirt and clean, olive trousers tipped his cap.

"Good day, ma'am. I'm with the Ace Tree Trimming Company. My supervisor asked that I come and give you advance word of notice he received from the City."

"What notice is that?"

"The City arborist toured this area and designated certain trees as potential risk due to their overgrown canopies. Regulations in the City arborist's policy manual stipulate that no tree within twenty-five feet of a building shall exceed five times the height of its trunk."

"And so?"

"Our company does a perfect job helping residents conform to City guidelines. We offer advisement concerning how trees should be cut and pruned. We follow City specifications. Ma'am, we love trees. We're not the sort of trimmers who would butcher a beautiful specimen. We have contracts with the City to provide feeding and manicuring of all trees in City parks and boulevards. I have a list of referrals from private property owners who testify to thorough satisfaction with our services."

"Are you telling me then," said Gertie, "that the City has some sort of problem with a tree on our property?"

"Not today, ma'am," said the man gently. "It's just that the rubber tree out here looks as if it's growing rapidly. My supervisor mentioned seeing the species name on the City's list. They want to keep the tree disease-free and trimmed properly. The City administrators consider your tree a significant asset to the neighborhood. It is, after all, a notable landmark, visible for miles around. You must be very proud to have such a lovely specimen."

Gertie grew impatient.

"I didn't order any tree trimming, sir, and we've had no problems whatsoever with our rubber tree. I have to get back to my duties now, but I thank you for stopping by to compliment our tree."

"Ma'am, let me then just give you word that a letter will be arriving forthwith addressed to your head of household. It will be from the City notifying you that this rubber tree must be cut back within two weeks. The clerk of the City Arborist is, at present, typing these letters. Yours is one of the street addresses being notified. Our company will be very busy trimming large trees for residents who have reserved our services in advance of City notifications. We have proper equipment, ma'am, to handle a tree of this size. Other tree trimmers do not. I'm afraid that the only companies left for hire when our busy season begins will be the companies that the City and fine residential owners refer to as tree butchers. Their men are known to cut trees quite irregularly and to fall from limbs of superior height, whereupon they engage in lawsuits with property owners. Our company guarantees no such thing will happen. In addition to City notices that residents will receive, the City will mandate a new fine to be paid by non-complying residents for every ten feet that a tree exceeds their requirements. The fine will be due and payable ..."

"Stop. Please, stop right there. I don't want to deal with any City notices, new ordinances or clerks who'll probably send letters to the wrong addresses anyway. How long would it take your men to simply top off the branches and bring the tree to correct height?"

"Why ma'am, we could do it later this afternoon. We are completing the same kind of task at a residence ten blocks over. The men are carefully cutting and cleaning up branches as we speak. We could be over right after that."

"Fine. I'd like it if your men came here to complete this job quickly. Before your men start work, however, I want to see your contract guaranteeing in writing, with the signature of your president, that your company takes full liability for the men's safety on my property."

"Certainly, ma'm, my pleasure. We'll be over with our proper equipment to complete the job swiftly and neatly. We'll have the paperwork bearing the signature you require."

Gertie closed the door. It was better to simply take care of this matter while the right men were in the neighborhood on a sunny day. This was not some problem of great importance. It was simply a tree and avoiding a fine. It could become problematic in winter months if bored City officials started snooping around the side where her husband kept barrels of specialty fuel he liked to use in his roadster. The yard was hardly licensed as a filling station. This tree at the front of the house could be taken care of in the least disruptive way using this available service.

Gertie called the City. She asked whom they might recommend for tree trimming. The clerk recommended several companies and gave the highest endorsement to Ace.

The men came swiftly as promised. Three stocky men, wearing bulky, short, leather jackets fastened to their necks, climbed skillfully to the topmost limbs. They completed their task, leaving very few branches on the ground to clean up. Gertie happily paid the modest bill and didn't mention it to TR. She was greatly satisfied with her decision as the weather grew stormy into the week.

Chilly winds blew past the house, motivating Gertie to set up special evenings. Her family enjoyed cheerful meals, followed by reading aloud next to the fire while TR finished up business in the study. By the time the fire was roaring and hot chocolate being poured, TR came into the living room, sniffing the fragrance and asking his favorite ladies for his big cup of cocoa.

The winds gathered strength, turning to harder gusts as the week progressed. One night, storm clouds thickened darkly. The air was charged and volatile with warm currents blowing north from the Gulf of Mexico that collided with cold air blowing south from Canada. Angry, indigo swirls fought their way across restless Southland skies while the Gimble family enjoyed a hearty, home-cooked meal.

The family laughed through a humorous short story read by Gertie. They nestled snug and cozy before the fire. They chatted gaily and giggled at TR's jokes. Winnie played accompaniments on the piano to dramatize the effects of travel adventures TR told with a twinkle in his eye and a wink toward Gertie and Ty. Kate had joined the fireside gang and laughed as she drank hot chocolate and sat beside her handsome beau. She looked at Ty with dreamy eyes but changed course quickly to ask TR about the types of land he'd seen during his travels.

Lightening cracked overhead followed by rolling bursts of thunder. The family shrieked and comforted Winnie each time. The girl covered her ears and ran to bury her head in TR's chest. Her papa held her tight. When the peels of thunder subsided, Winnie would pop back up. The music and laughter continued.

One massive lightning bolt arced across the horizon and shattered the entire sky. The yard outside the living room window lit up in a blinding flash. A tremendous crash came roaring through the house.

Winnie screamed and froze, refusing to uncover her head. TR's large frame curled around the child as tiles crashed onto the floor above them. He shot up a second later. Gertie, Ty and Kate got up dazed from diving to the floor. Seconds after the lightning, thunder peeled in great waves. Nature's blasts shook the windows and doors. The loud thunder was the first sound that did not resemble the house crashing above their heads.

Ty flew up the stairs while TR gently but firmly passed his clinging child over to Gertie.

"Stay here," he ordered as he ran to the foot of the stairs.

Ty dashed out from the upstairs rooms and breathlessly leaned over the stairway railing.

"The rubber tree crashed through the roof!"

The night watchman pounded on the front door. TR let him in. The man was soaked and breathless.

"It's bad out front! The chimney and a section of roof are gone!"

Winnie started wailing while Kate and Gertie tried to comfort the hysterical child.

"We're not staying here tonight," commanded TR. "Ty, come and help me get the car."

Gertie left Winnie with Kate and went into the kitchen to try and call her sister. She came back and exclaimed, "Wait, Papa! I can't get through to Helen. The phone lines must be down. Should we go there anyway?"

"Yes," said TR. "It's unlikely the same bolt hit her house. You and Kate gather some towels and get ready to run to the car."

Ty dashed out the rear door and jumped in the roadster parked under a large tarp in the back yard. He slammed the dripping key into the ignition and pressed his foot on the accelerator while he pulled tight on the parking brake. The engine revved as the needles on the gauges flung straight up.

Ty brought the roaring, steaming car skidding to the front of the house. Rain pelted off the steering wheel, the leather seats and Ty's head.

Gertie peered out from the porch with towels piled high in her arms.

"Dad's sedan is at the garage!" yelled Ty. "We have to take this."

TR ordered the watchman to stay with the women. He ran to the car through the blinding rain. He and Ty struggled to get the convertible top unfolded and stretched across the top of the car. The relentless wind blew the canvas sideways, threatening to bend the struts that would otherwise hold taut the roof.

As soon as they got the roof attached safely on one side, Ty held down the other side while TR yelled at Kate, Gertie and Winnie to get in. The women held towels over their heads as they dashed toward the car. Ty had trouble getting the wet roof clasps closed over the front windshield on his side, so TR ran to help him.

Winnie was bawling her eyes out, trying to cling to Gertie's skirts as they crossed the driveway. Her mother stopped as the child stumbled in a puddle. As Gertie bent down to help the child up, Kate stopped, too, and yelled, "Where's Helen's house?"

"On the other side of town!" yelled Gertie through the next clap of thunder. "You'll have to stay with us tonight."

Then Gertie gasped. Winnie had slipped from her wet hands as she tried to grab the child under her arms.

"Get back here!" she yelled as Winnie ran toward the house.

Winnie saw one of her favorite dolls strewn across the porch banister, lying as limp and dripping as she had been a second ago in the puddle. Winnie ran to her doll. Gertie chased after the child as another strong bolt of lightening arced over the tree splintered around the house.

"Winnie!" screamed Gertie as she ducked to the ground. The child grabbed the wet doll from the porch, but then she stopped. Something she knew wasn't supposed to be in the doll's apron pocket was sticking out. Gertie came running over as Winnie grabbed the cardboard and unfolded it. With terrified eyes, Winnie screamed, "Mama!" Winnie collapsed into incoherent sobs.

Gertie scooped up the shaking child like a rag doll. Winnie clutched her doll in one hand and the cardboard in the other. Gertie and Kate ran across the puddles and slammed into the seats. In a pile of wet clothes, towels and rain-soaked leather, the family held tight as the roadster roared down the driveway.

"Don't worry Kate," said Ty, "This old beast makes it through the heaviest canyon storms in Larwin Valley. We'll be fine."

Winnie silently handed her mother the soaked cardboard from her doll's pocket. Gertie opened it and turned as ashen as Winnie.

"Papa!" screamed Gertie.

"I'm trying to drive through a monsoon here!" yelled TR over his shoulder. "Can whatever you have to say wait until we get to Helen's?"

"No!" cried Gertie. "A note was stuffed in the pocket of girlie's doll. Look at this!"

Gertie threw the cardboard at Ty. The thick, red ink scrawled on the note had smeared and dripped off the edges of the paper, but the words were still visible, pressed deeply into the wrinkled fiber.

"No one in your family is safe. We can kill you," read Ty to his father.

Winnie wailed louder, gasping for air between her screams. Gertie curled around the girl's head trying to comfort her. Then the woman's head snapped up in rage.

"What in God's name does this mean, Thomas?"

Kate stared wide-eyed at Ty. TR said nothing as he drove. After several minutes, TR spoke calmly.

"I don't know yet, Mama. It could mean anything. It could mean things I'm working on or things I'm not."

Silence enveloped the sopping group in the car. Thunder broke in overlapping bursts outside. TR Gimble not knowing something scared his family worse than the storm or the tree crashing into the house. Ty sat still, hoping Kate would not depart after seeing this side of what really went on in his family.

That night at Helen's house, Gertie, TR and Ty drew close and spoke in quiet voices while Kate helped Helen prepare tea in the kitchen. Then TR and Ty went off and whispered intensely while Helen gave the women clean towels, fresh nightgowns and hot cups of tea.

Winnie could not be comforted. She was so withdrawn that she wouldn't look at anyone. Gertie could only sigh and hold the child until Winnie fell into an exhausted sleep.

CHAPTER 51

▼

Indigo skies, pelting rain and fierce winds gave way to sunshine in the neighborhood surrounding the Gimble home. Trees and shrubs pounded into irregular shapes during the storm shook off the moisture and filled out once again. The exception was one large tree in front of the inventor's mansion.

Winnie stared out the window as workmen from the Ace Tree Trimming Company cut up the branches of the toppled tree. Their saws and hatchets broke apart massive limbs. The sounds tore at the little girl's heart. The green grass and lovely shade where she spread out her tea parties and played with her dolls would never beckon her so delightfully again. Her mother's dear sewing room at the corner of the house, where she lovingly watched over Winnie hosting tea for her dolls, had received the worst damage of any rooms.

Two dark sedans slowed to a crawl on the street by the workmen's van. Winnie felt a lump in her throat but could not speak. She thought she saw one of the workmen hail the first sedan. She thought she saw a hand come out of a window rolling down on the second car, but she couldn't be sure. Everything looked blurry and distorted ever since the tree crashed into the house.

Winnie ached with loneliness. Her mother was in the basement where she could peacefully concentrate on developing pictures under a lamp's red glow. Aunt Helen had come to stay with them. She cared for Winnie while her mother spent hours alone in her photo lab until it was time to come help Aunt Helen prepare the family's supper. The little girl figured her mom felt safe down there.

Ty was gone a lot, working for Papa and attending business school. Billy was still at Nelson Naval Academy. Papa seemed just as distracted as Mama. Other than discussing repairs to the house and a new block wall to surround the property, not much was said at family meals. Aunt Helen honestly tried to foster distracting conversation. She came from the kitchen and hurried to the window.

"Winnie, you mustn't linger here."

Joey MacDermott stopped his bicycle on the street. As soon as he saw the article in the paper about the accident, he grabbed his jacket and ran. The news article that stopped Joey in his tracks that morning announced, "Giant Rubber Tree Hits Gimble Home." His heart beat wildly as he read the words.

"What is said to be one of the largest rubber trees in the United States, and which is located on the lawn of Thomas R. Gimble, was hit by the storm Sunday evening. One of the four large trunks of the rare tree was broken off at the ground, crashing down upon the northeast corner of the Gimble home and doing considerable damage to the roof as well as the inside plaster."

Joey jumped on his bike to go and see the damage after reading more of the article.

"A large chimney at the north end of the roof was jarred loose by one of the long, heavy branches."

Looking at the debris, Joey breathed a prayer of thanks that everyone in the family was spared from harm. The article did not mention casualties.

As Joey straddled his bicycle surveying the scene, his sharp eyes noticed the workmen's heavy, leather jackets zipped to the collar. The men seemed to look right and left every time they bent down to gather up something from certain branches and the lawn beneath those branches. Joey looked in amazement as the workmen swiftly untangled thin wires he could barely see. The workmen would unzip the fronts of their jackets and stuff the fine wires inside.

Joey slid closer onto the Gimble front drive. He pulled his bike behind some bushes. Now he could see the reflection of tiny metal pieces on the thin wires the men were quickly hiding. His pulse quickened as his mind whirled.

"Why wouldn't a world-famous inventor have a lightening rod on his house to prevent such an accident? Did Mr. TR have some other kind of device he used to stop this kind of thing from happening in other storms? Why would men from a tree company be pulling out wires? Did someone rig the tree to be a super lightening rod?"

Joey had too many questions to rest easy. He had to go and see Hiram. The boy looked right and left to cross the street. When he glanced up the street, he saw two dark sedans circling around someone's driveway where the street intersected with a large boulevard. Joey would have looked away, assuming these were visitors to the residence, but something about how slowly the autos circled without braking to a stop made Joey look again.

The windows on both cars were tinted dark. Joey saw no license plates on the grills. He decided to take a different route to the Gimble plant other than the direct route he ordinarily would. Joey started pedaling as fast as he could. He found his detour and careened through the alleys that would take him to the Gimble plant.

The guard at the door recognized him and said hello as Joey dropped his bike. Joey hadn't stood trembling on the narrow concrete steps leading to the inventor's workshop ever since Mr. TR helped him get his patent. Joey stood trembling as he knocked breathlessly now.

"Hiram!" exclaimed Joey as the door opened. "Have you gone by Mr. TR's house since the tree fell down?"

The inventor's assistant lowered his spectacles.

"No, but I heard all about it."

Joey told Hiram everything he'd seen. Hiram thanked the boy and assured him that TR probably did have some kind of lightening rod. He told him that such a thing would not involve fine wires or tiny metal pieces as Joey described the workmen untangling from the branches. When Joey told Hiram about the cars circling slowly near the Gimble residence, Hiram nodded.

"Those could be men who want Mr. Gimble to know they're watching him and his family."

Joey's adept mind flew into his customary million and one questions. Hiram set down the project he was working on.

"I think it's time to tell you about the way inventors sometimes have to invent their own survival."

Hiram and Joey talked for two hours. Hiram answered Joey's questions, including the one about the book Joey had seen on Hiram's desk. Hiram told Joey the story of the old knights recounted in the book that had the red shield with a cross printed on its cover. He told Joey about the dark, fiery rock and machines in the work yard.

Joey sat on a stool with his chin on his knuckles and listened. Hiram explained why Mr. Gimble didn't want his sons to join the Guild. He talked about Mr. Gimble's involvement with the Ancient Rite that hadn't lead to any discoveries about alchemy or the rock called shale. He and Joey discussed the new shale oil refinery at Red River and other places across the country, some being built and opened for operation, and some whose first shovel of dirt had never been moved to build a refinery at all.

Joey came to understand the inventor's world as never before. He learned that it had less to do with inventions and more to do with business, politics and intrigue than Joey ever would have imagined. Joey looked thoughtful as he gazed through the office window, seeing the outside world in a whole different way.

"I think Mr. TR is the most wondrous person I'll ever meet, but I'd never want to live a life so complicated. I'd like to work with Mr. TR someday, and maybe with Ty and Billy, too. I think what they learn must be fantastic. His boys see how their dad fulfills his dreams time and again. He works with intelligent men who build grand visions. That's beyond what I could ever hope to learn at a university."

"Perhaps you're right, Joey," said Hiram. "Now I want you to take down some telephone numbers of people you can call if you ever see those men in dark sedans again. Remember to watch for anything distinctive, like dents on the cars or anything to describe the men whose faces you might see. Anything you tell us might help the boss change things to make his family safer from those men."

"I will, Hiram. I'll help keep watch for Mr. TR."

"Thank you, Joey. You won't be alone. I and other men are looking out for his family's safety, too."

Gertie saw the news column about the fallen Gimble tree. She cursed the fact that she rushed the workmen trimming it. She shared her secret grief with her sister.

"Penny wise and pound foolish, that's what I was, Helen. If I'd told the men to do a more thorough job thinning the whole tree, this accident would have caused less damage or maybe not happened at all."

The news article drove home more guilt in Gertie's mind when she read the words that almost shouted admonishment.

"Its sister tree, which grew in the grounds of the Borden property on First Street several years ago, was cut down as unsafe."

Gertie suffered her anguish with Helen.

"My exactitude about the workmen's contract, rather than the tree, cost my family dearly! You know I hate bureaucratic intrusions. I was so angry about the City tree ordinance and Papa getting some letter about a fine, I didn't see things clearly. I must get more practical about new policies and laws instead of immediately reacting with such loathe!"

Helen spoke gently.

"Sounds somewhat like Billy, doesn't it?"

Gertie hugged her sister.

"You're right. I often get defensive or take insult when I oughtn't. I'm impatient like Billy, and he's like me. I'll call him and reassure him that we're okay. Ty will visit him soon. He'll tell Billy about the threatening note. Billy will remain safest at Nelson Naval Academy. He's learning everything from self-defense to reading maps, and certainly how to fire weapons. He might help our family yet."

TR was most apologetic to Gertie.

"I feel helpless to know what else to do other than to continue to work with my men to try and find out who's really behind these threats. I've hired another watchman to guard our house during the day. We must go to the hills in Riverside very soon. I'm supplying you with this powerful gun I modified. It'll knock your little self over if I don't show you how to fire it the right way. I want you to practice out there."

Gertie looked at the gun with the odd barrel. Somehow it didn't seem as imposing to her as when she'd first seen it and banned it from ever being stored inside the house. That was when she feared Billy might unlock it from the wooden box and harm someone unintentionally. Now times had changed. It was mostly she, Helen and Winnie alone at the house a great deal of time.

"Thank you, dear," said Gertie quietly. "Let me know when we'll go shooting. I'm ready."

Gertie sadly longed to return to the time before the accident, or even the cheerful hours right before Winnie stopped playing her music. The little girl hadn't sung a note, written a poem or laughed ever since the accident. The child was missing a great deal of school from becoming ill so often.

Winnie seemed to want only to sew. She and her mother set up a temporary sewing room in the middle of the house. Winnie sewed by herself for hours on end, her stitches crooked under her tearful eyes. She muttered the same thought to her mother on several occasions.

"I'm glad this room doesn't have any windows."

Winnie also seemed to like standing by the gardens close to the front door with the guard nearby. Gertie spoke to her daughter gently.

"Maybe we can spend time planting flowers together. Then we can make floral arrangements and decorate baskets."

Winnie's weary eyes brightened at the suggestion. Gertie was desperate to find any means to soothe her daughter. She longed for Winnie to smile and chatter again.

Hundreds of papers and news clippings had flown about from stacks on Gertie's and TR's desks, files and countertops. The percussion from the tree's impact blew papers that settled in every nook and cranny. For two weeks afterwards, Winnie silently collected each one. Gertie felt hopeful and complimented her daughter for helping so diligently to clean up the house.

As Winnie swept up plaster and shards of glass from sections of the floor, she carefully dusted off news and magazine articles. She slipped each one into the large pockets of the oversize apron she insisted on wearing to tackle this chore. She didn't stop until she collected every scrap of paper blown about. Gertie and Helen noticed but didn't say a word.

After she swept the floor, Winnie closed the door behind her in her new downstairs room. She slowly took off her big apron and emptied the papers she collected. Articles that bore news of her family or any men whose names she ever heard her father mention were tucked into boxes she hid under her bed.

Winnie also collected the cancelled checks she found strewn about the house after the devastation. Whenever she found a cancelled check from any bank account, no matter how old or from which bank, she placed these special treasures atop the others she'd found and tied them together with a pink satin ribbon.

The girl was certain she must be the keeper of these important papers. She obsessed about preserving all possible evidence that might help her father someday figure out the bad men that he didn't seem able to identify now.

Winifred Gimble secretly determined that someone in her family was definitely going to be killed. She wanted to sob into the stitches she would sew for the rest of her life. She wanted to be near flowers and learn how to make lovely garlands for the funeral to come. She whispered her secret terror to her dolls.

"All of you are going to outlive everyone in this house, even me."

CHAPTER 52

▼

"We've missed seeing you over at Amy's," said Twyla.

Kate hugged her friend amid the bustle of the downtown department store.

"I've missed all of you, too, but things got very busy for me after we delivered that land information to Barry. It looks like the group is executing a 1,000-acre oil lease in Van Nuys and trying to get another in Larwin Valley. I have two small parts in movies, and that suits me perfectly. My acting doesn't involve too much, just showing up on the set and getting fitted and made up. Then I read my few lines in front of the camera. I just wanted to earn some decent extra money, and I am. How are things with you?"

Twyla frowned.

"I thought things were going very well at my office. We've been busier than ever, and they gave me a modest raise in pay. The men have been traveling to meetings in other states and doing work all over the Southland. Regis Petroleum even became a client. My company hired new chemists for analysis they're providing on certain new Regis refineries. But then this jerk from Regis came in and started working with my boss in our offices. Quite frankly, the new guy is making my life hell."

"Why?"

"He's the most oighty-oighty man you ever did see!"

Kate's eyebrows rose.

"And that means?"

"You know, pretentious, stuck up, holier-than-thou. Mrs. Berkowitz used that word. It fits perfectly to describe this man's arrogance. I've just about had to become his personal secretary. I can't stand him. All the men in my office don't like him either. He's staying around more and more. The climate in the office has gotten so bad, I bet all the chemists who have to work under his supervision will quit and find jobs elsewhere. They've said as much to me."

"Is he a chemist, too?"

"Oh, yes, and he lets everyone know it, prestigious universities and all. His name is Regis Hamilton. What irks me most is that he goes around mumbling all the time about 'that damn nimble Gimble.' The men in my office work for lots of different business concerns, but Hamilton is simply obsessed with hating the inventor. Worst of all, one of the men came to me last Friday and told me Hamilton made an offer to buy our company! Why would he hate Ty's dad so much?"

Kate looked up at the Christmas tree beside them. The scent of pine, the colorful store displays and holiday music surrounded hearty, cheerful shoppers. It should have been the happiest time of the year, but this season seemed heavy to Kate. She sighed deeply.

"Isn't there some way you can temper your emotions, Twyla? Can't you find a way to work with Hamilton? You've been at that office three years. You have seniority over all the other secretaries. You could advance to …"

"To where?!" cried Twyla, her eyes filling with tears, "and to what? I'm already as far as I can go in that office. I'd need a university degree to go any farther. I have no interest in studying chemistry. I'm certain that the man who came in last Thursday to talk to Hamilton will become his new personal assistant. I saw his resume, and he has that degree. I'll be demoted, not promoted!"

"So what do you want to do? It sounds as if you've bumped your pretty, witty head against the ceiling there. Others will be moving ahead to the floors above you, but you'll be stuck below."

Twyla wiped the tears from her cheeks.

"You're right, Kate. I've advanced as far as I can with the nice chemists. They were good to me, but I'm not like Jules. I didn't even ask to read their scientific journals. I didn't invest in learning more about their business, but I doubt it would have mattered. Now I see my mistakes."

Kate took Twyla's arm.

"You worked very hard and learned new skills. What mistakes do you think you made?"

"First of all, I should've quit weeks ago like Nona. But she's engaged now, and I'm not. Secondly, I looked at going to work as a way to serve others the best I could. I just appreciated earning my paycheck, but I found out that men never look at their work that way. A young man thinks about his prospects for success at an entire company from the very first day he starts work. Mrs. Berkowitz said that I needed to find a way to make use of my inner talents. I thought about that. I concluded that the happiest I felt doing any work recently was when we were rushing around finding the title information and getting the maps for Barry. I'd like to see if I can find a job doing that kind of work, but I don't have the money to get my real estate license."

Kate thought a moment.

"Don't go blaming yourself entirely for thinking about work as an order of service different than men do. You should know that men generally want women to think about work that way. They keep women from growing by saying that lady workers do silly things and act grumpy once a month. Meanwhile, they gossip worse than ladies and act grumpy whenever they please. I'm glad you're casting aside old ideas that will not serve your best future interests. I might be able to help you. Mr. Sherman, who owns our company, has been purchasing land in Riverside. He's now working with developers who want to build homes there. There's an interesting project in El Lago to build nice homes on the hills around Annabelle Porter's mansion. Most of the lots will overlook the lake. The avenues and streets lights are already in. They just need to sell the parcels of land. There are lots of other projects like that, too. Did you know that Riverside County stretches from Orange County to the Arizona border? We're talking about enough land in that county alone to keep people employed in real estate for decades!"

"You've got me interested," said Twyla. "Keep talking."

"A man in Riverside that Mr. Sherman knows has acquired a lot of land there He needs a sharp assistant. The problem is, he can't find a smart secretary from LA to move out to Riverside so he can employ her. The place is rather wild and rugged with people who act that way. There are cowboys and ranchers and lots of moonshine from what I hear. That's the best way I can describe the place, but Mr. Donner, who's moved there for the real estate boom, is from LA. He's a polite, cordial gentleman. He likes the challenge of making money there versus downtown or the valleys around LA. Those places are already getting crowded with investors and realtors competing for land parcels whose values are skyrocketing."

"So if I wanted to work for Mr. Donner, I'd have to move to Riverside?"

"Yes. It would be too far for you to take the train out there and back every day. I've driven there several times with Ty. He adores the place. It's both hotter and colder than here, but very pretty with mountains and rivers and big trees. He likes that life moves slower there than in the big city. His dad has purchased four square miles. Mr. Gimble plans to build vineyards and move his family there. Don't tell anyone, though. Ty is excited at the thought of living and working in Riverside. He doesn't want to deal with so many characters in business like his dad has to. Men like Reginald Hamilton, who end up hating Ty's dad, do so for lots of reasons that Mr. Gimble can't help. It's jealousy, mostly. Ty figures, if you deal with fewer men, you live a simpler, happier life."

Twyla admired her friend's practical thinking.

"You're learning a lot dating Ty."

"I know," sighed Kate. "I have a much better understanding of how things are for Ty's family than I ever thought I would. I agree with Ty that a less complicated life than his dad's will make us happier than his mom and family have lived, even with all their money. I look forward to living a modest life in Riverside someday with Ty. It would be the most special thing to have you living out there, too. Think of the possibilities, Twyla, for us to work together in real estate. We could make some money and buy land like we planned to."

"Done!" exclaimed Twyla. Both girls laughed, remembering the women's exclamation after meetings at Amy Watson's. Twyla's eyes grew bright with anticipation.

"It sounds like Mr. Donner will appreciate the skills I have to offer. I'd ask him to sponsor my becoming a licensed agent in exchange for my willingness to move to Riverside and work very hard for him. I'd rather try to temper my emotions dealing with cowboys in Riverside than downtown with that Hamilton chemist. It sounds like more city people will someday move to Riverside, but I wouldn't mind owning a gun for my safety living in such a rugged place."

Kate clasped Twyla's shoulder and giggled.

"Do I ever know the right gun for you! You'll be safe alright!"

Practicing in the hills of Riverside, Gertie Gimble proved to be an excellent shot with her husband's modified gun. She lowered the weapon and winked at him.

"Nine out of ten. Only one can left standing. Maybe I blinked."

TR nodded.

"That was good. I'm putting the targets farther and farther out for you. We haven't begun to see how far you can hit a target at really long distance. I'm confident now that you can handle the gun."

"What a memory this is making, Papa. I never dreamed a city girl like me would be out shooting in open country with you. You know, my sister Helen has taken a liking to this gun's power as well. Thank you for bringing her out here last week. We're feeling safer with this weapon in the cabinet under my bed stand at night."

TR looked to the horizon.

"Just keep your eyes level and don't panic if it comes to using it."

On the drive home from Riverside, TR and Gertie went over their plan. TR kept a steady hand on the sedan's steering wheel as the wheels inside his mind whirred.

"All will appear normal at the office while I'm shutting things down. It'll be a year before I close all my offices in the Taylor Building. There are men and companies throughout the U.S. and other countries who'll be quietly notified, but not all, Gertie. There are those of whom I'm sure would be no part of a plot to put McDonnell and Ritz in charge of my business affairs. But there are more who won't care one way or the other or may become participants in payoffs along the way. I can only figure the odds as best I can regarding which clients I can trust. Men I already trust are helping me figure this out."

"Are you sure you can't fire McDonnell and Ritz and wrangle out in court whatever claims they try to put against you?"

"It's not that easy, Gertie. Threats to our family would only increase. Ritz has so much influence in Los Angeles, I can't be sure what would happen in the courts. It's better for me to simply shut down everything that's in operation downtown. Once we sell the house and move to Riverside, I'll register new patents. I've already got inventions I'm working on for steam-powered farm machines and other agricultural devices powered by hydrogen. There's little McDonnell can do to cash the royalties I've been getting for years, although don't put it past him and Ritz to try new legal maneuvers. We won't be able to count on anything from my past to set us up for a new life in Riverside."

Gertie watched the tall eucalyptus trees gliding past them on the road. In her eyes, they stood like centurions guarding the pathway to their step-by-step escape from Los Angeles.

"I won't breathe a word of this, Papa. Many things could change along the way anyway. I'll keep your gun handy and bide our time. We'll appear to live as ordinarily as ever."

As construction crews finished repairs to their home, the family started whispering almost always. Even with armed guards around the house, there was comfort in keeping everything hushed as possible. TR and Gertie trusted no man's ears. The Gimbles knew that workmen could be bought as easily as lady telephone operators. Skip stopped by the house frequently to survey the men working on the new block wall while Jacob Steiner paid records clerks to obtain copies of the workmen's employment and police records.

Hiram reassured TR that the large, brown envelopes containing newspapers with false headlines stopped arriving at the experimental plant. Ty checked with the men in the work yard and heard of no one lurking outside the fences there. No men bothered Billy Gimble at school, and Joey didn't see any more dark sedans.

TR whispered to Gertie one night.

"After I transferred my account for the coal and shale oil company from our local bank to the large bank downtown, the threats died down."

Gertie looked surprised.

"Where there a lot of threats?"

TR nodded.

"I have to admit there were."

"So what do you think?"

"I think, Gertie, that some of the men at the Merchant & Maritime Bank are in on whatever Ritz and McDonnell are up to."

"You're saying that there's a widespread plot?"

"I can't be sure. I'm saying be prepared for anything."

Gertie turned over but knew she wouldn't sleep. She tried to brace herself for the roller coaster to come as control of her husband's finances slipped from their hands.

CHAPTER 53

▼

Genevieve McDonnell surveyed her apartment's parlor. She glowed with appreciation at what she saw. Unlike Amy Watson's still-barren parlor, hers was filled with fine treasures. Soon, those treasures and the spotless, polished furniture would be moved from the flat on the downtown boulevard to a large, new home in a fashionable suburb. Her list of matching tables, lamps, chairs and lounges was growing. Ahead was shopping and ordering aplenty to fill ample rooms and patios. She promised herself to tackle this happy chore right after the holidays.

The wife of TR Gimble's head accountant brimmed with optimism as her husband brought home larger and larger paychecks. She admired his bonuses for his outstanding work for the inventor. She enjoyed the smugness of a wife whose financial status was ascending rapidly. She'd married a successful man.

The accountant's wife was shocked, therefore, to be abruptly cut off by Gertrude Gimble. It happened when Genevieve called to offer condolences to Gertie after the tree fell on the Gimble house. Genevieve reasoned that Gertie must be stressed beyond any woman's tolerance.

"The upheaval must be tremendous," thought Genevieve. "Trying to live in a half-open house under construction is too onerous to imagine."

Full of sympathy, Genevieve immediately sent a large bouquet of flowers and two pounds of Pig 'n Whistle chocolates to Gertie and Winnie. She received no thank-you's whatsoever. She decided not to bother her husband with a woman's slight at the time it happened. He had too much on his mind. But she wondered silently. She prayed she'd done nothing unintentional or misinterpreted to jeopardize Frank's fine position.

While her husband tossed restlessly one night in his sleep, Frank kept murmuring, "Damn Gimble, damn Gimble." Genevieve asked Frank the following morning why he kept repeating this in his sleep. Frank shrugged and said he was very busy at the office and never seemed able to catch up on his work.

Genevieve saw Frank changing. Worry and concerns bore heavily on his mind. He was seldom affectionate to her. She timidly tried to let him know.

"Honey, I'm going to end up as isolated and unloved as Gertie Gimble."

Frank chuckled cynically.

"That'll never happen, Gen. That Gimble broad's a prisoner in her own house. And she deserves no less. You're not a nag like her. You're free to go anywhere. Plus, you have a shopping budget that will surpass hers very soon."

Genevieve silently vowed she would go to any means to ensure she didn't become a prisoner in her own house. Frank was right about her shopping budget. She already had more treasures than Gertie displayed in her home.

The attorney named Harry Ritz called their apartment frequently. The increasingly friendly associate of her husband never called Frank at home before, but other new people were calling as well. Genevieve knew their voices. Frank eagerly ran to his study to return their calls.

There was a Mr. Tiemonet, who called occasionally. Genevieve liked flirting with the man with the French accent. There was the woman with the raspy voice who wouldn't leave her name. There was a persnickety-sounding man named Reginald Hamilton, and a gruff-sounding man who simply said to tell Frank there was a message from the Saint. Genevieve was extremely polite to everyone who called.

Harry Ritz and his bleached blonde girlfriends became part of the McDonnells' life. Genevieve was often left to chat with the blonde girls about simply nothing while the two men drank whisky and whispered in the corner. Genevieve was building up her courage to ask these women what tricks they used to keep a distracted man like Harry Ritz interested in relations with them. Genevieve was sure they knew things to do in the bedroom that she did not. Meanwhile, Genevieve breached conversations carefully with her often-irritable husband. One night, she thought she'd comment.

"I heard watchmen now guard the Gimble property day and night."

"Yeah," growled Frank. "I think the inventor is falling ill under the stress of his work. He's getting paranoid."

Genevieve carefully tried again.

"Dear, aren't you working as hard as possible to relieve Mr. Gimble of all the duties he once had overseeing business in his downtown offices?"

"Of course!" bellowed Frank. "But that damned Gertie still tries to stick her nose into everything. When Harry calls the house, she refuses to cooperate. She claims to not know anything, and we both know she's got dimes stashed in different corners. You saw all the cash journals she has!"

Genevieve tried to agree.

"I did notice how rude she's become of recent. She didn't offer a word to thank me for the flowers and chocolates I sent over. You'd think she'd remember that I offered to be her friend and help her with anything she needs, especially with her children."

Frank snorted.

"There's only one little girl left at the house now, and the kid's turned into some kind of mute."

"Do you mean she's withdrawn and shy? Maybe she was stunned by the tree accident."

Frank turned to his wife with a twisted smile.

"A tree falls into the house and the kid goes mute. That just shows you how weak those Gimbles are. In my professional opinion, I don't think they warrant all your concern. You are better than they are. You need friends of much higher caliber, friends who aren't afraid to get out and be sociable. We're going to be coming into an awful lot of money, my dear. You need to think about the social status you want to maintain for the rest of your days, not what happens to that family."

Genevieve couldn't help but become excited.

"What do you mean?"

Frank paused.

"I was going to wait until we finalized this deal, but you'll be joining me at County Records to sign your name on a very important oil and gas lease with the Gimbles."

"You're kidding!" exclaimed Genevieve. "I'm stunned. This is the last thing I expected with how chilly Gertie has been toward me. I'm delighted, Frank. I told you that I wanted to try and find a way to do business with them, but I never thought it would happen so soon. With the Gimbles having the drawbridge drawn up and locked tight around their kingdom, how did you find a way in?"

Frank grinned.

"This deal wouldn't have happened so fast except for Harry Ritz. You'll have him to thank for finding the right location and drafting the right kind of lease. I didn't have time for all that research. I haven't the right connections to track down the man who is the first lessee on this deal. He's bringing Oregon gold to guarantee the transaction."

Genevieve clapped her hands.

"It sounds so exciting! Please tell me more."

Frank shook his head.

"I can't right now. You'll learn the details after the papers are drawn up. All I can tell you is that this thing is going to be worth millions. There's a clever way Harry designed it so that only you and I and the Gimbles are involved with the land and the lease."

Genevieve was breathless.

"I'm dying to know more! But I can wait patiently as you ask of me. May I inquire where the lease is located?"

"As you requested, my dear, our business deal with the Gimbles is local. It's in Larwin Valley."

"I won't ask you any more questions, I promise."

Then her intensely excited eyes softened.

"I am still so in love with you, my dear Frank. You're exceeding any expectations I ever imagined. Can we snuggle mightily tonight?"

Frank yawned.

"Naw, I'll be too tired in the morning. I have to get to the office early. I've got a lot to do to set up the lease."

He reached for the whiskey and Waterford tumbler hidden in the cabinet at the bottom of the bookcase. As he stood up, the crystal glass tinked against the liquor decanter. Frank poured a drink and raised his glass.

"We'll snuggle mightily the rest of our lives, Gen, and we'll travel the entire world. You can bet on that!"

CHAPTER 54

▼

"Whaat?!" roared Buck Williams.

The timid county clerk stared at Buck Williams across the massive, elegant, heavy-beamed room on the second floor of the cowboy actor's mansion. Workmen were applying painted decorations to the exposed beams and wood columns. Large, colorful rugs were rolled up awaiting installation after the last planks of maple on the floor were laid.

The map of the actor's property and the valleys surrounding it lay on a large oak table in the center of the room. Pacing from window to window around the room, the actor stopped at every fourth set of long, beautiful window panes. The actor threw up his hands as he ranted.

"All this money for nothing! I so carefully laid out this home and all the exterior grounds to capture every last view I wanted. I deliberately installed walls with no windows facing the oil gulch! I don't want to see that mess when I wake up, or when I entertain guests or listen to music in this room. Now you're telling me I'll have views of a seventeen-acre refinery out these windows and views right off my party veranda toward a bunch of noisy oil derricks. That bloody, stinking refinery would be the first thing to greet my guests arriving at the train station. Their fine clothes will be covered in soot by the time they ride up to my house. Well, this is no goddamned Signal Hill, and I won't have it! The oilmen have more than 300 acres over in the Gulch. Why do they need to drill on this side of the canyon anyway? Even with all the damned land I bought around this place, it wasn't enough. What you're telling me is that my sanctuary will be ruined forever!"

The clerk's hand trembled as he groped in his vest pocket for a wrinkled handkerchief. He dabbed his sweaty upper lip and brow.

"I am so sorry to bring you this news, Mr. Williams, but my supervisor felt sure you'd want to know about this."

"Who's the dumb bastard behind this scheme?" shouted Buck.

"The proposal is submitted by the well-known inventor, TR Gimble."

"Gimble?!" roared Buck. "Holy Christ! Now I get to tango with a man who builds the most successful refineries on earth for the largest oil conglomerates there are! This is awful! I did not need this news right now. Well, at least you guys warned me. Please leave the plans behind. I'll pay for another set of blueprints for the county. Just get out of here. And you can tell the men on the planning commission and board of supervisors to be sure and get their rest. I'll be keeping everyone up extremely late with my testimony at the hearings. Gimble's going to get one helluva fight from me, and I can tell you this, I intend to win!"

"I'll let everyone know, Mr. Williams. I'll leave the plans. Your opposition to this proposal is what we expected. We'll gladly hear all your arguments, however long they take at public hearings."

The man scurried out the door, ran to his car and drove down the hill. He couldn't wait to get back downtown where the news reporter awaited him in the lobby at the county administration hall.

Francisco stared at the departing car. He prayed the county credentials the man showed him were correct.

Buck Williams picked up the phone and did not stop making calls until well past midnight. He knew he had to mobilize forces to oppose the inventor's plans. All the good souls Buck knew who were opposed to oil drilling and contamination promised to come to the public hearings to assist Buck's fight against the well-known inventor.

Buck and his lady pilot friend, Emily, flew over Larwin Valley. They took hundreds of pictures of the land to be included in the confrontation. The lady pilot nimbly swooped down low, and then pushed the plane higher into sharp turns to get the job done right. Emily's strong arms and capable hands guided the plane to all the angles and elevations Buck needed so he could take comprehensive photos from the air.

The hilly land and boundaries of the actor's estate in the valley were challenging to understand. Even Buck's own workers found it difficult to know exactly where the estate's boundaries ran. It would be even harder for planning commissioners to comprehend. The public officials who would vote on Gimble's proposal would do no more than drive out to the property for a look. Buck knew they'd be more curious to see his new home than looking across the hills to understand the intrusion that a refinery and oil drilling would impose.

The pictures from the air were developed. Buck hired draftsmen to ink the lines of property boundaries in white on the photos. Then he had them lay down the inventor's proposed scheme in red. He had them draw blue lines to show where visual impacts would occur from Gimble's oil drilling and refinery.

Buck knew talented artists who sketched designs for movie sets. He hired them to render illustrations showing how the views from his estate would be corrupted. He had the artists also sketch how the streets around the train station would become grimy and intolerable with rows of shanty houses for the oil workmen accompanied by drab eateries where moonshine and houses of prostitution would flourish.

Spending time in Larwin Valley taught Buck that disputes about the land were sometimes hopeless. It could take years for officials to understand the exact features of just a few parcels of land. Then they'd stall and delay, not knowing how to vote on a certain proposal.

The rugged valley with all its bounty also offered this curse of confusion. A person had to be well versed in spotting man-made markers and natural features to be able to understand how a parcel lay. Knowing this, Buck pulled out all the stops to bring reviewers of Gimble's proposal swiftly past any confusion about his land. He hired attorneys to advise him on the proper steps to set up his arguments and exhibits. He hired ex-petroleum workers to explain refinery workings and the damages to land and air that refineries caused in neighborhoods.

Francisco Alvarez and his family kept watch for the dark sedans with the men who once insulted the gatekeeper, but the same men hadn't reappeared in Larwin Valley since Buck's party. Francisco proudly showed his brothers, cousins and nephews the new gun rack filled with three fine rifles that Mr. Williams had installed inside the castle tower at the front gates of his estate.

When members of Francisco's family heard about Gimble's planned refinery, they argued pro and con about the jobs it would bring to Larwin Valley versus the intrusion to Francisco's employer and the guests the actor entertained. No one could seem to agree on which course might be better, so they decided to wait and see what happened when the millionaire inventor collided with the cowboy actor opposing his plan. The Alvarez men placed bets on who would win. Francisco was obliged to support Mr. Williams entirely, but he secretly wondered if the famous inventor would prevail.

Scoot Wynn was glad he hadn't been the one to tell Buck Williams about TR Gimble's proposal. He imagined Buck exploding with rage over Gimble's plan for drilling and refining so close to the actor's paradise sanctuary.

The experienced surveyor Scoot hired last fall had been more than worth the money the wildcatter paid him. They pored over geological maps and carefully drilled borings to test the layers of rock and soil. Scoot now had a good idea of how the minerals, hydrocarbons and groundwater sat, flowed and fit together on his land.

The wildcatter still kept horses grazing casually on his property, but he quietly installed a small oil well tucked into a cliff nook that was hidden behind large oleander bushes. He hit modest oil sands at a depth of only 2,800 feet. He was barely bringing up oil in any significant paying quantity, but he knew that Gimble likely had all the knowledge about where better veins of oil lay in deeper, nearby sands.

Scoot knew he could place his wildcat wells less than seven yards offsite from the inventor's property, but Scoot decided to let the inventor's showdown with the actor decide the course of events for his own next moves. It had always been his intention to ride the coat tails of the inventor. Scoot knew this strategy would save him the greatest amount of capital outlay in the near term and earn him the greatest return over the long haul.

The well-know inventor smoothed a stack of typewritten pages on the kitchen table where he sat with his wife.

"This oil and gas lease in Larwin Valley is called the Equity, Gertie. Ritz and McDonnell are trying to force this to be a limited partnership with only the McDonnells signing on, but I'm aiming for the oil group in Van Nuys to be the group of lessors we go in with."

Gertie looked through the pages of complicated legal terms.

"I don't see how Ritz and McDonnell can interfere with executing this lease. You've been working on it for years. The Equity sounds like a promising name."

"Details are far from final," said TR, "but this draft will help us iron out terms and conditions. This is the right lease to provide for you and the children for at least seventy-five years. Those are the kinds of quantities of oil and natural gas I know are in the ground in paying quantities on the six parcels we're acquiring. Plan to go with me to County Records next week to sign your name on the titles of the first four parcels of this lease. I finally got those titles cleared. I want them in your name as well as mine."

Gertie sighed with some relief. At long last, her husband was making progress selling off some of his smaller companies. He was setting up their children's security with reliable plans he didn't intend to alter. TR's inventions in petroleum were still yielding royalties. McDonnell and Ritz had not been able to lay their hands on that money yet.

Gertie's thoughts turned to what would come next. TR's schedule looked as if it would be more manageable. Their land in Riverside was being set up for vineyards. Ty and Kate would soon be engaged. Ty was ecstatic about operating an agricultural concern with his dad in Riverside, and he was getting Billy excited about it, too. Billy had shown great skill in his studies and was playing baseball at Nelson Naval Academy. He smiled proudly when his family came to see his games. Billy didn't seem to want much these days, but his letters and phone calls home remained quite cheerful. Winnie was attending school more often, although she still hadn't resumed playing her music.

The inventor's wife remained grateful for any small strides her family could make. Things were staying stable enough as TR transitioned himself away from his downtown companies. She feigned ignorance when Harry Ritz called and refused to talk to Genevieve McDonnell at all.

Skip Vanderhooten got the late night call from Buck Williams. Skip recognized the actor's voice.

"Howdy, Buck! You plannin' another party?"

There was a pause.

"Well, not a barbecue like we had before, Skip. This get-together involves your friend, Gimble. I'm afraid he's definitely coming to another sort of party in Larwin Valley."

After Buck outlined the problem with Gimble's proposed refinery and drilling in Larwin Valley, Skip paused at the other end of the line.

"TR's always got a lot of things going. Maybe it's a small, experimental refinery and not much drilling. There's no oil conglomerate named on the permit application he filed at County, is there?"

Buck rustled through some papers.

"No, I just see TR's name here listed alone. How do we know some other big company isn't behind this?"

Skip chuckled.

"We don't, Buck. And he might not disclose it if there were. Look, he knows how I feel about huge industrial contamination in any area. I agree with you and your friends on that. But I also know TR's always inventing things to make drilling and refining cleaner, safer and more compact than ever. I'm not so certain if it's right to come out with both guns blazing before we know the nature of what an inventor like TR is proposing. We should wait and hear the details. A general permit application doesn't tell us enough. Ellie and I will come to the public hearings."

"That's all I ask," said Buck. "I look forward to seeing you there."

CHAPTER 55

▼

The famous inventor entered his downtown office. The reception area on the seventh floor was groomed spotlessly with lush carpets and polished oak panels. A richly illustrated map of the world hung on one wall. A fine mahogany book cabinet decorated another. The burgundy velvet sofa with matching claw-footed chairs and mahogany tables glowed under the soft light of elegant Tiffany lamps.

Despite the fine furnishings, the large room stood devoid of the pulse of business. No visitors waited and not a telephone rang. The weary, vacant stares of his two secretaries strained with boredom told TR wordlessly that the women knew something was very wrong.

He handed each of the ladies an envelope. They took the linen parcels with trembling, ivory hands. Each suspected the inventor's good-bye. The ladies' envelopes each contained, not layoff notices, but one hundred dollars in cash and a sterling letter of personal reference. TR smiled kindly at the surprised women.

"First, buy yourselves something that feels fresh and special. I've included letters of reference seeing as you were the best administrative help a boss could ever want. Take your time finding a good place to work if you so desire. Mr. Steiner knows many fine employers so don't hesitate to ask for his help. I will not be around these offices any longer. You will not be fired or laid off by me, but I cannot say what others may do or when."

The women dabbed their tears and nodded silently. Too overwhelmed to utter words of response, the ladies finally knew the agonizing rumors were official. Every detail concerning how TR Gimble appeared to be removing himself from his offices in the Taylor Building was no longer cause for anyone's speculation. By letting his two secretaries know, the inventor was letting everyone on the seventh floor know as well. The inventor was laying himself off from his own companies headquartered there.

TR smelled the cigar smoke wafting from under the door of his former office. He knew Harry Ritz was inside with his feet propped up on TR's massive desk. TR knew exactly how the man was gazing down Sixth Street out the window. He heard him guffaw on the phone.

"That's right. Just about got him squeezed out. Oh, hell, the Equity lease is a piece of cake. S'more dough for parties and booze. Of course! We've got a way to trump the Van Nuys kiddies, too. Think gold. When the dollar slips, gold will trump everything. Hell, yeah. A guy from Oregon. Gold is how we'll reel that bugger in."

TR didn't knock or go inside. Instead, he turned toward Frank McDonnell's office. He opened the door to the accountant's roomy office.

"Mr. Gimble!"

Frank's shocked face admitted everything as he sprang up from his chair.

"Mornin', Frank. I see you're in here early. Hard at it, eh?"

"Why yes, sir! Wouldn't consider it a good morning unless I had a day's work done by ten."

"Good," said TR. "Sit. Ritz is on the phone and I've got to get going. I'll make it brief."

Frank sat down slowly, the shock on his face not diminishing. After weeks of not seeing TR enter his office, it seemed strange to see the inventor standing before him. TR turned his hat slowly in his hands. He spoke in measured tones, his green eyes piercing the accountant's mind.

"You and Harry will understand that I am going to execute the Equity lease with the Van Nuys oil group. We've spent five years putting this together. The land and mineral rights are in my name and Gertie's. I bore all the costs for exploring those veins of oil in Larwin Valley long before you crossed a 't' or dotted an 'i' in any of my books. The group has all the documents to prove my total investment. I do not want you and your wife on the lease with Gertie and me. Get rid of that thought. It had to be your wife's notion. Harry wouldn't care, and you're not that novel a businessman. I am walking away from everything in this office. Take what you want. Tell whoever's behind this scheme that I've left enough assets behind to build a refinery overseas or start twelve other businesses. I've shelled out all that I intend to."

Frank's deepening look of shock turned to impending nausea. TR turned on his heel as Frank's head dove toward his wastebasket. The famous inventor walked out of the Taylor Building for the last time.

Hammering out the details of the Equity oil lease and its participants was not proving to be an easy task for TR. The Van Nuys members, who belonged to the club of private, individual oil investors to which TR belonged, wanted TR and Gertie in on the lease with them. They did not like Frank McDonnell or Harry Ritz. They wanted those men out of the picture entirely. TR had some explaining to do.

"The men running the downtown Gimble offices are going to branch off on their own. Disregard their demands to put anyone else on the lease except the participants you want."

At times, the group would believe the inventor's words, but at other times, they doubted. They didn't want expensive lawsuits impeding the success of the lease. TR's campaign to win their full trust went on for weeks. Men who were members of the Guild found themselves face to face with men who supported Harry Ritz. Ritz assured the men that only Frank and Genevieve McDonnell would be on the Gimble lease with them. TR forged ahead on his personal contacts with every man and woman in the Van Nuys oil group. He was sure that a solution to the uneasy matter could be attained.

TR also attended the late night public hearings as the battle raged between him and Buck Williams over the proposed Gimble refinery in Larwin Valley. TR had drafted the proposed refinery to ensure the unparalleled success of the Equity lease. The inventor's oil wells in Larwin Valley would still make good money on the lease without the refinery, just not as much as if the refinery could be constructed and operating at full capacity. TR, Hiram and the men from TR's experimental plant worked relentlessly to get the refinery approved for construction.

TR patiently listened to everything that Buck Williams, his attorneys, friends and the townspeople of Larwin Valley had to say about his proposed refinery. TR and his representatives countered with fine exhibits of their own, showing how sleek, compact and non-polluting the new refinery would be. TR showed how trees planted around the facility would grow tall and thick to screen most of its buildings from view. TR assured county officials and Mr. Williams that the Gimble refinery would only hire workmen of quality stock who'd be good family men not inclined to drinking or gambling.

TR argued that the refinery would bring fine-paying jobs to the town. TR vividly described how a hundred men and women, who might otherwise have to travel to jobs in Los Angeles, could remain close to their children in town. His powerful words painted a picture of modern refinery workers as congenial towns-people, spending their money locally.

The town's businessmen applauded TR's arguments. They stood up to say that they vigorously supported the Gimble plan and would gladly welcome an enterprise bringing greater prosperity to all other businesses in Larwin Valley. One businessman noted that the cowboy actor's mansion, by comparison, pro-vided very few jobs to hungry families in the valley.

Francisco and his relatives continued to place bets on how the controversy between the actor and the millionaire inventor would play out. The big public hearings at the county administration hall brought out all sorts of characters who made long, impassioned speeches both for and against the Gimble refinery. Reporters took notes for dramatic articles they wrote about the unfolding affair. Photographers snapped pictures of the presenters and fine exhibits at the meeting hall. Even Buck Williams' horse and great danes were not spared public atten-tion. Whatever could add more life to the tale that readers wanted to follow was fair game for the reporters.

Francisco started getting worried when one of the Alvarez women, who had devised a way to witness all the activity, came back with some troubling news. The woman was allowed to sell her home-baked cookies at the entrance to the hall since the crowded meetings involved such long stretches into the night.

With her table of cookies, the Alvarez woman held a perfect position to see and hear everything that she could report back to her family. The odds-on favor-ites changed as quality exhibits and well-tuned arguments were brought before the public and described to the Alvarez family by the lady selling her cookies. She could see straight up the main aisle of the hall to where the planning commission-ers sat. She reported their remarks and how they quietly signaled each other indi-cating that their positions were shifting before their vote to approve or reject the refinery.

The woman told Francisco that she noticed six men always coming into the rear of the meeting hall together.

"Francisco, you must know that these six men arrive right after the pledge of allegiance just before hearings start. They sit hidden in the back row with their faces in the shadows. They talk to no one else. The sinister-looking men always leave early before debates are over for the night. They only whisper to one another once in a while. Now I must tell you something alarming. My heart must stop beating madly first. Last night, I left my table and followed behind them.

They went to cars in the deepest shadows behind the building. I did not go there myself, but I watched. I saw them get into two very long, black cars. These cars had very dark color on the windows. I wonder, Francisco, how can the men see out such windows to drive safely through the night?"

Francisco's heart started beating madly, too. He gasped.

"If those men have such interest in the proceedings between Mr. Gimble and Mr. Williams, then Mr. Gimble must be associated with the bad men in the dark sedans. Mr. Gimble could be El Diablo!"

Francisco wrung his hands. He had seen the inventor briefly in Larwin Valley several times when Mr. Gimble came with his wife and son. He'd seen the man laughing with Clay Henry at his filling station as if he were a lifelong friend. Francisco's words exploded.

"None of this makes sense! The inventor seems pleasant enough to everyone. What a convincing mask he can wear! I don't understand why Clay Henry seems to know him on good terms. We all know that Mr. Henry knows a drunkard or a conniver upon first sight! Why would the inventor be so friendly with the most respected Christian man in Larwin Valley? If the inventor is El Diablo, why wouldn't Clay Henry see this clearly and warn us?"

Francisco feared that nothing was as it seemed anymore. He pulled his wife and daughters close to his bewildered heart.

CHAPTER 56

▼

Francisco's anguish did not cease. He took his concerns about TR Gimble being El Diablo to Buck Williams. Buck had to agree that it seemed suspicious when the six mysterious-looking men showed up repeatedly at public hearings.

"Look, Francisco, I have no idea if those men are thugs of Gimble's, government watchmen or private investors. They could be any of those things. We'll put heavier locks on our gates. We'll add more men to the night watch around the estate. Let me know if you see anyone who looks like those kinds of characters around my property."

Francisco heaved a sigh.

"I remember the warning you got from the Saint. His men told you not to interfere with oilmen."

Buck squinted into the sun toward the oil gulch.

"Mr. Gimble is not so much an oilman as he is an inventor. In fact, I think this is one of the first times he's trying to build a refinery himself. Ordinarily, from what I hear, Gimble designs refineries with his patents. Then other investors build them. I'm still not sure what's really up with what he's planning. There is something more than a little odd about this whole affair."

Buck privately wondered how Mr. Gimble could be associated with thugs if Skip Vanderhooten was the inventor's lifelong friend. Buck had known Skip a lot of years. Skip never hid his loyalty to TR Gimble, but Skip had also never shown himself to be an opponent of Buck Williams on any matter, nor a friend of aggressive oilmen.

Buck saw Skip and his girlfriend attending public hearings, but Buck hadn't had time to talk to Skip. Buck decided to call him. He told Skip about the men he and Francisco observed at the hearings.

"You're right, Buck," said Skip. "Ellie and I noticed six men altogether in the back of the hall, too. No one I've asked seems to know who they are. I have to let you know that men of the same variety in the same kind of cars that we saw out at your place have actually been stalking TR Gimble and his family."

"You don't say!"

"It's true, Buck. TR has had men on the watch for the safety of his family for weeks. That incident when the rubber tree fell on his house looks mighty suspicious. They're trying to track down clues about that. Problem is, the same kinds of men we encountered at your barbecue were seen lurking around the Gimble property after the tree accident, almost as if they were verifying the damage. Gimble and his family have been receiving threats for some time, but that happened when we worked on the submarines, too. He's trying to close down whatever the men making threats want him to, just like he had to before."

"Wow. It sounds pretty complicated. I had no idea all this was going on."

Skip paused.

"Do you think it might be possible to set up a private meeting between you and TR?"

"Maybe that's the right thing to do, Skip. I truly don't want to attract sinister characters over this deal with Gimble's refinery. Maybe there's a way we can reach a compromise."

"Great," said Skip. "I'll tell him to call you."

Francisco couldn't believe it when Buck informed him that Mr. Gimble would be coming to the house. Francisco and his family thought the inventor wouldn't show. Francisco nearly fainted when he saw TR Gimble pull up to the entry gates in his roadster. The inventor smiled and greeted Francisco as if he'd been coming there for years. The gatekeeper scratched his head and wondered as the inventor's auto roared up the hill to Buck's house. Buck's great dane barked in friendly greeting as Buck threw open his front door.

The two men locked in controversy for weeks greeted one another as perfect gentlemen. Buck showed TR around his large home. The more they conversed, the more they found they had in common. They discussed their love of music, the great outdoors, constructing grand, new things, loyalty to family, unconventional views about business and politics, and their diverse friends and alliances that sometimes confused people who didn't know them.

The millionaire inventor and the cowboy actor then found that they were both one-time active members of different lodges of the Guild. Buck Williams still attended meetings sometimes, but TR rarely did. They found they were both raised to high degrees in separate lodges of the Ancient Rite. Each man told his story of what he'd learned inside their ranks. They could not deny their bond of passage through similar doors when they were both younger men.

They laughed about CJ Niles using the downtown country clubs and Guild meetings to sell his stock certificates, and they spoke about meeting the illustrious Annabelle Porter on different occasions.

TR roared hearing about Emily Browning's first low flight over Buck William's home. Then he told Buck that he didn't mind that the lady aviator had helped Buck prepare his fine air photo exhibits for the public hearings. The two men had a lively discussion about how exhibits for new projects using photographs and diagrams could transform the way that planning commissions and everyone could understand complicated design proposals.

Francisco couldn't believe what he saw by the time the inventor left. TR Gimble got back in his roadster and roared down the hill while Buck stood in front of his house, laughing and waving. Even Buster happily woofed hearty canine good-byes after licking TR's face at the front door.

As TR drove off, Buck yelled at the inventor to stop back in anytime. TR's long arm shot out of the top of his roadster, waving his customary one brief good-bye.

The men in the Alvarez family had to cancel all their bets. They never dreamed that any conciliatory ending to the men's confrontation would occur. They were rather hoping for a bloody duel.

The county planning commission voted down TR's refinery proposal, but the inventor got busy focusing on the Equity lease for oil drilling in the valley behind a ridge and out of sight from Buck Williams' large, stone veranda. The inventor's terse words to Frank McDonnell caused the accountant to back down in his eagerness to sign onto the lease. Whatever Frank told his wife Genevieve about their not participating, TR didn't know and didn't care.

After the dust settled from the controversy with Buck Williams, TR intensified his efforts to register more patents for refining shale. The Red River shale oil refinery flourished under construction.

Then TR registered the first of his patents for new farm machines. He and Ty built an irrigation system that would supply water to the planned vineyards and future Gimble home in Riverside.

Ty decided that one road on the large Riverside holding deserved to be named after the friendly downtown garage that modified TR's roadster. Ty and TR happily filed the name of Tally-Ho Road on their maps. They named another road after Gertie's family, and filed a main boulevard on the property maps as Gimble Road. Their realty associate, Mr. Sherman, wanted a road named after him, too. There was plenty of land with room to grow so he got his own street named Sherman Road at the site of the new agricultural concern becoming known as Gimble Farms.

Francisco and Buck Williams remained on the watch for evil men who called their boss the Saint. Members of Francisco's family spotted sedans from time to time prowling around the oil gulch. The family gave thanks that none of the men in dark sedans stopped to threaten Buck Williams or Francisco.

Scoot Wynn decided to bide his time until TR started drilling oil in Larwin Valley on the parcels adjacent to his. He got interested in collecting decorative Spanish silver saddles for his horses. His new pastime proved popular in Larwin Valley parades so he decided to join an equestrian group in love with the same silver saddles in Pasadena.

Everyone seemed to be moving ahead with what was lucrative for him or her, and then one afternoon, TR came home early from the work yard with a worried look on his face. He sat down with Gertie in the study.

"It seems a calamity is brewing over at my former downtown companies. Gimble checks are bouncing from accounts having insufficient funds. My vendors and suppliers who were used to prompt payments will now be calling the house, Gertie. They'll be inquiring why their payments are not arriving."

Gertie could not hide her grief. She started to weep.

"This is so terribly humiliating to me as an accountant. I'm so frustrated knowing that McDonnell and Ritz are entirely behind these accounting shenanigans."

TR clasped her hand.

"We'll just have to buck up and figure out something to tell these guys and their accountants. Jacob or I will go and see every vendor who calls. We need to prevent lawsuits and pay off those debts. Men are different in how they'll respond, but we must try in good faith with every one. I've heard McDonnell is riding hard the men who owe my companies money, but I can't pressure those accounts separately without upsetting whatever's going on downtown. Our family still has plenty of royalties coming in with no shortage of other assets to sell if things ever got really tough. This is a frustrating part of our transition. I couldn't have known it would happen, nor can I stop it right now. We have to ride it out as best we can."

Gertie's heart pounded. The two conspirators downtown were taking aggressive action to ruin TR's credit at his downtown bank accounts. The nerves in her head screamed thinking that these men were testing the waters to see how TR might react. There was nothing she could do without jeopardizing her family. And so large sums of money went missing.

TR and Ty spent more time in Riverside than ever before. Billy joined them every weekend he could. Gertie could see that her husband was trying to redefine his life in a less complicated way. As much as she worried about the evil being sown by the men who took over her husband's downtown offices, she was pleased seeing TR trying to build a simpler life than he ever desired to live before. Gertie tried to convince herself to be as confident as TR that all would be fine. She hoped that soon his downtown offices would simply close. Their family goal of getting re-established in Riverside was all that mattered.

Kate enjoyed discussing her plans with Twyla, who had relocated to Riverside to work for the nice realtor Kate introduced her to. Twyla was studying to get her real estate license and managing to save some money to buy some land with Kate. The two girlfriends took the train back to Los Angeles every other week, practicing Kate's lines and talking about the movie roles she received. There were no reporters following Kate. She kept her profile low and her income steady, just as she planned.

Twyla had fallen in love with the man for whom she worked in Riverside. Mr. Donner asked Twyla to marry him not long after Ty and Kate got engaged.

As snow dusted the beautiful mountains of the Southland, and frost began to settle on the farm fields and vast valleys of Riverside, the Gimble family saw happy new beginnings on the horizon.

The happiest day in a long time for Winnie was when her parents told her they decided to sell their big home in the suburb outside Los Angeles. Winifred Gimble knew she wouldn't miss living behind the six-foot block wall surrounding the renovated mansion, which stood under the irregular shadows of what was left of the butchered rubber tree.

Winnie longed to run and play outside in Riverside, free of armed guards, dark cars that crept by, and all the things she felt made her family unhappy.

Riverside represented hope for everyone. Winnie whispered her secret dream at night to her dolls that maybe there would be enough safety out there to ensure that no one in her family would get hurt.

CHAPTER 57

▼

Annabelle Porter ran to her car and threw a pile of blankets into the back seat. Her driver made a quick stop on El Lago's Main Street to pick up boxes of food and clothes. The boxes were swiftly stacked in the trunk and remaining seats of Annabelle's large automobile. Men in town with emergency supplies packed inside trucks and cars stood ready to caravan with Miss Porter 120 miles west.

The lady evangelist halted the convoy at the radio tower in Los Angeles. Annabelle rushed inside. She interrupted the choir broadcasting music to thousands of listeners. Her strong voice carried across the airwaves.

"Dear people, this is Annabelle Porter! A great tragedy has struck Larwin Valley where the San Demetrio Dam has burst! An enormous flood has carried bodies away. Homes of over a thousand are destroyed. The good people of Larwin Valley need your help! Gather clothes, food, blankets, whatever you can spare. Bring donations to the temple or come help the people right now!"

Buck Williams stood in the center of the large hall in the Larwin Valley lodge belonging to the Guild. He wept openly as muddy townspeople silently carried in bodies of men, women and far too many children. The poor souls were ripped from their beds with millions of gallons of water sweeping them naked into the early hours of dawn, only to deposit them on treetops and hills. Bodies wrapped in sheets were stacked together tightly on wet planks hurriedly gathered from the lumber yard. Clergymen prayed over the dead and blessed more bodies carried inside. Clay Henry knelt in a corner praying for the carrying in of the lifeless ones to cease, but it did not.

The rain poured as it had for days. People fanned out across the valley trying to locate survivors. Dazed residents wandered without aim as endless rivers of rain-soaked sludge and dead animals slogged through the streets of Larwin Valley.

Workers at Clay's Filling Station struggled to keep up with the flow of cars and trucks packing the crest of the highway. Frantic relatives screamed when they heard of entire families vanished. Anxious government engineers gathered around the remnants of the dam, skirting reporters who demanded that someone step forward to make an official statement.

At the Gimble home, the women hugged one another and wept for those who perished. Winnie ran to her room to gather toys to take to the children of Larwin Valley. Gertie and Helen pulled extra blankets, coats and sewing supplies from the closets. Gertie asked Helen to keep watch at the house. TR instructed Hiram to do the same at the plant. Billy called, worried his dad might have been caught in the flood. Gertie assured him everyone was safe. Billy said to call when they returned from taking help to Larwin Valley.

Ty loaded boxes into the trunk of TR's sedan, while Gertie and Winnie slid onto the back seat. Gertie put one arm around Winnie and placed her other hand on her purse. Inside her handbag was the blank check Gertie carefully tore from the page of checks belonging to one of the family accounts. She knew its balance precisely.

The engine of the large sedan idled while TR sat waiting with his large hands folded quietly atop the steering wheel. Ty hopped inside. The Gimble family joined the line of cars on the boulevard heading for the highway out to Larwin Valley.

Cars inched forward with men patiently steering while women sat reading Bibles and clutching rosaries deep in prayer. Children peered at one another through rain-soaked windows.

Nearing the crest of the highway at Clay's Filling Station, people's horror and panic became apparent. Cars heading back to Los Angeles were filled with sobbing women, wailing children and somber men. The clog of traffic going both directions had people getting out of cars that could barely inch through the throngs.

Groups of reporters interviewed travelers and flood survivors at car windows. Worried men and women milled about under sopping oak trees at Clay Henry's park beside the filling station. The line of people waiting to pay for supplies at Clay's small market included fine-heeled visitors in cashmere coats alongside men and women from the valley drenched to the bone and still caked in mud. Many a Christian act took place right there.

Annabelle Porter grabbed her umbrella and left her driver with their idling automobile stuck in traffic. She started walking from car to car, clasping the hands of terrified souls. She bent her head in prayer with all who reached out to her.

As she advanced down the line of cars, she reached the Gimble sedan and stopped. Through the steam on the front windshield, she thought she recognized the famous inventor. Annabelle slowly raised her hand and touched the jeweled cross from which dripped tiny droplets of rain. The rain splashed down her long, blue coat. TR nodded, acknowledging the famous lady preacher from behind his closed window.

"Oh, please Mama!" cried Winnie from the back seat. "I want to meet her! I have all the news articles you ever saved about Annabelle Porter!"

Gertie looked down at the child who'd been so silent that she rarely knew what Winnie was thinking anymore. Gertie wondered why her pile of paper clippings always seemed to dwindle toward the end of the week. Now she realized that her daughter was following all the same stories that interested her. Touched, Gertie rolled down her window.

"Miss Porter," said Gertie, "My daughter would like to meet you."

"Oh surely!" cried Annabelle. "I recognize your husband. You must be Mrs. Gimble. What is your daughter's name?"

"It's Winnie!" cried the girl straining to come closer to the wet window. "I'm Winifred Gimble, and this is my mother Gertrude Gimble."

"Pleased to meet you," said Annabelle.

She shook the hands of the millionaire's daughter and wife.

Ty looked over at his dad who smiled slightly. TR shook his head imperceptibly. Ty knew what it meant. His dad was telling him, "Do not engage this woman."

TR watched his wife and daughter in the rearview mirror of the car. Annabelle's soft clasp remained around Winnie's outstretched hand as the evangelist looked into her eyes.

"Do you want to say a prayer with me? Would that make you and your family feel better while you wait here in the rain?"

Winnie smiled brightly.

"Oh no, Miss Porter. We pray all the time every minute in our hearts. I just wanted to meet you and see your eyes."

Annabelle laughed.

"My darling child, not only can you see my eyes today, I want to invite you and your family to come and visit me anytime you want at my new home in El Lago. I have traveled from there to this flooded valley today bringing emergency supplies and God's comfort. I'd like it sometime if you visited. I think you would like my house. It's on a hill above a lake."

Winnie hadn't smiled or acted excited like this in what seemed like forever, so Gertie responded amiably.

"Sometimes we go to Riverside, Miss Porter. We might be able to stop by. I appreciate your invitation and thank you on behalf of my daughter and family."

Annabelle Porter knew all about the Gimbles' large holding in Riverside. Realtors were one group of businessmen she truly enjoyed speaking with and receiving donations from. The lady preacher knew exactly where the Gimbles were planning to move. The opportunity of meeting the non-sociable family here on this rain-soaked highway on her way to deliver help during a catastrophe was nothing short of a miracle.

"Mrs. Gimble," said Annabelle, "we have an entire caravan of believers stuck here in traffic with you and me today who are carrying hope to the people of Larwin Valley. We expect the survivors to need many things. I'm collecting donations to help us help these poor people in the coming months."

Gertie looked up and saw one of TR's green eyes wink at her in the rearview mirror.

"Oh, Miss Porter," said Gertie. "I brought but one check with me today. Our donation is to the Guild. We heard that those who perished are being cared for at the lodge in Larwin Valley, but conditions are primitive at their temporary morgue. The dead must be buried properly and soon. Our family will assist the men performing this horrible task. We've brought emergency supplies for survivors, along with our donation to help with burials. We'll donate more to the lodge if needed."

Gertie saw TR nod slightly.

"That's wonderful!" exclaimed Annabelle. "Bless you for your generosity. It will be a true miracle for the people of Larwin Valley to receive your aid. I still want you to stop by my home in El Lago sometime when you can. Now I must be on my way. It looks like traffic is starting to move again."

As Winnie waved an enthusiastic good-bye to the lady preacher, Annabelle swept around to walk back to her car. Suddenly, Winnie and Gertie screamed as a car swerved toward them, throwing Annabelle Porter's body against the Gimble sedan. Miss Porter's umbrella handle smashed on the pavement as TR and Ty jumped out in one swift leap from both sides of the car. The lady preacher lay on the ground stunned. The heavy, wet wool of her long, blue coat was heaped around her body.

Gertie and Winnie scrambled out of the car. Annabelle moaned and grabbed the top of her left arm. Ty and other men ran out to stop cars in both directions, shouting and waving their arms. Reporters and photographers ran forward, slipping on the rainy asphalt and falling over each other to get to the scene.

Annabelle twisted slowly on the muddy pavement. Gertie saw blood spreading across the coat near the woman's upper left arm.

"Quick!" shouted Gertie, "She's bleeding. We need help!"

Gertie lifted the woman's large jeweled cross that was lying across her neck. She carefully opened the woman's coat. Once she saw the gash on Annabelle's arm, she wrapped a hankie around her hand and pressed it firmly on the wound.

Annabelle murmured, "I must have cut my arm on your window."

"There, there," said Gertie, "Lay still. Help is coming."

Winnie looked horrified for a stunned second. Then she ran out onto the road. She pulled hard on Ty's coat.

"Unlock the trunk, Ty!"

Ty looked down in disbelief and shouted.

"Get off the highway, girlie! Get back in the car!"

By now, reporters and photographers were swarming from all directions. Traffic couldn't have moved unless God Himself parted the sea of cars. Ty ceased waving his arms and reached down. He grabbed his set of car keys from his pocket with one hand while scooping up Winnie with his other. He took her to the trunk of the sedan, knowing from experience she'd run off and try something dangerous on her own if she had a mind to.

As soon as Ty lifted open the car's trunk, Winnie wriggled out of his grasp. She reached inside to grab one of her dolls lying in a box of donations for flood survivors. She ripped off the doll's apron and dropped the toy on the ground. As the doll's ceramic head cracked open on the wet pavement, Ty looked down and saw it was the doll that had carried the threatening note to his family when the tree crashed into their home.

Winnie flew to the side of the lady preacher. The girl clutched the doll's apron. As she careened to a stop, she nearly knocked over her mother, who was cradling Annabelle's head and keeping her hand pressed over the deep gash on the lady's arm. Before her mother could object, Winnie reached gently inside Annabelle's coat and quickly tied the doll's apron as tightly as she could above the cut on Annabelle Porter's arm. Gertie looked in amazement at her quick-thinking daughter and then remembered all the news articles on family first aid that she had clipped.

"Good girl, Winnie," said her mother softly as she tied a second knot with the strings of the doll's apron.

Winnie bent down and whispered in Annabelle's ear.

"I'm giving you the apron from my doll named Dottie. Dottie was going to help children who needed her out here anyway. You needed her first."

A tear slid from Annabelle's eye just before she passed out.

The crowd around the accident scene had grown monstrous. The horrified family in the car that struck down Annabelle Porter was wailing together like a pack of wounded animals. The man driving the car turned hysterical. Ty thought the poor man was truly going to lose his mind over the incident.

Being tall enough to see over the heads of all the people, TR saw a man running from Annabelle's car.

"Let him through!" boomed TR.

People stopped in their tracks at the loudest man's voice they had ever heard in their lives. The throng of people parted like the Red Sea.

Annabelle's driver ran uphill carrying a black leather bag.

"I'm a trained medic!" he yelled.

TR all but lifted the man past the last few people in the crowd. Soon Annabelle's driver was at her side applying a proper tourniquet and disinfectant.

In what seemed like a flash, the lady preacher was carried off the road and back to her car. The driver swiftly turned the car around and sped off in the other direction. Time was precious, and there was scant care to be had from overwhelmed doctors and nurses at the small Larwin Valley Medical Clinic. Men at Clay's Filling Station telephoned the highway police. Patrol cars with sirens flashing helped to clear the roads as Annabelle Porter's driver rushed the preacher to the nearest hospital in Los Angeles.

TR told his family to get back in the car. People recognized the inventor and let his sedan through with rousing cheers and well wishes.

TR and his family drove to the sobering scene at the Larwin Valley Guild lodge in the middle of the mud-soaked town. Ty lifted boxes of his family's donated goods out of the trunk and handed them off to the men who were stacking them in trucks that would head out to help families in remote parts of the valley.

Then Ty got back in the car to stay with Winnie while Gertie put a fresh kerchief over her nose and walked swiftly with TR to the back entry of the lodge. TR handed the men the check that Gertie had quietly filled out in the back seat.

The return to the Gimble home was filled with cheers and good wishes from people along the way. Flowers and cards from Annabelle's faithful did not stop arriving at the inventor's home for weeks.

CHAPTER 58

▼

In the weeks after the San Demetrio Dam burst, millions more gallons of water and debris flowed from the upper mountain reservoirs through the Los Angeles valleys that lay west of Clay Henry's ranch. Tons of muck slogged through the mighty water channels of the great Southland until the sludge finally oozed its way into the Pacific Ocean.

The people of Larwin Valley mopped up the mud, dead livestock and wild animals gone awash on both sides of the destructive swath. The townspeople demolished buildings that could not be saved. Although the lodge belonging to the Guild was not damaged, that building in the middle of town was slated to go down, too. No one could bear the thought of all the large and small bodies that had lain inside.

Clay Henry wrote the most moving public eulogy to the perished souls and brave people of Larwin Valley that anyone in California ever saw. Buck Williams attended the memorial services for the lost children dressed in his finest cowboy clothes. He wiped his eyes with a red kerchief and held his big hat in his hand while brawny movie stuntmen wept beside him.

Not a soul in Larwin Valley who'd opposed the Gimble refinery felt right anymore about the inventor not being able to start his well-planned enterprise near the train station. The town's businessmen felt that human spirits damaged by the recent flood could be restored with new construction and plentiful jobs. Their businesses were in definite need of a boost from the kind of work the refinery would bring. Men excitedly discussed quality improvements that could be made with the capital that the Gimble millionaire would bring to Larwin Valley.

Buck met with Clay Henry and the town's business owners. They reviewed TR's plans and decided that everything he proposed would create a beneficial facility that man and nature could coexist beside.

Buck sent word to TR Gimble on behalf of the men in Larwin Valley, telling the inventor that he should appeal the negative ruling from the county. Grateful followers of Annabelle Porter offered to pray for a single public hearing where all the officials' votes would be cast in Gimble's favor.

TR jubilantly told his fellow members in the Van Nuys oil club about Buck Williams' change of heart and the people of Larwin Valley inviting him back to get his refinery approved. The private investors were heartened that the Equity oil lease would now be a phenomenal success.

Frank McDonnell and Harry Ritz were not pleased. They renewed their efforts to sow seeds of doubt among the men and women. They started rumors in country clubs and Guild lodges stating that TR Gimble's credit was slipping and may not be in good standing very much longer.

Skip and Buck Williams called TR to tell him. TR told Gertie about the downtown men's latest shenanigans, and her heart pounded.

"What do they want you to do?" she cried. "Are they worried you'll make some money they can't lay their hands on?"

TR shrugged.

"Likely, but we need to support this family's departure to Riverside and getting our vineyards set up. Until we can sell more assets, I'll keep trying to finalize the Equity. That lease involves good men and women who may come to realize that McDonnell and Ritz are not on their side either."

"You may convince them yet," said Gertie. "I spoke with three of your vendors who called the house. The two you paid are very grateful. They offered to speak with others. One of the men said that the same thing is happening with two other men in San Francisco who are battling to rid their businesses of men who seem to be leading their affairs into ruin. It's odd, Papa. They described those other professionals acting just as brazen as Harry and Frank. They're acting as if no one on earth can stop them."

On a morning not long after, Jacob Steiner read the paper as he sipped his tea and ate his favorite bagel at Emile & Bonnie's downtown diner. It felt pleasant to return to his favorite morning haunt. There'd been much disruption to the flow of clean water that came from the north into the Southland ever since the San

Demetrio Dam collapsed. The people downtown had been speaking of little else except that catastrophe for weeks

The hoarse whispers of the men sitting three booths down caught Jacob's attention. He kept his face low in his newspaper as he listened.

"It's got to be now!" whispered one man desperately. "That damn actor is resurrecting his refinery plan. That cowboy horse-kisser has the whole goddamned town ready to throw garlands at the plan. He's all but guaranteeing it'll get unanimous approval on first vote at the appeal!"

Jacob had no doubt about which movie actor, town or refinery the men were speaking.

The whispers of the unknown men continued as an authoritative voice cut in tersely.

"Look, we've got the men ready in every position. It's taken years to set this up. What remains is not going to happen overnight. All this may take five years, maybe more, but nothing like a small refinery getting approved is going to screw up the plan now."

"Here's how it's gotta go," said another apparent leader's whisper. "The shale plants are getting shut down one by one. A lot of them never got to operating, but his damn plant opened with enough fanfare to have news of it wired all over the world. They're shouting about cheap shale gasoline from the rooftops, and the people say his mix runs great in their scooters, but that whole scream has gotta be silenced—and silenced completely—enough so that it's never more than two-month newswire feed that got lost in history, just like his subs. Sure, some men'll squirrel away a gallon or two of the stuff, but with no refinery, it won't matter. There's a plan to get that dean hushed up at the college, too. He'll be no problem with one more near-miss from a bullet since he's got a wife and three kids. The town'll forget about the shale plant cuz lots of things go bust out there, but we have to figure out how to get that persistent bastard who's organizing the whole affair to go down with the ship. Hampton's gonna be a problem."

"What about the shale patents?" asked another whispery voice.

TR's patent attorney three booths over didn't breath. A gravelly whisper responded.

"The whole deal with his patents is that they have to become worthless. They're his primary flow of cash. That flow has to be broken apart so the guys downtown can continue to break down his credit. Getting his funds redirected off Uncle Sam's turf is gonna take time. The accounts will keep getting shallower, and then the bottom will become apparent. We figure there'll be a reaction with some sudden moves by the broad, but we can keep her in line. We've already scared her kids enough. That'll rein her in."

Another voice asked, "What about all the king's men?"

"The chums?" asked the first voice.

"No, the workers," answered the second voice. The authoritative voice whispered confidently.

"As long as workers keep getting paid, they're gonna stay loyal. He'll keep runnin' the plant til he moves. And he'll keep starting up new operations, too, even as he goes. Everything's hard enough to keep track of as it is. Don't worry about his men. By the time we're done, no one's even gonna want to say they worked for him. They won't even mention his name!"

Another voice of authority whispered.

"His shale patents are gonna go bye-bye, along with all his other patents. Older patents will expire, and no one will renew them. If you break that extra cash flow from the new shale patents first, then men won't get paid. Loyalty will drop off. He can't get men to work if he gets any kind of rep for not paying them. That'll happen soon enough. Then all his other deals will start busting up, too, new companies, partnerships and everything else he can't capitalize."

Jacob heard the men pause, then one of them whispered anxiously.

"He gave five of the shale patents to the Feds."

The confident one responded.

"No problem. They're already buried. The government boys who like him and still go around encouraging other shale operators are going bye-bye real soon, too. Headlines will scream that they wasted millions of taxpayer's dollars on worthless shale plants that did nothing. The Saint used Hamilton to screw things up with those experiments. Shale's gonna become a very unpopular idea. No one will want to dig his donated shale patents out of the files."

Chuckles followed.

The hoarsest whispering voice that first brought up the Larwin Valley refinery persisted.

"What about the people in that valley? With the way his family helped save that lady preacher, they'd work for him for nothing and smile doing it!"

The authoritative voice that spoke of making the patents worthless whispered impatiently.

"Look, they're counting on his bucks coming in to help save the economy there, so beat up the actor and tell him to withdraw his support. Then twist his arm way back so he makes every last call to all his earth-loving buddies to get in there and blast the refinery proposal back down again. Then there'll be no saving the valley and no hero antics with the inventor's money. That damn actor will know once and for all to keep his nose out of any kind of business with the Saint. We don't need that horse-kisser being a constant thorn in our side."

Jacob covered his mouth to keep from coughing up his bagel. He wiped his sweating forehead and quietly took a sip of cold tea.

"How's it going with the pinhead and the playboy?" asked the first voice.

"They got it wired, so to speak," answered another voice.

The men chuckled low and heartily again. One man couldn't stop snickering as he whispered.

"Damn, that was a good job on the tree!"

Jacob could only imagine that the pinhead was McDonnell and the playboy was Ritz. He shook his head. The tree, of course, was the accident that delivered the first irrefutable threat to the entire family in a way that TR could not hide from his wife.

The first authoritative voice spoke again.

"We got the playboy preoccupied with all the bimbos he needs for his limitless libido. We got a steady supply of booze being delivered to the pinhead every week. He drowns his head in that stuff every night. His old lady's beginning to look as dissatisfied as the inventor's!"

The man with the loud snicker couldn't stop himself from reacting. He had to blow his nose. The first leader continued.

"The pinhead has the longest haul ahead of anyone. He has to hang in there for a lot of years once he's headin' up everything. We need to make sure he's liquored up enough to last, but not so blasted that he can't think. He has to be locating accounts and assets that he doesn't even know anything about right now. If he can't nail down any more accounts after a few years, then those assets probably aren't locatable. Then we'll go ahead and ship him off."

Another voice queried.

"Is his place in South America set up?"

"Not yet," said a second voice. "He ain't gonna need it for a lotta years. I'd give my right testicle, though, to see the look on his old lady's face when she disembarks. She's joining social clubs and prancing around LA like her old man already did the job!"

The snickering man collapsed in giggles and blew his nose again. One of the leader's voices continued.

"She gets to enjoy a lotta years kissing royalties from the Equity before they leave. That's the pinhead's incentive to gut it out. He still has to get rid of that oil gang group of investors in the valley, though and get himself and his old lady on the lease with no one else but the inventor's family."

"Ritz has that covered," whispered another tense voice. "He's got the guy from Oregon with the gold. That'll shoot past anything the oil investors think they have to negotiate with. They didn't think that far ahead."

"Hey, speaking of shooting," said the second leader, "we want those special little daisies he invented. They fire damn far. They'd come in real handy."

"Sure," whispered an anxious voice. "We'll get those, too."

The man with the apparent runny nose snickered.

"Hey, we gotta go. Saints be praised, guys!"

"Only one needed," said another voice.

A third voice concluded, "Yeah, the one who pays!"

Jacob kept low in his booth until the men left. As they exited out the back door, Jacob was fairly certain that parked in the rear of the diner were two dark sedans with tinted windows.

The patent attorney thought to himself that being short and dumpy probably kept him safer than if he were tall, dark and handsome. The young waitresses didn't come to his table as often. He breathed a great sigh of relief because he wanted to remain as invisible as possible to hear all he could of the men's conversation.

One thing Jacob knew was that TR's affairs were so complex that just about no team of experts could soak out everything the inventor had. Whoever the Saint was, or whoever might be acting behind the Saint, wanted as much of Gimble's money as they could siphon out of the country. Every move the inventor made could cause changes that might upset the whole plan these goons had obviously taken years to put in place.

For what purpose Gimble's fortune was needed did not matter. The inventor had earned too much and was on someone's hit list to be laundered out. Someone wanted TR to simply allow the taking to happen without putting up a fight.

Jacob knew TR was confident enough to always land on his feet. The person Jacob worried about more was Gertie. Her exactitude trying to count all the Gimble pennies was not going to benefit the challenges that lay ahead for her husband. She needed to redirect those skills to sheer survival in outwitting a network of downtown enemies. Although it was a matter of personal pride to her that her family affairs should run like clockwork, Jacob knew that none of this ordeal was going to run like clockwork. He knew what he must do. The Gimble woman had to learn these bloodcurdling details before she made any moves that might interfere with the Saint's plan and cause one of these goons to inflict more harm on the Gimbles.

CHAPTER 59

▼

Jacob Steiner pulled up to the gates at the new block wall surrounding the Gimble property. The brawny, young man in the dark coat and hat standing beside the gates looked like he was counting flowers.

"Does she love me or does she love me not?" teased Jacob.

The man looked up with a grin as he recognized the inventor's patent attorney.

"I thought we were all done with these bouquets, but there are still some straggling in. If I have to check the bottoms of one more bunch of flowers, I think I might just puke from the smell!"

Jacob laughed as the young man put down the flowers, opened the gates and hailed him in. Each lovely card, gift and floral bouquet that the grateful followers of Annabelle Porter sent to the Gimble house was checked thoroughly before ever being laid upon the Gimbles' front porch.

"Good day, Mrs. Gimble," said Jacob when TR's wife opened the door.

"What a surprise, Jacob! Come inside."

Gertie closed and locked the door. She smiled wryly.

"So friend, what brings you across the meadows and over the moat to visit us today?"

Jacob chuckled. It was odd how terror and threats laid upon people over a long time transformed human emotions into a muted, dark humor in the heart.

"You haven't sold this old homestead yet?" asked Jacob.

"Not yet. Are you coming to tell me of a prospective buyer? That would be welcome news indeed."

"I have no prospective buyers today, Mrs. Gimble. Have you secured any offers?"

"Nothing in writing, but we could be getting closer. All the pictures I took and developed in my photo lab of the home's interior and exterior have been helping Mr. Sherman advertise this property to many more people. Even though it hasn't sold quite yet, I've been packing up some things and getting rid of other things. It'll sell soon. I'm delighted at the thought of a comfortable ranch house in Riverside where Winnie and I can plant a few flowers outside and have less cleaning on the inside. Smaller is better for us, I assure you."

Jacob looked at the woman who was trying to remain optimistic. He truly didn't want to upset her.

"Speaking of comfort, I have some things to share with you."

Gertie looked at him closely.

"Please sit down, by all means, Jacob. In fact, come into the kitchen, and I'll make you some fresh, hot tea."

"That'd be wonderful, Mrs. Gimble. I could use some."

Gertie did not cry or get angry when Jacob told her what he'd overheard three booths down at the diner. Gertie smiled.

"I'm relieved to know, actually. I thought we'd all be dead by the time we ever found out. The answer to what they want from my husband is simple. They want everything, don't they?"

Jacob nodded. His tone was serious.

"My main purpose in coming here was to let you know I think there'll be a lot of messing up by these characters along the way. Just from hearing their discussion, they have a mammoth project ahead for years, but there are far too many variables for things to not go the way they want. That will lead to them pulling more stunts like the rubber tree. I don't think you can be too defensive, but moving to a less populated area will be significantly to your advantage."

Gertie folded her hands.

"I agree with you completely, Jacob. You never can tell how various characters will react. I never dreamed so many hundreds of people would respond as viscerally as they did to Winnie's kind act of tying her doll's apron around Annabelle Porter's arm. Our family did not save the lady's life. Her driver and the doctors did. All we did was buy her a few precious minutes to get out of the throng on the highway. Few men or women can control all events, just as no one could have predicted what would happen to Miss Porter or us just for talking with the lady at the moment we did. I don't have any tears to cry over these circumstances with

TR's money, not at all. One had only to watch the way those men have been interfering with TR's business affairs downtown. And those guys never earned such big salaries, mind you. McDonnell was only some low level accountant, and Ritz has never been anything but a drunk and a playboy. I should have known sooner that all they were doing was creating more and more leverage over TR's affairs so that other men could come in and help them finish the job."

"Well," said Jacob, "It does appear that they and the other culprits are in their positions now. I'd have no idea how vast their network might be. I only regret that my specialty is patents and not any other kind of law. Otherwise, I'd know more judges, officials and private practitioners who can be trusted. I don't know who I'd recommend, other than your husband's closest friends, to see him through this transition until all of you can get enough assets out of your name and get moved to Riverside. Few greedy men would want a farmer's lot."

Gertie laughed.

"That's true, Jacob. You've done me a high honor coming here fearlessly to inform me of what you heard this morning. I'll never forget that. I'll wait to see what my husband says. We'll revise our exit from this downtown madness accordingly."

"Thank you," said Jacob. "All I wanted was to see you and your family do whatever it takes to stay safe."

After Jacob left, Gertie slowly closed the door, leaned against it and closed her eyes. Winnie came around the corner. Gertie jumped.

"Oh, you startled me, sugar! I thought you were upstairs in your new bedroom taking a nap."

"Sorry Mom," said Winnie. "I'm afraid I heard everything."

"Oh, dear. Are you okay?"

"Sure, Mom. I'm sort of relieved like you. Now I know that the rubber tree didn't get butchered for no reason, and that the men didn't shoot at Dad in Red River for no reason, and that shale oil is not going to go away for no reason. All these things have reasons now, so how I can be scared anymore?"

Gertie couldn't hide her surprise.

"How did you know about Papa being shot at? I just learned about that recently. You weren't in the house."

"Ty told Billy, and I got Billy to tell me. I was sure something happened in Red River just because of how you and Dad and Ty were acting. Billy knew I could take it. He said he didn't want me to lollygag in the folds of your skirts sucking my thumb forever."

"Is that why you were so brave helping Annabelle Porter?"

"Yes. I have nothing to lose being brave. I have everything to lose cowering behind fear. I don't want to take fears with us to Riverside."

Gertie pulled the child close. They hugged silently and did not cry at all. Winnie looked up at Gertie.

"I have one small idea, Mom."

"What's that?" asked Gertie.

Winnie straightened and stood tall.

"I think we'll be busy selling the house and moving. Who knows what Dad will have to manage at the plant and Riverside and everywhere else? What I thought is that you could start taking money from any accounts where you can still sign checks to withdraw cash. Dad could do the same. If you take as much as you can, then we can hide money inside the heads of my dolls. If burglars try to rob us, then we'd have some money leftover to live on and get safe. Robbers would try to take papers or checks or cash from your desk or Dad's. The last place they'd look would be inside my doll heads."

"That's a novel idea, Winnie. I'll discuss it with Dad. If he says to do it, you and I will reattach the heads on the dolls and sew their outfits back together securely around the neck."

"Good," said Winnie. "I was hoping I could offer one safe place."

Gertie hugged her smart, brave daughter again.

CHAPTER 60

▼

As Ty adjusted the rear view mirror on his dad's roadster, Billy looked over at Winnie in the back seat.

"Hey, girlie, did you bring water to drink and a bowl to pee in?"

"Of course," said Winnie. "I know it's eighty miles, and there's no place to go to the bathroom along the way."

"Smart girlie," said Ty.

Winnie looked at Ty in the rear view mirror.

"Did you and Billy put every single box in the trunk?"

"Why yes, dear," said Ty, smiling over at Kate in the front passenger seat. "Let's get going."

As the three Gimble children and Kate rode east along the highway, the wind blew their hair wild and free. Leaving Los Angeles behind, the promise of Riverside sang in their hearts.

Winnie had made a special request to go and visit Annabelle Porter in El Lago. Gertie had winked and assured Winnie that she would take very good care of her dolls for the afternoon. Ty and Billy chided Winnie while dragging out all the boxes from under her bed and deep in the back of closets to put in the trunk of the roadster. Winnie and her mom had added the latest news clippings to the collection of articles, journals, cancelled checks and photos that Winnie carefully arranged in the boxes.

The most recent articles made Gertie smile. They talked about the pinnacle of TR Gimble's career as the Red River shale oil refinery opened to wild acclaim and operated just like the inventor said it would. The line of cars waiting for fill-ups with the new shale gasoline created local headlines in all the towns around Red River. Reporters announced that the shale gas was cheap compared to petrol, and that people's cars and trucks ran quite smoothly with improved acceleration.

Gertie remembered the thrill when the news tapped along wires across the Atlantic to be broadcast on radios around the world. Newspapers had to reprint stories about the refinery, its inventor and the new Red River Oil Products Company with its thousands of acres of shale holdings. Newspaper offices got hundreds of calls from interested investors wanting more copies than the presses had printed or editors ever planned on selling.

Excited reporters tried to write stories about all the stages of the complex refinery. They used words like contraptions, gismos, and gadgets and every other word except the right terms for all the refinery processing. The plans and elevations for the new refinery had been stolen from the Red River Planning Department. Reporters could not consult the drawings to write accurate descriptions of the new technology. Threats to her family had already begun at the time, but Gertie cherished the memory of her husband's achievement they quietly enjoyed. She lovingly smoothed the folds of the newspapers that told these stories. She hoped they would endure.

To the young people in TR Gimble's roadster, the ride to El Lago didn't seem as long as eighty miles should last. Ty kept a heavy foot on the accelerator the same way his dad did. After they drove up the winding road to Annabelle Porter's white hilltop mansion, Billy walked through the odd gateway with the gold and blue tile dome. He strolled past the fragrant herb gardens and climbed the steps to the double blue wooden doors inscribed with a gold star and a cross. Billy lifted the square brass doorknocker. A lady in a crisp, white dress answered.

"Is Miss Porter in?" asked Billy.

The maid greeted Billy, introduced herself as Maria Alvarez and went to get Annabelle.

Annabelle rushed to the door. She grasped the young man's hand as Billy grinned.

"Billy Gimble, Miss Porter, reporting for duty on behalf of Winifred Gimble."

"Oh sweet heavens!" exclaimed Annabelle. "You are just as good-looking as the rest of your family. Did they come with you?"

"Yes," replied Billy. "They're getting Winnie's boxes out of the car."

Winnie, Ty and Kate came up the walk. Annabelle exclaimed once more over all the delightful young people she so adored and how wonderful it was that they drove all the way out to her mansion. She brought them and their boxes inside and showed them the most unusual home they'd ever seen.

Miss Porter's paintings, rugs and murals came from around the world. There was more decoration representing every different faith from every corner of the globe than the Gimble children or Kate had ever seen assembled in one place.

"It's like the most unusual museum in the world!" exclaimed Kate.

She couldn't wait to tell Amy about seeing all these styles of Moorish, Asian and Western decoration altogether. She wondered if Annabelle's potpourri of various designs could start a new trend for home furnishings that Amy Watson and other ladies would be delighted to learn about.

Annabelle took her visitors down some stairs to her underground catacombs. She flicked one switch that lit rows of beveled glass wall lamps. The lady preacher showed her guests the hallways.

"These tunnels were dug when the house was built. Maria's Uncle Francisco was in charge. He was so diligent supervising construction that all the work was done without one accident. Look at all the features Francisco had the workmen build. These beams every fifteen feet with metal struts in between and heavy tiles below ensure that the heavy, clay soil stays firm and dry. Your treasures will be safe inside these cool passages."

The Gimble children and Kate caught their breath seeing all the gold and marble decoration along the hallways. Trunks of every sort were stacked along the walls. Annabelle showed them the special place she reserved for Winnie's boxes. She assured Billy and Ty that Winnie's treasures would be safe here and to come back whenever they wanted to pick them up.

Winnie never breathed so easy in her life as when gazing out to the beautiful lake below Annabelle's mansion on the hill. Hawks circled and played overhead, riding the wind currents that Annabelle told her guests were created between the nearby mountains and lake. Lush eucalyptus trees swayed in the breeze while Annabelle and her visitors sipped tangy herbal tea beside the blue tile swimming pool behind the mansion that overlooked the lake. Too soon, it was time to go. Annabelle waved good-bye and told her young guests to please return often.

Refreshing wind currents lifted Winnie's hair in all directions on the drive home. The young people in the powerful roadster felt ready to fly happily toward tomorrow.

CHAPTER 61

▼

Colorful spools of sewing thread sat on pegs along the length of the wooden rack on the wall. A black, metal sewing machine and straw sewing baskets cast their humble shadows on the modest pine table. No light, other than from two lamps that TR and Ty had mounted high on the walls, flooded the sewing room. Winnie and Gertie sat side by side in the warm glow, carefully matching thread colors to different dolls outfits. Two doll heads lay on the large ironing board while mother and daughter examined miniature clothes that would be resewn around the base of the doll head necks.

"It's good we kept our sewing room in the middle of the house," commented Gertie.

"I know," said Winnie. "At first, I didn't care about not having big windows to look out while we sewed. Now I see how handy it is to be doing this where no one can see us."

Mother and daughter carefully sewed small linen pouches to seal the tightly rolled dollar bills in various denominations that would go inside the doll heads. Ty, Billy and TR were helping assemble a stockpile of money by quietly visiting various banks and businesses to retrieve all they could from multiple sources. They were thankful that time remained on their side. It was taking as long as TR thought it would for Frank McDonnell and Harry Ritz to break apart the Gimble empire downtown.

Gertie no longer threw a fit or blinked an eye when she heard about payments not being made. The family silently paid outstanding debts with minimal discussion, and vendors responded with polite discretion and thanks.

Jacob Steiner and Skip Vanderhooten reported to TR what was happening downtown among the businessmen, movie people and bankers. Downtown people no longer saw TR at his elegant offices where Harry and Frank now openly met and drank whisky with men plotting to steal as much of Gimble's fortune as they could.

"He'll be swept clean from history," boasted the drunken men. "Our network is so vast that only shadows of the man will remain. We're getting rid of entire years of newspaper repositories and public records where we can buy off clerks. People will think his family is crazy for even mentioning that a man such as TR Gimble existed. They already know what happens when they step out of line. He'll be a fantasy, a legend at best, and that is all."

Annabelle Porter called Winnie to let her know that the lady preacher's assistant, Maria Alvarez, reported something bad from her Uncle Francisco. Winnie and her mother never saw a word of this mentioned in any newspaper.

Francisco Alvarez found the badly beaten body of Buck Williams one morning, lying behind the white castle tower near the front gates of Buck's estate. Francisco had trouble making out what the actor was murmuring because the actor's mouth was too swollen. Some of his teeth had been knocked in.

The cook quickly tried to call a doctor up to the house, but all the local doctors were gone on calls. Francisco put the cowboy's body on his bed and told Buck he was going to find a doctor. Buck cried out and mumbled to Francisco to go keep watch over the actor's invalid sister instead. While Francisco was trying to wheel the woman's chair to the bottom of the stairs so she could call up to her brother's room and comfort him, Buck somehow rolled himself off his bed and down the entire flight of stairs. Buck lay face down, groaning at the bottom of the stairs in front of his horrified sister and Francisco.

Francisco left the cook in charge of Buck's sister and picked up the actor's body once more. Buck insisted in screaming agony combined with a heavy lisp that he must not be attended by any local doctors. That's when Francisco realized that word of Buck's assault must not reach the ears of news reporters. The cowboy actor, fearless of risky stunts, wanted to hide his own beating. The cook knew of a certain doctor in Los Angeles known to keep reports of such matters under utmost discretion so that's where Francisco had Buck taken by the gardener.

After Buck was stitched up with his jaw and broken bones set, Francisco then searched high and low for the actor's favorite dog. The gatekeeper finally found the great dane limping with a cut rope dragging sadly behind him. Buster was picking through trash boxes for food behind the businesses on Main Street near the Larwin Valley town square.

Within days of his beating, Buck withdrew his support for the proposed Gimble refinery in Larwin Valley. The businessmen, concerned about their town still recovering from the great flood, spoke in whispers of what might have happened to the stocky and fit beloved cowboy actor.

No one believed he fell down the stairs, but they knew that a man's pride must never be challenged or judged. Like Francisco earlier, they suspected that Gimble might be a wolf in sheep's clothing, and it probably would be better if the inventor's money never tarnished their fine town. Buck's earth-loving friends wrote letters of protest to the county planning commission. The planning staff and commissioners agreed to completely table the Gimble appeal for his proposed refinery.

Upon hearing this news from Winnie and Gertie, TR sent word to Clay Henry not to get involved. Clay quietly took TR's advice and told Francisco to let his family and the other good people of Larwin Valley know that the Gimble refinery would not be coming to town.

The Gimble ladies read in the news the reports about what was happening to CJ Niles. He and his eager assistant had printed and sold far too many oil and mining stock certificates. Many of Niles' ventures weren't likely to ever pay off. As investors' hopes and dreams were dashed, angry men and women cried fraud. They talked to reporters who expanded the hysteria. Stock values for the man in the white straw hat went crashing.

State and federal officials got involved with the Niles scandal. Men with political aims were soon launching investigations, and reporters had more stories than they could handle. Gertie and Winnie nodded silently to each other, knowing indictments would be handed down soon.

Only the wealthiest men who initially bought stocks in large pools from CJ Niles were able to capture the lions' share of any dividends to be made from his illustrious schemes. In private meetings at movie producers' offices, fine country clubs and lodge meetings with the Guild, men boasted of piles of money they made from CJ Niles. Men and women of lesser means, who invested their dimes and nickels, got washed into the sludge of meaningless court battles, just like the tiny bodies swept away when the walls of the San Demetrio Dam exploded in the dawn's early light.

"That's America, folks!" cried the bankers, as the travesty with Niles' investment schemes unfolded. Then some of the bankers were pulled into investigations, too. Several men at the Merchant & Maritime Bank got indicted, but they smoothly paid small reparations to angry investors and never served any prison time at all.

Gertie looked at TR's roster naming his brethren from the Ancient Works and saw that one of the indicted bankers was listed as a high-standing member in TR's lodge. She knew it probably made the man angry that TR never invested in stocks from CJ Niles. The men going after her husband would have loved to have TR investigated, too. As a group, the stock investors at the bank and elsewhere were expected to live the high life in jolly fashion, and then get in and out of trouble together. TR Gimble never chose to run with their gang.

Things didn't read much better for thousands of shale oil investors than they did for small-time investors with CJ Niles. All two hundred American shale oil plants, including the Gimble refinery in Red River, were closed and vandalized.

Dean Atkins sent a news clipping to TR showing how government men raided their once-magnificent refinery after bootleggers set up operations inside.

"That moonshine must have been highly toxic," noted TR. "The shale tailings were all over the stills and tanks."

Fulfilling predictions that Jacob Steiner overheard at the diner, shale oil quickly became an unpopular idea. Government men, who once vigorously supported the shale oil entrepreneurs, were swept into silence. The shame of the great failed alternative fuel experiment silenced scientists and engineers, too.

New royalty deals for Gimble patents ended abruptly for Mr. Steiner in mid-negotiation. Existing royalties dropped off from TR's shale patents licensed for use in the U.S. while Jacob took a trip overseas. The Empire of Japan showed interest in buying the remaining Gimble patents. Jacob and TR thought the foreign deal could provide a lucrative conclusion to all the work they'd done that wasn't going to pay any more dividends in America.

Gertie wondered if the sale of TR's shale patents was going to topple anyone's dominoes in other countries. As the U.S. moved relentlessly toward petroleum in all things fuel-related, Gertie figured that no one ever knows for sure about everything going on between other countries.

Kate sat once again in Barry's big Hollywood office. The movie director hadn't changed, but Kate chuckled at how she'd somehow found a polite way to speak his language. She was able to talk to him comfortably now.

"Am I getting too senior to play the older maidens?"

Barry chuckled.

"Hardly. You still got it, kiddo. You actually come off better now than when I first met you."

"Thank you, Barry. That means a lot because, being married, a woman doesn't know if she sparkles as much as when she was not."

Barry roared with laughter.

"Toots, the young man is doing you a world of good. Don't kid yourself. Men can see these things."

Kate blushed and smiled.

"Why did you call me in?"

Barry got serious.

"Folks in our group are happy with all the work you and Twyla and Mr. Sherman did to help us launch our oil lease. We made some decent money, considering the oil sands were shallow. The wells will be drilled dry with no more royalties to come in maybe five years. They want to move forward with something else, but the men and women have some concerns."

"About what?"

Barry rubbed his hand across his chin.

"I don't meddle with anyone's family affairs. I keep my nose out of anything actresses have going on with their husbands. It's in my best interests, but there are some things bothering the oil club investors about your husband's dad."

Kate breathed slowly as she replied.

"I wouldn't doubt it with so much controversy regarding everything to do with oil investments these days."

"Well, it's a little more complicated than that, kid."

Kate arched her eyebrows but said nothing. Barry continued.

"People I know have been trying to get another lease together with Ty's dad. They've been diddling around with it a damn long time. It's out in Larwin Valley, and you know, some weird things have been going on out there. The people from the oil investor's club don't live out there so they don't know what to make of what they hear. No one has their ear close enough to the ground."

Kate knew better than to try and comment on Larwin Valley. She hoped she wouldn't have to.

"I know little about what Ty's dad is launching in Larwin Valley or anywhere else."

"I figured as much," said Barry, "but some of the folks in the club thought I should let you know that they're beginning to think that men in the Gimble organization ain't on the up and up anymore. The people in the oil investor's club want to do this oil lease real bad with Ty's dad. It seems like the accountant and lawyer in Gimble's office are blocking their involvement entirely. That doesn't make sense to anyone. Aren't Gimble's downtown men supposed be putting together deals as he wants them to?"

Kate looked up sharply.

"That's a loaded question, Barry, and you know it. I can't comment on things like that. Now that I'm a Gimble, I can't risk saying a word to you or anyone that would end up in the news."

"That's all I needed to hear from you," said Barry. "If things were going peachy keen in Gimble's downtown office, I'd be getting assurances right and left from those doughballs, as well as Gimble himself."

"Draw your own conclusions," said Kate.

Barry winked.

"I did. Oh, here's a new script for a part I think you'll like. It pays nicely and won't be too much work. I'll keep you in the loop, Kate. You'll probably need some ongoing employment."

Kate didn't reveal a thing on her trained actress's face.

"Thank you, Barry. I always appreciate your help."

He lifted the phone to make a call and winked at her again.

"No problem, kiddo."

Kate told Ty and TR about Barry's words to her. Gertie listened with her arms folded across her chest as Ty and TR discussed the men and women in the oil club. TR made the decision to write the oil club investors telling them that he was temporarily suspending his interest in executing the Larwin Valley oil lease with them. TR noted Gertie's questioning look.

"I can only hope this change doesn't upset anyone's apple cart all that much. After our family's settled in Riverside, and the goons in my office are long gone with the furniture and money they want to take, I can resurrect this oil lease under better conditions. I can leak the word on that through Jacob and Skip."

Gertie hated to see her husband forced to change course, but she knew there was no choice. She loved Kate and wondered if Kate regretted marrying into the Gimble family. Kate didn't appear to be unhappy. She was having a wonderful time playing her bit parts in Hollywood and working in real estate along with Twyla.

Gertie wondered what it would have been like if she'd been so lucky as to have an occupation or two other than as wife and mother. It didn't matter now. She was a millionaire's wife, and her husband's assets were crumbling. She'd have a full time job just trying to secure enough funds so they wouldn't end up in bankruptcy court. They had to make it to Riverside. That was all there was to it.

CHAPTER 62

▼

Larwin Valley was known for years as an agreeable place for men and women to make money on private oil leases. The collapse of the San Demetrio Dam did not affect oil and natural gas underground. Men rebuilt pump stations and fixed their oil wells with little reason to think that lucrative drilling for men and women investing in oil couldn't continue.

Donald and Lillie Reynolds had signed on to a small, private oil lease with TR and Gertie Gimble several years earlier. The modest asset was doing just fine, but even a seasoned wildcatter like Scoot Wynn started wondering when Donald's wife and mother both got killed under mysterious circumstances only a week apart.

The brakes failed on the couple's car, which they had just picked up at the repair shop. That terrible accident was how Lillie got killed. When Donald was still recovering from his injuries, his mother was struck down on Main Street near the Larwin Valley town square. No one noticed the kind, old lady crossing the street, but after the woman was hit, witnesses saw a dark sedan with tinted windows speeding off. There were no license plates on front or back.

After attending both funerals, Donald promptly terminated his rights on the oil lease and told the inventor to do the same. After TR and Gertie dispensed of the lease with the Reynolds, the stunned widower picked up and left Southern California for parts unknown.

Scoot was not as surprised to hear what happened to the beloved cowboy actor. The wildcatter figured Buck Williams was going to get thunked by oilmen someday, just for being so popular and having strong opinions in a place where oil was very important. Big oilmen didn't generally like colorful characters other than their own. They particularly disliked influential Hollywood-types discussing drilling or refineries one way or another.

When Buck's bloody body was dragged out from behind the castle tower by the front gates of his estate, Scoot kept his clever ears to the ground to try and learn what happened. The wildcatter traded some tools to acquire the real story from Buck's gardener.

Scoot didn't think it so usual when Buck didn't reappear in town for over three months, or when Buck abruptly changed his mind about supporting the Gimble refinery, or when no one uttered a word about the actor's beating in any newspaper. What happened to Buck and what he didn't do about it shouted a message louder than any headline. Oilmen wanted their way in these parts, and they were getting more anxious about challenges on turf they intended to claim. The oil game in Larwin Valley was getting tricky.

The wildcatter kept his nose clean, maintained his little oil well hidden in the canyon nook on his property, and waited to see when TR might start drilling on the land near his. Scoot hadn't much more to do than collect his royalties on his oil rigs in other parts of the Southland. He polished his silver horse saddles and bided his time.

Scoot had been fairly lucky to get in with some Hollywood types. Anyone who collected fancy Spanish horse saddles automatically belonged to a group of esoteric collectors. They swapped information about all the decor and silver engraving. They found ways to make the saddles more comfortable for riders and their glamorized steeds. They were very popular in parades.

A lot of people in the movie business liked owning horses on their ranches around the Southland. Owning his horses and renting out his silver saddles for movie filming was how Scoot came to know actors and actresses, as well as Barry, the movie director.

Some of these people started calling Scoot, seeing if he could guide them into their own private oil leases. Several mentioned wanting to steer clear of the men from Gimble's downtown office. It was clear to Scoot that not too many people trusted those men anymore. Scoot scratched his head and wondered if he could get some business going directly with the inventor somehow. He also wondered if TR Gimble would open the doors to bigger fortunes with some new finds in Larwin Valley anytime soon. Scoot knew the inventor definitely had it in his head that there was money to be made in parts of Larwin Valley, so Scoot wasn't giving up hope of his chances to do the same. All he knew was that he had to be very quiet putting any deals together.

After Scoot heard about TR Gimble's departure from his downtown office, Scoot got very interested in knowing what the man intended to do next. He put away his silver polish and pulled out the most modest suit and hat he owned. He decided to go and get to know the new clerks over at County Records.

Scoot spent weeks prowling through hundreds of title records bearing the inventor's name. He was flabbergasted to see how much TR Gimble owned. Next, he scoured the titles for properties and leases bearing the names of anyone he ever heard of who was associated with the inventor. He was surprised to see mostly the same couple of clerks' names notarizing many of the signatures on those documents. He made friends with those clerks, too, which was not easy because they were in fancier offices upstairs.

Scoot took special note of the names of Frank McDonnell and his wife Genevieve. They appeared to have purchased land in Larwin Valley near TR's. Scoot didn't know who these people were, so he asked Barry, the movie director who seemed to know everyone.

Without revealing why he was asking, Scoot got an earful from Barry about how much the oil investor's club hated the Gimble accountant and attorney who were blocking the potentially sweet deal their club spent a lot of money trying to put together with the Gimbles. The wildcatter figured that, if the McDonnells were moving toward doing business with the Gimbles (and they didn't even sound like they had good social skills), surely Scoot could find a charm or two in his bag of tricks that might work with Gertrude Gimble.

Scoot already knew that the inventor saw him as just some two-bit wildcatter, but Scoot knew that the wives of successful men were often an easier target to get to know than their busy, distracted husbands. Scoot devised a plan to send chocolates and flowers to Gertie.

"Dear Mrs. Gimble," wrote the wildcatter, "I must thank you behind all the other people who have written and sent things to express their appreciation for what you did helping to save Annabelle Porter's life after the horrible accident at the San Demetrio Dam. Many people have mentioned to me how they simply couldn't have gone on in their faith without Miss Porter's inspired leadership to show them the way. They feel they have you to thank, and I do, too. I have been utterly busy up to my wide, flapping ears with all the oil wells and meetings I've had to take care of since that time. Please accept this delinquent, but ever-fresh bouquet, and this five-pound box of Pig 'n Whistle chocolates as testimony of my deepest appreciation for your family's selfless acts of kindness. I am an acquaintance of your husband and wish to send him my fondest regards as well. Sincerely, James 'Scoot' Wynn."

The letter and gifts were intended to merely get the attention of Mrs. Gimble. Scoot Wynn knew that it would take more correspondence and additional reconnaissance to finally meet the woman and show her that he meant business.

The weeks unfolded with the Gimble men working long and hard to get their Riverside farm established. TR, Ty and Billy sped out to Riverside many times. They'd gotten the new irrigation system working, and the tedious chore of planting the vines had begun.

TR wanted to keep his farm in Riverside as unremarkable as a man could. He opened a small checking account at the Riverside bank and kept only enough money there to handle farm expenses. Most of his Riverside neighbors didn't know him as more than the tall man working the fields with his sons. Gertie said she didn't think there was any way to keep his old railroad overalls sewn together any longer so TR got some baggy dungarees like his boys.

The Gimble men worked until their hands bled, spending twelve to fourteen hours a day breaking apart stubborn clay soil and rocks to put acres of vines into the ground. TR had a caretaker on the property and hired a few farmhands to help maintain the irrigation trenches and place the chains and stakes that measured how far apart the vines needed to be.

The drives to Riverside, as well as the manual labor, helped TR to relax. He slept fitfully on the nights he was physically drained. As soon as he got back to the fine suburb and his mansion, he and Gertie resumed the strain of selling their large home, hearing the downtown scuttle and strategizing how to sell more of their land.

Men like Victor Atkins, out of state in Goldenvale, could not see the changes occurring with TR. The enthusiastic professor, however, witnessed with shock what happened to men who persisted in shale oil. Some of the men mysteriously disappeared. Several were killed. Then he read alarming news about JE Hampton, the Midwest man who had formed the Red River Oil Products Company.

The entrepreneur unfortunately tried to save his company from total demise. Not willing to believe that the future of shale oil could be over almost as soon as it started, JE Hampton set out to Washington, D.C. He met with senators, congressmen and military officials, hoping to find ways his company could stay in business by supplying shale gasoline to government agencies.

What Hampton got for his persistence did not involve the continued operation of his shale oil refinery or even his company. On one of his trips to D.C., he wound up in a Maryland sanitarium. The man whose hard work formed the company that used the Gimble shale refining process, and whose new company had investors falling over themselves to buy stock after the stunning success of its opening, mysteriously died in a Maryland mental hospital with barely a line in the Red River newspaper to mark his passing.

Sadly, Victor Atkins clipped the news article and sent it to TR and Gertie. No personal note was needed to explain. TR and Gertie knew that the professor would wisely retire and never mention shale oil again.

Gertie continued to write out checks for cash. She emptied their local accounts where bank men knew her. Downtown bankers weren't going to release a dime to her or TR without the intervention of the pinhead and the playboy. She knew those men would ensure no money ever touched her hands.

"Papa, I suppose my accounting days for you are over," she commented grimly.

TR nodded.

"That part of our lives is done. We'll get along fine with what we have. You and Winnie should come to Riverside tomorrow with the boys and me."

Gertie bit her lip.

"You're right, Papa. It's time we set to our work out there like you men already have."

Arriving in Riverside the next day, TR and his sons showed Winnie and Gertie the fine irrigation system and their rows of vineyards spreading across the acres. Neal Tompkin, a quiet neighbor, watched the hard-working city family inspecting their land.

From his property, Neal could see down the road and over to the shack where the Gimbles' caretaker lived. A rundown farmhouse stood up a gravel dirt road from the shack. The house appeared to be getting the start of some making over. Neal figured the family would go at fixing the farmhouse and moving in after their fields were planted.

Neal saw the woman and young girl leave the men in the field to go take a look at what would become their new home. Neal could also see a strange-looking sedan parked in the shade of a large tree, situated down the road from the farmhouse where the family could not see. What looked strange to Neal were the windows of the car made to look like midnight instead of regular glass. What looked even stranger was the tall, thin man in a cape as black as the sedan he leaned against. Neal saw him light a cigarette and wait.

Gertie and Winnie looked at the wood-frame farmhouse with large trees beside it.

"These trees need fertilizer and the soil some good tilling," said Gertie sternly. "I can imagine the rodents inside the place."

"Oh, Mom, I can see lovely gardens blooming!" exclaimed Winnie. "I'm going to study where the light falls on each side of the house and make a list of the kinds of bulbs and flower seeds we can order."

"Good, dear. I must see what's needed in the kitchen."

Gertie stepped inside while Winnie surveyed the grounds around the house.

Neal saw the thin man throw his cape over one shoulder with what looked like a stunted hand. Neal leaned forward on his tractor as the man walked quickly toward the farmhouse. He knew the men in the fields could not see the man approaching. The trees were in their way.

The man strode purposefully toward the young girl. Neal decided to fire up his tractor's motor as the girl looked up at the approaching man in the cape.

"I'm with the realty company," said the Frenchman.

Winnie looked at him in surprise, noticing little else except the man's odd, yellow-orange teeth.

"Oh? Then you must talk to my mother. She's inside."

Gertie glanced out the window and saw the man in the dark cape. She reached inside the pocket of her skirt where TR's powerful gun was hidden.

"Girlie!" she screamed.

Winnie whirled around toward the house at the sound of her mother's voice.

Louis Tiemonet grabbed the girl by the throat.

"Let her go!" barked Gertie, cocking the gun.

The Frenchman laughed crazily. Gertie pulled the trigger. The blast sent the man staggering backward as Winnie fell to the ground. Gertie ran outside. The man was holding his shoulder with his stunted hand, his cape hanging in shreds. A large hole was blasted into the ground beside him. As Winnie sat up dazed, the man crawled backward. Then he staggered to his feet and ran to the waiting car.

As the dark sedan roared off in a thick cloud of dust, TR, Ty and Billy came running.

"We're alright!" shouted Gertie. Neal pulled up in his tractor as TR grinned proudly at his wife and hugged his brave daughter. Then he turned to Neal.

"Howdy. TR Gimble and family. We're the new neighbors."

CHAPTER 63

▼

Kate and Twyla disembarked at the LA train station. A brisk north wind bent large palm fronds to the ground as travelers pulled on gloves and raised coat collars. Winnie saw the young ladies. She bolted out of the car and came running. Billy closed the car doors and locked the sedan.

"Kate!" exclaimed Winnie in a hushed whisper. "You won't believe it! Mom shot at a guy in Riverside!"

Twyla's eyes grew wide. Kate hugged her sister-in-law tightly.

"What on earth happened?"

"He was so spooky," said Winnie. "He had yellow teeth and a black cape. He said he was a realtor out there. He grabbed me by the neck!"

Twyla looked at Kate in alarm.

"No one by that description is a realtor in Riverside. I hope he didn't hurt you, Winnie!"

The girl shook her head.

"No, he couldn't because Mom had Dad's gun. She saw him out the window and told him to let go. He laughed like some lunatic so she shot the ground next to him. He went running alright!"

Billy joined the girls. He heard Winnie's story and grinned.

"Just another day in the wild west!"

Kate studied him.

"Do you know who this perpetrator is?"

Billy grew serious.

"Yes. He delivered threats to Dad. I never saw him before, but Ty says he came by the experimental plant every once in a blue moon. We've marked our territory out in Riverside, though. Even the neighbors, like the guy Neal who saw what happened, will know. Every one of us will have one of Dad's guns from now on. I hope you're not sorry marrying into this family."

Kate shook her head.

"No, I'm not. It's for better or for worse with Ty and me, and your family as well. Where's Ty?"

"Dad and Ty are on their way back," replied Billy. "The irrigation developed a hitch in its getalong, one of the pumps, I think. They called and said they got it fixed. They'll be home later tonight."

Just then, Twyla spotted Amy Watson and her husband.

"Amy!" she called out.

Amy and her husband looked up in surprise. They hurried over.

"Where have you lost souls been?" cried Amy.

Twyla and Kate hugged their friend.

"What a surprise!" exclaimed Amy to the group. "I haven't seen you famous people since Ty and Kate's wedding."

"You two look well," said Kate.

Amy looked at her husband and blushed.

"We just got back from winter vacation. We journeyed to Tahoe. We simply had to get things back on track. Life turned on its ear for a while."

Kate smiled.

"You don't have to explain that to me. It's a wonder anyone can keep their head on straight anymore with so many things pulling us in every direction. Do you two have time to get some hot chocolate? It could be forever til we see you again."

Amy's husband grinned. He gazed at his wife who looked at him expectantly.

"Any indulgence your heart desires, my dear."

Amy blushed deeply and smiled at her friends.

"Let's catch up before we all have to get running again!"

The waitress at the station diner brought six mugs of steaming cocoa. Amy and her husband described the whirlwind they'd been on.

"Disbanding our ladies' meetings was only the tail end of a lot things that started happening," explained Amy. "I worked on Harry Ritz's staff never knowing he had any designs to take over Mr. Gimble's downtown office. Once I found out Genevieve McDonnell's husband was in cahoots with Mr. Ritz, I couldn't bear the thought of her snooty airs ever tainting my parlor again. She's now flouncing around all the big LA parties, and I hope she's happy. Most of the older ladies can't stand her now. They say they had a hunch about her lying through her teeth anyway."

Kate laughed.

"I hid my association with a Gimble, too, when I first met Ty, but you were all so sweet hosting an engagement party for me. I'm sure we'll be like the older ladies as we age, having our intuitive hunches, and then waiting for life to bring them forward."

Twyla scowled.

"Nothing Genevieve said ever added up in my book. I'm glad her role in this whole downtown debacle with Mr. Gimble is on the table. It allows the rest of us not to get caught up in any shenanigans with her."

Winnie chimed in.

"She sure was nosy when she came to visit our house!"

Amy looked at the girl in surprise. Kate hugged her young sister-in-law and explained.

"The Gimble children have had to grow up fast and hard in the face of some of the things their parents have had to endure. It wasn't like they had anyone explaining all these difficulties to them either. Talk about having to live by gut instinct and the seat of your pants! These youngsters really had to and still do!"

Billy grinned, wondering if he should admit his past secret. He looked at Amy happily clutching her husband's hand. He thought to himself in silence.

"Nah. I'm gonna let that secret rest. If Ty blows it open, then I'll admit I listened under the Watson parlor, but not now."

Amy studied the young man.

"You know, Billy Gimble. I did find out who crawled under our parlor."

Billy's mouth dropped open.

"How?"

"You ran into a neighbor lady of mine one time. You were all covered in dirt. Then, almost a year later, two other neighbor ladies peeking out their windows at different times saw you backing out from under the same shrubs. It took Doreen, Eva, Susan, Harriet and I to prowl around the house and gardens, and then figure out who the mysterious, tow-headed boy was."

Billy grinned.

"The only chemistry you know better than men is the kind that visits you once a month."

Kate squealed.

"How rude and crass, Billy Gimble!"

Twyla and Kate slapped Billy on his arms at the same time. Winnie blushed awkwardly as Amy smiled and explained.

"Harriet said those words when we were trying to discuss lady chemists. You weren't there that day, Kate."

"You smart aleck!" cried Twyla, slapping Billy again and blushing. "You may not be invited to my wedding. I wouldn't want my sister to meet you now, you little sneak! I can't believe you heard things from that long ago!"

"I heard all of it," admitted Billy, "except when I was sick and couldn't attend."

Amy's husband laughed.

"Then you know more than me!"

Amy hugged her husband and gazed into his eyes.

"Well, you caught up with Billy learning secrets, didn't you? Who ever would have known that Harry Ritz had designs to pull you into the Ancient Rite?"

"True," said Amy's husband. He turned to the group.

"At first I was flattered, then I became intrigued learning what some of the men are studying with castor beans and odd metallic potions. Talk about secrets. This goes way beyond. Now it's apparent to me that pharmaceuticals have become an interest for some of those men. I can't imagine why, unless some of them want to form a company making medicines that no one else is making. They never fully described their aims to me."

Twyla looked suspicious.

"What if those men wanted to try and inflict harm? Do you think they'd ever try that?"

Amy looked at Twyla in surprise.

"I never dreamed of that. All I was concerned about was all the time they wanted him to spend at the lodge. That's what nearly drove us to divorce court! There were all the meetings and rituals, and then additional study sessions for only the plants and chemistry. I finally blew my top when they asked him to set up a special laboratory."

"Rightly so," said Amy's husband. "I was getting pulled into their ranks so far and fast, I couldn't see straight. They said they'd elevate me to 33rd degree faster than anyone else. They talked about gardens of giant castor bean plants in thirteen different varieties out in the country at this man's estate. They said there was a fine building where they wanted me to set up research. They wanted Amy to move out there with me, too."

"Can you imagine?" said Amy to her friends. "I'd have been cloistered in some secret life, away from the city, my family and friends! I had to put my foot down and say no."

"I'm glad you did," said Kate. "Having seen firsthand what it's like for a family to live with secrets involving research, I wouldn't want that life either."

"It's not very fun," said Winnie.

"Sure isn't," added Billy.

"I'm glad I stepped back and didn't join," said Amy's husband. "I came to realize they were seeking a pharmacist, any pharmacist, not just me."

Amy sighed.

"Well, here's to hoping that we're choosing lives in the light of day where we can simply enjoy ourselves and do some good for others. I know that's how I want to live. We were able to help families with their medicines after the San Demetrio Dam collapsed. I want to be able to assist like that wherever needed, not stay cloistered and hidden."

"As do I!" proclaimed Amy's husband. "I surely don't need to attend lodge meetings anywhere to help people."

He paid the waitress for everyone's hot chocolate and smiled at the group.

"Well, we must get going. Wonderful seeing all of you."

"I'll call you, Amy," said Kate. "I want to discuss furniture and decorations. We saw Annabelle Porter's house. Talk about unique decor!"

"I can't wait to hear," said Amy. "I'll tell you about my new job for the probate judge, too. We'll make time next month."

Kate, Twyla, Billy and Winnie waved good-bye.

Billy turned to Twyla.

"Sorry about being a smart aleck."

Twyla grinned.

"You're forgiven, and I suppose we'll invite you to the wedding. You better behave, though, in order to meet my sister."

Billy laughed.

"I will."

He paused.

"You know, my mom used to give me castor oil all the time for upset stomachs. Why do you think castor plants could do harm?"

Twyla furrowed her brow.

"When I worked with chemists downtown, there was this man, Reginald Hamilton, who came to work at our office. I quit before he bought the company.

One time I overheard him whispering with a visitor in the lobby. They talked about poison in the beans of castor plants. The visitor said one bean could kill a child in a day and that it would take three days to kill an adult. He called the poison ricin."

"Oh," said Billy. "I never knew that. Well, I never died, and I must've drank enough castor oil to float a submarine!"

Twyla looked serious.

"The poison's not in castor oil if it's processed correctly. Ricin poison is in the bean. The strange part is that Hamilton and this man were both joking about the Ancient Rite. They whispered that injections of ricin create symptoms like sudden pneumonia attack. I had to strain to hear that part. The point is to never allow children around those plants. That's what I was thinking for Amy's children if she would have ever considered moving someplace where her husband would do such research. It sounded ominous to me, plus it's too dangerous for children."

Kate stood up.

"Well, none of those plants will ever be around my offspring! We need to get going. We have to drop Twyla at her house, and it will take some time to get back to your house, Billy and Winnie. I'm glad it finally sold. We'll have tons of work to get the farmhouse put together, but it's a whole new project I'm looking forward to, including getting my own gun like Twyla! I hope to be as good a shot as your mom. I'm going to call her now and see if Ty and your dad are back yet."

CHAPTER 64

▼

As Billy, Winnie and Twyla put on their coats at the train station diner, Kate went to call the Gimble house. Gertie answered breathlessly.

"Hello?"

"Mrs. Gimble. This is Kate. Billy, Winnie, Twyla and I are at the LA train station. We're going to drop Twyla off at her parents' house. Are Ty and your husband back from Riverside?"

Gertie broke into tears.

"They're back, but they're at the hospital. Papa had trouble breathing, and his heart was racing. He didn't want to go to emergency, but I insisted when Ty called me asking what to do."

Kate trembled.

"We'll be right there, Gertie. We'll take you to the hospital."

Kate ran to the table and told the group. They raced outside to the car. Billy drove quickly to the Gimble home in the beautiful suburb.

Amid stacked boxes and covered furniture prepared for the family's move, Gertie stood pale and shaking. She had a satchel prepared with things for her husband. They piled in the sedan and drove to the hospital.

The hospital attendant directed them to the correct floor. Ty's anguished face greeted them at the top of the stairs. He was pale.

"It came on suddenly! He could barely walk. I had to drag him to the car!"

A doctor closed the door to the inventor's hospital room. Ty and Gertie rushed to the grim physician. The man looked at the anxious faces.

"Best to let him sleep. He's sedated now. His breathing is labored but steady. We'll have to keep watch through the night. We'll give him oxygen straightaway if he doesn't improve."

Ty looked toward the room.

"What do you think is wrong?"

The doctor shook his head.

"I can't be sure. It seems like sudden onset of pneumonia. It's not good that his heart rate is fluctuating so much. He must have rest and quiet."

Gertie put her face in her hands. Winnie's tears dripped onto her coat. Kate and Twyla surrounded the Gimble women while Ty and Billy talked in low tones off to the side. Ty came to the women.

"I'm staying here through the night. I want to be here if he wakens, even for a second. Billy will take you back to the house. Come back at first light tomorrow morning. That's all we can do."

"I must see him!" declared Gertie.

Ty went to ask the nurse if Gertie could peek inside her husband's room. The nurse nodded. Gertie tiptoed to the door with Winnie and Billy behind her. Gertie gasped when she saw her ashen husband on the bed.

"It's impossible!" she whispered. "He was fine just today. How could he suddenly be this ill?"

Ty gently pulled his anguished mother away. Billy held Winnie, who did not want to leave.

"You must go," said Kate. "I'll stay here with Ty. Get some nourishment and try to sleep. We don't know how long we'll be waiting in these halls tomorrow."

The night passed in agonizing silence as the clock ticked on the wall of the hospital waiting room. Ty and Kate would doze and then waken each time the nurse went into TR's room to check on him. At three a.m., the nurse shook Ty's shoulder. He bolted upright while Kate groggily lifted her head. The nurse beckoned Ty to come to his father's room. Ty sprang to his feet and followed her in.

TR's head was turned toward the darkened window. He slowly turned it toward the door as Ty entered.

"Dad!" exclaimed Ty. "Kate and I are here. Mom, Winnie and Billy will be here in two hours."

TR tried to shake his head slowly but failed twice as his eyelids dropped. He struggled to breath, his gasps shallow. His voice was barely a whisper.

"Jus ..."

Ty leaned closer.

"What, Dad?"

TR struggled to gather more air. He labored to move his lips.

"Just you and me, son ..."

Ty clasped his father's large, limp hand.

"That's right, Dad. I'm here. The others are on their way."

TR's head dropped and then slowly rose. His eyelids fluttered open.

"Just us ... We'll open a fruit ... stand ... in Palm Springs ... No one else ... The girls can't come."

TR's exhausted head dropped to one shoulder. Ty whispered urgently.

"Dad! Dad!"

Kate stood tearfully at the half-open door to TR's room. She spoke softly.

"I called them, Ty. They're on their way. The nurse is getting the doctor right now."

Ty didn't look up from his father's face. TR's eyes fluttered open again. He drew air into lungs that rattled. The inventor gazed tearfully at his son.

"I did not ... tell you ... of the Final ... Work."

Ty put his hand on his father's shoulder.

"I've achieved the Great Work Dad. I didn't have to go to any lodge to do it. I'm good."

TR slowly moved his eyes right and left. His head would not follow. He breathed words in shallow gasps.

"This ... is ... the ... Final ... Work ... It's what ... they've done ... to me."

Ty drew back in alarm.

"No, Dad. You need to rest, that's all. You'll get better. The doctor's coming."

TR's head drooped to one side. He did not open his eyes or try to speak again.

The doctor hurried into the room. He brought an attendant and nurse. After checking TR's vital signs, they hooked up oxygen. As Ty stepped back toward the door, the doctor gave TR an injection.

Kate gathered the inventor's sobbing, eldest son in her arms and led him back to the waiting room. She held his head as he collapsed into incoherent groans and restless slumber on the chair beside her.

Gertie, Winnie and Billy came running up the stairs.

"How is he?" gasped Gertie.

Kate shook her head.

"He tried to speak to Ty. I don't know what he said. It upset Ty greatly, though. We must let Ty catch some sleep. The doctor put your husband on oxygen and gave him an injection, a sedative, I think."

"He's already slept so much!" cried Gertie. "Is a sedative what he needs if his heart is slow?"

"His heart was racing when he first came in," said Kate. "The doctor indicated the sedative and resting are keeping it stable. He didn't give us any more detail than that."

Ty awoke and stared out the window, barely acknowledging his family. Gertie came and sat beside him. She wordlessly took his hand. Billy immediately went to try and peer inside TR's room. The nurse sternly admonished the young man to return to the waiting area.

After three long hours, the nurse stepped out from her check inside TR's room.

"He wants to see you," she announced.

The Gimble family hurried in frantically. Ty nearly fainted. His father was sitting up in bed, appearing to be a new man.

"Geez!" cried Ty. "You sure know how to scare your family!"

TR reached for Winnie's hand on one side and Gertie's on the other. He smiled and spoke softly.

"Well, it was bothering me with my feet hanging over the edge of this bed. You have no idea how uncomfortable that is."

The family laughed and wept simultaneously. The oxygen appeared to be reviving the inventor. They spent two hours by his side, seeing him improve by speaking longer sentences and even telling them jokes they'd not heard before.

CHAPTER 65

▼

One by one, the ladies who were friends from Amy Watson's meetings called each other. They shared their grief hearing TR Gimble was suddenly in the hospital. Twyla called Nona, who started to cry.

"Oh, that's terrible! Richard is with the men at the Guild lodge right now. As soon as he comes back, we'll come to the hospital."

Twyla paused.

"So how is Richard doing with the Guild?"

Nona sniffled and then revealed excitement in her voice.

"He was just raised to 32nd degree in the Ancient Rite! That's a special higher order for men who qualify by ..."

"I know," interrupted Twyla. "I know what it is."

Twyla's heart pounded after hearing what Amy's husband had described.

"What's he doing with the men right now?" asked Twyla.

Nona took a short breath.

"Oh, that's never discussed outside their lodge. There's a whole group of young men who are very close to Richard, and they are being sponsored by older members."

"Swell," said Twyla flatly. "Are they out at some man's estate in the country?"

"I don't know, Twyla. Richard said he wouldn't be back until this evening. Why do you ask?"

Twyla paused again.

"Just be cautious, Nona. Be cautious about how much secrecy you allow in your life with those men."

Nona gasped.

"What do you mean? Richard is ecstatic being in their ranks. He's done nothing but improve in every way since joining. I couldn't be prouder of him. Mrs. Rhodes and Mrs. Graham have become very close with me and the other wives of the young men. We're family now and, in some ways, more loving and loyal than my own blood relatives! What are you getting at?"

Twyla swallowed. There was no point going any further on this subject with Nona. Twyla sighed.

"I'm happy enough for you. I hope the men will be praying for Mr. Gimble as we will."

"Of course!" said Nona. "I'll let the other wives of the men in the Ancient Rite know. Maybe we'll see you at the hospital."

"Thank you," said Twyla. "I'll call Mrs. Berkowitz and Mrs. Finny. Kate already called Susan and Jules. They'll tell Doreen, Eva and Harriet. We already know Genevieve McDonnell will hardly care."

"Now wait a minute," said Nona. "We know Harry Ritz, and he's sponsoring Frank McDonnell into the Guild right now. Genevieve would care deeply."

"Sure," said Twyla. "Look, I have more calls to make. Thank you for your prayers."

Twyla's hand trembled as she hung up the phone. It was clear that the ladies' group was divided forever. Their opinions about men's secret societies were already sealed.

Hiram called Joey MacDermott, who rode his bike as fast as he could to the hospital. Hiram called Skip Vanderhooten, too. Before Skip left his home, he called Buck Williams. By the time Skip and Ellie joined Hiram, Joey, Jacob and the Gimble family, Buck had sent over a giant, horseshoe-shaped bouquet of flowers to TR's room. The message read, "Get Well, Pardner!"

TR slept and then visited with friends and family throughout the day. As night drew near, he seemed exhausted again. He never uttered another word about a fruit stand in Palm Springs or anything to do with the Final Work. Ty told Kate it might have been delirium that had his father talking that way.

The exhausted family gathered around TR who'd awakened from an hour's slumber. He looked weak, but still he smiled and held their hands.

"We're going home, now," said Ty. "We all need some rest. We'll be back bright and early tomorrow. Soon we'll have you back home, and then you'll get sick and tired of seeing so much of us."

"That'll never happen," said TR. "I wish…. Can at least one of you…."

His head nodded to one side. He started snoring loudly. Winnie giggled.

"That's the old snoring Papa we know and love!"

Gertie nodded.

"He's done that ever since I've known him, just drops his head right in the middle of writing or reading and takes his forty winks. I think our old pop is on the mend!"

"Let's let him sleep through the night," said Ty. "I'm too exhausted to think."

"Me, too," said Kate. "We'll be at his side round the clock to nurse him back to health at home."

"My sweet daughter-in-law," said Gertie with a smile. "Thank you."

Winnie and Gertie hugged Kate. The family left the hospital with hopeful hearts and tired bodies.

TR Gimble died late that night. Shock waves ran through the family and across the great Southland when people heard of the inventor's passing at the age of fifty-one. Gertie didn't have a tear left to cry. Winnie sobbed enough for four other people. Ty rushed over to the plant, but his dad's and Hiram's files were already stolen.

By the time Frank McDonnell and Harry Ritz arrived at the mansion the following day, Gertie signed over her executorship of the Gimble estate with numb hands and a numb heart. Louis Tiemonet did not have to come visit the family with any more maniacal threats. Frank showed Gertie debts of TR's downtown companies piled higher than the widow could ever hope to repay. The family knew, as soon as the dark sedan pulled up carrying the pinhead and the playboy, what was expected of TR Gimble's widow.

Billy thrashed boxes in the rear yard of the house until his fists were bloody. Winnie rushed out to comfort him as he sat crying inside his dad's beloved roadster. Ty and Kate were inconsolable as they wondered about what kind of future they could ever have for their children.

"I'm lost without Dad!" cried Ty. "All I've ever been has been his vision for what I could be. I was shaped and fashioned in his likeness. He was the only one who could show me which direction I could go, especially now with so much gone wrong."

"We'll figure things out," said Kate softly. "There are more than one identity and career for every soul."

Ty looked at his wife. She had already fashioned two careers for herself in movie acting and real estate. He wept yet felt some small comfort.

TR Gimble's funeral was as somber and enormous as the passing of other Los Angeles notables. Procession cars stretched for miles along downtown boulevards, idling through ornate, black, wrought iron gates at the Glendale cemetery. Twyla's eye caught sight of the emblem at the top of the gates, a knight's white helmet perched atop a red circle held up by two black lions. Within the red circle was a shield, etched with lines of water and a fountain with the word 'Eternity' emblazoned across them. Hiram gripped Joey's shoulder as they looked up at the shield as well.

Winnie clasped her mother's arm as TR's body was laid to rest. She gazed at the horseshoe garland sent by Buck Williams, much finer than any she could have fashioned. The words on the garland read, "Good-bye, Pardner."

Winnie no longer wanted to sob into stitches she would sew for the rest of her life. She was certain she'd been wise to stow her father's papers. She never stopped hoping they might someday help identify the bad men that her father hadn't been able to stop. She would ask for a puppy and kitten and a new bird and fish to keep her company. She'd feed and care for each animal with utmost tenderness. And she'd whisper to her dolls, "All of you are going to outlive everyone, even me."

Hundreds of men that her father had not mingled with at Guild lodges in years filed into the cemetery. The indicted bank officials and other men from the Ancient Rite all turned out in their fine cars. Kate gasped, seeing Nona and Richard riding in the same car as Frank and Genevieve McDonnell. Twyla gripped Kate's arm, spotting Mrs. Rhodes and Mrs. Graham chatting quietly with Harry Ritz. The one-time friends from Amy's parlor divided themselves between those encircled with the Guild and Ancient Rite, and those who viewed them with suspicion. Ty and Billy looked at the faces of all the men in their fine cars, and Billy spat on the ground.

CHAPTER 66

▼

CALIFORNIA 1949

"Shall we?" asked Billy raising his champagne glass.

"A toast!" declared Ty. "To Mom surviving seventeen years of probate."

The group of adults stood in a circle around the stone veranda in Ty and Kate's backyard. Lawn chairs beckoned quiet relaxation under fragrant eucalyptus trees that swayed overhead. As in backyards of thousands of other Los Angeles tract homes, amenities at the Gimbles' tidy property thrived abundantly. Petite rubber plants and lilies with orange flowers grew in clusters around the outer edges of the patio. An American flag swayed in the gentle summer breeze, its shiny, silver pole topped with a bronze eagle. The flag was attached to the end of a large blue and white metal play set that sat on the lawn beyond the patio.

Three little girls giggled and squealed, pushing each other on the swings and climbing the ladder to slide down the six-foot, metal chute. Ty looked at his daughters playing and remembered the covered metal chutes at the LA railroad yard nearly three decades earlier, where tons of shale rock used to slide down from boxcars freshly arrived from Red River. He shook his head, trying as he always did, to erase those memories now. He never could tell what simple things might bring such images searing back into his mind.

Pink, juicy hamburgers and hot dogs simmered enticingly on the barbecue before him. The redwood picnic table stood ready, draped in a bright red and white-checkered tablecloth. A pitcher of lemonade decorated with daisies sat beside tall glasses etched with matching flowers. Plastic bowls filled to their snap-on lids with potato salad and cool gelatin desserts awaited the modest celebration the group would enjoy.

"To us!" declared Winnie.

"To the dolls!" exclaimed Gertie with a wink.

"To the love of the Gimble family!" proclaimed Billy.

They sipped the fine champagne and hugged each other tightly. Laughter and music seemed a fitting way to conclude the long journey closing the final chapter on the now-disappeared men who made sure the family fortune vanished.

The group settled into lawn chairs while Billy adjusted the large stereo in the playroom just inside the screen door. He toyed with the knobs and found a radio station playing orchestra music. Ty gently flipped hamburgers and turned hot dogs arranged around the barbecue grill. Winnie poured her mother a tall glass of lemonade as the woman set aside her champagne. Mom seemed ready, more than anyone, to do some talking today.

Ty glanced at his family seated around him. He wondered if contentment might settle into their lives at last. As he tended the grill, he spoke over his shoulder to the group.

"I wanted to wait another year after the end of that whole deal to have this celebration."

He turned to face the jubilant adults.

"We know for certain now that the pinhead and the playboy have truly disappeared. At times, I wasn't sure who might keep popping up, but I think all the boogey men are finally gone."

Billy grinned.

"Tiemonet's suicide would have passed right by us if Jacob hadn't seen that French newspaper."

Winnie leaned over to hug her mother around her shoulders.

"You made it, Ma," she said, giving Gertie a peck on the cheek.

"You too, dear," said Gertie, patting her daughter's hand. She remembered vividly the Frenchman's grip on her daughter's throat. The inventor's widow gazed at her sons.

"Sorry I sent you boys running all over the state to every bank we ever dealt with. I couldn't believe the men got their hands on every dime."

Ty chuckled.

"I've had enough time to accept the whole ball of wax, Mom. I'm at peace with all the bank records vanishing, too. I have my lovely daughters and Kate and all of you as my eternal treasures. That's worth more to me than all the money in the world."

"How are the guys at Regis treating you?" asked Billy tentatively.

Ty shrugged.

"Same 'ol, same 'ol. I act like I never worked for Dad a day in my life. I'm on the road a lot with the sales team. I just stroll around the LA headquarters when

I'm there and grin. There's nothing they can pull that ever surprises me. At least I've got a job for life, whether any manager likes it or not. They never want me out of their sight working anyplace else."

"Does it ever bother you?" ventured Winnie.

"Not really," said Ty. "No job anywhere could ever top my days working with Dad. That was the best adventure a young man could ever want. I've been with the best. I doubt there's any employer out there who could ever make it as exciting as it was with Dad and his men."

Ty looked back at the group with a wide grin.

"Or as profitable for each of them, I might add."

Gertie smiled.

"I liked working for him, too. You may be surprised to hear that, but Dad and I had a partnership I could never imagine with anyone else. I got a postcard from Jacob Steiner, by the way. He and his family are doing well."

"Where did they end up?" asked Kate.

"Up north," replied Gertie. "They're in a small town not far from wine country. I've read here and there that a lot of Dad's old friends in the oil business ended up retiring in towns around there, too. Did you know that men may have tried to shoot at Jacob when he was in Japan?"

"Gosh, no!" exclaimed Ty. "You never mentioned that."

"I don't know if I should mention it now. I kept zipped lips as things unfolded all those years in probate. Like you Ty, I stayed mum, not knowing who or what was going to pop up from which corner of the world. I lost track of Jacob after he petitioned the probate judge to sell Dad's shale oil patents to the Empire of Japan. With the Depression and World War, I didn't try to contact Jacob again."

"Silence was wise to maintain," commented Billy.

Gertie continued.

"After Jacob sent me the clipping about Tiemonet, I completely lost track of where he was. Then his postcard arrived six months ago. I saw the postmark and knew it was the town up north. Jacob simply noted he was retired and happy that his travels to the Far East were concluded. He wrote that he was somewhat surprised, but then again not, when tinted windows rolled down in Tokyo. That sounded too much like what happened to Dad and Victor Atkins in Red River. I concluded that Jacob lived through a dangerous incident or two. In all, I'm glad he made it back safely. Have you heard anything about what Hiram is up to these days?"

Ty looked at Kate.

"You tell her, honey."

Kate laughed.

"I was on my way to see old Barry at the movie studio. I just about fainted when I drove past a new store on Rodeo Drive. The sign said 'Hiram's Haberdashery, Gentlemen's Fine Clothing.' I thought, no, it couldn't be, so I turned the car around, parked and went inside. There was 'ol Hiram, unleashing his typical humor while selling men's suits!"

"Unbelievable!" exclaimed Gertie. "I bet he's doing well. Did he remember you?"

"Of course. We talked a bit, and I told him the whole mess was almost cleaned up. He said, 'speaking of cleaned up,' and showed me how clean his hands were. We laughed remembering all the oil he constantly had under his fingernails. He says he has a woman who gives him weekly manicures and a stylist who found ways to cut his unruly hair. He looks so refined and dignified, you'd hardly recognize him if you saw him on the street. He said to raise a glass for him, too."

The group lifted their champagne glasses.

"To Hiram!" they cried.

The little girls on the lawn glanced over with curiosity, but they obediently continued to play, waiting until the adults told them it was okay to join them.

"What about Joey?" asked Billy. "I remember what a neat kid he was."

Ty smiled.

"Joey went on to college like we thought he would. He actually attended the American School of Mining Geology and got degrees in chemistry and engineering. He's heading up the research division of a company developing plastics. He never stopped experimenting with phonographs, trying to find better ways to amplify sound. He's a silent partner with a Canadian outfit that makes music systems. Talk about diverse talents! He must be a millionaire by now. He's registered sixty patents at last count. Dad pegged him correctly alright. He also learned from Dad, I suppose, not to make a big deal of being a genius. He lives quietly with his wife and kids in Connecticut and stays far afield of news reporters. I see his name mentioned in articles once in a while when audio innovations are written up in technical journals. He doesn't strive to be a legend. I consider how he's living and fulfilling his dreams a notable triumph."

"That's great to hear," said Billy. "When you get a chance, I'd like to have Joey's address. I could drop him a line, maybe even catch lunch with him when we go back east to see the fall colors."

Twyla's younger sister beamed up at Billy. Then she looked at the group.

"Seeing the autumn trees is the most wonderful thing we do each year. We've talked about retiring back east."

Ty looked at the two of them.

"Follow your hearts, kids. Just be glad you're alive every day, and don't look back."

Billy hugged his wife, then winked at Winnie.

"Looking back should be a special treat you indulge in only once in a while, sister. I've got something in the trunk for you."

Winnie laughed.

"Really? A surprise?"

Billy smiled mischievously.

"I was on my way back from Riverside and decided to stop by your old friend's place."

"Annabelle!" cried Winnie. "How is she?"

"She's getting on in years, but she's still up and about. Her place still looks the same. It's still painted bright white and has all those odd decorations with the big, gold cross and pool and all. It's still sitting on that hill where you can see it from almost anywhere in El Lago. The homes that were going in on the streets around her mansion never got built with the Depression. Kate, you probably know more of the details about all that property than I do. The private party cabanas on the beach, the big paddlewheel boat and that two-story pier at the lake are all gone now, but Annabelle's house still stands as pretty as ever. She had your boxes stored exactly as Ty and I stacked them in her tunnels. I saw Maria, too. She's married now with a big family."

Winnie's eyes sparkled.

"I'll go and see all of them as soon I can get off work for a few more days. I want to drive around out there, stay overnight, and just remember how it felt. Thanks for getting the boxes, Billy. I think I'm ready to sift through those old things without crying my eyes out. Are you able to keep them in your apartment, Mom?"

"Of course, said Gertie. "Billy and I discussed it. We cleared out space in my closets before he went and got the boxes. I think Ty will probably keep them here after I take a look through them. I think one last peek will do just fine for me. Ty hasn't decided if any of it will be shown to his daughters."

Kate looked at Ty inquiringly.

"I think not," declared Ty. "I enjoy telling my daughters how it felt to be around Dad more than having them look through piles of information that would be meaningless to them. It's far more important for me to have them know about the twinkle in Dad's eye and the love in his heart. That's all I want them to carry in their memories."

Kate joined Ty at the barbecue.

"Are those burgers about ready?"

"Yes," said Ty. "Let's get the plates so we can start our little feast."

As Kate departed for the kitchen, Winnie drew close to Ty and spoke softly.

"I agree with you about not telling your daughters anything, at least not while they're young. Mom should have a peek at those old things and rest fitfully with her memories. I need to do the same. Then time will pass, and none of the things that once happened will linger over us any longer. Maybe someday, one of your daughters will want to drag out those old boxes and take a peek, too."

Ty chuckled.

"It will have to be long after I'm gone."

Kate returned with the plates and silverware. She started arranging settings on the red and white-checkered tablecloth. Before Winnie went over to help Kate, she hugged Ty.

"Whatever you decide to do, Ty, is perfectly fine with us. I was wondering, have you been out to Larwin Valley?"

Ty nodded.

"Kate and I will take you on a drive there next time you visit. I know you can't stay long on this trip. I was out in Larwin Valley on a sales run last week. Clay's Filling Station is still at the crest of the highway. The cemetery he owns now spreads across that big hill that faces town. Buck's old estate still overlooks the train station. He's getting old, but I hear he still shows up in town from time to time. The guys in the field say he never mentions a word about oil drilling or refineries. I can't believe his movies are considered classics now."

"Speaking of classics," said Winnie, turning to her mother. "How is that old coot, James 'Scoot' Wynn?"

Gertie laughed.

"Let's eat first. The burgers and hot dogs will get cold if I start telling you about the wildcatter before we eat. You can hear about that old buzzard with dessert!"

CHAPTER 67

—————————— ▼ ——————————

Kate opened the screen door to the back porch and walked to the picnic table where the Gimble family was seated.

"I'm not going to serve dessert right away," she announced. "Let's sit and watch the girls play awhile longer and hear what Mom has to say about the old wildcatter in Larwin Valley."

As the family settled into lawn chairs around the stone veranda once more, Gertie declared, "Well, you know, Scoot Wynn got the whole Equity sewn up in his name, or so he thinks."

"The Equity is the oil and gas lease in Larwin Valley, right?" asked Kate.

"Yes," said Gertie. "Before Dad died, the old coot sent me personal notes and gifts."

"Really?" asked Kate. "It sounds as if he was trying to find some way in with you."

Gertie smiled.

"Scoot Wynn's words were flattering to the whole family. His first note arrived with a bouquet of flowers and five pounds of chocolates. I disregarded his offerings, just as I refused to acknowledge anything Genevieve McDonnell sent me. I couldn't figure out what this man was up to. I hardly trusted anyone outside the family at that point. I never returned his calls or subsequent notes."

"Gosh," said Ty. "I never knew he was hounding you."

Gertie looked sternly at Ty.

"Dear, a lot of men were hounding me, especially after Dad died. Many were the worst sorts of characters you'd ever want to meet. Men and women came out of the woodwork with claims against Dad's estate. The judge threw out many such claims. You were gone a lot of the time and didn't have to answer the door to frantic bill collectors and people who got over the fence to ring our doorbell. They thought I was the richest heiress on earth. You remember, don't you, Winnie?"

"Certainly!" exclaimed her daughter. "I think I got to acting as sternly as you with all the people who'd stop me on the street trying to sell me things when I was simply walking to the store. The people who stood quietly in line at the back door where I was handing out food were extremely polite and grateful. Our guard in back didn't have to chase any of them away at all."

"At Dad's funeral," explained Gertie, "Scoot Wynn acted like he was some lifelong friend of mine. That confused me so I was very chilly toward him. Well, it turns out, he snooped himself silly down at County Records and made a few friends down there, which I'm sure he gave a few gifts to, as he did to me."

"Sometimes I see people trying to do that in public records offices," said Kate. "Their supervisors are supposed to catch any favor-takers and discipline them. If the clerks don't give back the gifts, the supervisors are supposed to fire them."

"Dear," said Gertie quietly, "Scoot would have been buying gifts for the supervisors as well. He only needed to compliment the clerks, and that part he was very good at. Those days were different than now. When you and Twyla first got the title records you needed for Barry, your pretty smiles were the greatest gifts you could have given the men clerks at that time."

Kate blushed.

"We just wanted the quickest service possible. We were so excited getting a chance to prove ourselves in real estate."

"You sound like Dad," said Gertie. "All he ever wanted was the chance to prove himself as a great inventor. Once he died, the conniving wildcatter never stopped trying to worm his way in with me on the lease. But Scoot didn't succeed making it into that deal. Through much of probate, there was a fight going on with the oil club people still wanting to be in on the Equity lease. McDonnell and Ritz kept trying to elbow them off, which they finally succeeded in doing. They used the leverage of gold during the worst time of the Depression. The oil club couldn't raise the same amount to secure the lease. At one of the court accountings of the estate, McDonnell showed up with a draft lease naming only the Gimbles and he as lessors. That's what the judge approved. That's what became the Equity lease."

"Sounds complicated," mused Billy. "What a struggle between the oil club investors and McDonnell. You know, Dad's friends in the oil club were prominent men and women of means. I bet they were discouraged losing out on the lease."

"Or scared," commented Ty. "No one probably knew who was working with whom for what aims. There was probably personal leverage applied until each of the oil club investors opted out, just like Mom and Dad decided to do when Donald Reynold's wife and mother were killed. But it doesn't take killing anyone to apply a slow kiss of death. These boogey men probably didn't want to create any obvious massacre of like-minded, associated individuals. They smartly gave that group of people the option to wake up and end a potentially deadly nightmare for themselves. That's my guess about what happened."

Billy's eyes clouded.

"There were deadly things going on around the time Dad died."

Winnie looked serious, too.

"The way the governor died suddenly of a pneumonia attack was odd to me. His demise was reported in the news several weeks later, almost word for word the same as Dad's death. The report of the governor's death even bore the same headline!"

"That was strange," admitted Billy, "especially knowing how the governor rallied Congress with JE Hampton to keep the shale oil refinery going in Red River."

"What about the gas explosion and fire in Fushun that killed 3,000 people?" asked Winnie. "That travesty occurred only eighteen days after Dad died. Talk about a deadly nightmare! I've often wondered what was going on over there and why Dad got pulled into designing a shale oil refinery there like you said he did. He must have known the dangers that existed there for centuries with scientists and engineers who tried to work with the Russians, Chinese and Japanese in that region. That place bore such violent controversy since the war there in 1904, and now the massive annihilation from that accident. It makes you wonder."

Billy nodded.

"All that intrigue is too wild for the boldest imaginings. Dad's involvement in Fushun and other places was all mixed up with activities and motives from men in our government and other countries. The Japanese wanted the kind of inventions Dad could provide to their Fushun industrial center. The Secretary of the Navy who came to visit Dad's experimental plant was old friends with Hirohito's top naval officer. How do we know this top official from our own government wasn't inviting Dad to help the Japanese, throwing out the welcome mat and writing letters of introduction? Yamamoto ends up bombing the U.S. at Pearl Harbor and Midway, so what about that old friendship? We know so few details about shifts in international relations as Japan got more aggressive. Dad was probably not the only inventor swept up in those goings-on. How do we know that Japan didn't want Dad's money to overhaul the old facilities that the Russians first built in Fushun? How do we know Dad's money wasn't taken and used for takeovers or coups elsewhere in the world? The timing sure fits."

Ty looked at the group and spoke softly.

"I did hear at Regis that the chemist, Reginald Hamilton, headed over to Manchuria after buying out the chemical engineering concern where Twyla and Nona once worked. If anyone was willing to get involved in science on a major, experimental scale, it was Hamilton. Maybe he's not even living anymore. I don't ask questions about things like that at work. The less anyone knows about what I saw or heard regarding Dad's work, the better. I can tell you that Regis had developments going on in Fushun before the war, with both the Japanese and Germans. Then they entered the silent war against those nations. That was the oilmen's thrust to cut off supplies as Japan prepared to mount attacks against the U.S. I was never involved in those affairs. I was selling petroleum products to gas stations in California, and that's what I'll continue to quietly do until I retire."

Billy's wife shook her head.

"My sister Twyla thinks there were many ominous forces at work during those times. She remains convinced that men involved with secret societies had something to do with America's involvement in the war."

"You have to admit things were going every which way," said Billy. "The French government of Prime Minister Steeg fell the day after Dad died. Things that happened with French banking scandals during that time seemed as sinister as the large banks' involvement with CJ Niles and other stock swindlers in the U.S. All this corruption happened in a frenzy that had people going mad losing millions and committing suicide rather than living with the dishonor of being indicted or becoming paupers."

Gertie sighed.

"What happened in France corresponds to the timing of Tiemonet's suicide as well. Who really knows about those events during the Depression? Various schemes could have been tied together in ways we'll never know. When it comes to the Equity lease in Southern California, both Billy and Ty may be right about how pressures collided. Scoot Wynn moved right in after McDonnell and Ritz disappeared. I sent police in search of the pinhead and the playboy but, as you know, they vanished completely. Scoot got signed on as the only lessee. Now he controls all the drilling. He even has the lease registered in his name with the state, and I tell you, I'm not challenging that either. Ty, you don't even realize that you are on the lease as well. You signed what you thought was just another piece of paper. I didn't explain what was going on at the time because I didn't want you or Kate doing anything to upset the delicate balance of those affairs. At first I thought, if I complied during probate, I'd somehow come out of it with money leftover for our family."

"Gosh," said Ty, "my head was definitely in some kind of fog for years. All I wanted was to go driving and boating. That was simply stunned grief as I see it now."

"We had fun times despite your grief," said Kate. "But I had no idea what your mother was going through when you said you had to run to McDonnell's office all those times to sign papers. You didn't want me to ask about any of it."

"I remember insisting on that, Kate," said Ty. "I figured anything I signed was worthless junk on paper anyway. I still feel that way. I'm not in any state of will-ingness to start wondering what I ever signed that had anything to do with that messy probate. You understand, don't you Mom?"

"I do," affirmed Gertie. "You have your family's safety to think about. That's the only thing I was thinking of when I signed over executorship of Dad's estate to McDonnell. No one needed to twist my arm. Of course, I never dreamed those men would bilk every last penny, but I needed all the debt and lawsuits cleared up that involved my name. They convinced me all those things would carry over into your lives if they weren't resolved and paid off. I didn't know any better at the time. Lawyers and judges I begged later on to help me refused to become involved. My petition to gain back executorship of Dad's estate was flatly denied in one hearing. Right after that, the men proposed to cut my widow's allowance entirely. We would have starved, so I never petitioned again."

Kate looked guiltily at her mother-in-law.

"Gertie, I have to tell you that Amy Watson did mention your petition to me. She was as devastated as you that you could not win back executorship of your husband's estate. She mentioned seeing your husband's original will naming you as sole executrix in 1916. She said McDonnell was never mentioned in your hus-band's will and that Harry Ritz was no part of the original filing of the will either."

Gertie looked surprised.

"I begged Amy not to tell you or Ty. I didn't want to burden you with that. When I met Amy at Superior Court, she seemed knowledgeable. She was work-ing for another probate judge. She knew more about legal terms and what to put in my probate petition than men who refused to help me. My sister Helen was impressed, too. We typed up my petition together."

"I know," said Kate. "We were holding our breath that the judge would grant you back your executorship. I promised her I wouldn't tell you back then. There was a group of ladies ready to help you, but we cannot say for certain what was going on with the judge. Seeing what happened to you changed Amy's views forever. That's why she's studying to become an estate attorney."

Gertie sighed.

"Well, perhaps what I went through helped someone after all. And you learned about some of it, too. I never felt more helpless in my life. Eventually, I came to want only one thing. I wanted to feel the kind of contentment we feel getting past these things now. It became a challenge to me to see if we ever could."

Winnie leaned over to hug Gertie.

"We're finding ways to settle these things with the past. I'm glad we're talking about it."

Gertie took a sip of lemonade and set the glass down carefully on the small table beside her. She looked around the group.

"I can stop talking about it if you want me to. Maybe that would be better."

"No," said Kate, gently touching her mother-in-law's arm. "It's better that we go into the future knowing just a little."

The other members of the Gimble family quietly nodded. It was a step that they felt would free them a bit more as a family. If it was a difficult step, it was no more so than the steps taken by other people with ties to those perilous times.

CHAPTER 68

▼

Gertie got comfortable in her lawn chair, ready to talk to her family some more.

"This is the last part of what happened with the Equity lease. The man with the Oregon gold was signed on as the first lessee. After the lease was approved in probate court, I tried to sell off the parcels of land related to the lease that were in joint tenancy between Dad and me. There were no offers on the land for quite a few years. Through that time, 'ol Scoot Wynn kept popping up like Prince Charming to help me find land-buying prospects until some buyers finally got interested. A few deals fell through before the land finally sold."

"That sounds like an arduous process," said Kate.

"Like slow roasting over a fire," chuckled Gertie. "We really needed the money after the judge cut my widow's allowance by half. I have to say that Scoot helped me get the money for the land while still sending me chocolates and holiday cards, but he ended up with the lease that was always supposed to keep generating royalties for us. He dribbles out a check for something he calls royalties once in a while to me, but the paperwork on the whole thing is about as messed up as can be. I wouldn't hold your breath thinking that anything will ever come of it. I wouldn't want you stirring up the wrath of old ghosts anyway."

Billy mused.

"It sounds like stirring up anything to do with the lease would be like Ty quitting Regis Petroleum and announcing to the world he's going to start his own shale oil company with some long-lost patents from Dad. He could stir things up further saying his new company would be financed with unlimited capital from the Merchant & Maritime Bank!"

The group chuckled at Billy's fable. Gertie continued.

"Let's just say that stirring up anything to do with the lease wouldn't go over very favorably with certain characters."

Ty shifted in his chair.

"You don't have to worry about me, Mom. Life for Kate and me is about raising daughters who will never have to deal with the kind of turmoil you endured."

Kate looked reflective.

"What you just shared with us about Scoot Wynn and the lease must stretch for miles of paperwork over time. Being in real estate, I can just imagine what a tangle it is. And that was just one lease you had to deal with. I can't imagine what the rest of probate looks like. Did you keep notes on these things?"

"Very little," said Gertie. "In my journals, I made sure you kids would know what weather we had every day, which you will only laugh at. I respected what Dad advised for the safety of the whole family. I wrote in general terms only about my daily activities, but I did note in my journals when I signed documents with various parties. If ever someone wanted to, they could go through my years dealing with probate to see what I wrote. They could pull titles and transfers corresponding to all the lease assignments and deeds of record I ever signed. I'm not saying all the records will be in the public files they're supposed to be in, but my job of following through has been completed."

Kate grinned.

"As interesting and challenging as all that sounds for one heckuva title search, I'd rather spend time with Ty and the kiddies right now."

"I don't blame you," said Gertie. "I feel the same today as I did at Dad's funeral. I've done all I can. I never had the chance to be as confident about things as you, Kate. In some ways, I envy you that way."

"Oh, I didn't develop confidence entirely on my own," said Kate. "There were many things I learned from the ladies who used to gather in Amy Watson's parlor. The older ladies are now passed on, but they were a source of inspiration to show the rest of us young women how we needed to appreciate rights and privileges women earned in this country. As we found out through your experience, Gertie, we still have a long way to go!"

Ty smiled proudly at Kate, thinking of the advantages their daughters would have to learn and grow in her care. He grew pensive.

"No women in our family except Winnie and Mom will have the kind of insight into the workings of evil men who can make just about anything happen when it comes to money and leverage that people would kill for. It'd be interesting to know if some person or group was really known as the Saint."

Billy interjected.

"I bet it was some hidden network like the guys who never gave Dad the alchemy secrets. There had to be international connections as well."

"You think so?" asked Ty.

"Sure," said Billy. "That's why I spat on the ground at Dad's funeral. Just looking at the faces of those hypocrites who stood by as their supposed brother was taken down by giants made me think that more men than just the pinhead and the playboy had to be in on it, too. All that nonsense about holy knights and courage and loyalty means nothing in the end. If the Saint or anyone else decides to put a tag on a man, that's it. The most influential men in the Southland could not prevent what happened to Dad or Mom. Hundreds of them were all making money with what Dad invented and built. Something or someone bigger than they ever stood scared them into knowing that they had to let their brother fall. If it wasn't that they were scared, then they were part of the profits taken away by the pinhead and the playboy. Whether that many men were merely silent witnesses or profit-takers doesn't matter much. The Guild is supposed to be about all brave and honorable characteristics with charity toward your fellow man. Few men ever came fearlessly forward to help our parents in their time of need. I think all the Guild and Ancient Rite baloney is a bunch of hooey myself. Those groups are no different from regular business, politics or any other kind of supposed order men pledge themselves to. I'm glad we never got involved with them."

"Hmm," said Ty. "I guess we'll never know who played what part in the whole thing. I did like some of the ideas Dad shared with us about ascending higher though."

Ty put his arm around Kate's waist and tickled her. Their daughters giggled from the lawn, pointing at their parents' flirting.

Billy looked sincerely at his wife.

"I'm glad we get a chance to love and honor as we see fit. I'm in agreement with Joey's way of life. Maybe we'll move back east sooner than we think."

"You could," agreed Ty. "You're freer to run anywhere with the wind than I am."

Billy threw his arm around Ty's shoulder as Winnie wiped away a tear.

The side gate opened, and the family looked up to see Skip and Ellie Vander-hooten walking into the back yard.

"Hey there, Skip-eroo!" exclaimed Ty. "Kate must've let you know we'd be having our little celebration tonight."

Skip and Ellie greeted the gang while Ty opened two more lawn chairs. Skip surveyed the yard.

"This stone patio looks a little like Buck William's sun deck. I like the eucalyptus trees."

"Where do you think I got the idea?" asked Ty.

Kate introduced Ellie to the little girls who ran over eagerly once she beckoned them.

"Mommy met Ellie when we acted in a movie together a very long time ago," explained Kate.

The girls exclaimed how Miss Ellie was just as pretty as Mommy. Then Kate gently told the girls to go back to their dolls and coloring books. She told them that the adults were almost finished talking and that they'd get cake and ice cream in just a minute. The girls clapped their hands in excitement, waved to Miss Ellie and returned to the big, plaid blanket on the lawn next to the swings.

Skip and Ellie settled into their chairs.

"These days, I'm with a group called the Caretakers," said Skip.

Ty laughed.

"I suppose that's better than being with a group called the undertakers."

Skip handed Ty his business card.

"It's sort of a humorous thing, a play on words regarding my old days with your dad's submarines. We put my favorite daisies on the logo, too. They look sort of high tech in there."

Kate leaned over Ty's shoulder to see the business card.

"Oh, I see the flowers!" she exclaimed. "How neat!"

The rest of the family also wanted to see Skip's everlasting tribute to TR Gimble embossed on the card, so they passed Skip's business card around while Skip explained.

"Our company is hired to clean up industrial spills and waste left behind after men and buildings move off a property. We're called in when companies disturb large areas of plants, wildlife and waterways, such as with oil drilling, mining or manufacturing."

"Gosh," said Ty. "Do I detect a bit of the earth-lover in your company's description?"

"Of course, my friend," said Skip. "Now that I'm older, I feel I want to come out forcefully as an earth lover. I knew you'd understand better than anyone what happens with oil drilling and industrial contamination, especially over long periods of time."

Ty nodded.

"I do. Actually, cleaning up earth messes is not as complicated as cleaning up men's business, is it Mom?"

Gertie shook her head vigorously and smiled.

"I'm glad some things actually can be cleaned up start to finish."

Skip, Ty and Billy caught up on the latest news with each other and recounted old times while Gertie listened. Skip asked if anyone saw someone they recognized on television riding with the men and women on horses during the National New Year's Day Parade.

Gertie grinned.

"You mean that fat cat wildcatter with his big belly hanging over his Western belt buckle and his plump legs bouncing against his fancy silver saddle?"

Skip roared.

"Good eyes, Mrs. Gimble. You caught that, too. I should have known nothing like that would get past you."

"Well," said Gertie, "that goes with being trained by Dad, who had the best magic eye of all. It's all about seeing details and having your heart keeping watch for details, too. Things pop out clearly when your heart knows the truth. As I understood Dad's definition of the magic eye, it means seeing the good details, as well as unpleasant ones. What I see around me represents certain ironies, but these things don't upset me because it's much more important that my family has survived and is okay. People cheer because Scoot Wynn's saddle and tassels and big hat and pony are so pretty, but few people will ever know where his money came from. No one will know how the wildcatter got so rich except us. Families who picnic and play at Wynn Park in Whitman City have no idea of the story behind the man for whom their park is named. But we know, and every year we can laugh as he rides by with his belly bouncing over his silver saddle. The truth is, he outsmarted and outlived a lot of other people who could never bounce along so carefree, with the public cheering them on to boot! I think that's pretty humorous in perhaps a dark sort of way, but yet that's what life is. Sometimes, as I know Dad felt, you have to let certain men and circumstances pass by in the parade."

After the little girls had dried their hands and scrambled to their places on the red and white checkered cushions at the picnic table, the little girl with the widest green eyes looked at her daddy and asked, "What were all of you talking about for so long?"

Ty reached down and brought the little girl onto his lap.

"We were talking about reaching compromises with fate."

He hugged her tightly as he added, "And, my little angel, never losing sight of the magic eye."

About the Author

Ann Mauer provides environmental services to Southern California real estate developers. Ann applies her field experience and associations with talented engineers to this vivid portrayal of an American inventor's story that sparked her imagination.

978-0-595-47504-9
0-595-47504-3